Down on B-Dock

A Dewey- Rehoboth Novel

Paul Dyer

Spy Press

Rehoboth Beach

Down on B-Dock
Copyright 2013 by Paul Dyer

This is a work of fiction. Any resemblance to actual persons,
living or dead, is purely coincidental.

First Edition

ISBN-13: 978-0615816494
ISBN-10: 0615816495

Spy Press LLC
Rehoboth Beach, DE 19971

Cover design by Crystal Heidel

ψ

For Betty and Dick

From Whom All Blessings Flow

ψ ψ ψ

Book One

ψ ψ ψ

Joe's Story

'When the roads were as many
as the places I had dreamed of
And my friends and I were one'

-Jackson Browne

Chapter 1

Gypsy Joe Margarita

3 Parts Dulce Vida Blanco   1 Part Fresh Lime Juice
Shake with Ice and Strain into Martini Glass
Splash or Float Cointreau   Add Orange Wheel

Joe Rath sat on the finger dock staring at the Gypsy. His long legs didn't quite reach the water which was fortunate because at the end of the summer season this end of the bay consisted largely of jellyfish and muck stirred up by boats entering and leaving the marina. Idly, he ran his fingers across the rough grey boards as the afternoon sun baked his tanned shoulders.

Studying the classic lines of his trawler calmed him. He could close his eyes and picture every inch of her, inside and out, but watching the Gypsy bob gently in her slip, light reflecting off her glossy white paint, was like meditating. Only the fringe of green scum attached to the hull swaying up and down in the water like a hula dancer's grass skirt bothered him. Joe knew he needed to get in the water and clean off the vegetation. He reviewed everything else on board in his mind. And knew it was shipshape.

Shipshape. He loved that word. All of its connotations. The ends of the lines coiled into perfect circles on deck, teak polished inside and out. He'd lived in apartments, houses, condos. Nobody said houseshape or condoshape. He loved that distinction. Loved the self-contained world he could sail away in at the drop of a hat.

Shipshape. His life had seemed in order and in control until a week ago. Turned on end in just seven days. His stomach knotted thinking about the money. Money in his life had always equaled trouble. The timing couldn't have been worse. Two days before Labor Day weekend. Two days before these two little beach towns became a nightmare of drunken tourists and summer workers intent on one last fling.

The palm trees swaying in the breeze along the edge of the deck of the Rusty Rudder across the crescent shaped lagoon caught Joe's eye. The owners let the palm trees die every year. Sometimes they'd last almost until Christmas if the fall was warm. That was a couple months longer than the bars. Dewey Beach folded faster than... Joe tried to come up with a comparison, but finally realized that autumn in the little town was more like dominoes falling. The Cork would go first, followed by most of the little bars. The Starboard would last until mid-October and even the Rudder, which had tried to make it through the winter for years with a truly lame ladies' night, had announced it would close in October.

By the time the palm trees died, the half mile stretch of downtown Dewey Beach would be dark, the five traffic lights turned to yellow, for there was no reason to slow the cars on their way north to Rehoboth Beach or south to Ocean City. It reminded Joe of the ghost towns he'd seen in the mountains around Telluride. His little town would not begin to re-awaken until the Starboard had their annual St. Patrick's Day opening party.

Four lines. Slipped through four cleats. He glanced again at his boat. The Gypsy ready to roam. Gas tanks topped. Everything he had in life was on board. Ready. Joe thought of all the times he'd driven the old Ford pick-up across the country. Detouring to Panacea, Florida to see if it was. A long side trip to Dime Box, Texas, because he'd read about it in *Blue Highways* and liked the name. Wanting to stop and petition the elders in the ugliest town in America, Butte, Montana to drop the E, until he learned that blessedly, the town was subsiding into the copper mines cut beneath it and was slowly solving the problem on its own.

The road. His old solution for everything. It could still be, he thought. Untie the Gypsy and go. Get in the pickup truck and go. He stood and said, "Just go," but only a solitary swallow perched on his starboard rail noticed. It chirped and flew away. Joe sat down again. The trouble was, he no longer wanted to go. Irony? Paradox? He never remembered which was which, or if they were the same thing. Bubbles would know. She knew everything. But she wouldn't speak to him unless they had 'the conversation.' The talk about the baby thing which made him lock up like the Tin Man without his oil can.

A squawk signaled the swallow's return. It let loose, missing him by inches, but spattering the side of the Gypsy from the cabin windows to the top of the hull with an audible splat. Joe watched it run down the side thinking, insult to injury. Slowly he stood and uncoiled a hose from a piling. He couldn't help but smile and mutter, "Shipshape."

Chapter 2

Urkontinent Belgian Ale

Dogfish Head Brewery
Est. 1995 Rehoboth Beach Delaware

As always, Joe had felt like he was surfacing slowly through layers of murky water that morning. He reached his hand across the bed in the normal way, waiting for her to take it, pull it around her and run her finger along the callous on the inside of his left thumb raised by opening thousands of beer bottles. "Just to make sure it's you," she would say. This morning, he felt only a cool sheet.

He reached over and grabbed the pillow from the other side of the bed and pushed it down on his face. Nothing. How had her scent disappeared so quickly? One week and nothing. Could he live without her scent? He pulled the pillow away. His mouth was dry and his head throbbed. Seven nights of trying to drink her out of his head was taking its toll.

He looked up at the giant map of the United States she had put up on the ceiling over the bed as a joke. She claimed he roamed across the bed relentlessly. He thought that living on the boat, with its constant motion had cured him of his old need to drive across the country. She said he had substituted with nightly drives over the mattress. Coast to coast then back. She told him she had wanted nothing more than to cling to him through the night to make up for sleeping alone for her first twenty-five years.

She said in the beginning, she waited on the far edge and held on for a few moments before he resumed his slow travel. She told him he always spoke a single word, rarely the same one, like the ding at the end of an old typewriter's carriage run before rolling over and heading back the other way.

She had no experience with anyone else and said she couldn't imagine a person sleeping more heavily. He didn't remember making love in the middle of the night although she said it had happened more than once. She told him it took her a whole year to adjust her rhythms to his, but she refused to miss any nights together.

But everything was wrong that morning. The sun was already high in the sky. He rarely slept much past dawn. Joe had tossed and turned most of the night thinking of the two numbers, 48.325 and 2.6 million. Maybe, just maybe, he thought, the first number was the answer to the problem with the second... So, he kept returning to 48.325, glancing back up at the map, wondering where latitude 48.325 would be, daydreaming of calcareous soil and bicycles in the basement. Now, light reflecting off the water cast dancing circles across the map, breaking the dream yet again.

Joe sighed, rolled out of bed, stepped out the back door and climbed the ladder to the upper deck.

Something else was wrong. He glanced over at the soft tub, saw the three shot glasses glimmering in the sun on the table by the tub. Right where they should be. He looked at the rolled up hammock where they slept most nights. He thought he should unfurl it and check for some sign that she had been there, but didn't because he knew it would depress him if there wasn't.

He knew if he turned to the east and jumped, he could see the ocean. No real need to prove it. Still, he turned to the east, jumped and saw the ocean. Everything seemed right but didn't. Maybe coffee would set the world straight. He climbed back down, cut through the cabin to grab his phone, trailing his hand along the teakwork as he always did, then stopped.

The duck chart.

 Laid out on the map table.

He hadn't put it out. It was early September, way too soon for ducks. His breath caught. Bubbles? Had she been back?

In the fall, ducks descended on the marina and stayed through the winter. Joe had become enthralled with the birds and made his own duck collection poster. With rules of course. Bubbles had asked about it their first fall together and he had explained the system. The ducks must have landed in the marina. They must be positively identified and he told her the difficulties involved in distinguishing the subtle differences between say, a lesser scaup and a greater scaup.

It became a game, a competition between the two of them. She would set down his binoculars and definitively declare, "Barrow's Goldeneye." And move to put a checkmark on his chart.

Joe would pick up the binoculars and examine the duck in question and contradict her. "Common Goldeneye. The Barrow's range is only as far south as Long Island." He would then move to erase her checkmark. She always tried to stop him and it would devolve into a wrestling match with clothing removal. Now, Joe's breath caught again as he thought that only with Bubbles would a duck poster make him think of sex.

As if he could get any more morose, he thought of his first autumn with her when she saw the long low boat being put into the water on the ramp near C-Dock. Three men in camouflage got in, motored out into the bay and disappeared. A short time after, she asked about the thunder reverberating across the water, how that was possible on a clear day. Not thunder, shotguns, Joe had answered without thinking and she'd seen him glance at the duck chart.

Horrified, she'd asked him if it was legal and if they could stop them. He didn't answer. He just told her about the time he'd visited the redwood forest. He had walked out into a grove of the huge trees and said it had felt like a cathedral with no one around and the streaks of sun penetrating the gloom looking like light through stained glass windows. He said a thought had come to him unbidden that anyone who chopped one down was destined for hell.

Christ, he thought, gotta think about something else, anything else. Get to the coffee shop and complain bitterly about the tourists, the favorite pre-Labor Day pastime in Dewey and Rehoboth. That's it. Pin the chaos he'd mostly created on his own on the out-of-towners. Beautiful. Already, he felt better and headed down the dock.

Chapter 3

Mocha Blanca

3 Parts Van Gogh Double Espresso
1 Part Godiva White Chocolate Liqueur
Stir. Serve over Ice with Chocolate Curl

If Joe closed his eyes, he knew exactly where he was on the short walk to the coffee shop just by the different textures on his bare feet: The rough wood of the finger dock. The smoother feel of the planks on the long walk down B-Dock, where the boards had been recently replaced. The left turn onto the sun-damaged wood of the walkway along the edge of the parking lot. The one step up onto the concrete retaining wall before jumping the couple feet down into the cool sand of the tiny bay beach, still damp from the humid night air. And then onto the blacktop of the parking lot with its scattering of sharp pebbles and occasional bits of broken glass from bottles dropped by the summer partiers.

Alice's Subaru was parked in the lot. Bumper stickers all over the back—*No food without farmers, No nukes*—any liberal cause sticker which would further obscure her rear window. Joe had bought her a *BuckFush* sticker a few years ago, but figuring out what to remove to make room for it must have been too traumatic for Alice to deal with.

Soapbox Alice, the coffee crew at BooksandCoffee called her now for her penchant to go off on a rant with very little provocation. And provoke they did. Steve, the manager, had said to her just a few days ago, "Alice, you hear this one? Baby seal walks into a club." Alice couldn't respond from behind the counter, she had to charge her short barrel-like frame around to a table in her little green apron, grab a chair to keep her from rocketing into the air and yell at the group, " Idiots. Killing baby seals is…." blah blah blah, and she was off.

BooksandCoffee. Joe loved the fact that somebody believed that a bookstore could exist in a beach town devoted solely to the consumption of alcohol. Dewey Beach, a strip two blocks wide between the ocean and Rehoboth Bay. One half-mile packed with fifteen plus bars and little else. No taffy. No T-shirts. Just restaurants, bars and the coffee shop that Joe thought of as his own.

The Thursday before Labor Day weekend. Joe knew that the town would start filling up tonight with refugees from real life in Washington DC, Philly and Baltimore intent on one last summer bacchanal. Dewey was about a two hour drive from each, but it seemed to draw mostly young professionals from the DC area ready for a break from running the world. The big bars—the Starboard, the Cork and the Rudder—would be packed for the weekend with the smaller bars catching the overflow.

Joe hesitated at the door to the bookstore, hoping to get the funny Alice, not the still bitter about the five-year-old divorce Alice. As he pulled the door open, he yelled "Aliiiice," going for

Gleason. No answer. The place was empty. He looked at all the vacant chairs and wondered again why this day felt so different.

Joe weaved through the cafe tables in the brightly lit section with the cathedral ceiling, past the fireplace and the bestseller shelves. He eased behind the counter, pulling a tall paper cup from the stack on the back bar. As he placed two shot glasses under the little wands and punched the button to start the espresso, Alice entered from the other side of the counter area. She moved next to him. He towered over her by nearly a foot and as she looked up at him, scowling, her glasses reflected the fluorescent lighting.

"Joseph, this is not self-service."

"Alice, if you're gonna disappear for hours, I'm going to have to take matters into my own hands. I just sold two Americanos and a bearclaw."

"I was gone for two minutes. Move out of the way."

Joe reached out and tugged the edge of Alice's apron. "The boys and I were thinking of having a benefit, maybe raise some money to replace this whatchamacallit."

She sighed. "It's a smock." Only one sigh Joe thought. If she was really worked up there would be two sighs with a "Joseph" in the middle, as if he were her cross to bear, her Sisyphean rock.

"Perfect, we'll call it a Smock-a-thon and get that Scooby Doo looking long haired dude and his anorexic girl friend to play some tunes. I figure if we lock the doors and she starts screeching, people will pay good money to get out. Maybe we'll have enough left over to buy her a hamburger."

"Ben and Darla are wonderful performers." She turned from Joe, but not quickly enough to hide her smile.

"All the feral cats showed up the last time she sang. Thought they'd lost one of their own." Joe grabbed the hem of Alice's apron again. "I was thinking maybe beige, blend in better with those coffee and pastry stains you got there."

The opening notes of *Some Enchanted Evening* began to emanate from Joe's pocket. His phone. And it finally hit him. The song. The stupid joke about his siblings' Sam and Janet. His father, Dick Rath, would never sing the punch line again.

Joe felt emptiness surround him. His father was gone, the anchor removed which had tethered him through countless troubles. He missed Bubbles more at that moment than in the whole week following their blow-up. His new anchor. Maybe she was gone now as well.

And why would his sister be calling, he wondered, especially after how things had gone yesterday? Janet and Sam should be winging their way back to Tucson, where Dick Rath would spend eternity in an urn on their mantle. Of course, a single day could seem like eternity at his siblings' house, he thought.

A horrible feeling hit him that maybe Janet had phoned Bubbles and was calling to yell at him for not telling her about his dad. One more reason to dread going to work today. Joe realized that Alice was poking him.

"Are you okay?" she asked. "You looked lost."

Startled, he remembered. "Knock Knock."

"Who's there?" Alice turned towards Joe and held out her left arm. Joe slid his hand behind her back, grabbed her left hand in his right and waltzed her out among the easy chairs and rockers.

"Sam and Janet," he said as the ringtone went on.

"Sam and Janet who?" said Alice.

"Sam and Janet evening," they crooned together, drawing out the words until the phone went to voicemail. Joe collapsed into an easy chair, his easy chair, the one between the two bay windows in the corner that looked out over the parking lot.

"You were a little slow on the uptake, Joseph. We do that every time your sister calls."

"Could be one of the last times. Janet's really hot about the funeral."

"Funeral?"

"Yeah, my dad died."

Chapter 4

Grim Reaper

1 Part Kahlua   1 Part Bacardi 151
Stir and Pour over Ice   Add Dash of Grenadine

J oe stared out the window at the Lighthouse bar sign flashing the
same message over and over, Taco Toss Every Friday 4 till Close,
thinking he should go get his hammer and permanently remove
the second L. He thought about his dad.

When his dad got rich, they moved to a big house overlooking
Long Island Sound. It had mostly been his mom's idea. Flaunt that
wealth. His dad's only stipulation had been his private room.
Soundproof. Acoustically perfect. Bang and Olufsen quadrasonic
audio system.

The room was kept locked and Joe had only gotten glimpses of
the walls lined with shelf after shelf of LP albums. He had dragged
a ladder around once and climbed up to peer in the bay window
which looked out at the Thimble Islands. A single battered leather
chair sat in the center of the square room, facing the water,
surrounded on three sides by the rows of records.

If you sat just outside the room, you could hear the music. If
you placed your ear against the door, the sound was quite clear. A

vibration made its way through the walls of the surrounding rooms and when he felt it, Joe would go sit by the door and listen. Sad songs mostly. Scratchy old recordings of men selling their souls for love, following her to the station, all their love in vain.

The door opened one day and he toppled into the room. Dick Rath stared at him with an amused look. Joe took the outstretched hand his father offered and was pulled to his feet. "I...."

His dad grinned. "I've known for a while. Come on."

And so, Joe learned music and a few things about his dad as well. No classical. No jazz, but just about every other kind of music, sorted by type and alphabetized in each section. Some twenty thousand records his father had told him, which prompted Joe's first question.

"Why do you listen to those sad ones over and over?"

His father had looked at him with an expression that Joe couldn't interpret at age twelve, but had never forgotten. Sad? Wistful? Then he had smiled and said. "Tamp down the joy," which was as baffling to Joe as his expression. When Joe tried to get him to explain, he just asked Joe, "What's your favorite?"

"The one about the train station."

"Mine too. Robert Johnson. *Love in Vain*. Where it all began. Over here."

And he took Joe over to the section where the shelves had labels marked *Blues*. Joe noticed a path worn in the thick beige carpet to this exact spot. His dad pulled the album from a protective sleeve, showed Joe how to hold it gently by the edges and ease it onto the turntable. It was smaller than the records Joe had seen before, a 78, his dad said.

A dark blue label Joe would learn by heart. *Vocalion* arced along the top. *Love In Vain Blues* just below. The word Blues to the left of the center hole. Guitar Player to the right. Robert Johnson just below.

His dad had always seemed just old to him. He traveled several days a week on business, visiting corporations all over the country. Consulting, which meant nothing to Joe. Consulting must have been tiring though, for he spent most of the weekends sleeping. Until that day, Joe and his father were essentially strangers living under the same roof.

Darkness had fallen outside. His father sat in the chair and Joe moved next to the window and looked out towards the little islands just off shore. A light blinked on in a house.

"Roger's Island," his dad said as Robert Johnson felt so lonesome all he could do was cry.

And the islands that Joe had explored since he was old enough to paddle a boat or even swim to the closer ones, changed before his eyes. The lights which began to appear with the darkness seemed to flicker like fireflies dancing on a summer breeze.

His father continued to name the islands as the lights appeared.

"Money."

Thirty-two houses and a library, thought Joe.

"Governor."

Fourteen houses. Been in every one, thought Joe

"Cut in Two."

"Cut in Two West." Joe glanced back at his father who had a big grin on his face.

"Cut in Two West indeed. Good to know we have two Thimble Island experts in the family."

Robert Johnson's train pulled away from the station taking with it his woman and his mind. Silence descended on them and Joe felt the first threads of a connection with the man in the chair. It was a connection that he would never let go of.

But now, his dad was gone. A tap on his foot brought his attention back from the window.

Alice stood by his outstretched legs with a look of concern. "Your dad died? Were you planning on telling anyone?"

"What would you have done if I told you?"

"Whatever it is that people do, Joe, say how sorry I was, give you a hug."

"That's what I was afraid of. I needed a couple days to get him fixed in my head just the way I wanted, before everyone tried to sanctify him. I wanted to remember plain old Dick."

Alice shook her head and started to speak, but a customer came in then and ordered a string of complicated drinks and Joe returned to staring out the window. A black Porsche pulled into the parking lot at the Rudder and a man with long, fuzzy gray hair emerged. If Dewey Beach had Big Kahunas, Joe thought, this was the biggest, the head of the group that owned half of the town and in Joe's mind, thankfully, the man who kept Dewey out of the hands of the 'let's turn it into a family resort' crowd. Joe's hero and evidently, a great lawyer.

Lawyers.

ψ ψ ψ

Yesterday, the three of them, Joe, his sister Janet and his brother Sam, had sat in front of the desk while the lawyer spoke to them, glancing down occasionally to pull a number from the document spread before him. Joe had zoned out after the lawyer had said the words *at least 2.6 million.* Not 2.6 million divided by three, but at least 2.6 million each. The figure seemed to hover over each of their heads in black cartoon bags with yellow dollar signs.

Joe had focused on a picture just over the lawyer's left shoulder. The lawyer shaking hands with Ed Rendell, governor of the evil empire. Rendell looked nice enough, big square head, like a solid dairy farmer maybe. Pennsylvanian through and through, though, probably thought tipping was a sacrilege.

Joe was staring out the lawyer's window at the brick buildings of downtown Lancaster thinking that a little brick was good, but a little too much and you strayed into penal institution territory.

Janet poked him and said, "He asked if you had any questions."

He thought back over the steady stream of words—*assets, legatee, probate* and a few in Latin that he hadn't comprehended. "In the two hundred plus years since the founding of the republic, how is it that the legal profession hasn't taken the time to translate everything into English?" he asked, still staring outside.

"That is beyond the scope of our purview," said the lawyer, whose name Joe had already forgotten.

"Jesus, Joseph, please," said Sam and Janet in unison.

"No further questions your Honor."

Janet and Sam skewered Joe with a couple more laser looks. They hadn't been happy since he picked them up that morning. He had taken a little too long checking the lines on the Gypsy, stopping for coffee in Newark and of course, he always had to pull over for a pep talk before crossing the Pennsylvania line into enemy territory. So, Joe had arrived about a half hour late. When he knocked on the door of his dad's apartment in the retirement home where Sam and Janet had stayed after flying in from Tucson the day before, Janet had stared at him in the doorway.

"Shorts and sandals, Joe?"

"Brand new, black and appropriately mournful I would say. And check out this shirt." Joe grabbed Janet's hand and ran her thumb along one of the sharks formed by raised yellow dots. "Kinda looks like one of those Lite Brite panels we used to make." This actually elicited a smile.

"Very classy, Joseph," she said.

"Let's go, we're late," said Sam. "You can change before the service."

"I guess we're postponing the family love fest til later then?" said Joe, reflecting on the barely touching un-hugs favored by his mother and siblings. After his mom died, Joe had initiated bear hugs at all family gatherings, persisting even after Sam clocked him the first time Joe tried.

They walked back down the hallway with its garish carpet. Joe always expected to turn a corner and run into a roulette wheel or a baccarat table. At the pick-up truck, Sam balked at sitting in the little flip down seat in the back.

"Ever think of having a salad once in a while there Porky," joked Joe. Sam reached out and rapped him on the head with his knuckles. Joe tossed him the keys and jumped into the little seat.

"You drive then."

Chapter 5

The Sweet Hereafter

½ oz Each: Cruzan Coconut Rum
Kraken Spiced Rum/Chambord
1 oz Cointreau   5 oz Pineapple Juice
Splash of Sprite   Garnish with Fresh Pineapple

Joe had practiced his eulogy almost all the way up from Dewey Beach. In retrospect, he thought as he dodged his way around another Amish buggy on Route 896, heading home, maybe he shouldn't have slammed his hands down so hard on the little podium when he shouted "You don't know Dick," at the beginning of his speech. It was supposed to be funny after all the other speakers, including his brother and sister, had deified his father. Captain of industry, family man, and on and on.

For most of the service, Joe had sat alone in the front row on one side of the aisle in the bright room. Sam and Janet had pointedly sat on the other side, still miffed that Joe was wearing the shark shirt, even after Joe explained that their Dad, who hated computers, had mastered the intricacies of the internet to buy it for him.

All the other speakers had climbed onto the raised stage and spoken down at the assembled group. Joe had gone up and carried the lectern down so he could look more directly at the people. Also, in hindsight, maybe Joe should have left the box with what was left of Dick Rath on its pedestal on the stage. The podium had felt pretty solid, but when his hands came down, something had broken and the box slid backwards down the sloping wood. Joe caught it before it fell, but the lid popped off releasing a small cloud of Dick and something hard that bounced once and rolled towards the audience, stopping at Janet's shiny black shoe.

Joe thought he had recovered nicely by saying, "Glad you could join us," eliciting a group chuckle from his father's breakfast crew, the only people who had seen fit to join Joe's section. He had played golf with these guys once a couple years back and they had kidded him every time they had seen him since then about losing twelve balls in nine holes, christening him Joey Twelve-Balls on the spot, since shortened to simply Twelve.

"Way to go, Twelve," one of them had hooted. Joe had looked out at the audience for a moment, maybe forty people sitting behind his sister and brother, a few wheelchairs pulled up alongside the aisle and the breakfast club on Joe's side, Joe thought of them now as the Black Sheep Squadron.

Joe had launched immediately into the stories that he loved about his dad. The time when he bought the house with the pool and had refused to let someone show him how to light the pilot on the pool heater. Luckily, when he and Sam had stuck their heads in the box that housed the heater and pump and lit the match, the resulting explosion had been small, but had blackened his glasses and singed off his and Sam's eyebrows. The time after his dad had gotten the big deal consulting job and bought the Henry Kissinger black frame power glasses. Joe had ridden him unmercifully, asking for Dr. K whenever he called home. Joe had given him credit for sticking with the glasses for a whole year anyway.

He could have gone on longer— he even had the serious side of the room laughing now— but he saw the lady from the retirement home giving him the cut sign from the doorway. They had another group coming in after, maybe another after that, death being the only constant in the place. Joe's sister had actually given him a real hug and told him how good his words had made her feel. Joe was able to retrieve the hard thing and return it to the box when she and Sam had turned to thank everyone for coming. The Black Sheep Squadron had surrounded him, shaking his hand, telling him to come visit. The one named Walt asked Joe what it was.

"What?" said Joe.

"That thing that rolled across the carpet."

"Thought you geezers were supposed to lose your eyesight."

"Still 20-20, Twelve."

"I think it was a tooth, thought I saw some gold."

"Wouldn't surprise me. He was gold, Joe."

"I know, Walt."

"He loved you."

"I always felt it."

As Joe crossed the Delaware line back into safety, the money had occupied his thoughts once again and a crazy idea began taking shape in his head as he passed between the corn and soybean fields south of Dover.

Chapter 6

Money Shot

1/3 oz Amaretto Di Amore   1/3 oz Baileys
1/3 oz Midori
Shake with ice   Serve in shot glass

Alice tapped Joe on his bare foot with her shoe rousing him from yesterday's memory. She held his coffee in one hand and a plate with a bagel in the other. "You forgot your coffee."

"Yeah, weird morning. Where are my people?" He always sat with Steve, the manager of the coffee shop, Jeff, the owner of a couple local restaurants and a rotating cast of other semi-regulars. Time spent catching up on town gossip and trying to provoke Alice.

"Joseph, you're late. They were here hours ago."

"What time is it?"

"Almost noon."

"Can't figure out why this day feels so different. I never sleep this late." Joe got up and walked over to the new book section, noticing the cooler feel of the hardwood floor on his bare feet. He stood in front of the non-fiction bestsellers to the right of the fireplace. He always read novels on the boat, but for some reason was drawn to read science or history with his coffee.

"Alice, where's that book I was reading?"

"I sold it this morning."

"How many times do I have to tell you not to sell them before I'm finished?"

"That would entail you actually paying for them."

Joe figured that he had read at least a hundred books for free since the place opened. He'd linger after the morning crowd left and read a few chapters of something that he could discuss with Bubbles when she woke up.

He wandered back into the main book area of the store past the poetry rack, wondering again if it was possible that a single poetry book had ever been sold to the alcohol-sodden Dewey Beach crowd. It was probably no coincidence that Joe picked up the McInerny book again. *Bacchus and Me.* Nobody could capture wine like McInerny could, comparing the pale beauty of champagne to Greta Garbo or a Condrieu to a Tahitian painting by Gauguin. Joe turned to the champagne chapters for what must have been the tenth time.

"Hey, can you Google latitude 48.325 for me," he shouted up to the counter where Alice sat at the computer.

Alice looked up and scowled. "Joseph, if you had paid attention in geography or history class, you would know that parallel 49 is the border with Canada.

"Come on now, don't forget my generous offer to improve your wardrobe situation."

"48.325 runs just below the Canadian border through Maine and out west in Washington and Idaho."

"Maine's too cold. Go west, young woman."

"All through Washington state and the panhandle of Idaho into Montana."

Joe thought, too wet in western Washington, too flat and dry in eastern Washington. "What's in Idaho? Gimme a town."

"Little town called Bonners Ferry almost right on the line."

He smiled and moved to the counter. "Any mountains?"

"It's right near the Selkirk mountains." Alice leaned forward and squinted at the computer.

"Any water?"

"A river runs through it."

"Saw it. Meryl Streep in a totally unbelievable role showing off her muscles."

Alice rolled her eyes. "No seriously, a river runs right through the town."

Joe moved behind the counter to look over Alice's shoulder. "Show me."

She moved aside and Joe studied the map. "This could be the place," he said.

"What place?"

"Pinot Noir country."

"Wow, something to do with alcohol. I'm shocked. Does this involve money?"

"Maybe."

Alice sighed. "Joseph, you never have money."

He pulled a twenty dollar bill from his pocket and waved it at her. "What do you call this?"

She shook her head. "About a quarter of what you owe. I'm sure Bubbles will stop by soon and settle your bill."

It was the end of the season. He and Bubbles usually made a round of the bars and restaurants in town after Labor Day and made sure he was current with everyone. "How could I possibly owe that much? For coffee?"

"You and your morning buddies are like hobos. No money. Barefoot. Dressed like street people. You always say you've got it when they come in. This isn't a charity. Someone's got to pay." She nudged him away from the computer. "Speaking of paying, where has Bubbles been?"

Crap, he thought, he'd managed to not think about her for five whole minutes. Every mention of her name felt like a punch in the chest. One of the ladies from the offices upstairs came in before he could answer and Joe walked to the door and looked out across the beach between the Lighthouse and the Rudder where a game of two on two volleyball was in progress. Boys against the girls under the bright sun glimmering on the baby waves rolling onto the sand.

He thought again about the money and tried to push the thought away. He didn't do well with money, hated the thought of it. Years ago, before Bubbles, he'd given all his tip money to Jamie to hold. Somehow if he left the restaurant with it, the money would rarely make it home with him. When he needed money to buy the boat, he called Jamie and asked her how much he had. A little over eleven thousand dollars she'd told him.

"How soon can I get it?" he'd asked.

"Let's just say it kind of became a loan. I had to use it to make payroll in February. I can definitely get it to you by the end of August."

And he was upset, but he understood. Few people were aware of the difficulties of running a seasonal restaurant, the income dried up so quickly that everyone had to borrow to get through the winter. If she hadn't used his money, there might not be a restaurant.

But he had switched to the Bank of Bubbles. He just handed his money to her at the end of the night and if she was off, he'd peddle his bike to her apartment as fast as possible and leave the tips there.

Bubbles had told him that her father had taken her and her brother to a bank when they were very young and opened savings accounts for them. They were expected to record each deposit and balance the accounts at the end of each month. She still felt the need to know exactly how much money she had and he would jokingly accuse her of knowing how much change was rattling around in the bottom of the big purses she carried. He knew she didn't really understand why he went to the post office twice a month to purchase money orders to pay his bills, not trusting banks. He wasn't exactly sure why himself.

He never wanted to know how much he had stockpiled. Sometimes Bubbles would have an involuntary relapse into her old world and tell him he should have his money working for him. Invested in something. He would laugh and reply that he just wanted his money to relax and enjoy its brief time with him before being traded for a mask and snorkel in Isla Mujeres or a café au lait in the south of France.

The two bikini clad girls, sand sticking to the sweat covering them, raised their arms in victory by the volleyball net and ran to the bay to rinse off. Joe turned from the door. The customers had gone and he moved towards his chair then turned back to Alice. "How would I get there? This Bonners Ferry place."

She returned to the computer and Joe watched her stubby fingers work the keyboard. He waited at the counter looking at the accumulation of check-out junk; clip-on book lights, Starbucks mints, a wind-up flashlight. Stuff that seemed new until it sat there for a whole summer.

"You'd fly into Spokane, drive over from there. It's a little over a hundred miles."

"Book me a flight."

"Mr. Impetuous."

"Decisive Alice, impetuous is when you don't know what you're doing." Which of course, Joe thought, he didn't.

"Impetuous," Alice repeated.

"Story of my life," he said. "You can see how well it's worked out so far."

Chapter 7

Quiet but Quick

1 1/2 oz Effen Vodka   ½ oz Kirschwasser
1oz OJ   Shake with Ice
Martini Glass with Dash of Orange Bitters/ Cherry

So much for planning Joe thought as he walked back to the boat. Alice had booked him on a flight just two weeks away. Time enough to give notice at work, do some basic research, really come up with a plan. He realized his feet were burning on the hot pavement, jogged around the corner of the little shack that housed the boat rental office and jumped onto the cooler sand. His father popped into his thoughts again.

It was too soon to think of him as gone. Passed away. Departed. Across the miles. All the supposedly gentler words which wouldn't change the fact that he now resided in an urn, probably touching down in Tucson right about now. Joe thought of his mother and felt guilty. He had probably thought more about his dad in three days than he had about his mother in the five years since her death.

They had never been close. Never had the connection he felt with his dad. He had been an accident, as she liked to announce frequently. Joe had arrived in her country club years and he just kept her away from the bridge games, tennis and her new wealthy friends. At a young age, he had stayed away from her and their home as often as possible, spending days outside and nights at friends' houses whenever he could.

Sam and Janet blamed him for their mother's death. His father and mother came to see the Gypsy soon after he got it. She had taken one look and announced that it was the worst thing Joe had ever done, flounced away toward terra firma and promptly died three weeks later. That Joe or his boat could have caused a brain aneurysm seemed impossible to him, but the connection would always be there in his siblings' minds. Family. He wondered if he would ever see them again.

As he stepped onto the sand of the little beach, he noticed Sheets standing on the Jet Ski dock, probably working on a wave runner. Joe always thought of Tarzan when he saw the man. Lord Greystoke. *With the sinuous curves that told at a glance the wondrous combination of strength and speed*, to steal a line from old Edgar Rice Burroughs.

 Long black hair almost maroon along the edges where it had been washed out by the sun, tied in a ponytail down his back. Shirtless, sun darkened skin. Umber, Bubbles called it. Reddish, Joe would say, because he had no idea what umber was.

Joe thought back to the day he had driven the Gypsy into the marina five years ago, slamming into pilings and nearly colliding with the neighboring boats. Two days later, they caught a nor'easter with big winds. Sheets had knocked on the side of Joe's boat and asked if he needed some help with the lines. To be truthful, Joe knew boats, but mostly little boats. It had been a minor miracle that he had been able to pilot the Gypsy through the Chesapeake Bay from Richmond where he'd bought it. Sheets had said very little, just showed him some basic knots and told him to check the lines every day, because his new ropes would stretch.

Sheets owned a forty-one foot Morgan Classic sailboat. It was moored down B-Dock from the Gypsy. He didn't appear to have any means of support, but did odd jobs at the marina, repairing jet skis and engines, sometimes helping out at the gas dock. Joe didn't even know if he asked for money. Maybe he just traded for his slip fees. When they first met, Sheets didn't speak much with anyone. He would sit on his deck with a guitar and a bottle of what looked like Tequila most evenings, strumming and sipping quietly. Joe quickly saw Sheets as a project. He would stop by and ask for Sheets' help with something boat-related and finagle a way to stay and try to engage him in conversation.

A mostly one-sided friendship developed, Joe providing virtually all of the talk, Sheets listening, providing any nautical expertise needed. Joe discovered that while he loved living on the water, Sheets was *of* the water, as comfortable in it as out, swimming straight out from the beach every day no matter what the conditions, a half hour out and a half hour back.

Now, six years later, he looked at Sheets and tallied what he knew about the man;

Name: No

Age: No

Previous Occupation: No

Joe realized that he basically knew nothing about the man except that he considered him the brother he should have had instead of the really weird one he did have.

He calculated that it was about forty feet across the small patch of sand to the retaining wall of the marina, then another five feet of dock between himself and Sheets, who was bent over with his back to Joe. He ran as fast as he could, leaped to the top of the wall and launched himself towards Sheets in a perfect line of attack. But instead of landing squarely on Sheets' back, he grasped empty air, then landed in the shallow water just beyond the row of jet skis. He sank a foot into the sand, muck and god knows what else that had accumulated in the corner of the marina over the years. He turned back to the dock saying, "What?"

Sheets stood upright now, smiling, stroking an imaginary goatee. "You have much to learn Grasshoppa," he said in a bad oriental accent. "Feet make squeaky squeaky sound in warm sand, give away apploach." He reached a hand out to Joe to pull him from the water. Joe launched himself into deeper water to rinse as much mud from himself as possible, then stroked back to the dock and pulled himself out in one smooth motion.

"I can't accept help from someone with such a putrid Kung Fu impression." Joe still had bits of seaweed stuck to his legs. "How did I miss you anyway?"

"Ancient Chinese secret."

Joe couldn't help but laugh. "Shut up."

As they stood together, a man with a beer gut walked down F-Dock approaching them. He held a silver can in a meaty fist and his sunburned torso glistened with sweat. He glared at Sheets and said, "I'm paying you to fix my waverunner, not fuck around with dock trash."

Sheets tossed the socket wrench he was holding to the man who tried to catch it, but only succeeded in dropping his beer, which soaked his flowered shorts. "Think I'll go for a swim instead."

"Asshole. You made me spill my beer."

Joe and Sheets shook their heads and spoke as one, "Not beer. Coors Lite. America's Shame." Sheets stepped up onto the main dock. As Joe was about to follow, the fat man took two steps and moved to kick Sheets. Without looking back, Sheets jumped up and grasped the guy's ankle as it came up between his legs. He twisted the leg and held on, causing the man to flop onto the dock.

He let go of the leg, turned to the guy, and said softly, "Just let it go." Then he held out a hand and pulled the big man to his feet. "You won't be going out today anyway, your fuel pump's shot."

He extended an arm to Joe, pulled him up beside him and they headed toward B-Dock.

"What the hell was that move?" Joe asked.

"Physics." Sheets smiled at him.

"Quantum mechanics? String theory? Brownian motion? Something along those lines?"

"A little more basic. Levers, pulleys. Like that Greek guy who said, give me a lever and I can move the world. Some torque, a twist, and down they go."

"Jesus." Joe stopped by the gas pump and stared at his friend. "Where do you learn…?" He shook his head. "Forget I asked."

And he wondered, how can you know someone so well, and yet, know nothing about them?

Chapter 8

Highway to Heaven

1oz Cruzan Coconut Rum   1oz Midori
1oz Flor de Caña White Rum
3oz Pineapple Juice   1oz OJ
Mix in Hurricane Glass/ Splash with 7Up
Garnish with Fresh Pineapple

"Did you notice anything different this morning?" Sheets asked, as they walked along the section of dock bordering the marina parking lot.

How would I notice, Joe thought? Everything's been different, screwed up for a week. "I've been sleeping so late, nothing's seemed right."

"No ultralight. It went down off the end of Rehoboth Avenue yesterday. Sheets raised a palm towards Joe.

As he slapped the hand, Joe thought, how the hell could I have missed that? The ultralight was not a popular subject. Little more than a hang glider with a two-stroke engine, it offered scenic tours of the ocean and bay. Unfortunately, the marina lay directly in the path of its ascent, and the flights started early in the morning.

When it passed overhead, it sounded as if you were being attacked by lawnmowers.

"Any survivors?" Joe said.

"The pilot and passenger were fished from the ocean unharmed, but the bird sank like a stone." They exchanged another slap.

"Calls for a celebration," Joe said. "B-Dock crew, late night, bottle of Mezcal until the worm is gone or the sun comes up. If you see the pilot, invite him. He's gonna need some consoling. The wind picked up, ruffling Sheets' ponytail and the breeze and the warm sun brought back a memory of a day from his first year on the dock. Although they'd hang out most evenings, Joe was still initiating the conversations, and truthfully, finishing them as well. Sheets would rarely even utter a complete sentence and Joe wondered if he felt the bond growing between them that Joe did. Until a day, just like this one, late in that first summer.

ψ ψ ψ

"Get up. We've got to leave right now."

Joe flopped out of the hammock on the top deck and looked down at Sheets, who was rapping on the side of the Gypsy. The August sun, already warm, was just above the horizon. "Leave for where and more importantly, what the hell time is it?"

"Time for you to learn the joy of sailing, which you've been trashing since you got here."

"Gimme five minutes."

Joe climbed down from the top deck and stood brushing his teeth in his outdoor shower, thinking that he owed Sheets the chance to at least try to show Joe what was so great about sailing.

Point A to point B, he thought, never really understanding the thrill of having to turn a boat twenty times to get where you were going. He wandered across the dock in his black bathing suit and T-shirt to the stern of Sheets' sloop, hoping that Sheets had laid in plenty of alcohol to help Joe make it through the boredom of a day of sailing. But at least it was a perfect day, just a few clouds, and crisp, with a fifteen knot breeze from the northwest. He laughed at himself. Without Sheets he'd know nothing about either kind of knots.

Sheets motored out of the marina and raised the sails. The breeze was freshening and with just the mainsail up, the boat began to move rapidly south down the bay. A line of catamarans from the sailing club was circling in front of them, racing in the perfect conditions. Joe assumed that Sheets would have to detour to the west to get around them, but he picked a line and shot through the little boats without ever deviating from his course. Joe was amazed, as always, by Sheets intuitive feel for everything on or in the water. He reclined against the front of the cabin and dozed off in the embrace of the sun and the breeze.

The hard turn into Indian River Bay rolled Joe onto the starboard deck and nearly into the bay as Sheets laughed at him from behind the wheel. The sloop lost some speed when Sheets tacked to the east and began picking his way through the mass of boats attempting to pass through the inlet into the ocean. A few people were already returning from pre-dawn fishing excursions creating a watery traffic jam. Sheets again was able to hold a line through the traffic out into the ocean, earning a few epithets, honks and fingers from the powerboats he got close to. The Arabs will love the Jews before sailboat owners and power boaters get along, thought Joe. Sheets continued straight out into the ocean and Joe dozed off again.

When he woke up, Sheets was on the bow pulpit lowering the anchor. Joe could still see land, but they were far enough out to make it impossible to see people on the beach.

"What's for breakfast?"

"A ride in the sky," said Sheets as he unfurled a large triangular sail on the bow. "Watch and learn." He grabbed a line attached to the lowest point on the sail and was lifted from the deck as a gust filled the sail. He rose on the breeze to a level far above the deck and was lowered back towards the boat as the wind diminished, making a perfect landing on the deck. Another gust quickly lifted him again, but this time at the peak of his ascent, he released his hold on the sail, did a couple back flips and knifed into the water. He re-appeared moments later, shook out his long hair, and swam back to the boat. "Your turn."

Joe stood on the deck as Sheets waited for the wind to bring the line from the sail back into reach. Sheets handed him the rope as Joe said, "What do I do?"

"Not much. Just let the wind and sail do the work. Don't try and land on the deck the first time."

A powerful gust lifted Joe from the deck, nearly pulling the line from his hands. His timing was way off and he released the line well before the peak of his rise and plummeted feet first into the white-capping water. He bobbed to the surface, looked at Sheets and said, "Wow." He scrambled up the ladder, moved to the front of the boat and grabbed the line from Sheets.

"Why haven't you shown me this before?"

"You've not been ready, Grasshopper."

Joe was pulled off the deck again, releasing the sail closer to the apex of the rise and executing a decent swan dive. He felt as if he'd been thirty feet in the air before slicing into the deep green ocean. Even a mile from shore, the water was warm and he couldn't remember ever feeling more exhilarated, more in touch with the world.

Joe would look back on this day as the time he was fully accepted into Sheets' world, allowed to see the perfection that Sheets sought in the natural world of sun, wind and water. They spent several hours riding the spinnaker, as the sail was called. Several boats stopped to watch the aerial acrobatics, applauding each ride.

Joe forgot time, alcohol, food, everything, caught up in the wonder of it- the closest thing to flight he had ever experienced. When they pulled up the anchor, Joe was as tired and sore as he ever remembered being, but the exhilaration lasted for days. Sheets and Joe hadn't spoken more than a few words the entire day, except for Sheets explaining that he'd not been holding out on Joe, but that days when the conditions were ideal for riding the spinnaker were few and far between.

ψ ψ ψ

"What happened over there?" The grizzled Dockmaster's cigar bobbed as he attempted to speak around it. Sheets paused to talk with the man Joe called Cig for the, disgusting, drool sodden stubs which never seemed to leave his lips.

"Catch up with you later." Joe waved his hand and kept on going.

The man never used anyone's first name and was famous for his frequent vague warnings. Joe was pretty sure the guy was about 80% deaf and since Sheets rarely spoke more than a few words at a time, their conversations resembled bad mime. Lots of pointing and grunting on Cig's part, while Sheets mostly just nodded. Sheets had once told Joe that the old guy was an Ex-Navy lifer with a sound of real respect in his voice, so Joe just kept his feelings about Cig to himself. He avoided the marina office like the plague though, with the stale cigar stench seemingly embedded in every surface.

"You watch yourself, Rath," Cig called after him.

Chapter 9

Roy Rogers

6 oz Coca Cola   1oz Grenadine
Tall glass   Straw   Cherry Garnish
Add cheap rum as needed

A s Joe walked out towards the Gypsy, deep in thought, he missed the left turn to his boat and slammed his foot into a red and yellow Big Wheel. He collapsed onto the bench of the picnic table in the center of the big square where the dock turned 90 degrees to the left and pulled his foot up to assess the damage, when he noticed the little kid watching him. The child was wearing long flowered yellow board shorts and nothing else.

"No Lilliputians allowed out here," said Joe.

"What's a Lilliputian?"

"Don't you read?"

"I'm six, Joe."

"What's your name," said Joe, rubbing his damaged toes.

"You know my name. I live here on the weekends."

"Refresh my memory."

"Jason"

"Jay Sin, gimme some skin."

"It's Jay Son and I'll give you a ton," the kid said, whacking Joe's outstretched hand with both of his little paws. Joe jumped up and flopped into the seat of the Big Wheel, pulling his long legs back in a fruitless attempt to use the pedals. He planted his feet on the dock and propelled himself and the trike forward towards his boat yelling, "Grand theft, Big Wheeeeel." The child pursued him, laughing. As he reached the Gypsy, Joe leaned back, fell off, bounced once and watched as the trike clattered over the remaining boards, hung in the air for a millisecond, then splashed into the bay. He shouted, "Man overboard Slim. Gaff," as he lay on the unforgiving wood.

Joe watched from his back as the kid hustled onto the Gypsy and passed the hooked pole down to him, and the skinny runt reminded him of himself with the boundless energy he'd had at that age.

"You might have to handle this, Slim. I believe I'm hors de combat."

Jason jumped down to the dock, grabbed the gaff, extended it fully and managed to hook the yellow steering wheel and drag the rig in toward the dock. Joe crawled over to the edge, leaned over and pulled the trike out of the water. It had snagged a jelly or two and a hunk of sea lettuce which reeked like garbage.

Jason put his arm around Joe and whispered, "Whore's a bad word,"

"*Hors de combat* means out of action. Where did you learn that word anyway?"

"When my dad drinks beer, it's what he calls my mom's sister, then my mom yells at him. So maybe we shouldn't tell my mom you said it." The kid stared at Joe. "Can I sit in the hot tub?"

"That is blackmail, you scrawny weasel." Joe gave the kid a long look and wondered about the lessons he was learning. Most of the boat people drank a lot, but Jason's parents sometimes got ugly and violent. Sheets and Joe had to intervene one evening when things got out of hand. Sheets had pulled Jason's dad, Moose, aside and spoken softly to him and there had never been another incident, but Joe worried about what happened when the kid wasn't here.

"All right, hose down your rig and let's go." Joe waited on his front deck looking eastward across the line of sailboats on the south side of B dock toward the marina office. A pontoon boat was loading up to go fishing at the gas dock, piled with coolers, fishing poles and orange life jackets. A couple sat with their feet up on the white railing of the porch of one of the third-floor condos overlooking the marina. A steady stream of traffic was moving south on Route 1, heading to Bethany, Fenwick and Ocean City, a stream which would have all the coastal resorts filled to capacity soon. He sighed, thinking how much he was dreading dealing with those crowds this weekend.

Jason finished hosing off the Big Wheel and moved to climb onto the boat.

"Forgetting something, my little pal?" Joe held his arm across the break in the rail.

"Permission to come aboard," Jason said, snapping off a salute, which made Joe laugh.

"Bow down to the Gypsy." Joe tried for a stern voice and failed.

The kid stretched out his hands and bent at the waist, his fingers touching the bow, his long sun-bleached hair covering his face.

"Come aboard."

Jason leaped up and ran down the port companionway, waiting for Joe on the rear deck. Joe hoisted him up on the ladder, then climbed up behind him to the top deck. He lifted the lid off the soft tub, held out his arm which Jason grabbed, and chinned himself up. Joe raised his arm and lifted the kid over the edge and deposited him into the blue lined pool. He then punched a button on the side of the tub and watched as bubbles obscured the skinny body. He thought with sadness of the seven nights without Bubbles, right here, their favorite place.

Joe pulled his workout bench and dumbbells into the center of the deck. "Count for me, Slim." He started a set, then glanced over at the kid and dropped the weights to the padded mat below the bench. Kids. What was his problem? He liked having Jason around, gave him free run of the Gypsy. Why had he crucified Bubbles about that baby book? Maybe it was the book itself, the original Dr. Spock baby manual, the same one his mother had given to his wife and him when his ex had become pregnant. It's all you'll ever need to know about parenting she'd said, which made Joe cynically wonder if she'd ever read it.

Something about seeing that book, with that name on the cover, in Bubbles hands last week, had brought back all the guilt and pain he felt whenever he thought of the pregnancy and the end of his marriage. And he had exploded at her and turned away from her shocked look with no explanation for his outburst. She'd tried to talk to him several times that evening, but he hadn't been able to respond. He knew if he told the story of what had happened fifteen years ago, that it would end their relationship. Christ, he thought, he was stuck, with only a half-assed plan to count on. He picked up the weights and pushed them violently into the blue sky.

He was halfway through his first set when Jason called over.

"What's this? It stinks." He was holding up one of the shot glasses, his nose crinkled.

Joe finished his set before answering. "Aztec medicine."

"What's wrong with you?"

"Immediately or globally?"

"What?"

"Immediately, two broken metatarsals and a sore coccyx. Globally, lack of focus and follow-through."

"What?"

Joe pulled the bench over to the side of the tub. "Were you here earlier? The duck poster was out this morning."

"No. We got here about ten minutes before I saw you."

Weird, Joe thought. Did she stop over last night? Was he too drunk to remember? Did he get it out himself? Maybe he was going crazy. Too much happening at once.

"You alright? Jason flicked some water into Joe's face.

Damn good question, Joe thought. "What would you do with a million dollars, Slim?"

"Is it enough to go to Disneyworld?"

"Maybe two or three times. Wouldn't work for me though. I'm not a big fan of the Mouse." Before Joe had to explain anything to the kid, a voice came from the dock.

"Joe, you up there?"

"Yeah, Moose."

"You seen my son?"

"He's soaking in the hot tub with a six-pack and a couple Jager girls from the Rudder. What are you doing here on a Thursday?"

"Sheets called and said the boat looked like it might be taking on water. Had to take a day off work, come check it out."

"Everything ok?"

"Bad seal around the propeller shaft, but I repacked it temporarily. Can you send the little guy down? We gotta drive home. Got to work tomorrow. We'll be back Saturday."

Jason was climbing out of the soft tub. He turned to Joe and said, "Mum's the word on saying whore, Joe."

"Mum's the word? Where do you come up with this shit? I thought you were six. Oh no, no, pretend I didn't say that."

"Looks like I'll be spending a lot of time in the hot tub."

"Get out, you little cretin. Spawn of Satan."

Joe watched as Moose hoisted the little guy to his shoulder, water from Jason's still wet trunks darkening his father's white t-shirt. As they moved away towards the parking lot, Joe thought that when the rapture took him away, he actually might miss that kid.

Chapter 10

Egg Crusher

1 oz Appleton White Rum   1oz Tia Maria
1 Cup Eggnog
Shake with ice   Strain into Snifter
Dust with Nutmeg

.

Joe lowered the dumbbells back to the deck and sat up on the bench. He glanced to his left, down the bay, watched a pair of sailboats with matching red and white striped sails crossing the shallow water from the boat club. Joe loved living on the water, couldn't imagine not living near the ocean. The marina was only one long and one short block from the beach and he went over almost every day to run a few miles along the shore towards Indian River Inlet. He loved the ocean, especially during the solitude of the offseason when the sanderlings retook possession of the beach with their maniacal dashes towards and away from the surf line, taking flight in synchronized, ever-changing patterns.

But he thought of the ocean as an autistic child with its endless repetition, in and out and after a run he'd sit, mesmerized, locked into the rhythm of the waves, and an hour would pass mindlessly.

That's why he preferred the bay, the hyperactive child. Constant activity. The barn swallows that lived under the dock dive-bombing people as they walked over their nests. Gulls jockeying for position on the pilings. Boats of every type entering and leaving the bay from the canal which spilled into the bay near the marina. The live music from the Rudder deck, which started promptly at 4 p.m. and went on until the bar closed late at night.

Now, Joe looked to the seawall behind the boat. A few summers ago, a flock of pelicans had moved in for a month, dominating the pilings on the wall. Joe missed having them around, thought they looked like living fossils, a connection to an earlier time. The pelicans brought back memories of a Costa Rican evening, sitting on a rock overlooking the Pacific, the red sun just beginning to drop into the water when four of the prehistoric birds crossed the sun just above the waterline, etching the scene in his memory forever. He'd check several times a day each summer, hoping for their return.

Joe did one more set, then stood up to stretch the kinks from his shoulders, sweat rolling off him from the effort and the heat of the day. A voice from the dock below cooed, "Ooh, how manly."

Joe didn't bother to turn around, just raised his arms to shoulder level, flexed and said, "Not easy maintaining the body that men envy and women adore."

"How would you know, skinny?" said the voice.

Joe grinned and turned to the voice—Egg from two slips over. Egg because she lived on a beautiful old Egg Harbor motor yacht. She had moved in this season. He stepped over to the rail.

"Party for the demise of the ultra tonight," Joe said. "Clothing optional."

"Like you haven't checked me out already," Egg huffed, "You know the sun reflects off the lenses of your binoculars." Egg was in the habit of sunbathing naked on her top deck which could not be seen from the dock, but was slightly lower than Joe's.

"Terrorist watch," laughed Joe, "Top secret project, which is why I can only peek over the rail surreptitiously."

"Jesus, Joe, that is so lame."

"Hey Hey Hey. I'm not the only one. You should be happy the ultralight went down. I believe our favorite pilot was targeting your boat. Called it 'Flight of Porn.' I think he had your picture in this year's advertising brochure."

She shook her head, her long black hair swaying across her face. Joe knew her big brown eyes would be flashing behind her sunglasses. God, she was something though, he thought. Black bikini against deeply tanned skin. Italian temperament. DiAngelo or DiAvellino. Joe couldn't remember her name. The only person at the marina who used last names was the foul tempered dockmaster who never used anything else and he could make everyone's name sound like a disease.

"That little…." Her head shook again.

Joe loved it when she got fired up. She smoldered. He and Sheets had been sitting on the Rudder deck one night, where she tended bar, when a guy had come on to her a little too hard. Sheets was already moving towards the man when she clocked him with a straight right hand delivered across the bar.

"Well at least our little friend never stole his own father's boat."
Joe decided to tweak her, feeling fairly safe on his top deck.

"Borrowed, not stolen." Egg had not taken the bait.

They were distracted by a pair of waverunners honking, the
riders waving at Egg as they passed through the break in the wall
that protected the marina from the bay. She blew them a kiss and
they nearly collided. She had a look. Those brown eyes, full lips.
Sultry. That was the word. Her tip jar was always overflowing. As
much as six or seven hundred dollars on weekend nights.

"Why did you steal your Dad's boat again?" Joe had heard the
story multiple times over the summer, but it made him laugh every
time. He stood and stretched, then moved under the bimini cover.
The early September sun, directly overhead now, was beginning
to bring back his hangover. The breeze shifted and he picked up
the smell of chicken grilling. A picnic in progress on the beach by
the lagoon.

"Requisitioned. He neglected to attend my graduation."

Joe laughed, "The bastard. Stealing his boat was the least you
could have done." Joe felt a little sympathy for the guy. He knew
Egg was twenty-eight and had just graduated in May.

"Not stolen. Short term loan. He couldn't take a half a day off
from sinking the economy to come to Boston for his only
daughter."

"Capitalists. Can't live with em. Not allowed to shoot em.
Who's he work for?"

"Chase Stanley Sachs Stearns. Who knows? Every time there's
trouble, a few of the names merge to take off the heat." She pushed

her dark glasses down her nose and stared at Joe. "Summer's almost over. What am I going to do?"

"You thinking of driving that thing back to The Hamptons? Maybe turn yourself in?"

Moisture seemed to be appearing in her eyes. "One hundred percent Dago. We don't give up on grudges. Joe, I like it here. Sheets, you, even that midget pervert pilot. Bubbles already seems like the best friend I've ever had."

She must have seen him flinch at the mention of Bubbles' name. "You haven't found a way to screw it up have you? Oh crap. She hasn't been here all week."

"I... we...." Joe turned and concentrated on the one fluffy cloud hanging on the western horizon.

"What have you done? You idiot. How could you? She loves you."

Joe moved to the helm, sat down in the captain's chair and laid his head on the cool metal of the wheel. There were no answers.

Chapter 11

Banana Republic

6 oz 10 Cane Rum   6 oz Mango Juice
2 Bananas   2 Fresh Pineapple Rings 1 Cherry
Blend until Smooth   Serve in Collins Glass
Splash with Ginger Ale

Maybe the town wasn't completely devoted to alcohol, Joe thought as he biked past Vavala's Beach Things which doubled as the Dewey Beach Post Office. The town had a few of these strange combo businesses: A place called Sun Medicine, which also sold beach chairs. Jeremiah's; formerly a record and tape store which now sold hot dogs and beach chairs; and the strangest one of all, the Exxon station, which except for a new canopy over the gas pumps, looked to date from the 1950's. If you went in to the small attached building to pay for your gas, you could also buy a beach chair.

He passed through the residential area named Rehoboth by The Sea, which of course was in Dewey Beach and not Rehoboth and then across Silver Lake bridge into Rehoboth Beach proper. The two towns could not be more different, he thought. Dewey looked like a traditional beach town. Sparse vegetation. A shade on the run-down side. Everything worn and sunbaked.

When you crossed the bridge into Rehoboth, tall trees appeared as if from nowhere, rising above elegant homes with manicured shrubbery. Two freshwater lakes, ponds really, adorned the north and south sides of town. Rehoboth was filled with excellent restaurants and had a mile long boardwalk with arcades and a miniature amusement park. A family town. Only the most cockeyed optimists would call Dewey Beach a family town. Hedonism III would be much closer.

And if the towns were completely different, the politics and administrations of each were also light years apart. Dewey, with a year round population of less than 350, seemed to operate like a banana republic. The town sued businesses. Businesses sued right back. Accusations flew back and forth between rival factions. From the safety of the marina, which was technically not part of the town, Joe thought it was like watching a food fight.

In Rehoboth, on the other hand, things always seemed to go smoothly. A guy from an old Rehoboth family had apparently been elected mayor for life. The names on the city council rarely changed. In all, he thought, the city ran quietly and effectively. No food fights. And so he rarely had any cause to think about the people who ran things and even fewer occasions to come in contact with them. Except for one memorable evening.

ψ ψ ψ

The bar was set up on the lawn of the Art League. "We need these people," Jamie had said. "They can help the Emerald." And though Joe knew she already had one of the most successful restaurants in town, he also knew she had some desperate need to be accepted by the power elite. Bound by Joe Rath rule number one, 'Never say no to a friend,' here he was.

He largely avoided Henlopen Acres, the location of the Art League. Its manicured lawns and huge houses reminded him a little too much of the Pine Orchard neighborhood he'd grown up in on Long Island Sound. Joe recognized the people as well. Immaculate. They hewed to some dress code that he couldn't quite put his finger on. Some fabric which didn't wrinkle that only they had access to. Movers and Shakers.

He wished the bar had been set up so that he could see down to the little private marina on the canal. Then he could picture Sheets sailing up, running up to the private function in his ratty red swim suit, and like Tarzan, carrying off a young Jane.

Joe guessed that there was a hundred people spread across the grass in clusters of four or five, some leaning against the tall oaks. Most everyone had a drink in hand at this point and he scanned the faces. He recognized very few. He thought that in Dewey and Rehoboth he knew 80% of the bartenders, most of the restaurant owners and workers, and scores more people who ate regularly at The Emerald. Maybe the sushi revolution had yet to reach the blue bloods of Sussex County.

Some people complained that the town of Rehoboth was changing too quickly, cottages torn down to put up mansions which overfilled the small lots. Others said it never changed at all.

Joe guessed that the people on the lawn represented a large chunk of the power in the Rehoboth and except for the occasional sound of a cell phone, this event could have taken place thirty, forty or even fifty years ago. These people or their ancestors had probably run the town since the first Methodist tent was raised in the 1800's.

And honestly, he thought, let em have it. Divine right of kings. Noblesse oblige and all that. After all these years, they were pretty good at running things and they would be doing it after he was long gone. If Jamie felt the need to hang out with these people, she'd need to start getting up early enough to do Sunday brunch at the Back Porch where the power elite met to get a post-church buzz on with Mimosas and Bloody Marys.

He saw Bubbles out among the crowd in the starched white shirt and black pants the organizers of the 'Save the Whatever' fundraiser had required them to wear. She was talking to a guy who was standing far too close for a mere chat, giving Joe that falling feeling in his stomach that he still felt every Thursday night when she went dancing at the Rudder. The man had that perfect look that most of the people here had about them.

Handsome. Pink shirt rolled up exactly two turns. Hair manicured like the neighborhood lawns, perfectly placed patches of gray on each temple. Mid-thirties. Deeply tanned. She was smiling at the guy.

Two ladies strolled up at that moment, holding empty glasses, beaded with condensation. Matching beauties, they could have been sisters. They looked to be five years younger than him. Only their weathered hands gave away the fact that he probably had ten years on them. Light blond hair on one, dark on the other, curved out and returned precisely to the nape of their necks. Gotta give them this, he thought, they maintained.

"Mezcal shots, ladies? From my private stash." Joe pulled the bottle of Ilegal from the ice bin. He thought that he and Bubbles would sneak a shot during clean up.

"Mezcal?" Blondie said.

"Like Tequila, but better. Aztec medicine. Surefire cure for scurvy, impetigo, just about anything that ails you."

"Set em up, barkeep," said dark hair grinning at her friend. "And one for yourself."

Joe glanced out at the crowd, heard the low murmur of conversation and saw Bubbles being steered toward the periphery, handsome man's hand on her sleeve. Panic. This was the world she came from, the world her father had been grooming her for. Had she finally realized that this was what she wanted after all? His heart was racing. He needed a shot now.

He grabbed three plastic glasses and poured a perfect shot in each. Taking his fruit knife, he cut large orange wedges and ripped open a paper packet of sea salt. Licking the curve between his thumb and forefinger, he tapped some salt on the damp spot.

Seeing them hesitate, he said. "Moisten up ladies." And passed the salt.

"So ladylike," said the blond as she applied the salt.

Dark hair giggled. "Ready."

Joe raised his glass and touched theirs. "Save the...." He paused. "What are we saving again?"

They glanced at each other. Dark hair giggled once more. "I've forgotten."

"So many lawns. So little time." Joe licked the salt, downed his shot and the ladies followed suit. He handed them the orange wedges and they all sucked loudly. He was truly beginning to like these two. He scanned the area for Bubbles. All he saw was the constantly changing groups of four or five people milling in the gathering dusk. Maybe one more shot with his new friends.

"Let's do another," said dark hair

"We must," said blondie.

But the moment was ended by a woman approaching who gave Joe a withering stare. She flicked her eyes towards his shirt and he followed her gaze to an orange stain on the starched white. Cause for dismissal by the host, he was certain. He looked back up at her.

Magnificent, Joe thought. Still beautiful, she was probably every bit of seventy years old, but the only concession was a touch of neck crepe. Impeccably outfitted in a dress of that same material he knew naught of, a single strand of pearls, she had a presence that spoke of old wealth and status and all the power that came with it.

"Your husbands are looking for you." Her tone was quiet, but firm. He wondered if anyone had ever said no to that voice. He started to speak, but caught himself. What would be the point of asking her if she enjoyed life? He knew he would never comprehend these people, these fabrics, these lawns, these lives, money, power, any of it. And with one last 'you'll never be back here' look at Joe, she turned on her heels and his two new friends followed meekly behind her. It was exactly the type of performance his mother must have thought she could do just by joining the Country Club, never realizing that it takes new money decades to grow authority, if ever.

Magnificent, he thought again as he felt a tap on his elbow. Bubbles. "I need a perfect Manhattan. And quit flirting with the hoi-polloi."

Joe filled a glass with ice to chill it. "Is this for your new friend?" He could hear a touch of bitterness in his voice.

"He owns the biggest house on the beach in North Shores with a hot tub overlooking the ocean. And I'm invited."

As he filled a shaker with Crown Royal and a splash each of sweet and dry vermouth, his heart fell. "What did you tell him?"

"I never got to answer. He got a call and said he had to take it. A big deal about to happen."

"You gonna go?" Joe added ice to the mix and shook it violently.

"Well, I wondered if I went to the biggest house on North Shores and sat in his hot tub overlooking the ocean and put my head back and looked at the sky, if he would be able to tell me when the moon would be in Venus."

He felt his heart restarting. He looked at her as he slowed his shaking motion.

"I wondered if he would know exactly which cowboy song to play to make me want to dance naked with him under the stars."

I'm an idiot, he thought. Relief rushed through him. He set the shaker down.

"I wondered if he would know exactly when to go to the kitchen and bring me that split of Champagne. And you know what?"

"Your life is full of wonder?"

"I said to myself that none of that mattered. Because he was so good looking. Because he likely had taken the time to be sure his deep rich power tan covered his whole body, not like some people I know who let their shiny white butts glow in the moonlight." She paused and gave him a two-handed shove. "Jealousy doesn't suit you, Joe Rath, but god that was fun."

Joe felt as if he had just gotten off a rollercoaster. Shaky with relief. She was his own Mover and Shaker. "Think I'm gonna go find me some rich dowager, help me drown my sorrows." He started to walk away, then turned and took her in his arms and twirled her around, banging the table and spilling the drink. "You evil thing."

Chapter 12

Novocain

4 oz Southern Comfort   4 oz Remy Martin Cognac
Chill   Strain into Martini Glass

Joe locked his bicycle to one of the rings on the side of the restaurant and sighed. Thursday, the last day before Labor Day weekend. A drop of sweat stung his eye, the result of his two-mile ride and lingering hangover. Three days of hell after tonight then the hard part would be over for the year. He glanced up at the sign over the door. It was supposed to be a wave breaking with sea spray coming off the top, but Joe had always thought it looked more like a crayfish or shrimp caught in a maelstrom. As at the end of every summer, paint was peeling off the shrimp, leaving it raggedy looking, like all the service workers in town. He sighed.

The hot vinegary smell of freshly cooked sushi rice from the kitchen assaulted his sinuses as he pushed open the front door. He turned to the right into the bar, flipped on some lights and saw that the brightly-colored stools shaped like Trivial Pursuit wedges had not been pushed back under the round glass tables along the angled right wall. The bar top was littered with half-filled glasses and he knew that Jamie had closed the bar in his absence. Joe figured since she owned the place, she thought everyone should clean up after her. Or maybe she was drinking Novocains in Joe's absence because he refused to serve them to her after a broken window incident late one night.

Another glance past the hanging glass racks to the back bar revealed the liquor bottles turned with their labels facing in all different directions. Joe moved behind the bar and began straightening the bottles, his bottles, making sure they were in their correct places. The beer cooler was making an unusual clicking noise. Joe thought, go away for one day. His attention was attracted by a family passing by the bar room window, a mom and two kids pulling a cart piled high with beach toys and chairs. Sitting at the tall table by the window was Bubbles, her short hair back-lit by the sun, and he was instantly filled with pain and regret.

The hair had been the first thing Joe had noticed about her when she started at the restaurant three years earlier. She had always kept it short and it seemed to pick up the ambient light in any room. Light blond, nearly white, it created a halo effect when lit from behind.

Joe had originally called her Angel, which she hated, but Joe could not bring himself to call her by her real name of Wanda, never once deviating from this policy.

Bubbles head turned from the window and she met Joe's eyes. A cold look, none of her usual warmth.

"Hey, you," said Joe, moving from behind the bar and approaching the table.

"Hey." Dispirited.

Joe reached out and touched her shoulder. "There's something I need to tell you."

"I already know. Janet called me. I'm so angry and upset that I had to hear this from your sister. I loved your dad."

Joe lifted his hand from her shoulder into her sun dappled hair. She pushed the hand away. "I'm sorry, Bub, really, but I just couldn't talk about it."

"Sorry Joe? Sorry? We shared everything til a week ago. Then you just shut me out completely? We've never even had a real argument before. And a baby book set you off? It wasn't even mine. A gift for a friend."

He didn't respond, just looked past Bubbles out the window. Saw David, the bartender from the restaurant across the street sitting on their entry stairs smoking a cigarette. Listened to the air conditioner cycle on from the roof. He finally said, "Just a baby book."

"Give me some idea why it was so upsetting to you." Bubbles picked at some white fuzz on her black uniform shirt.

"I don't understand it myself." A lie, he told himself. Had he ever lied to her before? It made him feel hollow. He'd carried the guilt about the baby around for fifteen years, had never spoken to anyone about it.

"That's not good enough. A whole week. Getting Jamie drunk and letting her drive home. Not telling me about you dad. What is wrong with you?"

What to say? He knew he couldn't talk about it. It gave him lockjaw. "I. I can't," was all he was able to get out.

Bubbles stood and pushed Joe hard in the chest with both hands, knocking him back.

"Fuck you, Joe Rath."

Joe reached for her with both hands before she could push him again, put his arms around her, lifted her up and twirled her 360 degrees, depositing her back where she started. She pushed him again, but half-heartedly.

"That won't work this time."

"Twirlabouts always work."

"Twirlabout? I need one. Labor Day weekend coming," said a long haired woman coming through the bar entrance.

"Sorry, James, didn't drive the forklift today," said Joe. She turned on her heels and stormed back the way she came. Moments later, he heard her office door slam. Joe turned to Bubbles. "What was that? We always kid about her weight."

"Hormones."

"Thought hormones were next week."

"Different hormones. She's pregnant."

"Pregnant? Pregnant as in …." It finally sank in. What Bubbles had said before. The baby book had nothing to do with her. He was losing her…and it really was over nothing.

Bubbles pushed past him and headed toward the kitchen. She turned. "Go talk to her. See if you can make her as miserable as you've made me."

ψ ψ ψ

"I'm sorry." Joe rapped on the door to Jamie's office, really just a converted closet next to the host stand. There was no response from behind the door. The sound of the pump and falling water from the pond she had built behind the reception area was all he heard. "Come on, James. Open up." He knocked again. "Congratulations."

"Go away."

Silence fell once more. Crap, he thought. Everything he'd done for the last week had turned into a nightmare. Turned people he loved against him. It had been a good summer. A great year. How had it gone so bad so fast? Make her laugh, was all he could think.

"Who's the father?" he said to the closed door.

"Shut up, idiot. My husband." Jamie sniffled a couple of times.

"The big man? Is he still around?" Her husband, Rick, ran the kitchen. He hated Joe. Last Thursday's night drunken revelry at the bar had her husband riled up. Just another item on his week long list of screw-ups. He had been drinking to try and forget his encounter with Bubbles and Jamie had been angry with Rick for something.

The door clicked open. Jamie sat behind her desk, tissues pressed to her eyes. "Go away. I've got to finish with the reservations." She paused. "Asshole."

"Stand up." Joe did the come here motion with his index finger.

She shook her head. He moved behind her chair and lifted her from it. He carried her into the reception area, spun her around, moved her back into the office and set her back in the chair. "One twirlabout as per your request."

"What's this baby thing Bubbles is so upset about?"

Crap, he thought, were there no secrets here whatsoever? He just needed time to think. Get this plan straight in his mind. "Gotta go. Prep time. Somebody destroyed the bar last night."

Joe hurried back to the bar and tapped the CD player to life, preventing any further discussion. And what else would come on but Counting Crows. The lyrics that most reminded him of her;

"*And all at once you look across a crowded room*

To see the way the light attaches to a girl"

He looked to the table by the window, but she was gone.

Long gone.

Chapter 13

Angel Hair

Remove Zaya 12 year Rum from Freezer
Pour ¾ oz in Shot Glass
Add ¼ oz Dr. McGillicuddy's Peach Schnapps from
Freezer
Hold up to light. Tendrils of filament will appear

Before Bubbles became Bubbles, she was Angel. Her parents had named her Wanda. A girl called Wanda. Seriously? He had thought the day they were introduced. Nobody names their child Wanda. He had taken one look at her short hair, platinum blond, so nearly white that it looked like a halo and promptly dubbed her Angel. She protested, but as best he could recall, no one had ever called her Wanda again.

Joe and Angel had not been close for the first year. She was just going to be a seasonal wonder, a summer at the beach, like so many others, before going off to B school at Wharton. But, she fell into the rhythm of the ocean and decided to postpone real life for a year. Angel had confided in Jamie that business school and the corporate world had been more of her father's dream for her than her own vision. As Joe knew all too well, secrets burned like habañero peppers in Jamie, spit out quickly to the next person, usually him. He filed the information away, not sure at that moment how he felt about it.

It was easy to see at the end of that first year that she was hooked and could no longer see a future without a beach. Mountains for some, he thought, deserts for others, the ocean captured a few people every season and never let go.

In that first season, Joe and Angel had worked side by side as servers, never getting very friendly, mildly competitive. Joe felt a little resentful when Angel began to get close to Jamie, because he and Jamie had been best friends, sometimes more. During that first year, Angel and Jamie became like sisters and Joe felt like the odd man out.

Two years earlier, Jamie had decided to build a bar in the restaurant and told Joe he would be the bartender since he made most of the drinks for the servers already. They spent the winter remodeling the Emerald to include an eight seat L shaped bar. She told Joe that she wanted to upgrade the wine list. Joe, being a shots and beer guy, knew little about wine and protested. Angel pulled him aside and told him that she could help.

It turned out she knew a lot about wine. Her parents served wine with dinner and let their two kids have small glasses right along with them from an early age. Her father was a collector, mostly Bordeaux and high end Napa cabernets. He insisted that she and her brother learn the basics of wine and wine appreciation. She came to have a passion for the subject and amazed Joe with all she knew, grapes, wine regions, food pairings.

Wine reps would leave bottles for them to taste. She and Joe would wait until after closing, sometimes getting the kitchen to make them an entrée to try to pair with whatever they were tasting. They would move to a table in the back and sip the wines. They agreed to each write a description before comparing notes, so they wouldn't affect each other's opinion.   Joe quickly came to appreciate the subtle differences of the wine world. That a Napa Valley chardonnay tasted almost nothing like a White Burgundy made from the same grape. That a Pinot Noir was vastly different from a Syrah, even if they were similar in color. They slowly put together a solid list of about forty wines, heavier on whites because of the sushi and other seafood on the menu.

Their conversations were not always about wine. Joe learned about her life as well, growing up wealthy on the Main Line outside Philadelphia. Private schools, music lessons, gymnastic training. Her older brother, Peter III, who everyone called Three, had ruined his father's plan to have him follow in his footsteps as a big time business consultant by being artistic and gay.

So her father had turned his attention to Angel, and she excelled. Valedictorian in her private school, on to the University of Chicago, accepted and ready to go to graduate school at Wharton until the ocean intervened. Joe had met her parents when they visited after that first summer in an attempt to talk her back into the life they wanted for her.

Actually, it was only her father, Peter Junior, who wanted it. He turned out to be everything that Joe had hated about corporate America in his mercifully brief contact with it. Loud and opinionated, Peter hated everything about the town and the restaurant and let everyone know it, from Jamie to the bus staff, to Joe who had waited on their table. The only fun was the fact that the whole staff acted baffled when he asked for Wanda, who by now was universally known as Angel.

She and her parents had sat at the newly finished bar before dinner one evening in June and her father had ordered a bottle of Caymus Napa Cabernet, one of the most expensive bottles on the menu. Angel was not a fan of big Cabs, preferring lighter, more nuanced wines. Peter declared the wine great. Angel took a couple of tentative sips and began pronouncing it Camoo and called it pointless. Her mother, caught with a mouthful of the wine when Angel said this, had snorted in a most un-ladylike fashion and had to press a napkin to her nose to prevent wine from escaping.

Marie, Angel's mom, was the surprise though. Soft spoken, she seemed only to have her daughter's happiness at heart, constantly reaching out to touch her as they spoke. And, she was almost a dead ringer for her daughter, longer hair and a slightly different shape of her mouth, possibly even a little better looking. Joe had always thought it was most important to meet a girlfriend's mother so you could see how bad things might get. He thought whoever wound up with Angel had a great future.

Angel had resisted her father's crude efforts to shame her into getting back into his world, smiling throughout as her father's anger grew and his voice got louder. He finally stormed out of the restaurant leaving the embarrassed but gracious Marie behind. Joe watched as she held Angel for several moments, whispering to her.

She had seemed composed after he left, but she had sat at a table with Jamie after closing, their heads nearly touching, and it looked to Joe as if she had been crying.

As the wine menu neared completion, Joe noticed a glaring omission. They had no new sparkling wines, just the same tired list they'd always had. Cheap and boring, a customer had once complained. Joe asked Angel when they would revive the sparkling list. "You do that part," she had said.

"What? You don't know about Champagne? You know about everything else."

"I know plenty about it, too much. I shouldn't drink it. Don't drink it."

Joe smiled and asked, "What's the problem with it?"

"Seven seconds," she'd said and walked away.

Chapter 14

Karma Killer

1 oz Myer's Dark Rum   ¼ oz Cointreau   ¼ oz Peach Brandy
Pour Liquors over Ice in Highball Glass
Stir in 1 oz each of Orange, Pineapple and Grapefruit Juices
Add Orange Wheel

The bottles were all straight, labels facing out. The upside down glasses in the racks above the bar were all polished and reflected the light from the window. Three shakers were lined up on the black bar mat with the bat logo on the raised red Bacardi letters, the sink below mounded with the round crystal chip ice he preferred. He checked the sake warmer. A red light glowed on its face. Ready. His favorite part of the evening. The calm before the storm.

Joe loved the purity of the restaurant world. The concept was easy. Give people good food in a nice setting and they gave you money. They would came back again and again. Yet, some 85% of new restaurants failed. He'd watched it happen over and over in Rehoboth and Dewey. Bad service. Mediocre food. Good chefs invariably leaving for a better offer or a bigger stage. He liked that The Emerald had avoided the pitfalls to become one of the signature dining destinations in the resort town. Due in large part to Jamie's charisma and hard work, but he knew that part of the success was that people saw the same friendly faces from year to year, including his.

Bartender. He'd come late to the party, wished he'd found it earlier. Bartending was like a cult in the two towns. Moves were hot gossip. Big Bill's leaving The Summerhouse? He's been there for fifteen years. Mark and L.A. have left the Starboard? It won't be the same. Denise is back for another summer at Big Fish, charming every man, old and young. David, with the leopard spotted hair, still getting all the after-hours restaurant workers across the street at La La Land.

Joe liked being part of that crew. He thought of all the jobs he'd bounced through. The telephone company sales job he now thought of as his cubicle phase, where your stature was defined by the height of the dull grey dividers around you. Dividers that while offgassing formaldehyde, also seemed to syphon off his will to live.

He had found something to like about most of his other jobs; cutting grass as a kid, he'd liked the way the rows appeared from nothing; while doing stock work in a Barnes and Noble, he'd sneak off to a hidden corner and read stuff that looked interesting as he'd unpacked it. He had gotten so caught up in *Like Water For Chocolate,* that he'd told his boss he was sick and gone to see the movie. Even driving around the D.C. area as a courier, he'd loved the challenge of finding new routes to avoid the horrendous traffic.

He would never have defined himself by any of those things he had done, though. But he loved calling himself a bartender, loved knowing he had a home on any bar seat around the area, knowing that sitting at any bar in the world, he was a member, a confidant of the person making his drink, pulling his beer.

A few early customers had been seated and the gray printer on the service counter began to spit out the bits of paper with the orders that would dominate the next five hours of his life. Karma, he supposed, the first ticket with the name Angel on top. Two hot sakes and a Kirin Ichiban. He slipped a carafe under the nozzle of the sake machine and reached into the cooler at the same time to grab the beer. No wasted motion. The start of a long, non-stop aerobic routine of bending, reaching and shaking.

He set the two carafes and the beer on the service bar, slipped the ticket between the sakes and waited, hoping to catch her eye when she picked up her order. But she sent a busboy and he saw her across the dining room, hip cocked, hand lightly touching a man's shoulder in the way that made them all fall for her.

Fall for her.

Fall for her.

Chapter 15

Krug Grand Cuvée
Non-Vintage Champagne

"Seems like you left a gaping hole in my wine knowledge." Joe stood in front of the table, where Angel sat finishing the evening's closing paperwork, two hands behind his back. The dining area was dark except for the glow of the dimmed paper lanterns above the sushi bar.

"What have you got back there?"

Joe pulled his left hand from behind his back showing her a bottle of sparkling rosé wine. "Champagne"

"That's Cava, Joe. It's Spanish sparkling wine, good, but definitely not Champagne."

"My education continues." Joe stuck the bottle in the wine chiller attached to the side of the table.

"And the other hand?"

"Ta Da," Joe said as he pulled the second bottle from behind his back.

"Oh no. Do you have any idea what that is?"

Joe glanced at the label. "Krug." He pronounced it like bug. "The rep dropped it off today. Said it was really good stuff. She wanted to thank us for buying so many wines from her."

"It's Kroog." She drew out the oo, made it sound like oooh. Her voice seemed to drop an octave as she said it.

"Kroooog," Joe repeated, drawing it out, lowering his voice. "Sounds kinda sexy." He felt his throat catch as he thought of the late nights sitting next to her when their legs would touch under the table as they evaluated the wines. The electric feeling. Neither pulling away.

Angel looked at him as if she was making a decision and said finally, "What do you think of me, Joe?"

Joe stared through the window behind her, saw the little bridge over the pond Jamie had put in the center of the outside dining area. He looked back at Angel, pulled out the chair opposite hers while he deposited the Champagne in the second cooler at the table. "You're the best server, hands down, in all of Rehoboth Beach." He paused "And you smell wonderful."

She smiled. "If we open that Champagne, you may wind up feeling differently about me. I'm not sure it's a good idea."

"Let's have that Cava first then. I wanted this to be like my graduation ceremony from Angel's wine academy." Joe pulled the foil from the bottle, twisted the cage free and allowed the cork to explode from the bottle ceremoniously." He poured a flute for each of them and they clinked glasses, then each took a small sip. "Wait." He stood and weaved his way back through the tables in the dining room and grabbed a platter from atop the refrigerated case on the sushi bar. In a moment, he was back at the table where

Angel sat, watching him. "I had Dim Sum make us up a little sushi," he said as he lowered the platter to the table, a beautiful collection arranged artfully the way only a master chef could do. The wasabi was carved into figures of a man and woman. The chef had even put tiny daikon sprouts into the woman's head making it look remarkably like Angel's hair. "I think maybe Dim has a thing for you."

"It's Zheng Quan and he has a wife and three children in China."

"How do you get this? The man knows five words in English."

"My father correctly predicted that the pan Asian region would be economically powerful in the coming decades and had his children learning Chinese languages from age five."

"Always painful when assholes are know-it-alls. Sorry. I didn't...."

"That's okay. Peter the Great is an asshole savant."

Joe immediately thought of several people who qualified. "I like that. Sheets will love that. A whole new a-hole category." They went silent for a while, eating and sipping, giving him a chance to reflect on her earlier question. What *did* he think about her? He wouldn't call her beautiful, but she was a magnet for all the young boys that worked with her. Some kind of indescribable charisma. Physically she was tall, big, but not heavy, good muscle definition. Nose maybe a touch too big, lips maybe a little too full. Damn close to beautiful.

He wondered if she would just swallow up a man mentally though. She might be the brightest person he had ever known, but she never flaunted it. It had taken him most of that first year to realize just how smart she really was.

They came to the end of the first bottle and Joe lifted the Krug and started to remove the foil. Angel put a hand on his arm, stopping him and moving to the chair next to his.

"I need to tell you something before you open it." She paused, then continued softly, "I've only ever been with one man in my life and I...." She went silent for a moment. "I'm not sure it was consensual."

"Not sure?" Joe hoped his startled reflex hadn't showed. What the hell did that mean? he thought. He started to speak, then noticed a look in her green eyes that he'd never seen before. Sadness? A wave of emotion rolled over him. He felt in that moment that there was nothing in the world he would rather do than protect her.

"There were several bottles of Krug involved, and I never was certain if I had participated willingly. I only know that I felt awful about it the next day and have never been willing or able to be with anyone since."

Joe began to put the bottle back in the ice bucket, at a loss for words for once in his life. He finally came out with, "That sucks so bad. Sorry to bring up crappy memories," realizing immediately how lame and childish it sounded.

He couldn't help but think of the small-town rumors that surrounded Angel and her legendary Thursday nights on the deck of the Rudder dancing with the young boys and the equally legendary rumors of what happened afterwards on the Jolly Trolley rides back to Rehoboth.

As if she had read his mind, she said, "I know about the rumors, Joe, but it's only ever been about drinking and dancing at the Rudder."

He looked at the bottles and the sushi platter on the table and his stomach tightened with a terrible thought. "God, I hope you don't think I...I really just wanted to celebrate the...." And of course then had to ask himself if that's what it had been about. But no, she was 25, he was 35. He'd put that idea to rest long ago.

Hadn't he?

She laughed and picked up what was left of the wasabi woman with her chopsticks and moved it back and forth. "Big barman seduction scene, eh?" she said with an oriental accent. A piece of the woman broke and it landed face down on the remains of the wasabi man. They both stared at the platter for a moment.

As if that had made a decision for her, she stood and walked to the bar and returned with two fresh flutes. She pulled the bottle out of the bucket and with three swift moves the cork released with a small *pfft*. She poured the Krug.

"I'm confused. Are you sure about this?"

"I have to go back there." She raised her glass and they clinked, then drank. She made a sound deep in her throat. "I'd like it to be with you."

He just stared at her. "This is the best thing I ever tasted."

Chapter 16

Seven Seconds

7 oz Ti Amo Prosecco   7 Drops Chambord
Serve in Flutes

"What was the seven second thing about?" Joe held his flute up to the light and watched the bubbles rise.

"Carbon dioxide. Sparkling wine hits your brain in seven seconds." A drop of champagne slipped from her lip and rolled down her chin onto her throat. "Don't let that go to waste."

Joe moved to get the drop with his finger, but she grabbed his arm.

"No hands, Joe Rath."

He moved closer and caught the drop with his tongue as it moved into the little depression at the base of her throat. The taste, if possible, was even better when it mingled with her scent. She tilted her head back and let a small stream roll down. He was unable to catch it all before it made its way under her black uniform blouse. Angel worked open the buttons enabling him to get it all before it reached the barrier of her black pants. Joe worked his way slowly back up where all impediments had now been removed, taking his time to make sure no traces had escaped to the left or right.

Then he stood, said one word, "Jesus," and pulled the tablecloth off the next table. They laid down on it with the bottle between them. As he lay down, Joe thought of the words from the McInerney wine book she'd had him read, where he'd talked up a certain wine as being the finest to lick off the body of your lover. Joe thought if it hadn't been Krug, McInerny had gotten it wrong.

Chapter 17

Appletini

6 oz Van Gogh Appel Vodka
2 oz Marie Brizard Manzanita
Chill and serve in Martini Glass
Float Kiwi Slice

The man rose from the round table near the bar room window nearly blotting out the incoming evening sun. He picked up the drink from in front of the woman sitting with him and headed towards the bar. Joe looked at the blue Nittany Lions T-shirt stretched across the massive chest, 73 in a circle below the letters. O-line was Joe's first thought, but offensive linemen usually have a big gut and an air of intelligence about them. This dude was rock hard, the sleeves of his shirt cut along the seams to accommodate his huge upper arms. An aura of violence surrounded the man. Definitely D-line.

He watched the man approach. Take the easy way he told himself. Then he thought, screw it. It was his bar. It had been a long summer. He was still ruffled by the mess he'd made with Bubbles. He didn't want to set precedent by giving in to every customer's every whim over the long holiday weekend. Okay, he admitted to himself, maybe he was just feeling vindictive.

At that moment, premature death at the hands of a defensive lineman didn't seem like the worst fate imaginable. He glanced at the clock on the back bar, 7:35. The night was peaking. Jamie was surrounded by people waiting for tables, but there was a lull in the action at the bar, a party of seven he'd been serving had just been seated.

The guy actually had to duck to get under the hanging glass racks. It looked like someone bending over to peer in the windows of a dollhouse. He set the drink down, slopping some liquid over the edge of the oversized martini glass. Joe looked at the fruit island with the umbrella floating in a green sea, rather taken with his own creation. He could almost see himself and Bubbles reclining alone on the kiwi beach. He mentally added a tanned cabana boy to fetch them drinks. And thinking of her, his resolve dissolved. Just do whatever it takes to get through the night, the weekend, he thought, and smiled at the giant.

"Molly says this isn't like the Appletinis she gets at Mo's in Reading. Says maybe she'll get a beer instead."

"No need." Might as well make a friend, he thought. "Mo's in Reading. Hold on." He pulled his phone from his black cargo pants and tapped a few keys. As he waited, he dumped the old drink and iced down a clean glass, wondering how normal it was to have a bunch of bartenders on speed dial. "Mac, I need your Appletini recipe." He grabbed bottles as he listened and poured differing amounts into a shaker. "Thanks. Next Thursday? I'll be here."

"You know Mac? He's the best bartender I've ever seen."

"Until now." Joe shook the drink, poured, then inserted a fresh kiwi island with a new umbrella. He grabbed a can of whipped cream and built a little volcano on one side of the glass. He filled the depression with Midori. The deep green liqueur slowly ran down the slope and started to turn the drink a deeper green.

"That's beautiful," the guy said extending his hand. "Sam Fisher."

"Joe Rath, Zen Mixologist," he said as his hand disappeared in a huge paw.

"Good God. I hope you're not a proctologist." One woman of five approaching the bar spoke as she looked in awe at the big man.

Sam smiled. "Veterinarian."

"Barkeep," said another of the group, "Cosmos all around. We've got a bachelorette to get drunk."

"Let us help you." Two of the girls moved behind the bar. This was obviously not their first drink of the evening.

But, what the hell, he thought, no need to be a party-pooper. He filled two shakers, raised them to shoulder height and began rattling the alcohol and ice with a little extra gusto and a twist of his hips. The five woman thrust their arms up, shouted and sang;

"Shake Shake Shake
Shake Your Booty"

It was when they insisted on pictures with their new favorite bartender, including some hugs and kisses, that he realized someone was watching from the service bar with tears in her eyes.

Chapter 18

Aftershock

2 oz Drambuie   2 oz Malibu Coconut Rum
2 oz Cherry Brandy   4 oz Lemonade
Serve over ice in Brandy Snifter w/ Lemon Twist

The empty bottle of champagne stood between them. They reclined on their sides, heads on their hands, looking at each other. "No hands," said Joe. "I wouldn't have thought that was possible."

Angel sighed. "Soccer sex."

"I grew up playing basketball." He reached across and put his hand on the curve of her hip. "Much more hands on."

She covered his hand with her own. The patio light coming through the window caught in her hair and partially illuminated her face. "Do you know why I stayed here after that first summer, didn't go to B school."

"Charmed by the sun and the surf?"

"Partly that, but mostly you."

"Me? Why me?"

"I got intrigued by the way you live. You didn't seem to care much about what happened beyond the boundaries of these two beach towns. That there was enough here for a whole life. Like you had put up walls around it."

"Walls?"

"Walls. Have you ever paid attention to how you treat the new summer help?"

"Like a shepherd tending his flock?"

She laughed at this, slapping his hand. "More like shepherd who doesn't give a shit about his sheep. You never give them the time of day. They're on the other side of Joe's wall. Sheets said you're the same way at the marina with new people." She ran her hand through the sun bleached hair along his arm.

"Sheets? I've never seen you talking to him here other than to say hi."

"Oops, uh. It wasn't here." Her blushing was mostly hidden by the soft lighting.

"At the dock? You've spoken to Sheets at the dock?"

She laced her fingers through his and squeezed. "I told you that I was intrigued by your life. I stopped over there one night last fall when you were closing here. I knew what your boat looked like from that picture behind the bar. I just wanted to look. To see if it told me anything about you. But I couldn't stop myself. I got on board and snooped around. I wound up sitting on the top deck for a few minutes. I was entranced. The stars. The gentle rocking motion. The lights across the bay. Joe, it's so you. I learned more about you in those few minutes than in a whole summer working together.

"Sheets was standing by the boat when I hopped off. It was like he just appeared. He scared me so badly, that he actually apologized. I was so busted, but he just told me to come along and we went and sat on his boat for a while. I kept talking non-stop, still a little rattled by what had happened. He finally stopped me and told me that if I felt something up on that top deck, then that was you in a nutshell, I either understood you or I didn't. I begged him not to tell you I'd been there. He smiled and said it was in the vault. It's pretty apparent that he loves you."

"Hey, hey, hey. I'm all boy."

"So I noticed."

"Sheets never said anything else about me?" Joe was hoping that the Thursday nights he had gotten Sheets to sail around and tie up at the Rudder dock so Joe could watch her dance without her knowing hadn't been mentioned. He thought of how she moved, how she looked to be in another world with partners merely in orbit around her. How the tufts of her hair would catch the light and bob like the antennae of the bees in the old Saturday Night Live sketch. He wanted to run his fingers through that hair.

He maneuvered himself closer and moved his hand from her hip into her hair. His motion was arrested by a thought. For fifteen years he had moved away as quickly as possible after encounters like this. Where was the usual voice in his head screaming, *Run*?

"No. He didn't say anything else about that night," she said.

"That night?"

"I might have gone back a few times."

"A few?" Stalker, he couldn't help but think. Rabbit stew. But he realized that he felt good that she'd been drawn back.

"Certainly less than a dozen."

"Gotta speak to Sheets about that vault," Joe muttered.

The sound of the outside kitchen door opening startled them. They scrambled to their feet and started grabbing clothing. A head poked through the curtain behind the sushi bar and quickly disappeared. From the kitchen they heard, "*Madre de dios. Lo siento.*" The kitchen door closed again."

"Ezekiel," they said simultaneously.

"I think he stays here some nights," said Joe. "Sleeps on that bench in the back dining room when he's too tired to drive back to Georgetown. Guess that means this cat's out of the bag. Dishwasher telegraph. Half the town will know by tomorrow. You ok with that?"

"Joe, honestly, I didn't know if this would ever happen for me. I feel so good, I don't care if everyone knows." She reached out and pulled him to her, smiling. "By the way, does this get me inside the wall?"

Joe scowled. "You think a little champagne tongue bath will get you inside the walls of which I knew nothing before tonight? Your fingernails are barely scraping the top and it's a long fall back down to the bottom."

She actually looked shocked. "Joe?"

He leaned over and picked up the champagne bottle and held it up." Listen up, Bubbles. The champagne bath was nice. Scored a few points. But when you add a term like asshole savant to the Joe Rath lexicography, the gate is opened. You are in"

"Bubbles." She looked at him and smiled. "Bubbles."

Chapter 19

Jack and Coke

3 Parts Jack Daniels   1 Part Coca Cola

The crowd around Jamie at the reception stand had dissipated and she caught his eye and mouthed the words, *all in,* meaning all the reservations had been seated. It must be close to ten o'clock, Joe thought. She'd let stragglers in for another half hour or so. The night had passed quickly and the bar customers had reminded him why he loved doing this.

Five martini glasses filled with ice water lined the bar mat. Joe shook the mixture of Stoli O., Cointreau, a touch of fresh lime juice and just a little cranberry juice. Girlie drinks should be pink and too much cranberry made a Cosmopolitan red. Shake vigorously and ice from the edges of the Cristal Chips would shear off so that when he poured, they would shimmer and sparkle in the glass. Dump the ice water, then pour the five glasses full— with a strainer—no ghetto pours for Joe Rath, Zen Mixologist.

"Sex in The City." Tom drained his Sapporo and used the empty bottle to point at the five glasses. "It ruined bartending for me. The end of the Jack and Coke era." He shook his head. "I don't think I'm coming back next summer."

Another old school bartender gone, thought Joe. He had never seen the TV show, but, Tom was right, it had ushered in the fancy drink era. Martinis with every sort of flavored liquors and exotic mixers. Tom, from somewhere in the Midwest, had been coming to bartend at the Bottle and Cork every summer for over twenty years. Joe pulled another beer from the cooler and set it in front of Tom, who occupied the end seat at the short end of the L shaped bar. "Have you ever actually made a Cosmo?" he asked. The Cork with its concrete floors, plastic cups and shots and beer ambiance didn't cater to, in fact, discouraged the Martini crowd.

"Hell no." The flat O dragged out at the end.

Minnesota, thought Joe. "A last stand for tradition." Joe pulled his own beer from the ice and they touched bottles. He glanced at the service counter. The five drinks were still there. "Duty calls." He lifted the drink tray and headed into the dining room.

"Well?" said Tom, as Joe moved back behind the rail.

'*God don't make ugly girls,*' Joe sang. "Bachelorette party. They're heading to The Cork from here. Told them to hit the corner bar and see Tom. I better give you the Joe Rath quick Cosmo course."

"I'll wing it. I better head down there." He looked over Joe's shoulder. "Hey Bubbles. When you going to dump this guy? I've got a beautiful shack in the woods in Minnesota."

Joe turned, but she was already moving away.

Over her shoulder she said, "Soon."

Hot Tub

¾ oz Grand Marnier   ¾ oz Blue Hen Vodka
¾ oz Cristalino Cava Brut   ¾ oz Chambord
Pour 4 oz Cranberry Juice over ice in Rocks Glass
Add Liquors   Garnish with Cherry

"Tell me about the boat." The warm water lapped against her chin.

"Long version or condensed."

"Long. We've got all night."

Joe looked west over the bay and saw the quarter moon low on the horizon, knew the night was nearly over. Another new feeling for him. Wishing this night wouldn't end. He reached across the hot tub and grabbed Bubbles' hand, turning her so she wound up sitting in front of him. A small wave accompanied her and water sloshed over the side. He curled his arms around her, still unfamiliar with the feel of her against him.

She squeezed his leg and said in a deep voice, "C'mon George, tell me about the rabbits."

Rabbits. *Of Mice and Men.* George and Lenny. How could she know this? Coincidence? Knowing Joe's internal code for unfulfilled dreams. It wasn't the first time she'd done this, pulling something from his private thoughts. A chill ran up his spine. The lyrics that had been in the back of his head all night came back:

'*And I had a lover*

It's so hard to risk another, these days'

A stillness settled over them as Joe reached out and turned off the pump and the water became still.

"The boat is really all Jamie's fault. Some guy was hitting on her at the restaurant and not getting anywhere, so he offered her comp tickets to the trawler show in the fall on the Chesapeake Bay. She dragged me to this show with her as cover and man, I was taken by the trawlers as soon as I saw them. Looked like real fishing boats. When I saw the Island Gypsy, I knew right away she was the one. I think I looked at every square inch of that boat.

"I was really fired up about it. Guess I made a mistake of not wearing my Topsiders and ascot that day, cause the salesman kind of cringed when I asked him the price, obviously not impressed by my Eat at the Emerald T-shirt and flip-flops. Half a million bucks brand new. Then he took some pity on me and told me I could probably find a used one on the internet for under a hundred thousand."

Joe paused and took a drink of Fernet from the glass on the table by the tub, ice rattling, the only sound on the breezeless night. "Sip?" She just made a quiet hmm and pushed more closely against him.

"I started searching on Jamie's computer. Six months of looking and nothing. Always too expensive or the wrong model. Then I found one that looked good. Old, but it seemed to be in decent shape from the pictures. It was in a marina on the James River south of Richmond. I drove down there that day.

"It was in the middle of nowhere. Chilly day in March. Only a couple boats in the water. Rickety old docks. And right in the middle of everything, this beautiful Gypsy. I mean, pristine. Nobody in the marina office, so I just walked down the dock. There was an old guy in a wheelchair out there, looked like he was asleep. He had an oxygen tank next to him and those whatayacallems up his nose. Cannolis or something.

"So I'm admiring the boat and thinking since no one was around, maybe I'd sneak on and have a look."

"That would have been so wrong." Bubbles made a little snorting laugh.

"Sure, remind me of your criminal trespassing. Should have you arrested." Joe pressed his nose into her neck. He pulled back. "Eucalyptus?"

"Partly. Okay, a guy with cannolis up his nose, asleep. What then?"

"I had a hand on the rail to climb up and a voice says '1978 Island Gypsy Europa. All original equipment. Mint condition. Worth a fortune.'

"It was the old man. I told him I didn't have a fortune. Asked him if I could have a look anyway since I'd come all the way from Rehoboth Beach. He said all right, but he'd like to go with me. He started to push himself toward the boat, but started wheezing, so I pushed him up as close to the Gypsy as I could. He tried to stand and couldn't, muttered something about his damn emphysema.

"I asked him if he could hold the canister. He hugged that thing to his chest and I picked him up and carried him aboard. Couldn't have weighed more than 80 lbs. The cabin door was open. I put him down on the settee and looked around and knew immediately that I had to have it. He told me to take my time and check everything. He was still breathing heavily, but said he'd be okay in a few minutes.

"I spent an hour poking around and when I went back to the main cabin, I noticed a built in shelf filled with books and pulled one out. Tarzan. He told me they were first edition Edgar Rice Burroughs. Asked me if I'd ever read any when I was a kid. I told him I'd read every one, most of them twice. I knew I could never afford any of this and I guess he read that in my face.

"He asked me my name and told me I might recognize his, John Winstead. I told him I didn't follow the news. He said he'd been a lawyer for Phillip Morris for 45 years, many of them spent fighting the tobacco settlement. Family tradition, he said. Work for the company. Smoke their products and fight to the death to keep the deadly stuff on the market. He smiled and told me that in a double dip of irony, he was not only dying of lung cancer, but that he had also received a substantial settlement himself when the companies had finally signed the agreement.

"My whole life was wrong, he said and told me that getting away on the Gypsy was the only peace he'd found. He'd sail out into the bay alone and read. He looked me in the eye then and said he'd like me to have it. I looked down at the book and said I didn't think it would be right to break up the set. Not the book he said, the boat. He'd had more than forty people come to look at the boat, but what he really wanted was someone who would love it like he did, said I was the first one who had the right look and feel.

"I wanted it badly, but that didn't seem right. I asked him if someone in his family wouldn't want it. John said his family, even his wife and sons, had turned their backs on him when he went to the press to apologize for what he'd done over the years. He said his granddaughter was the only one who still spoke to him, that she'd put the boat on the internet for him.

"I smiled and told him that I didn't think a geezer like him had figured out websites and that maybe he should sell the Gypsy and give her the money. He called me a wise ass, pulled some fancy phone out, punched some buttons and held up her picture. Said she was getting all his money. Soon. He coughed some again and then asked if I wanted it or not.

"I asked him what he thought it was really worth and he told me he might be able to get $100,000 because of the condition, but said that if I'd been looking on line, I should know that old boats didn't get big prices. He said how about if we settle on $50,000. I hesitated and he said to take it or he'd think I was too much of an idiot to own the thing. And, he told me there was one caveat."

"What was it?" Bubbles asked.

"He wanted one last ride."

End of story, and the end of a perfect night as well, Joe thought, as he saw the first hints of pink in the eastern sky begin to reflect in her hair.

Chapter 21

The Other Half

Pour ¾ oz Patrón Citronge in Shot Glass
Layer in ¾ oz Disaronno Amaretto
Top with Bacardi 151 Rum   Extinguish Lights   Ignite Rum
Blow out Flame   Serve Immediately

"Last one for nine months." Joe passed the lit cigarette to Jamie. They sat on the low railing of the bridge over the little pond on the patio. Their nightly ritual after all the customers were gone. The glass of wine he had poured for her was resting on her knee as she pulled deeply on the cigarette in her way that reminded him more than a little of possibly hazardous oral sex.

"I'm going to miss this," she said, inhaling again.

Not me, he thought. Smoking was disgusting enough without turning it into a simulated sex act with an inanimate object.

The low lights on the perimeter of the patio provided just enough illumination for Joe to see her staring at him. He knew from years of working with her that a blast was coming. She had no filter, especially with him. He looked back, waiting.

She glanced away, leaning her head back and blowing a plume of smoke into the thick night air. The sky was invisible in the glow of the bright lights of the town. Looking back at Joe, she fixed him with a scathing glare. "I knew you would find a way to fuck this up."

He smiled at her. "I thought the night went perfectly. All our wonderful customers looked pleased as punch when they left." Thursday night done, only three days left until the peace of the offseason was what he was really thinking.

"Shut up, Joe. You know exactly what I'm talking about. She was crying in my office after your argument and I know what she's feeling. I've been there with you."

He bit down hard on his tongue. His relationship with Jamie, other than work, had consisted largely of the two of them falling into bed after drinking too much when she was between men. When she needed comforting or needed him to reassure her that she was still attractive. He looked at her. Four years younger than him and after one daughter with another child on the way, she still was.

Still hot, actually. Male customers followed her to their tables with their eyes on her long legs. And if she wasn't quite beautiful, she was damn close. Plus she gave off that vibe that somehow said *maybe* to every man and even some of the large lesbian contingent in town. Still trying to change the direction of their talk, he said, "You cried over me? I'm touched. Shocked to my core because I didn't think you tough women could cry, but touched none the less."

She coughed out some smoke as she attempted to stifle a laugh and told him to shut up again. "Bubbles is my best friend and by the way, by far my best employee, present company included. If she leaves, I'll kill you."

And maybe that was the problem, he thought. She could probably do just that. She *was* tough. He had watched her outwork every man on the job when she was building the restaurant. He had actually despaired of her ever finding a long term relationship because of this. Jamie would never settle for someone weaker than herself, but luckily, a guy as tough and smart as her fell into her life. Joe often wondered if Rick had just conked her on the head and dragged her home like a caveman.

But her words had hit him hard. "If she leaves, you won't have to kill me." He started to stand.

Jamie put her hand on his arm and pulled him back down. "Ah, Joe. Come on. Just talk to her."

"I can't have the conversation she wants."

"What's it about? I thought I knew every sordid detail in your life."

Joe recognized the fake eagerness in her voice. She was trying to get him to laugh. Jamie did know most of the details of his life after all their conversations, drunken and sober over their years of working side by side.

"Seriously. Did you cheat on her?"

He glared at her. "Don't be ridiculous. Hell, I'd been with her every night for two years until last Thursday, when I vaguely remember getting drunk here with you. One of us fell off a barstool. It must have been you because I'm not sore. Ring any bells? And someone insisted on driving home and blaming it on me."

"Jesus, Joe, don't ever serve me a Novocain again no matter how much I threaten you. It still hurts."

"Any repercussions with the big man?"

"I've got a get out of jail free card after he got drunk and drove off the road that night last summer and had to call me. He does want to kill you though."

Joe stretched his legs across the narrow bridge to un-kink the tightness in his muscles he always got after a long bar shift. "He's wanted to kill me since the day you two met. Tell him to just give me a couple of more weeks."

She locked eyes with him again. "A couple of weeks for what?"

"I've got a...a plan. It'll, you know, smooth things out."

This time Jamie laughed out loud. "A plan? A Joe Rath plan? Bumper Car Joe, bouncing off everything in life, mostly women, and heading in the other direction? I've got to hear this."

He stared across the parking lot at the line of people waiting to enter the bar next door. He could hear the sounds of the band playing through their front door. "It's a good plan. I think she'll like it."

Jamie took his chin in her hand and turned his face to hers. "Tell me."

Joe pulled away and looked down into the black water. "It's complicated." Probably far too complicated and farfetched, he thought, but he needed something to hold onto. "Don't want to get into the details here, but I'm going to get her back. Whatever it takes."

He stood and looked down at Jamie, the cigarette burned nearly into the filter. "I'd love to hang here and get more of your loving support, but we're partying at the dock tonight to celebrate the downing of an enemy aircraft. Feel free to stop by, if you'd like to continue beating the crap out of me."

With that, he turned and walked over the hump in the bridge. She called after him. "Just talk to her."

Joe raised his arm in acknowledgement and continued walking down the flagstone path between the patio and the restaurant towards the sidewalk.

Don't think about her. Don't think about her. Joe thought of something he'd read about Tolstoy, about how he had a club as a boy. To get into the club, you had to sit in a corner and not think about a white bear. White bear. White hair. She hated when he described it as white. "It makes me sound like an old lady, she would protest. Okay, that wasn't working, he thought as he pedaled his bicycle left onto 1st Street.

Delaware, Brooklyn, up to Laurel with the two churches occupying what passed for high ground in the flat beach town. Better, he thought, concentrate on the streets. 1st Street jogged to the left and became King Charles. Accelerate down the hill past Hickman. Close your eyes. Pedal. Skip the next one. Her street. Faster. Catch the breeze. Make the lake. Five blocks.

Joe pulled to a stop on the high ground west of Silver Lake and looked across the light studded water. He always mentally divided his ride home into four sections; the ten block ride from the restaurant to the edge of the lake, the section along the lake, the dark residential area known as Rehoboth by the Sea, and finally, the ride through the bright lights of downtown Dewey.

Now, he dismounted and sat on a patch of lawn, damp in the late night humid air. He and Bubbles usually rode to the Gypsy together, frequently stopping right here. They would pick one of the eight houses on the little spit of land on the far side of the lake and come up with a story about the people who lived in them. Mansions really, built over the last ten years or so, each subsequent house seeming to try to outdo the one before. Bubbles had decided that, as in Newport, the owners would call them cottages.

Without Bubbles, the houses had no appeal to him. He had watched as they appeared one by one, turning the one patch of wild left along the beach into just another pocket of affluence, another section of beachfront closed off to the unwashed. But, at least the houses were distinctive and the ride past with their lights reflecting in the black water became their favorite part.

Joe lay back in the grass and looked up at the sky. The moon had already passed by on its nightly transit west and the bright dot of Venus was the only object visible through the light haze from the two towns. He thought of the times he and Sheets and sometimes the three of them would walk up the beach from Dewey, cross the dune and sit on one of the porches in the off-season when the owners were long gone. They would bring a bottle of something to pass around and Bubbles would insist on calling the porches verandas. It was one of those nights that he had told them about Nick.

ψ ψ ψ

When he was about ten, he became aware of the looks his mother sometimes cast at him, looks that he translated as resentful. She seemed to hate the time she had to miss with her new Country Club friends because of him. Sam and Janet were out of the house by the time he was six or seven and his Dad traveled during the week, so it seemed it was usually just him and his mother.

So, his mother palmed him off on neighbors or friends. One of the neighbors had a son named Nick who Joe knew from school. Nick was a couple years older, so they hadn't hung out together before. Nick's parents both worked, so he had a lot of free time. He and Joe wound up bonding quickly, united by the neglect they felt.

They also were connected by their fascination with the Thimble Islands. Nick knew them even more thoroughly than Joe. And together they developed the game. Not only did they have to have visited each island, but they tried to 'occupy' every house on the inhabited islands. The occupation could consist of sitting on the porch, but they gave themselves extra points if they went inside. The houses were rarely locked. Evidently, people felt pretty secure living on islands. Nick and Joe would walk up, knock on a door and if no one answered, they went to the kitchen and helped themselves to a glass of whatever was open in the refrigerator, and then left their glasses in the sink as evidence.

They were caught only once. Sitting at a kitchen table when a woman appeared from upstairs with a towel wrapped in her wet hair. She didn't seem upset in the least and just asked them if they'd like something to eat with their orange juice. She told them they were the talk of the islands and that she'd be famous for catching them.

When their faces fell, she laughed at them and said their secret was safe with her. She asked them why they did it. They had looked at each other and Joe realized that they had never talked about why. Stupid kid game, Nick told the lady. Then she popped the big question. Had they done the mansion on Rogers Island yet? When they didn't answer, she laughed at them again. She told them her name was Suzy and to come back when they were master criminals and had cracked the toughest nut in the Thimbles. Said she'd buy them a drink.

The mansion had been an Inn at some point, but was now privately owned. It was the only property on the island and had a broad expanse of lawn running all the way to the shore. The lawn, and indeed all of the surrounding grounds, were patrolled by two of the largest dogs Nick and Joe had ever seen. Dobermans. Spiked collars. Lots of bared white fangs.

Joe and Nick had circumnavigated the island many times looking for a way to get to the house, but even at night, the dogs were on duty. But now, the gauntlet had been thrown down and they had to find a way. And they came up with a plan. They enlisted the help of another kid, Mickey, who was always begging to let him come along with them. Mickey was a nice kid, but he was overweight and couldn't swim, so they did the Thimble excursions without him.

The plan was for Mickey to drop the two of them from the little skiff a ways off the shore of Rogers. He would then motor closer in and draw the attention of the dogs and lead them to the far side of the island. Nick and Joe would swim in, run to the mansion, touch the door, then run back and hopefully be in the water before the Dobermans got back. They practiced several times, making sure Mickey could handle the skiff and that the dogs would follow him.

The day came and disaster struck. Joe's mother announced that there was a mother/son golf tournament at the club that day. Joe told her that he had plans, but she was adamant. As he got in the golf cart she used to go back and forth to the club, he saw Nick watching him from his yard with a questioning look on his face. All Joe could do was shrug his shoulders and look away.

Nick and Mickey went ahead with the plan. And, it nearly worked. Nick swam in, ran to the mansion and made it back to the water. No one ever really knew why he died. The shock of the cold Long Island Sound after the run. Too much adrenaline. The fact that Mickey didn't have the strength to pull him from the water. They finally blamed it on a faulty valve in his heart, but Joe never believed it. He'd thought his best friend was indestructible.

Joe blamed Mickey, was sure he could have saved Nick had he been there, but mostly he blamed his mother. He would feel bad about it later, but he browbeat Mickey into taking him back out to Rogers. Joe slipped off the skiff and waited til Mickey led the dogs away. He swam in and ran to the mansion, touched the door and headed back. He knew he wasn't as fast as Nick and before he reached the water, he tripped and fell.

The Dobermans were on him in a moment and promptly began to lick him while he laid and cried for his fallen friend. All for nothing he had thought, the dogs were harmless. He had returned to Suzy's house and told her everything that had happened. She had told him how sorry she was and held him when he broke down again.

ψ ψ ψ

The only sounds when Joe finished the story were waves easing onto the beach and palms in planters on the veranda rustling in the late night breeze. Bubbles had broken the quiet by asking what Nick looked like. Joe thought, but couldn't bring up a mental picture, and got frustrated. He had begun to pace the wide plank floor of the huge porch. Bubbles had finally grabbed him and pulled him next to her on a chaise lounge. "Just describe him," she had said. She told him to slow down and began to rub the back of his neck, as Sheets watched from his seat on the stairs leading to the beach.

Nick's mother was half Pequot, a Connecticut tribe, Joe told her, and Nick began to come back to him. He had only been fourteen when he died, but he already had a long lean swimmer's body and was handsome enough that the neighborhood girls all hung around in front of his house. Dark hair to his shoulders.

As Joe continued to describe his first best friend, Bubbles turned to Sheets, sitting on the porch rail. "Sound familiar? Can you two think of anyone else who fits that description to a T.?

They all went quiet. Joe stared at Sheets, outlined from below by soft landscape lights

"No way." Joe shook his head. "Completely diff... No way. Christ" He fell silent.

Chapter 22

Seething Jealousy

1 oz Noilly Prat Sweet Vermouth
½ oz Johnnie Walker Black   ½ oz Cherry Brandy
½ oz OJ
Shake Well with Ice   Strain into Rocks Glass

His shirt and pants were now nearly soaked through from the dew. He remounted his bike and reluctantly headed toward the dock. He wasn't really in the mood for a party, but a few shots of Mezcal might help. As he went down the little hill past Lake Comegys, he began his nightly count off of the streets; Chesapeake, Carolina. He picked up speed as he approached the lights of Dewey: Jersey, Cullen, Chicago. At the traffic light at Coastal Highway, the East of Maui surf shop was lit up brightly on his right.

It still amazed him that so many people could fit in this tiny town. After midnight and the sidewalks were full. Labor Day weekend was officially underway. The crowd waiting to get into the Starboard spilled out across the sidewalk into the street. A Friday or Saturday night drive through the town was a test of braking agility. Most of the bars were on the west side of the road, the pizza joints and sub shops on the east. Since the crowd started drinking early, sometimes at breakfast, they rarely looked as they crossed the four traffic lanes plus two breakdown lanes.

The state legislature had sent a busload of elected officials to town one summer Saturday to see firsthand what was called 'The Dewey Problem' and as Joe could have predicted, a drunk jumped in front of the bus and was hit. Unhurt of course, for Joe felt that the Lord had a soft spot for the weekend hedonists of Dewey Beach.

The light changed and Joe made the left turn into town, and skirted around the Starboard crowd. He pulled over in front of The Bottle and Cork, just The Cork to locals, to see who was playing. The doormen at the front corner entrance dressed in Zoot suits hailed him. Joe pointed at the suits and raised his eyebrows. "Squirrel Nut Zippers," they responded. "Whole crowd's dressed up," said one. Joe looked in the door. He could see the stage. The band dipped their saxophones and trombones in time with the swing tune they were playing. The crowd was filled with men in cool old suits and women in flapper dresses and hats with feathers. Bubbles would have loved this, he thought, and then wondered if maybe she had forsaken the deck of the Rudder to be here tonight.

The Cork was one of the few places in Dewey with any history. Joe had a photo of the place from 1936 when the sand road had ended at its door. 1936. He thought of his dad and tried to remember what year he'd been born. Definitely before the Bottle and Cork. He pedaled on past the Sand Palace Motel which, of course, wasn't on the sand and the Atlantic Oceanside Inn which was only on the side of the ocean in a global sense. Both had already put *Low Fall Rates* up on their signs. Joe wondered if this referred to their prices or if maybe fewer drunks had tumbled from the balconies this year.

An old pickup passed him heading north on the other side of the divided road. His pickup. Joe slowed and turned his bike around, wondering where Sheets would be going at this time of the night. He watched as the truck made a U-turn at the light at Bellevue and pulled into the parking lot at the liquor store. More Mezcal, he thought, when he saw Sheets exit the driver's door. Joe was about to call to him when he saw Bubbles appear from the passenger's side.

The two of them converged at the rear of the truck and she threw her arms around Sheets. Joe let his bike fall to the sidewalk and leaned against the wall of Jeremiah's Beach Store He felt as if he'd been punched in the stomach. He lifted his head as they broke their embrace and she turned towards the entrance to the Bottle and Cork. Her short black skirt swayed as she walked and colored feathers bobbed in her hair.

It's not what you think, Joe told himself as he slid down the wall and crouched with his head between his knees, acid gathering in the back of his throat. A steady stream of revelers detoured around his bicycle, many of them dressed for the show. Joe couldn't stop thinking about the two of them now. Movie-star-handsome, she'd called Sheets, and now he thought of movie night at Bubbles' apartment. She would sit between Joe and Sheets on the sofa and hold both of their hands. For a moment, Joe saw himself removed from the picture, just Sheets and Bubbles together.

His best friend. The best he'd ever had, but it wasn't how it had looked, he told himself. No way. He started to push himself up the wall and immediately slipped back down, felled by the thought that Sheets' boat had been out last night when he'd gotten back to the dock from Pennsylvania, but was there this morning. Where had it been? A romantic midnight cruise under the full moon? Who could resist the quiet man? Joe could see him, foot on the wheel, leaning back, profiled in the dim light, arm around…. Stop. Jesus. Sheets went out on many nights. He said he slept better out on the ocean. It didn't mean a thing.

Shaky, Joe stood and retrieved his bike and started to swing his leg over. He didn't seem to have the energy to do it and wound up just walking it down the breakdown lane. The pile of crap building up this week seemed mountainous. His dad. The money. Bubbles. Add in the insanity of Labor Day. It was too much to deal with. He didn't need to be questioning his best friend. Someone called to him from the bar as he passed McShea's. Sammy. Dancing Sammy, who was regular enough to have a medallion with his name on the bar in front of the seat he occupied. Joe gave him a desultory wave.

He took a deep breath. Buck up, soldier, almost home. Eyes forward. Don't even think about the Cork or who she might be with. Talk to Sheets. There's a simple explanation. You have troops to entertain tonight. Mezcal to drink. Christ, on top of everything else he was becoming an alcoholic. He needed a drink.

Many drinks.

Chapter 23

Ilegal † Mezcal Reposado

100% de Agave Espadin   Handcrafted in Small Batches

"I saw you at the liquor store." Joe tried to smile, but the lingering doubt and hostility made it impossible. Sheets just held Joe's eyes with one of his inscrutable looks. He had been sitting by the fire pit next to the Queen when Joe walked out the dock. Joe had motioned to him and they were now standing in the shadows by the Gypsy. "How is she?"

"Anger, pain, confusion. I could go on. You've really put her into a tailspin." Sheets dark eyes flashed in the dim glow cast from one of the few working dock lights. "She called and asked for a ride to the Cork, but I think she really wanted to see if I could tell her anything."

"And?"

"And she'd obviously been crying. I don't know what's going on with you two, probably don't want to know, but she needs support and I could never say no to her."

"When I saw you with her by the pickup, I thought—"

Sheets interrupted with a harsh voice. "I know what you thought. Everything you think passes across your eyes like a banner behind one of those summer ad planes." His voice softened. "Joe, you know me better than that."

Relief flooded him. He did know better. Why, he asked himself, was he making life even more difficult than it already was? "Yeah, I do. Sorry. Let me get changed and I'll buy you a drink." He still felt unsteady as he stepped up onto his boat.

"Hurry, you've got an audience with the Queen and I believe the rich pageantry of the B-Dock drama is about to start." Sheets turned to go then stepped over and punched Joe in the arm. "And by the way, could you just fix this fucking thing with her. It's making everyone crazy"

"I've got a plan." He sighed. A plan, he repeated to himself as he stepped into the cabin of the Gypsy.

ψ ψ ψ

Joe watched as the dark-skinned Yemeni crept down the dock towards the six people sitting in beach chairs surrounding the large fire pit, their faces tinted orange by the glowing embers. Their conversation was nearly drowned out by the music playing from the deck of the Rudder's outdoor bar just a couple of hundred yards away across the darkened cove in the bay. The music also covered the sound of the man's footsteps as he moved from piling to piling to hide his approach to the group. From a crouched position behind a piling just a few feet from the closest chair, the Yemeni leaped towards the ring shouting, "die infidels!"

Sheets shot from his chair and confronted the smaller man. Joe couldn't help but laugh as he stood as well. The little man's head moved rapidly back and forth as the two men moved to surround him, his keffiyah snapping in the night air. After circling warily for several moments, the Yemeni plunged a hand into one of the many pockets of his black cargo pants and snarled, "Allah shall flay your flesh."

At that, the two of them dove simultaneously, each grabbing a leg of the little man, hoisting him until he hung upside down above the dock and shook him vigorously. "Your mothers are naught but rutting beasts," he howled into the night as keys and coins fell from his many pockets. "Any WMD?" Joe asked.

"Just this." Sheets plucked a cylindrical object from a pocket before it could fall to the dock. A pink pig's head topped the cylinder. Sheets pulled back the head and a blue rectangle appeared. "Cyanide capsules?"

"Pez. Allah shall rot your teeth. Satanic dogs."

A female voice came from the circle of chairs. "Joe, Sheets. Put him down. You're going to hurt him."

"Eternal vigilance is the price of a civilized society," said Sheets, as they lowered the little man gently to the dock. "The terrorists shall not win. Wait. What is this?" Sheets picked up a card which had fallen to the dock. He showed it to Joe. "Friend of the Philadelphia Zoo?"

Sheets and Joe grabbed the man again, hoisted him into the air and shook him. "Pennsylvanian terrorists, we shall not rest until you are gone from our fair land. No more shall you despoil our taverns and inns with your minimal tippage and slovenly apparel," laughed Joe. "By the way, where did you get that beautiful head scarf?" They lowered the man to the deck once more.

"Classy huh? It's a table cloth from Mama Maria's. I liberated it from the non-believers this evening."

"Yeah, I think there's a chunk of cannoli stuck on the side," said Sheets as he and Joe returned to their chairs. The music had stopped and everyone seemed to relax with the peaceful sounds of waves slapping the sides of the boats. The light wind rustled lines on the sailboats against the masts, giving off metallic pings.

Joe looked at the little man. Maybe 5' 6" tall, all flesh and sinew. He guessed he weighed about 120. His real name was Mpoki, so sometimes they called him Pokey, but usually Buzz, for the annoying noise of the ultralight, that he had flown over the marina for years. Buzz lived in an apartment over Mama Maria's, where he waited tables. Like so many others, he had to work two jobs during the summer in order to make it through the long off-season. Joe wondered if he had insurance to cover his downed aircraft and had the sudden inspiration that he had the money now to help Buzz if he wanted to purchase a new one. It would be a bit of irony after the constant bitching about the noise.

Sheets was the reason Buzz was part of the B-Dock crew. He had helped the little man keep the ultra flying. They would completely disassemble the thing and put it back together. Actually, Joe thought, Sheets would take it apart while Buzz handed him the tools he needed. Sheets did the same with Joe's old bubbletop Ford pickup. Without a manual. Like it was nothing. And it always ran better after he put it back together.

Buzz and Sheets had been huddled on the cove beach one day with the ultra in pieces on a blue tarp when Joe wandered over on his way back from the coffee shop. Buzz had been speaking in a foreign language. Yemeni or Arabic, Joe had guessed, and Sheets' answer had made it sound as if he were fluent in the same tongue. They reverted back to English when they saw Joe and he felt as if he were intruding. He never asked either one about it.

And that was the way of the dock. Give as much back story as you wished. In Sheets' case, none. With Buzz, Joe knew he had been born In Yemen, but had spent enough time outside Philadelphia to speak with a Mid-Atlantic accent. Wuter instead of water and so on. A fully developed American sense of humor too, always the quickest to pick up on a line. And his finest attribute in Joe's eyes was his total willingness to participate in the admittedly stupid fake terrorist attacks on the dock which Sheets and Joe found endlessly amusing, but much like the Three Stooges, the women found appalling and incomprehensible.

There were moments though, when he'd caught Buzz in a quiet, serious moment, and there was a faraway look in his black eyes that spoke of something dark that he kept hidden behind the façade of humor. Joe would wonder if he could only speak of it in that other language.

After a few moments of silence, Joe reached down for the salt shaker at his feet, shook some into the pad between his thumb and forefinger and passed it along. He then lined up seven shot glasses and filled them from a tall round bottle of amber liquid, passing one to each person.

"Buzz," Sheets intoned to the little Yemeni, "This one's for all the aircraft lost at sea and the men who flew them. May they be at rest in the deep." With that, each member of the group tapped their glass on the deck, licked the salt from their hand, stood as one and downed the shots.

"Praise be to Triton, god of the deep and hopefully, shallow polluted bays," said Joe. The crew turned to face west towards the tiny string of lights across the bay and one by one hurled their glasses over the row of boats in front of them. Six satisfying plops followed as the glasses sank into the water. Then one thud as shot glass met fiberglass hull. Joe turned to the woman beside him. "Queen, if you're going to hang with the boat people, you gotta work on that arm."

"First time jitters," she giggled with a slur. "Never had Mezcal before." She looked at Joe. "Do you harass that guy like that all the time?"

Joe held her gaze at he sat down. "Much like the Passion Play in Germany, it bears frequent repetition. There is so much to learn from our production."

"You are all very weird."

Sheets walked to the front of the largest sailboat at the dock and grabbed a chair from the deck. He returned to the circle, set the chair between his and Joe's and patted the seat. "Sit down, little man, and tell us the story of the last flight of Little Gull."

Chapter 24

Drunken Parrot

2 oz Parrot Bay Pineapple Rum 2 oz Parrot Bay Coconut Rum
1 oz Captain Morgan Spiced Rum
15 oz Pineapple Juice   4 Tbsp Sugar   5 Drops Vanilla
Fill Blender Half Full with Ice   Add Ingredients
Blend to Smoothie Consistency   Serve in Highball Glass

"Confession." The B-Dock crowd fell silent as they always did when Sheets spoke. "Buzz, I believe I may have accidently gazed upon the Piggy that went to market and possibly the Piggy that ate roast beef when your sister stepped up on my boat in her bathrobe the other day."

Buzz was silent for several moments. The little Yemeni then stood unsteadily and pointed at Sheets. "It is a burka you heathen mongrel and while in my land, the sight of the market Piggy is not a sin, gazing upon roast beef toe means you are now betrothed. Your cattle will be shipped tomorrow."

The crew dissolved in laughter as Buzz stumbled towards his chair and wound up laying beneath the picnic table. Joe looked at Sheets and felt some strange sense of pride, like a parent must feel when their child takes its first steps. Sheets? Humor?

Joe watched the woman sitting next to Sheets. It appeared as if she was having trouble holding her head up straight and it came to rest against Sheet's shoulder as her eyes closed.

"Queen, what have you got for us?" Joe asked.

Her head came off Sheet's shoulder as if she'd been awakened. "Whaddayamean?"

Joe figured she was pretty far gone at this point the way she ran all her words together. Queen was usually so reserved, maybe now she'd say something to unstick herself from Joe Purgatory, where she currently resided. Joe knew that she and Sheets had long meaningful talks about whatever, but Mr. Silent never gave up any details. Joe did know that she got sick as a dog the only time Sheets took her out sailing, which made any long term relationship problematic.

All Joe knew was that she was a local writer. He had met her through a bartending friend, but hadn't known her until she started working at the coffee shop. She had rankled him from the moment that he had casually asked if the picture of the woman on the cover of her book was her as he looked at one on the pile by the cash register. She said no rather curtly, then proceeded to leave his coffee an inch short of the rim. Joe had thought of her since as the Ice Queen.

Later, as she moved to the bestseller rack with a copy of the weekly *New York Times* list and began to rearrange the titles, he raced up to the counter and grabbed one of her books. He stuck it behind the book he had been reading and began feverishly comparing the cover woman to her. And although he did get sidetracked occasionally by mentally removing articles of her clothing when she bent over to rearrange the lower shelves, he was sure the picture was her.

"You're sitting in the ring of honor, he told her now, which requires sharing of some details of your life, preferably filthy or at least self-incriminating."

"Whaddabout those two." She nodded at the two young guys sitting together. "They never say anything."

Joe looked at the two kids who had moved into the marina that summer in a tiny little sailboat. He could only think of them as Mop and Broom, both skinny as rails, one with dreadlocks down past his shoulders and the other with yellow blond hair that grew straight up from his scalp. They sat back a little from the group in near darkness. Joe thought of them as a Greek chorus, for occasionally they would repeat something someone said and then look at each other and giggle. He assumed they were baked most of the time, judging from the near constant plume of smoke rising from the cabin of the sailboat and the pot smell hovering around their slip. "They're grandfathered in."

"WhyHow?" Queen stuttered. Joe figured he'd better hurry, she was nearly done.

"They live on B-Dock which confers a certain automatic status, but more importantly, their girlfriend looks and dresses like a librarian, wire-rim glasses, hair up in a bun, long skirts. She inspires me to vile and unhealthy thoughts which means they're in. Come on, give us something."

"Smile Train," Queen mumbled.

"Sooouuulll Train," said Joe. "Don Cornelius. What about him? Have you had relations with the man? This could be good."

"I think you're loaded my friend," said Sheets. "She said Smile Train."

I'm just getting started, thought Joe, wanting nothing more than to drink himself into oblivion and forget about Bubbles and what she might be doing tonight. The music from the Rudder had stopped, meaning she was either on her way over to the marina or riding the trolley back to Rehoboth.

"Smile Train? Smile Train?" He paused. "The little kids with the harelips?" He was baffled now about where this might be heading.

"Creft parrots. Harewips in't PC. I gotta go." She stood, then faltered and started to fall back into her chair. Sheets caught her and eased her back down.

Creft parrots? Creft parrots? It finally penetrated Joe's alcohol fog. "You mean cleft palates." He couldn't help but laugh now.

She smiled. "Yes. Yes. Creft Parrots."

"Wait," said Joe. "Don't leave us hanging. What about them?"

She hung her head and spoke nearly inaudibly. "Ushe the labels. No money."

It took Joe a few moments before the meaning became clear. "You use the address labels and don't send them any money? That is so wrong."

"I know," she whispered.

"Heinous," intoned the boys. "A crime against humanity."

"Stone her," slurred Buzz from underneath the picnic table.

Joe had dragged Sheets with him to the coffee shop the Sunday following his initial encounter with her, the only day the Queen worked. He wanted independent confirmation of her brazen lie.

When she again came over to work the bestsellers, Joe pointed at her back and the cover of the book, saying, "See."

Sheets glanced at the cover, then at her. "Look at the way she handles the books. She's lost in that world." He stood up, walked over and began to speak to her.

When the conversation was ongoing after a half hour, Joe disgustedly left the shop, vowing to continue his quest for the truth.

The next Sunday, she approached him. "Tell me about Sheets."

"Tarzan."

"Tarzan?"

"Raised by apes. Knows naught of our world or your ilk."

She smiled at this. "Ilk? I'm part of an ilk?"

"Females in general." Joe glanced at the table where her book lay covered by another, "Specifically writers who would attempt to decei...."

She had followed his gaze. "It's. Not. Me."

Chapter 25

Last Chance

1¾ oz Tarantula Reposado Tequila   ¼ oz Apricot Brandy
1 oz Fresh Lime Juice   1 Tsp Honey
Shake with Ice   Pour with Ice into Old Fashioned Glass
Add Lime Wheel

"How is he?" Bubbles stood with a pair of sandals hanging from her fingers, wearing one of the short black skirts she favored for Thursday nights dancing at the Rudder. Joe inhaled deeply, hoping to catch her scent, but got the odor of burned wood from the blackened pile he seemed to be hanging over.

"He told me he coveted my buttocks." Sheets' voice.

Joe's world turned and he lost his view of Bubbles. He seemed to be draped over someone's shoulder. It must be Sheets, he thought, for he had felt a vibration when he heard his voice. Joe wanted to protest, wanted to see Bubbles, but he couldn't seem to form words. Dark silhouettes of upside down boats floated in his eyes. Dots of light danced in the distance.

"Oh dear. Did he also proclaim his love?" Her voice. Like she was far away.

"Repeatedly. I've never seen him this drunk."

Joe felt the shudder in Sheets' back once more as he spoke. It felt soothing.

"And you? You capable of getting him to his shower?"

"Had a few. I told a joke." Sheets turned and started moving.

Bubbles came into view and Joe watched as she knelt among the plastic shot glasses littering the dock. She reached beneath the picnic table. "Buzz?" she said. "My god." She paused. "He's snoring. I suppose he's alive. That must have been some party."

Now she was somehow standing again, following him. Gone. Joe tried to move his head to find her. Nothing. His new world seemed to rise up and his head bobbed against Sheets' back. A railing and water appeared. A boat window a couple of feet away. He caught a brief glance of his own head. Upside down. Weird.

"Clothes on or off?" Sheets said and Joe felt himself touch down on a solid surface.

"Oh, just set him under it. Let him marinate for a while."

Warm water began falling on his head. Nice, he tried to say. Bubbles appeared, sitting in a deck chair. Another chair appeared and there was Sheets. The water was running across Joe's face and he found that if he blew out he could make bubbles. Bubbles for Bubbles. Communication. But she didn't seem to notice.

"Tell me about the party." Bubbles.

"Epic, even by B-dock standards." Sheets.

"Bbbb." Him.

His eyes refused to stay open. Concentrate, he thought. His head was like a revolving door, only opening on their conversation once with each rotation. A word or two at a time came through the haze. "Painful." "Worried." "Last Chance."

He felt something touch his feet and he opened his eyes. His legs were really long. They extended all the way to Bubbles' chair. He realized that half of them were hers. Their feet together. Perfectly aligned. He loved her toes. Tell her. One word. Love. Place tongue behind front teeth. Slide tongue downward while opening mouth and pushing out breath. His effort resulted in him biting his tongue, but it revived him a bit.

"How was he tonight?" said Bubbles.

"Funny. Caustic. Joe." Sheets' voice trailed off.

"And?" Joe saw one of her feet pull away from his and nudge Sheets' foot.

"And, with those eyes he can't hide anything. He's a mess. Hasn't looked right for a week."

"Those eyes. Shit. Look at him. I think he's more comfortable than we are." Her upper half disappeared. Her lower half moved toward the falling water. He felt her body next to his and her hip scooching him over so the water fell between them. She gathered a handful of water and tossed it at Sheets. "Get over here. I need all my men around me."

Then Sheets disappeared as well and Joe felt the wall behind him shake as if from an impact. He managed to glance to his right and saw six legs side by side. He felt Bubbles stretch her arm across his shoulder and pull him closer. Her scent. He tried to turn his head. That scent.

Bubbles voice. Soft. Distant. Her breath warm in his ear. "I can't watch this any longer. If we can't settle it tomorrow, I'll have to leave."

Joe felt the warm water changing to cold. "Bbbb," he said.

Chapter 26

Baby Mama Drama

½ oz 99 Bananas   ½ oz Stoli Strasberi   ½ oz Pineapple Juice
Shake Ingredients with Ice   Strain into Test Tube
Float ½ oz Bacardi 151 Rum

Joe rolled over towards the edge of the bed and tried to open one eye. Pain flared through his head and a nasty rumble started in his stomach. He reached up behind him and managed to slide open the screen. As he dragged himself onto all fours and moved toward the window, he noticed the scent. "Bub," was all that he got out before sticking his head through the opening and retching into the water below. Several minutes passed before he felt it was safe enough to pull his head back inside.

The sky was overcast, but still bright enough to send jolts of pain into his head when he opened his eyes. Even the far away sound of jet-skis felt like a belt sander attached to his brain. He realized as he pulled back into the room that there was someone else in the bed. He had no recollection of the prior evening past Sheets returning after delivering the Queen home in the Zodiac. Please let it be Bubbles, Joe said to himself, not Egg or god forbid, someone he didn't even know. He leaned over and inhaled.

Smelled like Bubbles. Slid his hand under the sheet, felt short soft hair. Another wave of nausea returned him to the window, but it passed. Joe saw a face in the galley of the neighboring boat and quickly slid back inside, closing the tinted glass behind him.

Joe lay back down and moved closer to the sleeping woman, now presumed to be Bubbles, putting his hand on her hip.

"Hands off," she said with the husky morning voice he loved, moving to the edge of the bed. She slid out and turned to face him. She was wearing one of his tattered green and orange Miami Hurricanes T-shirts, possibly nothing else, but his head hurt too badly to attempt leaning over enough to sneak a peek. "Let's talk about babies."

Joe covered his eyes with his arm and moaned. "My head," He groaned again.

Bubbles took the three steps up to the galley and returned with a glass of green liquid and handed it to him. "Drink this." Her herbal hangover remedies were legendary at the restaurant. He sniffed it first; he'd always thought that the worse they smelled the better they worked. This one was particularly vile. He drank half of it down. It soothed his stomach immediately. He drank the rest.

"Feel better?"

"It's amazing. I feel so much better, think maybe we could uh, you know, before we talk? It's been over a week."

Her face softened a bit. "God Joe, you're impossible," she said with a puff of breath like a half laugh. "How many of me do you see?"

"Only three."

"Did you have a plan?"

"Shoot for the one in the middle."

"You need to tell Mr. Revere there to stand down. We're going to get the baby thing settled."

Joe looked down and realized that indeed, Mr. Revere was recuperating nicely and decided to cover him up. No sense exposing him to the flak he knew was on the way. A feeble sun broke through, brightening the cabin. "No hangover pity?"

"Joe Rath rule number seven, no pity for self-inflicted wounds."

"Hoist on my own petard." I've got to stop making rules that I might break, he thought. He paused not really knowing where to start. "I was married," he finally said, then stopped again.

"I've met Bonnie."

"Well, she was my high school girlfriend. We went our own ways during college, but kept in touch, got back together after we graduated, got married that same year. It felt like love. Seemed like we both wanted the same things: house in the burbs, a couple of kids, the same things our parents had. And then…." Joe looked down, unable to meet Bubbles' eyes.

She reached out and touched his leg. "Then what?"

"Then she got pregnant."

"And?"

He continued to stare at the bed. "And, you'll think I'm a monster."

"Joe, I've known you for three years, been with you for two. I think I would have seen a hint of this monster by now."

He sighed. "From the minute she told me about the baby, something changed in me. I felt like my life would be over, ruined.

I blamed her. I was totally irrational. Went through the motions, Lamaze classes, buying baby stuff, but I was secretly hoping that something would happen and I wouldn't have to be a father." Joe paused and looked up at her. "I was completely unsupportive, a total asshole. And then—" He let out a long breath.

"Just get it out." She encouraged him with a half-smile. "You've been sitting on this for years."

"Then she lost the baby." Joe stood and moved to the door, looking out through the screen, forgetting he was naked. A ragged line of clouds loomed like a mountain range above the trees on the west side of the bay. He felt his forehead begin to throb anew. "All I could feel was relieved. And she knew. She just knew. I tried at that point to be good to her, but all the feeling between us was lost. She blamed me and I couldn't argue. It was like I wished that baby away. She moved back in with her parents in less than a month." A warm gust of wind raised the curtains against his legs, then the breeze died and they fell away.

Bubbles moved behind him and wrapped her arms around him, then moved a hand to his head, tugging on his hair. Joe leaned forward, increasing the tension on his scalp, easing the pain in his head. Another Bubbles hangover remedy. She spoke softly; "Pre-natal depression is fairly common in men. You're not the only one."

"Doesn't make it okay. Joe Rath rule number twelve: own what you are. I'm an asshole."

"I wasn't exonerating you. But fifteen years is a long sentence to serve for your crime." She turned Joe around and pushed him down on the bed. "And, you were about to commit another, indecent exposure; there's a boat coming."

"Still," said Joe. "I can't be trusted…you shouldn't trust me. You saw what happened last week with that baby book." He shook his head, wondering if this would be the end of things and when he glanced at her she had a stricken look.

"Trust? I don't even know what to say to that… if it would be possible to trust someone more than I do you. I can't wipe away what happened with Bonnie, but you're not that person anymore."

He sighed. "I hope not." A pelican hovered over the seawall and from his vantage point on the bed, it appeared to be landing on her shoulder. "Do you believe in signs?"

She looked at him quizzically. "Signs?"

He stood and turned her around and said, "Look."

The bird was settling on a piling and stretched its wings to dry its feathers. "Joe! Is that a pelican?"

"Yeah. It's been three years since I've seen one here." He paused. "But that doesn't mean it's a sign, showing up today of all days. You start believing that, and the next thing you know, you're dancing around pentagrams under the full moon."

She laughed. "We already dance under the moon." She pulled his arms around her and they watched silently for a while. "Magnificent," she finally said. "The first one I've ever seen," and laughed again. "Definitely not a sign though. We're thoroughly modern people. Just a coincidence. A sign. That's ridiculous."

"Total bilge," he said.

"Hogwash." She pulled him closer.

"How do you know about things like pre-natal depression anyway? Joe had returned to his place on the bed.

Bubbles smiled and said, "Baby books."

"Funny."

She got a serious look on her face. "I've been thinking a lot about babies lately. Thinking it's about time for me. It must be that biological clock thing"

He pondered a while, knowing she was tweaking him. She was years away from hearing any ticking, but he pictured Bubbles with a baby, lying in the hammock tossing it gently above her. He strangely saw it dressed in a tiny orange life jacket, but somehow couldn't see himself as the father. "You've never said anything about kids before," he said softly.

"How did you feel when I said that?"

He didn't answer, thinking of Jason and the strong feelings he had for the kid.

As if she had read his mind, she said, "What about Jason? You and Sheets are better fathers to him than his own dad."

"Yeah, I do like that kid."

"You love that kid. Your eyes light up when you see him."

"But still…you really want a baby?" He kept waiting to feel his usual panic, but mostly he felt oddly relieved, like a fifteen year burden had been lifted. He glanced at her. "It's weird, I don't feel all that badly about it."

"Well, you're not 21 anymore. Maybe it's time to go a little easier on yourself and not go all ballistic on your girlfriend for looking at a baby book."

"I know you said that baby thing just to get my reaction, didn't you?"

"Do I look like a girl who's ready to give up dancing and charming all the young boys in the Mid-Atlantic?" she said as she raised her hands and twirled about. A passing pontoon boat honked and the couple on board waved, then honked again. "Oops, even charming strangers." She reddened slightly and pulled down on the T-shirt to cover herself.

Chapter 27

Hanky Panky

1 oz Cold River Gin   1 oz Noilly Prat Dry Vermouth
4 Dashes Fernet Branca
Shake with Ice   Strain into Highball Glass
Garnish with Orange Twist

"That was pretty rotten, taking advantage of a person with a syndrome, this PND thing. What if that baby talk had pushed me over the edge into a state of catatonia or worse? I feel like a victim here." Joe grinned at her, feeling lighthearted now.

"Victim, my butt. I should have just let you suffer for another fifteen years."

"I feel the only place I could find solace would be in your ample bosom." Joe reached out to grab her. She turned and pulled the curtains across the door and turned back to him.

"Ample?" She pulled the T-shirt off and jumped on the bed, straddling him. "Ample? Substantially more than ample I would say."

"Ample is in the eye of the behold...." His voice was lost beneath her lips.

Chapter 28

Mr. P

1 oz Chopin Potato Vodka   1 oz Cherry Juice
½ Tsp Cherry Syrup
Pour Ingredients over Ice in Hurricane Glass
Fill with Sprite   Garnish with Pineapple Chunk

"We okay then?" Joe sat under the overhang of the upper deck, sunglasses on, still shaky from last night's partying.

Bubbles had moved a chair into the sun closer to the stern. "You're a little too late," she said, standing and moving next to him before pushing him with both hands, singing '*there's somebody new and he sure ain't no bartending man.*'

The pain flared in Joe's head again and he wasn't sure if it was the hangover or her god-awful voice. "No more. Please." But he smiled because he knew the song was code. All was right in their world.

She pushed him again. "Sing it, cowboy."

'*That's all right baby. If I hurry I can still make Cheyenne.*'

"Pretty good for a drunk." She sat down in front of him and Joe reached down and kneaded her shoulders. For a moment and they were quiet as they rocked on the gentle waves.

After a few minutes, Joe stood, moved to the shower on the rear deck and let hot water beat down on his forehead, teasing away some of the lingering ache. He looked down the bay. A couple of Hobie Cats were moving listlessly across the water in the intermittent breeze. He flipped the water to cold and thought that if he ever tired of the view from his improvised outdoor shower, it was time to pack it in and call Dr. Kevorkian.

The boat people were tolerant about nudity, so Joe had just used a few hibiscus plants as a shower stall which mostly shielded him from view. He turned and looked over one and saw that Bubbles had pulled her chair under the cover of the top deck. She had the Nordic skin that matched her platinum hair and couldn't stand much sun exposure. She was leaning back in the director's chair, eyes closed, with a book opened across her lap. *The English Patient.*

She usually just picked books of his at random. He had explained that if a book had earned a place on the Gypsy, it meant something special to him. He called them put downs, ones you had to put down frequently to think about. Now she would read them on the back deck and said that staring across the bay or at the birds or at the myriad distractions helped her focus on the writer's meaning.

She had picked up *The English Patient* one day, read the whole book quickly and told Joe she was puzzled by why he had kept it. It had no real plot, she said, and seemed to meander aimlessly. Joe said he'd had the same experience, but for some reason had kept it and read it again. He told her to give it a second chance, but read it really slowly. Take a week, even two.

Now Joe splashed some cold water over the hibiscus onto her face. She opened her eyes and said, "Listen," and read him a paragraph.

He put his head under the cold stream as she read. When she finished, he paraphrased a line from another Ondaatje book, "'A book so much a favourite, so thick with human nature, I wish it could accompany me into the afterlife.'"

Bubbles leaned her head back and closed her eyes. "Maybe this is the afterlife, Joe. Feels like heaven."

Joe slipped on his swim trunks and still dripping, pulled a chair out to catch some sun. He noticed she had idly reached out to the Mr. Potato Head glued to the stern rail as she read. Weathered by the wind and rain, it was now nearly completely white, with only one arm, one eye and a moustache without a nose. The remaining arm was cocked back above the missing eye in a salute to passing boaters. He and Bubbles had returned to the Gypsy one day to find Jason, only four at the time, busily gluing the spud's feet to the rail.

They hadn't been together long and she told him afterwards that she was concerned about what he might do, having seen his temper at work. His beloved trawler defaced.

Jason had smiled up at him and said, "You like it?"

Joe had looked seriously at the child and began to raise his arm which Bubbles had tried to grab, fearing the worst. But, he just continued raising his hand to his brow and snapped off a return salute to the potato saying, "Sir, Yes Sir."

Bubbles looked up from the book and Joe caught her eye. He pointed at Mr. P., smiled at her and said in a western drawl, "Faded." He reached up and tipped the brim of an imaginary cowboy hat and continued. "Like our love."

Her eyes clouded. "Don't say that word."

Love—saying it brought bad luck, she'd always said—but never told him why. "Sorry. It just slipped out."

He stood now to pull his chair into the shade next to Bubbles. He was still a little rocky and not ready to face the hot sun which had broken out fully. The freshening breeze was pushing the Gypsy to the end of its lines and the boat would snap back like a gentle teacup ride. It felt oddly soothing.

"Do you remember Creft Parrots?" Bubbles reached over and put her hands in his wet hair.

"Creft Parrots? What the hell is Creft Parrots?"

"It was the last thing you said last night. Apparently you admitted the Queen to the inner circle because of them." She smiled. "That's the most out of it I've ever seen you."

Joe sang a line from Lori McKenna. "'*I think I got a drinkin problem*'" "Wait. Wait. Creft Parrots, yes. Smile Train. Oh god, Queen. I might have to have a recount."

"Sheets really likes her."

A sailboat passed by, its outboard engine sputtering and trailing gas fumes. "Admiral Ross," Joe shouted, and received a snappy salute from the man at the tiller. As he stood to return the gesture, his faded orange swim trunks sagged from his hips. He glanced down. End of the summer and he'd lost the fifteen pounds he always did during the season. One of the best parts of the slow time was eating like a hog to gain it back before Memorial Day.

He sat down. "Are Sheets and Queen, you know…?"

"He says they're not."

"How come he doesn't tell me that stuff?"

"Because, when you ask about matters sexual, you sound lewd and lascivious." She reached down and pulled his suit up from his stomach. "Why can't I lose fifteen every summer?"

"Please. Look at you." Joe reached over and punched her rock-hard thigh.

"Shut up. I know you think I'm fat."

"Yeah. The quiver from that punch probably gonna start a tsunami somewhere. Millions dead, but it's all worth it cause I love me a plus-size gal."

"Asshole, I should have just let you suffer."

"A couple more days of drinking like last night and I might have been dead." Joe massaged his temples thinking he was going to have to rally soon to make it through tonight's shift. "I came up with a plan though."

"A plan for what?" Bubbles turned her head to the seawall where one gull had dislodged another, setting off a squawking round of musical pilings. The loser flew away as the others settled with a flutter of feathers. She turned to him.

"A plan to get you back." Joe laid his hand over hers which was still resting on his stomach. "I don't remember a worse week in my life."

She turned her hand up to grasp his. "What were you going to do?"

"You're gonna think..." He paused. "A winery.... Champagne."

"You were going to buy a winery? Where? God, Joe, what a thought, my—" She laughed. "Our own Champagne."

"Not buy one—I wanted us to start one. I found a place in Idaho. Same latitude as the Champagne region. It's got hills, water." Joe was kind of warming to the idea again. "You know, call it something like Bubbles Bubbles."

He could see the business-school girl eyes lock into place. Reality time.

"That would take a lot of money"

"Yeah, my dad left me 2.6 million dollars." His head started to hurt again just thinking about it.

"What did you just say?" "2.6 *million*?" "Oh, Joe. You must have been going crazy."

"Hey. I admit it's kind of a farfetched idea, but I'm not crazy. I was desperate."

"I meant about the money. I know how you are with it. Ah *crap*." And just like that she began crying. Between sniffles, she choked out a few words about how sweet he was to think about spending his inheritance to try to get her back.

Joe stood, pulled her up into his arms and held on until the little aftershocks in her back began to subside. It felt incredibly good just to hold her again after their week apart. As he looked across her shoulder, the pelican lifted off the piling, reminding him of something. "Were you here the night before last? The duck chart was out and Jason said he hadn't moved it."

She started to speak, then pulled him tighter. "I stopped by every night."

ψ ψ ψ

"So, do you want to go visit all the hotspots in Bonners Ferry, Idaho?" They had moved inside and Bubbles was cooking eggs, Joe's go-to, kill-the last-of-the-hangover remedy. "Alice booked me a flight. It's not for a few days. I could get another ticket."

She flipped the pan and the eggs eased over perfectly with the yolks intact. "God, it would be nice to get away after August. One of us should be here though. You said Jamie was cranky when she was pregnant the first time. Somebody needs to protect the crew. Keep her from wrestling an alligator or something stupid."

"I'll just cancel the flight."

Bubbles sprinkled something green into the pan. "You go. Get away for a few days. You deserve it after this crazy summer. Scout us out a new place to vacation." She smiled. "Buy a ranch."

"Yeah. Maybe I'll go have a look. Ticket's non-refundable anyway."

"Mr. Millionaire still counting his pennies."

"Jesus." Joe let out a long sigh.

Chapter 29

Up All Night

Pour 1 Can Red Bull into 16 oz Beer Glass
Fill Shot Glass with Jagermeister
Drop Shot Glass into Beer Glass

Joe eased awake again to the pinging sound of the slot machines from the casino down the hall. He hadn't really thought about it when he booked the room. Not a fan of casinos in general, this one was the particularly dispiriting kind with only slot machines. One-armed bandits no longer, the listless gamblers had only to insert bills and poke at colored buttons. Native American revenge, thought Joe. Every push of the button seemed to draw some life force from the player. Slowly sucked into the machine, leaving lifeless bodies programmed only to return with more money. The place was turning him morbid.

He glanced again at the lights from the other half of Bonners Ferry reflecting off the black surface of the river which bisected the town. He kept returning to the same dream each time he dozed off, falling from someplace that felt like home into the ocean. A swim to shore that he never completed before waking up again.

Bubbles would laugh at him. It wouldn't take Freud or Jung to analyze this dream. Here he was in a town two thousand miles from home, alone on a ridiculous mission. A vineyard. Who the hell did he think he was? Robert Effing Mondavi? Joe realized he hadn't been away from Bubbles for more than a day in two years and except for a couple vacations with her, hadn't been away from Sheets in longer than that. He glanced over at the alarm clock. 2:24 a.m. He couldn't think of anyone he could call without annoying them.

He flipped on the light on the nightstand, stood and checked out his reflection in the full length mirror on the closet. Damned cool. Black T-shirt. Block letter I with Vandals in script across the I. Who named their team the Vandals? Idaho, that's who. He wondered if their stadium was covered in graffiti, all the seats with names carved into them. He was definitely going to stop on the way to the airport and get more shirts. Make everybody on B-Dock wear them. Get drunk and go knock down some mailboxes. He smiled for the first time since arriving in the town.

He sat back down on the bed, knew he wouldn't sleep, wondering about his life. He used to drive across the country just for the hell of it. Loved the feel of the road, passing miles, no real destination. Restless, the Jackson Browne lyric always with him.

'*I can't help thinkin I'm just a day away From where I want to be.*'

Where did that put him now? Was where he wanted to be still a day away? He thought of the string of things that had happened to him since he'd turned thirty. Meeting Jamie, working at the restaurant, buying the Gypsy, Sheets and ultimately, Bubbles. Had to admit, he loved it all. Was it perfect? Could a life spiral up to perfection? No way, he thought, there were still plenty of things he wanted.

But when he tried to catalogue those wants and needs in his head, all he came up with was a new gas grill for the Gypsy. Joe laughed out loud at himself. Okay, life was good. He was happy. Even the baby thing he'd carried around like a medicine ball all those years had been eased by that talk with Bubbles.

Just the one problem left: What to do with the money?

Maybe he would give it away. Save the bonobos or something. Or give it to Rehoboth Beach if they'd let everyone park for free next summer. He'd be the most popular guy in town. Screw that, he thought, he was already popular with all the people he cared about. But Joe still felt the vague uneasiness he always felt about money, the sooner it was gone the better. At least Bubbles hadn't laughed too much about the vineyard idea.

The charade only needed to go on for one more day though. Then back on a plane. Back to the ocean. He was still kicking himself for missing four days in September, by far the best month at the beach.

He stepped to the window and pushed it open, thinking how warm it was for this far north. Bonners Ferry was actually a pretty little town, the Kootenai River running right down the center and tree-covered mountains in the distance. He'd driven around the area all day yesterday ostensibly looking for elevated south facing slopes ideal for champagne grapes, but really just killing time until he could get home.

One ranch had actually looked nearly perfect though, and Joe had noted the name of the real estate agency, stopped at their office in town and asked about the property which was called Elk Ridge Ranch. The lady had called the owners and made an appointment for him to stop by the following morning. Be careful up on that hill though, she had said, some of the neighboring ranch owners are less than welcoming.

Chapter 30

Lambada

2 oz Boca Loca Cachaca   2 oz Coco Lopez
1 oz Heavy Cream   6 oz Cherry Juice
Mix and Serve Over Ice in Hurricane Glass

Joe's usually infallible sense of direction seemed to have failed him. He hadn't slept well and had made the mistake of taking free coffee from the lobby that morning. My bad, Joe thought. He'd driven across the country countless times, stayed in scores of places offering free breakfast and the coffee was universally awful. He had passed a couple of local coffee shops and thought of stopping, but he just wanted to get to the ranch, then get out of this town. He couldn't pinpoint what didn't feel right about it.

Maybe it was the call from Bubbles at four a.m. She had forgotten about the time difference and woken him, saying she just wanted to hear his voice. They had talked for forty-five minutes and she'd made him laugh. The same things they always spoke about—the restaurant, Sheets, Jamie, bad customers, good customers—and he realized how much he enjoyed the details of his silly life. This town didn't have his friends, his boat, his ocean, his coffee shop, and most of all, it didn't have her.

The dirt track to the ranch house didn't look the same as it had the day before and the morning sun was striking the front windows of the house, which seemed wrong too. Maybe it was just the difference in the time of day, but then he noticed a camera mounted on the ranch gate as it tracked the rental Jeep when he turned in. He was definitely lost, Joe thought. There was no camera at the place he'd driven by yesterday. The driveway inclined about a half mile, up to a house, where he figured he could get directions.

It was just one packed dirt lane bordered on each side by grass, mostly dormant, but with a few patches of green left, glistening with dew in the chilly September morning. No trees until the fence line far in the distance. No animals grazing as there had been on the ranch he'd seen yesterday. Nothing being grown, no livestock. The feeling he'd had earlier about something being off returned.

As he neared the house, Joe noticed that the front door was ajar and a few minutes later, he was standing in the center of a huge living room. Large shaved ponderosa pine logs shaped a rustic post and beam superstructure. Impressive. The ceiling beams were more than two feet in diameter. A stone fireplace large enough to roast a calf in dominated the rear wall. Plank flooring from the same ponderosa pine but stained darker was partially covered with Indian rugs. Mounted heads from various animals completed the masculine décor. Not exactly a Martha Stewart situation, he thought. He'd rapped on the open front door and a voice had said to come in.

The minute he'd stepped inside, a large man with a shaved head had jumped into the air from one of the rugs, extended a leg and completed a full turn before landing. Then he turned to Joe. "Familiar with the Brazilian martial art of Capoiera?"

"No, but I've mastered a few steps of the Lambada, the forbidden Brazilian dance of love." Joe stepped across from the entryway to the man and extended his hand. "Joe Rath."

The guy's sneer and his hesitation before taking Joe's hand were enough for Joe to form an immediate opinion—douchebag. The man stepped close enough for Joe to clearly see the design on his black sleeveless T-shirt—a dagger inside of a red arrowhead. He finally reached for Joe's hand, applied a crushing grip and made no move to let go, confirming Joe's opinion.

"Buck," the man said in a raspy voice.

"Cool shirt. What's that design mean?" Joe smiled and cranked up the hand pressure, picturing one of his childhood toys: GI Joe with Kung Fu grip. Every bartending shift was a hand and wrist workout, but as Buck continued to hold on, Joe revised his initial thought—douchebag with a side of steroids. Apprehension flooded through him along with the real estate lady's words—'less than welcoming.'

"The shirt is my private business, Lambada." Buck used his grip to pull Joe closer. "Why are you here, anyway? Trespassing."

"Trespassing? No no. I was looking for Elk Ridge ranch and I got turned around. I was just hoping to get directions. I saw your door was open."

Buck was now looming above Joe. A red rash began to creep above the edge of his shirt and rise along his neck. "So you just wander onto private property and start snooping around? This is Aryan Nation territory. People have been shot for less than that."

"Don't worry. I'm usually a lot whiter, just a tan from living at the beach," Joe said in an attempt to lighten the mood. "Slower lower Delaware, where we rarely shoot intruders. Stop by if you're ever in Dewey Beach." He shook his hand free and turned to leave, but when he reached the open front door, he felt a heavy hand grasp his shoulder, spinning him back into the room.

"Not so fast there, Lambada. Did you say Delaware?" Buck continued to pull Joe's shoulder forcing him further into the house. "Delaware?" he repeated. "You just happened onto this ranch from *Delaware*? I don't think so."

Joe shrugged out of the man's grasp, apprehension changing to fear. The guy was as tall as Sheets, 6'4" but much bigger, at least 240 pounds. A nasty tang of sweat hung in the air around him. "I don't know what you're getting so worked up about. Just a mistake on my part. An accident. Wrong turn. I'll go."

"Accident my ass. Wandered onto this particular ranch all the way from *Delaware*."

"Come on man—"

"Shit, this is no coincidence. You're—you're not him—not that pretty boy." Buck ran to the front door and looked in each direction then came back and faced Joe. Sweat had formed across his forehead. "Where is he?"

Oh crap. Sweat. Paranoia. Rage. Joe realized this was more than steroids. And the asshole was now between Joe and the door. He eased a hand into the side pocket of his pants, where he had carried pepper spray since an ugly incident in the bar two years ago. He flipped open the lid and tried to calm his voice. "Who are you talking about?"

"You know who," Buck said, flecks of spittle appearing at the corners of his mouth. "Randolph. The Admiral's son." He advanced towards Joe.

"Go easy. I don't know any Randolphs or admirals." Joe began to back away. "You're confusing me with someone else. I'm just a bartender from a little beach town on vacation." Joe slid the plastic canister out and kept it covered in his hand. "I've got to go." He stepped to go around Buck, trying to leave room between them. "Bullshit. You're not going anywhere." As Buck moved to block Joe's way, a woman's sleepy voice came from the doorway.

"Bucky, who's here?" She walked to Buck's side and he took a step away from Joe. Black tangled hair fell halfway down her back. Green scrubs hung below her hips. Thin, painfully thin, she had smudges below her dark eyes. Joe would have called her beautiful, but her face was haggard as if she were ill.

"Renee, go back to your room."

"Bucky, I need—"

Buck grabbed a fistful of black hair and twisted, yanking her head backwards violently, displaying a dark bruise just below her jaw line.

"Now," he snarled.

Renee whimpered, collapsed against Buck's side and slid to the floor.

Joe had seen enough, knew he needed to run. When Buck looked back at him, he raised the pepper spray and gave Buck a shot in each eye. Buck yelled in pain, lunging at Joe, then fell to the floor, rubbing at his eyes. Joe looked to see if he would have to spray Renee as well, but she was sitting in the same spot, looking dully at him. An overwhelming anger filled him. He hadn't asked for any of this, just wanted directions and wound up in some steroidal maniac's delusion. Buck was still blocking his way to the door, one hand stretched across his eyelids and the other sweeping back and forth in an attempt to find Joe.

"You're dead, motherfucker. And so is that turncoat seal. We know right where he is. Right on that dock in Dewey Beach." Buck lunged forward with both arms as Joe took another step back.

Joe's voice shook. "One more time. No seals. No admirals. You've got the wrong guy, wrong dock, wrong everything."

"You won't get off this ranch alive and Randolph won't live out the week." Buck flailed his hand in Joe's direction.

The dock? How did this crazy man even know about the dock, Dewey Beach? No time to worry about that now. The man had just threatened to kill him twice. Just get out of this insane asylum, Joe thought. Anger was replacing fear, and when Buck's hand went back to his eyes, Joe kicked him hard in the side of the head. He was wearing sneakers and didn't think he could hurt the man too badly, but Buck slumped to the pine floor. Joe wished he'd worn boots. Really hurt the bastard.

"They'll kill you. You need to run." Renee had pushed herself to her feet. She limped to the front door.

"Kill me?" He realized he was panting, on the edge of panic, and moved next to her. "Who will?" Adrenaline had kicked in. He was shaking.

"Them." She pointed to a long black SUV turning into the ranch. "His Delta buddies."

"Delta? Seriously? Like the Special Forces guys?" Jesus, Joe thought, Idaho, packs of crazy people. What was I thinking?

"Yes. Quickly. Go. Around the back of the house, follow the track to the fence." She touched his arm. "Stay away from town. The sheriff is Buck's uncle."

"I saw what he did to you." Joe glanced at the bruise on her jaw. "You need to get out of here too."

Renee made a pathetic attempt at a smile. "I need what they have."

Joe looked at the line of brown along her front teeth. Oh god, he thought, emaciated, rotten teeth. All the signs he'd read about.

Tweakers

Crystal Meth. Shit. Shit. Shit. What had he stumbled into?

He sprinted for the Jeep.

Chapter 31

Undertaker

3 oz Stoli Vanil   1 oz Kahlua
1 oz Crème de Cacao   1 oz Chilled Espresso
Shake Liquors w/Ice   Strain into Martini Glass
Stir in Espresso

Joe jumped into the rental Jeep, circled the house and flew down the back road as fast as the rutted dirt surface would allow.

His heart was pounding. How could this possibly be happening? He tried to channel his inner Sheets. Calm. Think. But the panic kept rising as he nervously attempted to keep one eye on the rear-view mirror while negotiating the rutted dirt track. The dust rising from the wheels obscured everything behind him. About a half mile down the road, he could see a line of trees, possibly the end of the ranch property. He couldn't tell if the road continued into the woods.

He heard a ping as something hit the rear of the Jeep and the glass in the back window dissolved into shards. I'm going to die out here, he thought, and pictured Bubbles. He was sweating and one hand slipped from the steering wheel as the SUV bottomed out in a deep rut with a long scraping sound. His head slammed into the roof as he fought to stay on the road.

The blow to his head acted like a slap in the face. You're not dead yet, he thought, accelerating as he passed the worst of the dips. He knew virtually nothing about guns except what he had picked up from books. A couple Stephen Hunter sniper novels. He remembered something about the best marksmen being able to hit targets from distances of over a mile. He guessed, prayed, hoped that he'd come at least a mile from the house by now. Maybe the dust would prevent the shooters from sighting in on him.

He went down a short incline and a bullet ricocheted off the roof. The tree line was only a couple hundred yards away, but he could see now that a stockade fence gate blocked the road. Shit, she'd forgotten to mention that. A camera mounted on the fence tracked the progress of the Jeep. There was no time to stop and Joe figured the gate would be locked anyway. No choice now. He had the bizarre thought that the rental company wasn't going to be happy with his decision. Alamo. Not an omen, he hoped.

Glancing down, he checked his speed. Forty. If he stopped, he was dead. If he didn't make it through the fence he was dead. The road seemed to flatten a little as it approached the gate. He pushed the pedal to the floor and braced for impact, holding an arm up to shield his eyes from any flying glass.

And? Nothing but noise that sounded like giant fingernails screeching on a blackboard. He opened his eyes. The windshield was intact. He glanced at the mirror and saw dust curling through the remains of the gate. Bits of something flew up from the hood.

Plastic? Cheap bastards, he thought, relieved, and realized he was holding his breath.

The road was wider and flatter on this side of the fence and surrounded closely by tall evergreens. Through the trees, Joe saw filtered sun almost directly ahead. Heading south. He checked the mirrors. The road was hard-packed and he could see clearly. Nobody there. Yet. He wanted off this road, and found himself hunched forward scanning desperately to find a place to turn off. A road, driveway, something. But there was nothing. At least the Jeep seemed intact. No strange noises that he could hear above the relentless pounding of his own blood in his ears. Keep moving, he thought, then call Sheets. He knew that somehow the quiet man would know what to do.

The dirt road ran on through the trees for almost two miles, before popping him out on a paved surface. Just a two lane county highway with no one on it. More trees. No homes. No businesses. He'd instinctively turned west hoping the road led to Route 95. What would his pursuers expect, he thought as he watched the dirt road disappear in the rear view? They'd expect him to head straight to the police. Or back to his hotel.

Straight to the police. Crap. That woman had said the sheriff was Buck's uncle. Joe rechecked the mirror. Nothing. He saw a sign for Route 95. Two miles ahead. Right turn to Bonners Ferry? Get his stuff at the hotel? Joe slowed to make the turn. One more look back. Still nothing.

Renee, was that her name? Everything that had happened already felt distant and surreal. The morning was too quiet. The road deserted. Nothing but blue sky and green trees. Why was there no pursuit? Keep moving, he thought, do not go back to town. He had a weird moment of regret for leaving anything of his behind in this state, but there was nothing in that hotel room worth risking his life for.

His mind made up, Joe skipped the right turn and bumped up onto the two lane road heading south. Drive. Get out of this god-forsaken state. Leave the lunatics behind. He saw cars coming at him and some ahead and felt relief wash over him as he hit the gas pedal so that he could catch up with the other cars. He got behind a silver Prius with a kayak strapped to its roof. Stay with it until you turn off to Montana, he thought, wiping the sweat from his hands onto his black shorts. He took some deep breaths. Keep moving.

It was somewhere in eastern Montana before Joe started to calm down and stopped looking behind him every ten seconds. He'd picked up I-90 in Missoula and was pushing the Jeep at ten miles above the seventy-five mile per hour limit. There had been no cell service on the nearly deserted Route 200 and he realized that the long 4 a.m. call with Bubbles had nearly drained the battery on his phone. The charger was sitting in his bag at the motel. He had gotten through to Sheets after he hit the Interstate, but realized he was babbling when Sheets kept telling him to slow down. Then the low battery signal started sounding and he had to settle for telling Sheets to let Bubbles know he was on his way back and not to worry.

Not to worry. Jesus. He wondered how close he'd come to not making it off that ranch. He toyed with the idea of going to the police, but would he really be willing to go back to Idaho, swear out a complaint and confront Buck again? Joe had seen a sign for Ruby Ridge just a few miles from Bonners Ferry and vaguely remembered that a few people had died there when the government had confronted some Idaho crazies. No, he thought, just go and never see these people again.

Airports. Any of the Montana B towns—Butte, Bozeman, Billings—would have one. But the thought of trying to explain bullet holes and broken windows defeated him. 2500 miles home. Go straight through. Let the road calm him. His heart rate had finally slowed to near normal. The worst was over.

By afternoon, the morning felt like days ago. He tried to reconstruct the events, the exact words in his mind as he drove on. How could his innocuous beach town set someone off like that? Buck had latched onto Dewey and Delaware like a rabid dog. He'd even mentioned the dock. "A pretty boy on the dock," he'd said. Very few people you could call pretty among the scruffy weekenders there to fish and drink. Egg was pretty, hell she was beautiful, but all girl, and Sheets was handsome, but Joe couldn't imagine anyone calling him a pretty boy. Maybe steroids and meth had completely fried the man's brain. Still, how would he know about the dock?

After ten hours on the Interstate, he pulled off in the old cowboy town of Sheridan, Wyoming, feeling better about having a whole state between him and the crazies. He remembered a good bar there with Pony in the name that served decent food along with some sad country music. He'd gotten lucky on the way there and found a convenience store with a pay phone. He called Bubbles and tried to give her a sanitized version of what had happened, so she wouldn't worry. A waste of time, he thought after; she'd read his mind as always and dragged most of the details out of him. How long, was all she wanted to know when he told her he was going to drive?

Thirty more hours on the road plus a couple of hours sleep in a rest area. He wasn't going to risk registering the shot-up Jeep at a motel. He'd inspected the rental at the convenience store. Huge gouges in the paint down the length of each side, the rear window gone, a furrow in the roof and three bullet holes in the rear. It looked like it belonged in a roadside ditch in Iraq.

Now, as he sat at the bar in the Pony place with a burger and a beer in front of him and Radney Foster singing '*Went For a Ride*', Joe finally was able to clearly reflect on the day. I'm okay, he thought and though he'd been as panicked and scared as he could possibly imagine, he'd done alright, reacted pretty well. The beer had a mellowing effect and he risked one more. He began to think about how he'd tell the story at the dock and the restaurant. Make himself a little more heroic, tamp down the fear part. Then he laughed thinking about playing it out, with Sheets as the evil Buck and The Queen as the scrawny Renee. She was almost skinny enough. Jesus, he thought, it's good to be alive.

Chapter 32

Homecoming

1¼ oz Amaretto di Amore   1¼ oz Bailey's Irish Cream
Serve over Ice in Rocks Glass

The dock. The marina. The ocean. Joe turned right on Collins, the bright mid-day sun filling the space of the missing rear window and pulled into a parking space by the office. A gull lifted up from a puddle next to the Jeep with a loud squawk. After his odyssey, it sounded like welcome back. He leaned forward and rested his head against the steering wheel, back sore, eyes dry, that woozy feeling from extreme exhaustion settling throughout him.

Home.

Montana, Wyoming, Nebraska, Iowa. The trip was a blur of semis and Interstate mile markers. He smiled, thinking that for the first time in his life, he had been happy to see Pennsylvania, meaning only one state left to cross. He turned to the rear seat to get his bag before remembering he had left everything in Idaho. He was totally in a fog. I'll be useless for two days. He stuck the dead phone in his pocket, the only possession left from the trip.

As he got out of the Jeep, he glanced to his left towards the docks, but his view was blocked by the Murphy Electric van in the next slot. His legs were rubbery from fatigue and lack of use. He propped himself against the Jeep waiting for the feeling to return to them and took several deep breaths, hoping that the smell of the bay and the cool air would revive him. He glanced at the missing rear window thinking that it was a miracle that he hadn't been pulled over somewhere along the escape route.

And that's when he noticed a different smell. Gas? No. More like gas mixed with something acrid. As if someone had stirred up the cold ashes from a wood fire. A knot formed in his stomach. And then the truck backed out of the space and he saw the side-on view of Sheets' sloop rocking in small waves.

Something was wrong with the picture.

Something was missing.

The Gypsy was gone. His heart fell and he looked again. A boat he didn't recognize was in his slip. Why? He pushed off the Jeep and moved toward the dock, his legs still wobbly.

That strange odor assaulted him again, only stronger, leaving an acid taste in the back of his throat. It seemed to be coming from B-Dock. No one was around. The parking lot was empty except for his old Ford, the Jeep and the dockmaster's pickup with the camper top. Completely quiet, except for the sound of the pump in the bait tank. Something bad had happened, he felt it.

Knew it.

And began to run.

As he passed the marina office, the dockmaster stepped out and spit out his cigar stub. Joe heard him say, "Rath. Wait," as he raced by.

Book Two

ψ ψ ψ

Sheets' Story

'When I close my eyes I see her,
No matter where I am.
I can smell her perfume
Through these whispering pines.'

-Zac Brown

Chapter 33

A long December, but there's reason to believe
Maybe this year will be better than the last'

Impossible now, Sheets thought, as he picked out the opening notes to the old Counting Crows song on his antique Gibson Hummingbird guitar, desperately holding onto something he loved, while trying without success not to think about her. He scanned the dock and the parking lot looking for Joe for the hundredth time and willed himself not to look at Joe's boat slip. He needed to be the one to give Joe the news. That she was gone. Forever. He didn't even know if he could say the other word.

The picture of the three of them with their rakes in hand, bandanas on their heads was already overturned on his nightstand.

Gone.

It seemed impossible.

Joe Rath's rules for life would no longer begin to cover all the changes they would need to make if they were to get along without her, he thought. A whole new list was needed:

1. No bandanas. He hadn't had the heart to open the drawer and see the ugly thing, much less throw it away. Not yet. If he touched it, he would feel her behind him brushing against him as she tied it on, twisting his hair into a ponytail to fit through the back, her hand smoothing wrinkles from his shirt as she mock-scolded him for being such a slob.

2. No Champagne. Champagne had bubbles.

3. No cowboy songs. Especially no George Strait. Especially no *"I Can Still Make Cheyenne"* He'd think of her awful voice singing:

    > '*There's somebody new*
    > *And he sure ain't no bartendin man'*

4. No dancing. He'd never danced in his life. But, Sheets didn't want to see anyone dance. He knew he'd avoid looking at the spot in the center of the outside deck of the Rudder where she held court on Thursday nights, eyes closed, whirling, short hair bouncing, seemingly unaware of anything but the music. Dancing. Her escape.

5. No Breakfast Club. Maybe no movies at all. Movie night had meant her apartment, her between the two of them on the couch, her taking both of their hands during tense moments. *The Breakfast Club* had become their favorite. They watched it at least twice a year. Sheets watched fascinated, as if the high school kids were a different species. His school years were spent at military schools learning the skills of war, of killing. Bubbles' high school

years were spent in fear of failure in her father's eyes. Only Joe had any connection with the experiences of the kids on the screen. And yet they watched, absorbed, as if to answer- what if? What if they had had a chance to do it over? Who would they be? Who could they be? When Allie, Judd, Molly and the others danced on the railing, Bubbles would synchronize her feet with theirs, tapping Joe's and Sheets' until they joined in. Maybe, he always thought at that moment, that the road to how they lived now was less important than the destination. Correction. Lived. Past tense. How they *had* lived.

And what of her scent? The heady smell that he ruminated over like an archeologist with The Rosetta Stone and knew Joe did as well. How could he possibly avoid it? Would it rise from the pages of a book she had touched? Would it fall with the fat leaves of the sycamores in late October? Would it be blown to the edge of the ocean from the dune grass? Five. Ten. Fifteen years later, would it still startle him? What would he do when it appeared? Cry? Of all the lessons of life he'd learned from Bubbles and Joe, he had never learned to cry.

He needed to learn.
He would learn.

Chapter 34

Love.
Loss.

Emotions, Sheets thought. What kind of brave new world did he live in now? Watching and waiting as he sat in the cockpit of his boat, he realized he was anxious, worried about what to say when Joe got back. The thought surprised him. William Allen Randolph feeling emotion? WAR, as his father, the Admiral, had dubbed him shortly after he was born, having feelings? Sheets almost smiled, but the events of the last night killed it before it reached his face. He tried to remember if he had ever had a real friend before Joe.

He saw the shadow of his mast in the nearly flat water and knew from the angle that it was almost noon. Virtually no action in the marina. Even the two swallows perched on pilings seemed to be nodding off. Joe should be back by now. He'd called last night and estimated that he'd be here early in the morning. Maybe he'd hit rush hour somewhere or had to stop to sleep for a while. I want him back now, Sheets thought. The waiting was making him crazy.

Sheets had been a year into the process of sinking into the

blackness of his life when Joe arrived on the marina scene, incompetent but obviously in love with the Gypsy and his new water world. Joe's second day at the dock brought a late spring nor'easter, and though Sheets tried to ignore the sound of Joe's boat pounding into the pilings, he couldn't stand the thought of such a beautiful piece of work being smashed to pieces. So he'd knocked on Joe's hull and spent the afternoon showing Joe some basic marine survival techniques—ropes, knots—and figured that would be the end of it. But in the days and weeks afterward, Joe would stop at Sheet's slip and pepper him with questions about his boat and Sheets began thinking of Joe as a long-term project. Initially, he thought that he might kill Joe because of his incessant chatter. He hadn't spoken more than a few words to anyone in the previous year.

Sheets taught Joe how to maneuver the boat with the twin engines, going in and out of the slip countless times until Joe mastered the technique. He frequently marveled that Joe had managed to get down the James River, up the Chesapeake Bay, through the C&D Canal, down Delaware Bay and through the shallows of Rehoboth Bay without seriously harming the Gypsy, himself or anyone else. Joe told him that he mostly had used just one engine throughout the trip. Sheets suspected that Joe lived a charmed life.

Without him even realizing it, Joe began to pull Sheets back into the real world. Sheets found himself looking forward to Joe grabbing him when he came home from the restaurant late at night, sitting up on the top deck of the Gypsy, the ritual shots of Mezcal, Joe providing a wrap-up of the events of the day. Joe had talked him into going over to the deck of the Rudder for a beer one evening and Sheets had found that he enjoyed sitting there looking out at the bay through the palm trees, imagining them sitting at a bar on an island somewhere. Everyone at the Rudder knew Joe and there was a constant parade of people stopping by their table at the back bar area to talk. Sheets wound up talking with a young waitress who loved sailing and invited herself to go out on his boat.

The day sailing with the waitress had launched another aspect of real life for Sheets. He began to regularly take the summer girls out on the sloop for a day or evening sail. Joe naturally assumed that Sheets was sleeping with every one and constantly pestered him for details. In reality, Sheets found, for the most part, the girls were smart and attractive and provided him with information on how normal people, especially women, lived their lives.

The summer women were a revelation, their stories fascinating him and he picked up endless facts about pop culture with which he was largely unfamiliar. *American Idol*, Hobbits and *A Million Little Pieces* were the big topics of conversation. One of the girls told him he looked like the guy in *Pirates of the Caribbean*. When he'd asked Joe who it was, Joe just laughed at him and said, Sheets, you're good looking, but there's only three guys in the world as pretty as Johnny Depp.

Now Sheets stood and checked the parking lot one more time, empty except for Joe's pickup and the two-wheeled carts used to carry all the weekenders' crap down the docks. No Joe. He went below to use the head.

And of course, when Sheets climbed back on deck, it was too late to catch Joe as he ran toward the Gypsy, or what was left of it.

Sheets watched him reach his slip, still with the yellow police tape wrapped around the pilings, and turn as if confused, not recognizing the charred remains of his trawler, which had burned nearly to the waterline. The radar mast trailed behind the boat in the water, kept afloat only by the buoyancy of the Loran unit mounted near the top. The hot tub lay upside down on the blackened wood and melted fiberglass of the cabin.

As Sheets approached, Joe sat down heavily on the edge of the dock and collapsed onto his back. Sheets knelt next to him, wondering how and even if he could tell Joe that the Gypsy was the least of it.

"Joe." Sheets reached out and put his hand on Joe's shoulder.

"What the hell happened? Does Bubbles know about this?" Joe sat back up.

Sheets looked at the rumpled black shorts and T-shirt and smelled stale sweat as Joe started to get up from the dock, but Sheets pressed his hand down on his shoulder.

"Hold on. There's something I need to tell you." The smell from the remains of the boat was picked up by the cool northwest breeze, charcoal and a chemical odor from the melted fiberglass mingled together. They both looked up at the Gypsy, Sheets picturing Joe and Bubbles together in the soft tub on the top deck, a bottle of champagne as the sun set. Early fall, their favorite time of year. "Joe." Sheets' hesitated and his voice caught. "Bubbles was on the boat."

"What boat?"

"The Gypsy."

Joe again tried to stand up, but Sheets held him down.

"Where is she now?"

Sheets hesitated again. "She slept here last night thinking you might make it back before morning." Sheets was talking now just to postpone saying it. "She never.... She never made it off the boat." He choked on his words, could not get them out, still not believing what he had to say.

"What?" Joe pushed Sheets' hand away. "Where is she?"

A laughing gull hovered above them and gave three scolding squawks, its black head bobbing.

"She's..." Say it. Say it. Say it. "Bub—she's...." A highlight reel of images was playing in his head: in her black and white server outfit; at the helm of the Gypsy with the captain's hat she'd bought for Joe; laying in the hammock pretending to be shooting at the ultralight. The one in that stuck, though, was the one where she had Joe in a headlock, acting like she was trying to pound some sense into him. She was looking Sheets with her million-dollar smile and her hair askew and it felt as if she were asking him to take care of Joe. He took a deep breath.

"Bubbles died in the fire. She's gone."

"Gone?" said Joe.

Sheets opened his mouth to answer, but there were no words left to speak. He sat down by Joe and watched the mid-day sun reflect in the waves bouncing off the Gypsy's blackened bow.

"Bubbles is dead?" Joe's voice was a monotone as if he was trying out a foreign phrase that had no meaning to him. "Are you sure? How do you know?"

"Cops. Medical Examiner." Sheets motioned to the caution tape, still struggling to speak.

Joe lay down on the dock and put his arm across his eyes. After a few moments, he sat up, looked at Sheets and said, "Bubbles is dead."

It was still a question, but Sheets knew it was sinking in as slowly as it had with him when he'd sailed into the marina early this morning.

"Who'll take care of the cat?" Joe said, as he steadied himself with a hand on Sheets' shoulder and moved hesitantly down the dock.

Sheets stared at Joe, unable to move or call to him. He'd watch out for Joe, go after him in a little while, he thought, but it hit him then: who would watch out for him?

Chapter 35

As Joe walked down the dock towards the parking lot, he passed a woman coming the other way. His head came up briefly, but he kept on moving. Sheets realized it was the Queen, recognizing the toned runner's legs in khaki shorts. He shook his head. *Bubbles, Egg, Buzz, Queen* and the two kids Joe called *Mop* and *Broom*. Joe's world, Sheets thought. His stage and everyone a player with a part and a name supplied by Joe.

The Queen held a pizza box in one hand and a six-pack in the other. When she stopped at Sheets' slip, she looked up at him. "I thought maybe you'd be hungry."

"Hadn't thought about it, but thanks." He took the pizza and beer from her and she climbed aboard, popped open two of the bottles and went below to get plates. They moved to the picnic table on the dock and sat on the same side looking out to the bay. Only a few boats remained in the marina. The season was over. People had moved on to other pursuits, school, football. The nearly unobstructed view across the bay was empty now except for a lone sailboat. It was a beautiful late September day. Sunny and warm. The tourists left the town each year just as everything turned to perfection, he thought.

Perfection. Except. The chemical smell from the burned-out Gypsy rose on the breeze. It made him want to gag. "Did Joe say anything?" he asked.

"He mumbled something about feeding a cat?"

"Her cat. He's in shock. I just told him.

"Should you follow him? Make sure he's okay?"

"He won't be okay. They were…." He sighed. "I'll give him some time."

"So sad. I never really understood him. He'd come to the coffee shop, read, always seemed, I don't know, a little hostile, especially towards me." She looked at Sheets.

"You worked on the wrong day. Sundays. His people weren't there—Alice, Steve. Joe's a creature of habit. Maybe he has a little of that, what is it, OCD? Bub— She called him that sometimes." She. He couldn't say her name. "You had to see his bar set-up. Every bottle facing out, spaced equally. He used to tell me you didn't fill his coffee all the way to the top."

She brushed away a dragonfly hovering over Sheets shoulder. "Guilty. I hate the coffee part of being there—cappucinos, triple lattes, skinny, vente. I just want to play with the books. So why does everyone here love him so much?"

Sheets watched as the sailboat attempted to come about, the sails dying in the listless breeze, failing to complete the turn. What about just sailing away? Away from the trouble he could feel building. "He's got no box."

"No box?"

"That expression, think outside the box. He doesn't have a box to think inside of. He'll say something that sounds completely irrational, but if you think about it, there'll be some weird logic to it." He was my first exposure to the real world, he thought, and shook his head.

The dragonfly returned and she shooed it again. "Give me an example."

He took her hand as she raised it to keep the dragonfly away. "They don't bite," he said, and fell silent. This is what he enjoyed about her. When they talked about a book, she wouldn't let him just say he liked or disliked it, she'd push him to tell her why. Sheets held on to her hand and realized how good it felt.

"Come on." She squeezed his hand.

"Okay. Drunken drivers."

"What about them?"

"Here's Joe's take. Repeal all the laws against drunken driving. They don't seem to work anyway. A constant cat and mouse game between the cops and the drunks. So. No laws. Advise all sober drivers to get off the roads by midnight and stay off until an hour after the bars close. Send out tow trucks before rush hour to clear away the wreckage. He says the problem is self-limiting."

Queen pulled her hand away. "That's ridiculous."

Exactly, he thought. Ridiculous. Maybe their whole existence had been ridiculous. But it had been theirs. Had been. "That's what she always said."

"Okay, I'll admit there's a certain perverse sensibility to the idea." Queen paused. "He's not going to be alright, is he?"

"I don't see how." Sheets couldn't help but look at the remains of the Gypsy, crushed, looking like a hammer had smashed it down to half its normal size. At least the parade of cops, Coast Guard, Fire Police and gawkers had ceased and the dock had returned to its off-season quiet. "I don't see how," he repeated.

"How about you?" She took his hand and spoke softly. "You've said *she* and *her*. You haven't said her name."

Bubbles, he thought. The name had been fun. A perfect repudiation of the serious life her father had laid out for her. Now he wanted a different name to remember her with, a name which could represent her intellect, warmth, intuition, all the things that made him love her. The name left a taste of ash now when he tried to say it. He himself had been hiding behind a nickname for six years. "She didn't even know my name."

"What do you mean?"

Sheets looked at Queen, startled, not realizing he'd spoken the words aloud. "Sorry, it's not—."

"No, please. Tell me what you meant."

He blew out a long breath and repeated. "She didn't know my name." He paused. "WAR."

"War?"

"William Allen Randolph." He swallowed. He hadn't heard or spoken those words for six years and they felt foreign in his mouth. "WAR. Not an accident, even though my mother's maiden name was Allen. The Admiral's own little warrior." What am I doing? he thought, dredging up my old life of war and weapons that he'd thought life on the dock had squashed forever. "Sorry."

"Don't be. I know you loved her."

Sheets looked at her quizzically. "You did?"

"You positively vibrated when she was around." Queen gave him a wry smile. "Not that easy to watch when—" She glanced away.

"Hold it. Is that why...?" Sheets stopped. He thought of all the time he'd spent with Queen. Talking books, life, whatever. He loved her calm way. Tranquil, like the ocean on a windless day. But nothing had ever happened physically. Most of their time together had been at the bookstore because the sailboat made her sick.

She pulled off her sweater, tossed it on the table and rested her hand on his forearm. "War? The Admiral? Tell me."

He nodded. For six years, he'd kept everything about his life concealed through countless interrogations by Joe and everyone else on the dock. Even Queen, who was a novelist, a story teller, had never asked him about his past, as if she knew intuitively to stay away from it. Just like Bubbles, he thought. Maybe that was why he felt like telling his story. Maybe he wished he'd told *her* about his life before she died. He slid closer to Queen, craving more physical contact. Fuck it, he thought, just tell the tale.

"The Admiral was my father," he began. "He threw me in the river behind our house in Charleston when I was three to teach me to swim. Phase two of SEAL training includes learning to tie knots underwater. The Admiral tested me on that when I was seven. When he was at sea, I was sent to military schools specializing in preparing naval officers."

"Some father." She fingered her seashell earring, twisting a strand of her long blond hair around it. "What about your mother?"

"I think the schools were also about keeping me away from any love or comfort my mother might have offered. I barely remember her.

"You see, my father, or Sir, or the Admiral, never dad, was intent from the beginning on creating a weapon. No feelings. Duty to country, the Navy. Life in the service means moving around. No possibility of lasting friendships. Military schools, followed by the Academy, SEAL training and the plum The Admiral always wanted, SEAL Team Six. Something he failed to do. The only black mark in his career." Sheets wondered if he sounded as bitter as he felt.

"The thing is, I wanted it. Wanted to be the little warrior, please the Admiral. I knew nothing else. If he had stuffed me in a box, I liked the box. I was as hard and uncaring as anyone could be. I was the weapon he set out to create. Until...." Sheets stopped, aware that he hadn't once looked at her, hadn't eaten or taken a drink, caught up in the story he had never told anyone, even Joe.

A clam exploded as it landed near the picnic table and a seagull followed it down, eying them warily as it began picking at the broken shell.

"That scared the hell out of me." Queen reached over and wiped some goo from her leg and a fresh smell of seafood rose around them.

"Soon as the tourists leave, the gulls start using this as a platform to open shells. It'll be covered by spring. We wake up to that sound most mornings."

"You said you were trying to please your father until.... until what?" She moved her hand back to her earring.

Sheets pictured the Afghan boy with the big brown eyes, the red splotch suddenly appearing between those eyes. The picture he'd lived with for six years.

"Until I walked away." He picked up a slice of pizza, already cool, had a bite and a sip of beer. No taste for either one. He heard the reggae band begin to tune up at the Rudder. Nearly four o'clock. He should find Joe and try to talk to him. He looked at Queen again, wondering how shocked she was by Mr. Quiet actually talking about his own life.

"I got the thought this morning after everything happened, waiting for him, that Joe was the first friend I ever had. How is that possible? I was thirty years old when I met him. Jesus, I must have forgotten someone along the way."

She looked at him with a half smile. "You don't forget friends."

"Somehow, he pulled me out of The Admiral's box. Made me laugh. When we sat on the dock, he made people try to guess my name and what I did before, because I wouldn't answer questions about myself. He guessed pedophile priest one night and came up with a stupid name, Father Bonkin, and a whole back story to go with it. Had everybody in tears including me. The first time, you know, she guessed…" He stopped and took a deap breath. "She said Navy SEAL and never guessed again. She just knew. I don't know what Joe will do without her. What I'll do."

A loose plank creaked as someone approached them. The dockmaster with the ever-present cigar. One eye was partially closed to avoid the stream of smoke curling from the stub. He walked past them and stood in front of Joe's burned out boat. Moments later, he turned and motioned Sheets over with a twist of his head.

"Give me a minute." Sheets rose from the bench and made his way to the man's side.

The dockmaster continued to stare at the Gypsy and then pulled out the cigar and traced a circle in the air as if outlining the boat. "Wrong pattern." He plugged the cigar back in place.

"What are you saying?" Sheets looked at the wreck, the yellow police tape on the pilings flapping lightly.

"This wasn't an accident. Look at the scorch marks. I saw my share of boat fires in the Navy. Two folks died in one on A-Dock, year before you came. Looked nothing like this."

No way, Sheets thought, unable to process the meaning of this new information. "Are you sure?"

"I wasn't until this came." He handed Sheets a tri-folded piece of paper. "I opened it because I didn't recognize the name."

Randolph was written on the outside. The same feeling of shock he'd had when he'd spoken his name earlier hit him. It can't be for me, he thought. Don't let it be me. He lifted the top fold and two hand-written lines were revealed. He would never forget that neat lettering, styled to ensure that orders were always followed exactly:

Sending your friend to the ranch cost him his life.

I haven't forgotten about you.

Sheets looked from the note to the Gypsy and felt the world fall away. Six years. He thought it had been over. That they had forgotten about him. How could he have been so stupid? He had he lost his edge, he thought, thinking he was safe in Joe's world. His breath caught and he felt as if he were swaying. Why hadn't he run? Kept running? This was his fault. He'd gotten her killed.

He felt a hand on his shoulder and a gravelly voice saying his name. He glanced over and saw Queen rising from her seat with a look of concern. He held up his hand to keep her back. He needed to think. To concentrate. "Who brought the note?"

"Two guys. Military for sure. Cocky. Probably Army."

"Why Army?"

"Army smells different."

Sheets was aware of the foul scent of the cigar and wondered randomly if the old guy could smell anything. "Special Forces?"

The cigar came out momentarily and the dockmaster spat into the bay. "Could be. They had the swagger."

"When were they here?"

"They pulled up this morning in a black Suburban. Dark tinted windows. I've seen it in the lot at Ruddertowne a few times in the last couple weeks."

Shit, Sheets thought, someone had snuck in last night and set fire to the Gypsy and black SUVs were hanging around town and he hadn't noticed anything. Guilt descended over him. This life had left him dull as a butter knife. "You didn't tell the Coast Guard or the State Police about this?"

The old man eyed him from head to toe and was silent for at least a minute. When he spoke, his voice was barely audible. "I figured maybe you'd want to handle it yourself." He turned from Sheets and shambled back towards the office.

Sheets returned to the table and stood next to the Queen. "New information…." He found himself unable to continue, overwhelmed with thoughts of what the message meant and what he must do. "I need to find Joe."

She stood and put her arms around him, but he felt the tension of his old existence building and knew she would feel it as well. "Be careful," she whispered, and turned to go.

He gazed out across the bay, flat and peaceful in the quiet of the afternoon sun. He felt no peace or quiet. Anger coursed through him and he tried to push it away. Emotion had been useless in his old world, but it continued to vibrate in him. He felt himself clenching his fists, unclenching, clenching again. He'd been completely caught off guard once, it wouldn't happen again. If this was what his father wanted, it's what he would get.

Chapter 36

Sheets pulled open the door to Bubbles' glassed-in front porch and surveyed the masses of plants growing there. The space was still bright with the early evening sun, giving it the feel and smell of a greenhouse. Mostly herbs, Sheets thought, one of her passions. Probably none would survive; collateral damage along with Joe, everyone at the restaurant and to be honest, himself as well. If Bubbles hadn't been with Joe and if he had known anything about women, he would certainly have tossed his hat into that ring. He felt his anger building again as he walked along the sun's angled rays across the small living room.

He'd jogged up the beach to Rehoboth after stopping at his boat to pick up his SIG-Sauer pistol and dive knife. He'd not only wanted to give himself time to think, but also to approach from an unexpected direction if The Admiral had people watching. He suspected that the old man would most likely have pulled the Deltas or whoever was working for him out of town until they were sure that there would be no blowback from the murder, but Sheets wanted to be sure. He'd scaled the roof of a utility shed which overlooked the thin strip of grass behind her apartment and saw no one there or in any of the adjacent yards. Joe's rental Jeep was parked in front and Sheets' breath caught when he saw the bullet holes and realized how close he'd come to losing not just one, but both of them.

Surrounded by pillows, Joe was sitting up against the headboard of Bubbles' bed, staring straight ahead at an old black and white movie poster next to the window. The Three Stooges with a gorilla in *Dizzy Detectives*. Bubbles had come home from work one evening to find him and Joe watching a Stooges DVD. She was appalled. Joe had found the poster on the internet and they snuck in and put it up after signing it 'With love from Joe and Sheets'.

Joe reached absent-mindedly for the white cat sitting next to him. The cat moved just out of his reach, but continued to stare at him intently. Sheets passed through the doorway and pulled a rocking chair up to the side of the bed. He had waited a couple hours before coming, knowing exactly where he would find Joe. The bedroom was on the north side of the apartment and only one thin ray of sunshine across Joe's chest lit the space

Sheets looked at Joe, nearly buried in the fluffy flowered comforter. Wrinkled black T-shirt, black shorts, no socks or shoes. A dozen pillows surrounded him on the bed. Pure Bubbles. Joe idly fingered a white robe lying next to him.

A memory of the nights Joe stayed late to close the restaurant, made Sheets think of a similar robe of Joe's she always wore after showering on the back deck of the Gypsy; the one she climbed up the ladder to the top deck in; the one she slipped out of as she slid into the softtub, water still streaming from her short hair. Naked. Unselfconscious. Kidding Sheets about always leaving his bathing suit on. He knew she felt safe with him. After an hour or so, they would hear Joe's footsteps on the dock, hear the shower running, and see Joe appear, balancing three shot glasses. Rarely saying anything. All three savoring the late night peace of the marina, clinking those glasses, toasting their little world. Joe's world, Sheets always thought on those nights; leave your real name and the real world behind when you stepped onto B-Dock.

Joe touched the collar of the robe again, reminding Sheets that she wasn't here. Reminding him that the ugliness and violence of his old life had climbed the wall surrounding Joe's world. Sheets stood and gently took the robe from Joe, and desperately needing to put it out of his sight, went and hung it in the closet in the spare bedroom, then returned to stand by the bedroom door. He couldn't shake the empty feeling. Her bed, her room, her apartment.

He reached and touched Joe's arm. "You okay to talk?"

"I keep telling myself it can't be real." Joe looked vacantly at Sheets as he reached out for the cat, but again, it moved just beyond his reach.

"There's some things about my past I need to tell you about. It's connected to what happened to…on the dock." Sheets swallowed hard, struggling to continue, thinking the next words would end their friendship. "My past caused her death."

"What?" Joe jolted forward in the bed and looked directly at Sheets for the first time, his eyes narrowing. "What are you talking about?"

Sheets moved to the window where a little pot of something that looked like wheatgrass was growing, brushed his hand across the top of it and turned back to Joe. "The ranch in Idaho. It seems impossible, but you stumbled into some people who knew me or knew of me. People who want me dead."

"What? That doesn't make any sense."

"I know. But—"

"And what could Idaho possibly have to do with Bub—?" Joe stopped. "Jesus, Sheets, who would want to kill you? And why?"

Three questions, but how could he explain it? The who was the only easy answer. Start with that. "Ex-Delta guys, maybe current Delta guys."

"The girl on the ranch—Renee— said that Buck's buddies were Delta. The ones that were shooting at me. What do you have to do with Delta?"

"Nothing and everything."

Joe sat up on the edge of the bed, fully alert now, anger in his tone. "That's not an answer, Sheets. Tell me how this has anything to do with the boat, Bubbles. Why are these guys after you?"

For a moment there was silence. Only the distant sound of the surf and the hum from the plant incubator on the porch could be heard.

Sheets returned to the chair, sat down, leaned his head back, closed his eyes and tried to gather his thoughts.

"Why the hell do they want you dead?" Joe repeated. The last ray of the sun had disappeared from the room.

Where to begin? Sheets thought. He'd let his guard down and as a result, she was gone. Grief and anger flared through him. He'd known better, but he'd gotten attached to these people and this life. He said finally, "I stayed here too long."

"What are you talking about?"

"It goes back six years." He fell silent again.

"I don't care how long it's been. My life's been ruined. So just tell me, Sheets."

"It's a long—"

"Tell me."

Sheets gathered his breath. "The Admiral had the brilliant idea of teaming Delta and SEALs. Inter-service cooperation. Trust building."

"Wait, The Admiral? Buck said something about an admiral."

"My father." Why didn't I just finish the job, he thought? He pictured himself at the house in Virginia, leveling the gun at the old man's chest. "As his never questioning son, I was volunteered to go on the first mission with three Delta guys. Extract a supposed Taliban leader from a tiny village south of Kandahar. The Deltas joked with each other all the way in on the helicopter, let me know the SEAL was only along for the ride. Odd man out. We were dropped a few miles out from the village, hiked in, found the target's shack.

"It was the wrong man. No question. We'd been shown pictures of the target. This was a younger man. His wife and kids were there. It was just a one-room mud hut, smoky, no ventilation, filled with cooking smells. Two kids, a little girl, maybe five or six years old, a young boy, a couple years older. The Delta leader, Stan, smiled and looked at his guys and said, 'No witnesses,' His second in command, Donnie, pulled his gun up and shot the man."

Sheets rose from the rocking chair, moved to the window and pulled back the lacy curtains. A few high clouds were still visible in the purple sky. He listened carefully, but heard nothing stirring the air around the house. Get in. Burn the boat, then get out. That's the way he'd have done it. He assumed they were gone for now.

"Just shot the guy? The wrong man? Wait. You were a SEAL? You should have told me this." Joe moved on the bed and her scent rose from it. How much longer would it remain? Sheets wondered.

"Let me get this out. It gets worse." Sheets knotted the curtain in his left hand and spoke to the open window. "Then Donnie turned and shot the wife. The third Delta had some kind of mini digital recorder and was filming the whole thing. The SEAL teams had heard rumors about this, guys who made movies and sold or traded them. Nobody really believed it."

"What about the kids?" Joe seemed to be fading out again. His voice had returned to a monotone, unable to process anything beyond his own grief.

Sheets did not speak for several moments.

"Tell me," Joe finally said in the same flat tone.

"I froze. I had my gun up and ready, and froze. Donnie shot the little boy between the eyes. The closing ceremony of every day of my life since that night has been that red bloom appearing on his forehead." Sheets dropped the curtain, sat down on the end of the bed. "Ten years of service. Ten years of ops and I'd never witnessed a kid being shot. Never. An innocent." His mouth went dry and he remembered why he'd never told anyone the story, remembered the alcohol-fueled days in the year before Joe showed up in his life.

"So, I turned and shot the guy Donnie. Dead. Triple burst to the head. Dead. But it was two seconds too late. I'd trained all my life to react without thinking and I didn't do it. And that kid's dead because—"

"What about the little girl?" Joe was barely whispering now.

"Stan was about to shoot her when I took out his buddy. He turned to me and I kicked him in the head, put him down. The third guy was still recording the scene. I hit him in the head with the butt of my rifle, put him down too, flexcuffed both of them. I took the little girl to one of the other huts. I went back and the two guys were coming to. I took away their weapons, had one cut the other loose and made him pick up the dead one. Marched them back to the evac sight, cuffed them all back together and took off.

Joe was silent in the darkness and Sheets wondered how much of the story he was absorbing, but he finally spoke.

"You should have killed the other two."

"Maybe if I had…." He stopped. If. There were a hundred ifs. "It probably would have made my life easier, but it felt like a plug had been pulled. I didn't want to see anymore killing, wanted just to be done with all of it, Joe. My old life was over. No matter what, I'd killed one of my own and it didn't matter why, I'd be out, most likely hunted down and killed. Delta would not leave what happened unavenged." Sheets paused, but Joe remained silent.

"For thirty years, my whole life, I never had a day when I wasn't told what to do. Breakfast at 0700. Night drop into Kirkuk, Jalalabad, Quetta. Transport Hajis to Gitmo—"

"Hajis?"

Christ, Sheets thought, the words were carrying him right back to that time and place. "SEAL slang for the targets... the bad guys. I usually operated alone. Other than weapons training, I never rotated back to the States. He—The Admiral— never let me rest. I guess he didn't want me to have time to think and then when the shit went down with those guys, I had to.

"At first I had no idea what to do. I felt like the first amphibian that crawled too far from the water. All I could think was 'get back to the ocean,' and I did. I found a trickle of a stream, followed it to a river, followed that one to another, got to the coast in Pakistan. Took a month of walking."

"How'd you get back to the States?"

"I found a freighter headed to Baltimore. All the SEALs had extra passports in case of emergencies, so I just signed on. Told them I was a cook." Sheets involuntarily brought his hand to his nose. Six years later and the smell of potatoes still came to him when he thought of that trip.

Chapter 37

"I still don't get the connection between what happened to you and…and what happened to the Gypsy. Couldn't it have been an accident? Is there any proof?"

"Flip on the light." Sheets pulled the note the dockmaster had given him from his rear pocket, unfolded it and handed it to Joe. He leaned toward the soft glow of the lamp on the night table, scanned the lines, turned the paper over and read the name on the other side.

"Randolph? Shit." He looked at Sheets "That's the name that Idaho asshole said."

"My name, William Allen Randolph." It felt no more natural in his mouth than it had with Queen earlier.

"Wait." Joe looked down at the note. "Friend, ranch?"

Sheets knew the words exactly as written at this point: *Sending your friend to the ranch cost him his life.*

Joe went silent then looked up at Sheets. "They were trying to kill me? They think I'm dead?" The significance of what he'd said appeared to hit him. "She died because of me going to that ranch?" His head collapsed onto the pillow and he whispered, "That fucking money."

Sheets waited and thought that he'd come too soon, that Joe was in the mental state he himself had been in that morning; unable to think beyond the unreality of losing her, but after a moment, Joe raised himself from the pillow.

"Why are you saying it's your fault if they were trying to kill me?" Joe shook the paper. "Where did this come from anyway?"

"It was left at the marina office today." Sheets related the dockmaster's story. "I guess these guys have been in town since before you went to Idaho. They must have thought I sent you out there. It doesn't make much sense, but I think your death was supposed to be a warning… that they were finally coming for me."

"This is insane." Joe moved to the edge of the bed. "My going to that ranch was an accident. I mean, Sheets, what the fu… who does shit like this?"

Sheets took the note from Joe's hand. Looking at the familiar lettering chilled him again. "This is my father's handwriting," he said quietly. And he was suddenly uncomfortable sitting in the light of the room. "Turn out the light, I need to tell you about him."

ψ ψ ψ

"Breaking and entering now? Murder and desertion weren't enough for you? I should call the police."

Sheets was sitting in a dark green leather chair in The Admiral's home office. "Good to see you again too, daddy." Sheets tried to keep his voice calm, but his reaction to seeing his father had been immediate and visceral after what he had learned that day. Thirty years of trust gone with the spin of the dial of a safe "You might want to have a look at this before you start calling anyone." Sheets tossed a disc onto the big wooden desk, where it slid up against a laptop computer, the only item on the otherwise pristine surface. He went back to staring out the bay window to his right, across the expanse of perfectly mown lawn toward the rocks on the far side of the Potomac, as gray as the overcast sky in the late afternoon.

The Admiral sat down in the black desk chair and loaded the disc into the drive. Sheets scanned the room. Sixteen feet wide by twenty-four long. He had a knack for knowing exact dimensions. Boat lengths, distances to objects, square feet, cubic feet. They just appeared in his head. He never knew where the ability came from, but he'd had it all his life. He thought it had made him a better fighter, always knowing exactly where to position himself against any opponent.

The long axis of the room ran almost perfectly north south. North to the river. South to The Admiral's desk, butted up to the wall, photos of him with famous people, political and military above. The long wall opposite Sheets held hundreds of books on built-in shelves over cabinets of dark oak. Books of warfare, military strategy, weapons. The books of his childhood.

The room was silent except for the whirring sound of the disc beginning to spin. The Admiral casually moved his hand to the top drawer on the right side of the desk.

Sheets lifted the SIG Sauer P226 semi-automatic pistol from the hidden side of the chair and fired a round into the drawer near his father's hand. "Looking for this?" The sound reverberated around the small room, the smell of nitroglycerin leaking from the barrel of the gun. He turned away from the scene that had begun to play on the laptop, not needing to replay the death of the Afghan family, still present every night in his mind.

As the screen faded to black, The Admiral spun around to face his son. "This proves nothing. What is it that you were hoping to get from this?"

Sheets gazed at the man he had until recently revered. Still lean and in fighting trim at sixty plus years, only the scattered gray in his high and tight hair showed any age. He looked for something of himself in the older man's face, but found nothing, which pleased him. He'd had an irrational worry all day that he might carry the genes that had let The Admiral do what Sheets had discovered.

"Let's call this my exit interview. I want out. Out of the picture." Sheets fired another round over his father's shoulder into a photograph of his graduation from the Academy, obliterating his own face, leaving only the Admiral with his arm around a headless body. Glass from the frame tinkled onto the wood of the desk. "And we'll need to discuss my severance pay."

The older man smirked. "Did you lose your mind in the desert? You have no leverage here. You killed a fellow serviceman. It will be a miracle if you aren't hanged. Are you going to kill your own father as well? I raised you, made you the best—" The Admiral was interrupted by another roar from the gun. He turned to the bookshelves where a row of books had been set up to face the room. The first book was now lying flat, a thin column of smoke rising from it.

"Ah yes," Sheets, smiled through his rage. "Child rearing The Admiral's way. Let us review. That was *Ashley's Book of Knots*, memorized by the little warrior at age seven." Three more shots rang out and three more books fell. "*Battle of Midway, The Spanish Armada, Jane's Naval Weaponry*, ages eight, nine and ten." Sheets waited until the smoke lifted towards the ceiling before firing another three times, felling the last of the books. "I'm sure you know the names. It was your curriculum."

Sheets pulled two books from beside him in the chair and held them up. Two volumes by Dr. Seuss. "I found these in a locker in my old room upstairs. Obviously not part of my course work." He looked at the cover of one. *On Beyond Zebra!* A stylized cartoon zebra peered quizzically back at its own tail.

"Your mother," said The Admiral, ashen-faced now.

"Yes, tell me about her. Tell me about my mother. What happened to her?" Sheets had very few memories of her, just faintly recalled putting on a suit to attend a funeral when he was still very young.

"She was weak. She had a fondness for mint juleps which became an addiction. I was forced to keep her away from you. She would have spoiled you, made you soft."

"Soft." Sheets raised the two books again and stared at them, trying to recollect any tie to his mother, any softness. He came up blank, thought for a while. "So you removed her only child from her life, substituted bourbon." He paused and shook his head. "You cold fuck. This is for my mother." He raised the gun, pointed it at his father, put tension on the trigger, but hesitated, wondering how he'd never been able to see the manipulative bastard for what he was. The first thoughts and ideas of my own have come in the last month, he thought, and part of his anger turned inward. He should shoot the old man and then himself. Instead, he lowered the pistol and slowed his ragged breath.

The Admiral pointed at Sheets and shouted, "She would have kept you from your destiny. I—I created one of the finest weapons that has ever served this nation."

"Served this nation? Served this nation? You twisted bastard." Sheets dropped the books and turned to the picture window, firing two shots at it. Glass cascaded into the room. In the brick barbecue grill on the patio, sat a pile of melted plastic. Empty disc cases were scattered on the surrounding surfaces. A small plume of black smoke rose from the remains. He thought of the pain and suffering of the families involved with the killing shown on the discs. The video he'd watched to be certain of his father's involvement had sickened him.

"Snuff films? Your idea of serving the nation? What happened to you? At the very least, I always thought you believed in your country and the Navy. What happened to you?" He was shouting now, his heart racing.

"How did you find those?" A hissing sound could be heard as an occasional raindrop fell onto the steaming pile of melted discs.

"You forget, daddy dearest, that I spent some years here. Some of your lessons were drummed into me in this very room. I know all the hiding places."

"They were in a locked safe."

Sheets snorted. "There were 1196 sailors on the USS Indianapolis when it was torpedoed in the Pacific after delivering the atomic bomb dropped on Hiroshima. Only 316 survived the sinking and subsequent shark attacks. Add a one for Robert Shaw's masterful soliloquy in *Jaws* and you have the extent of your creative ability. You've used some variation of those numbers for every alarm or password all your life." He looked up at the old man, whose face had fallen. "Is there enough money in this—" He gestured to the patio—"to make it worth losing the career you spent your life building?"

"Millions." The Admiral looked dejectedly out at the charred remains. "And what would you know about my career? The career those bastards dead-ended."

I know nothing, thought Sheets, surprised to hear that The Admiral had been derailed on what had looked like a non-stop ride to the top at the Pentagon, maybe even the Joint Chiefs of Staff. He'd been kept so busy that there wasn't any down time to focus on what might have been happening in his father's life. But still...the nightmare of the video flashed, and his rage flared.

"So you get a negative review and you turn to this?" He motioned again to the window and sent three more rounds into the rubble.

"You don't understand." The sneer had returned to his father's voice.

Exactly, Sheets thought, he knew nothing about anything but soldiering and running ops. He was totally unprepared for any life beyond the Navy. Christ, he didn't even know how much money he'd need to try and run from all this. He'd never bought a house, a car, an appliance, anything beyond a restaurant meal and a few CDs. For some reason, the word dust kept coming to mind. Every place he'd been flown into for years had been dusty: Yemen, Oman, Kuwait, Afghanistan, Pakistan. Dust from planes, helicopters, Humvees, dogs. If he found an escape from this, he vowed stay near the ocean.

He looked at the old man. "I'd shoot myself if I ever started understanding any of this,."

"So did you destroy all the videos?"

Sheets knew that burning the discs had been symbolic, his acting out his rage and disappointment with his father. There were probably more being made while he had been emptying the safe.

"You pathetic old man. It took me a month to walk out of Afghanistan. I had time to think for the first time in my life and that's all I did—think. About you and that mission. Nothing added up. Me teamed with Delta. And then it finally dawned on me that I was carrying the answer with me. You had to have known what they were doing. The videos. You either wanted it to stop, or you were in on the deal and wanted to eliminate those three guys. So you sent me. You were counting on me to take all of them out once I saw what they were doing. What happened, daddy? Things get too hot for you? Afraid someone was catching on to your scheme?"

"What stopped you from finishing the other two?" The Admiral looked genuinely puzzled, as if the only thing that bothered him was that the weapon he'd created had failed him.

Sheets shook his head in disgust at himself and the man in front of him. How had he lived with this for thirty years and not seen the man for what he was? He started to answer—"Killing isn't that hard when you believe you're fighting for a cause…." He stopped. "I prayed I was wrong…." He motioned out the window to the plastic rubble with the SIG. "Those videos answered my question. Money. A dead soldier for what? A few million?" He struggled for another word to describe his disgust, but could only repeat, "Pathetic."

"It's more complicated than that. Way bigger than you could imagine. Enough to make you rich beyond belief. If you come back in—"

"Stop." Sheets stood and took the slip of paper he'd been holding and looked at the account number he'd written down along with the amount of money he'd intended to demand from The Admiral. But now, the thought of touching anything related to the man repulsed him. Just get out, he thought.

He released the disc from the laptop and pulled out two more from beside the cushion in the chair. "If anyone follows me, these will begin airing on the internet and I'll come back here to finish the job." He fired two more rounds into the chair, one on each side of The Admiral's head, "Remember what you created."

"I'll track you down. The Pentagon idiots put me in the Defense Intelligence Agency. I have access to every bit of intel around the world. You can't hide from me and my people."

"Send them. I'll be waiting." Sheets turned to walk away, then turned back to face his father and flipped the SIG to him. "Did you keep count old man? Fifteen in the magazine and one in the chamber. Basic knowledge in any firefight."

The Admiral turned the pistol and leveled it at Sheets' chest. "Thirteen." He pulled the trigger and the firing pin clicked on an empty chamber.

Sheets held out his left hand containing three cartridges and tossed them through the shards of glass remaining in the window, then picked up the children's books from the chair. He stared at The Admiral for a moment and shook his head. "My loving father." And walked away.

Joe had disappeared from view in the dark room as Sheets told his story and remained silent for several moments afterwards.

"Crap," he finally said. "That was your life?" He gave a low tuneless whistle.

"Until six years ago. Pretty much." Sheets heard a car passing on Hickman Street through the back window.

Joe sat up and his silhouette appeared against the dim light of the window. A pungent smell rose from the bed as he moved to sit on the edge again. Days of travel, fear, loss, despair and anger all seemed rolled into the palpable aroma. "I still can't see how this is your fault. You were just trying to find a life."

"I should have kept moving."

A long silence passed before Joe spoke. "No. This is your home."

Home, Sheets thought, and couldn't ever remember saying the word or having it said to him. He just wished it had come earlier, not at the moment he would be forced to leave at, and not at the cost the word now carried.

"Sheets, what are you...we going to do?"

It felt as if ice were settling around him, narrowing his vision to one objective. "I'm going to find him."

"Your father? And then what?"

"Kill him."

"Okay, but I want the other one.... Buck." Joe's voice was hard. "He's a part of this. He's just as responsible for her death as your father.

Sheets heart sank. Since the moment he'd received the note, he had only thought of what *he* would do. In the old life, he'd worked solo, but Joe was in danger as well.

Joe had apparently misread his silence as a rejection and said bitterly, "Fine. I'll go alone."

Idaho's as good a place to start looking for the old man as any, Sheets thought. "I wouldn't let you do that."

Chapter 38

Nearly fall, Sheets realized as he walked through the shadows behind Joe. This was exactly the type of night when Joe would have organized one of the evening bike rides. Warm air, heavy with humidity. So that moving through it felt like having velvet rubbed softly against your skin. Joe, Bubbles, maybe Buzz, and he would ride through the streets of Rehoboth single file, wheels turning on the pavement the only sound.

They wouldn't stop as they wended their way through the town, but Joe would slow as they passed the few occupied houses, brightly lit tableaux of family life, people sitting down to dinner, watching TV. Not looking voyeuristically, but feeling drawn somehow into each scene. As always in the little town, folks who were outside would recognize Joe and call out to the procession, but the group would only raise their hands in silent greeting and roll on.

The trips always ended at the oddly shaped house in the woods on the corner of Park and Gerar, where, as if pre-determined, the man would be sitting at the grand piano that nearly filled the living

room. They would dismount and sit shoulder to shoulder on the
curb, listening to the tunes through the open sliding doors. Sheets
knew nothing of classical music, but it seemed as if the player was
always able to capture the exact feel of the weather.

On their last ride, the notes had formed into something Sheets
recognized, a melody he had picked out on his guitar. "Bach,"
Bubbles had said and Joe had picked up on it as well and his voice
rose at just the right moment, singing,

'*That her face at first just ghostly*'

And the rest of them chimed in

'*Turned a whiter shade of pale*' stretching the last word as the
piano player began to clap.

ψ ψ ψ

Sheets watched as a streetlight shrank and then lengthened
Joe's shadow as he passed under. Joe could easily be picked from
a crowd with his confident stride, almost a prince of the city
swagger. Now it was gone. He was walking stiffly as if he had
suffered some brain trauma and had to plan each step before he
took it and Sheets' heart fell, wondering if his friend could come
back from his loss.

The SIG he'd held so infrequently for the last couple years felt
heavy and unfamiliar, reminding Sheets how lax he'd become.
He'd suggested to Joe that they head out of town immediately, but
Joe said he wouldn't go until he'd had a chance to say a proper
goodbye to her and dispose of the Gypsy. Sheets was appalled with

himself that he hadn't thought of having some sort of ceremony. Had six years of civilized life deserted him so quickly?

Joe said Jamie had called the apartment and told him that Bubbles' mother and brother were on their way to the restaurant and that he should come over as well. As Joe showered, Sheets did another reconnaissance of the area and saw no one and nothing out of the ordinary. The sight of a gun in Sheets' hand didn't even elicit a comment from Joe and he'd just nodded when Sheets asked him to walk ahead of him to the restaurant. Lost. The word kept repeating in Sheets' head.

Overhead, the fat leaves of a sycamore rustled in the breeze, the sound nearly stopping Sheets in his tracks. Ridiculous, he thought, but lost along with Bubbles, the Gypsy and maybe Joe, would be what they all looked forward to each autumn: Birdie's

Sheets and Joe had been sitting on the Gypsy the first fall after Joe moved into the marina. Joe had said that the only thing he missed about shore life was raking leaves, and he then fell silent, looking as if he was brooding about it.

The following Sunday, Joe had rapped on the hull of Sheets' sloop and tossed him a T-shirt that matched the one Joe was wearing. Under a huge oak tree covered with gold and red leaves on the back of the shirt were the words, "Birdie's Leaf Removal." Joe had just told him to put on the shirt and come on.

When they got to Joe's pickup, he asked if Sheets would mind sitting in the bed. So Sheets had climbed into the truck and sat alongside four brand new bamboo rakes. They stopped to pick up Buzz and the procedure was repeated. The three of them had driven into Rehoboth, pulled up in front of a house with a for-rent sign, piled out, and raked the lawn. Birdie's was born.

Sheets had never raked a leaf in his life. He fell in love with it. The different muscles it worked. The smell of the leaves. The pristine patch of green which slowly appeared as the leaves were removed, even Joe insisting that they ride in the back of the truck like migrant laborers.

Like Tom Sawyer's fence, word got around, and people at the restaurant and elsewhere started asking if they could come rake. After the first three Sundays, Joe added a rotating fourth person to the crew. He started by just picking someone randomly, but it soon developed into an interview process during which Joe insisted on being called Birdie and Sheets and Buzz were given veto rights.

Year by year, Birdie refined the business. Priority was given to the elderly, for people now clamored for their services, but the rules were strict. No yards outside the canal. Only yards with leaves enough to make an impressive pile. Birdie now constantly rolled a toothpick back and forth across his lips and frequently leaned on his rake talking with the homeowners while the others worked. He would curse them in Spanish. *Pendejos! Maricon! Mas rapido!*

The pay was lousy. Birdie would take them to a bar in Dewey, insisting that all the bars in Rehoboth were far too upscale for his crew. He bought them all a can of Milwaukee's Best, possibly the second worst beer in America after Coor's Light. After four or five hours of raking, to Sheets it always tasted like vintage Champagne. Everyone would put their hands on the bar when the first round was finished and they would vote on the best blister, which earned the winner an additional can of beer on Birdie.

The crisis came in the fall after Joe and Bubbles' first summer together. She casually asked if she would now be included in Birdie's. Sheets knew that Joe wanted her in, hated doing anything without her. As much as he liked her, Sheets worried that she might change the Birdie dynamic and insisted on the standard interview process.

Birdie recused himself and Buzz, normally the funniest and most caustic interviewer, became completely incapable of speech in her presence. Sheets had been left to ask all the questions. When Sheets told her that she lacked the experience needed to work at Birdie's, she smiled sweetly and pulled a package from under the table.

She pulled out four faded bandannas, stood and made her way around the table, tying one on each of the three of them, then covering her spiky hair as well. Sheets watched as everyone began to smile as they checked out the new look and Joe started to laugh so hard his toothpick flew across the table. Birdie's had a fourth permanent worker.

Bubbles brought along a new tool on her first Sunday, a wooden handle with a metal spike. It quickly became known as the bitching stick and Birdie would assign the person who complained the loudest to police the stray leaves that fell after they finished a section of lawn. And bitch they did, about the pay and working conditions and Birdie. Bubbles was on the stick more than the others, for she would curse Birdie fluently in several languages and pretend to stab him with the stick when his back was turned.

Birdie refused to rake wet leaves, so Sheets found himself obsessively checking the weather throughout the week. Six weeks, maybe seven, and leaf season would be over. They all hated missing even one day and would gather at the Lighthouse Bar, drinking and cursing the weather Gods on rainy fall Sundays.

As Sheets and Joe passed through another pool of light, they walked through a small pile of dry leaves which had accumulated in the gutter. The crunching sound of the leaves as they turned to dust under their shoes seemed only a mocking reminder that those carefree days were over.

Chapter 39

Sheets reached for the door of the restaurant. Locked. A handwritten sign was taped to one of the six glass panes set in the top half of the door.

Closed Indefinitely   Death in the Family

Uneven lettering with a downward scrawl. It looked as depressed as he felt. He glanced down at the gun in his hand. Twenty-four hours ago, he'd stood at this same door. Twenty-four hours and now she was gone and he was holding a weapon.

Joe was at the Emerald's reception podium. Sheets had watched for several minutes after Joe entered and seen no one except a couple who walked to the door of the restaurant and left after reading the sign. It reinforced his idea that The Admiral's people had pulled back. He jammed the semi-automatic into his waistband, out of sight.

Now Joe released the deadbolt and let him in. The lights in the reception area and bar were off, the hanging glasses in the barroom reflecting the streetlight onto the top of the bar. About seven thirty, and on any other September evening, Joe would be entertaining a few regulars at the bar, Jamie would have greeted him at the door, and music would have filled the space. Tonight the only sound was a hushed conversation from the dining room, dimmed paper lanterns above the sushi cases providing the only light. A door to the right of the table had another paper sign taped to it. Sheets knew the door opened onto the patio seating area with the pond and low wooden bridge. He found himself slipping into operational mode. Had they locked the front door? He tried to remember the sound of the lock snicking into place. How many points of ingress? Side door. Kitchen door. No roof access from the interior that he knew of.

Jamie stood and hurried to Joe, hugging him and starting to cry. Sheets glanced at them, then moved to the side door to check the lock. The patio was empty. Nothing but vacant tables and chairs sitting in the darkness, surrounded by a high bamboo fence that would prevent anyone outside it from seeing into the restaurant.

Sheets made his way to the table and knelt between Egg and Buzz, putting his arms around both. Eggs' eyes filled with tears as she turned into his chest and buried her face in his shirt. Buzz had the same lost expression as Joe. Sheets felt himself falling into their grief, but steeled himself against it and after a moment, stood and grabbed a chair, placing it so he had a direct line of sight to the side door. Joe and Jamie moved to the table and he watched as everyone exchanged looks, nobody knowing where to start. Finally, Jamie spoke: "Joe, Sheets, have you eaten? The whole staff was here earlier." Her voice caught. "There's plenty of food left."

"Yeah," said Joe. " I could eat. It's been a couple days."

Sheets nodded his agreement and as Jamie started to walk to the kitchen, he said, "I'll help," and followed her. She opened a refrigerator and Sheets moved to the outside door and checked the lock as she lifted out a platter of sushi. He moved to her side, and feeling a bit more confident that the restaurant was secure, took the food from her and carried it to the table. He and Joe dug in, and the group was silent again until Egg spoke.

"Joe, did the cops find you?"

Don't say anything, Joe, Sheets thought. Cops were a complication he didn't need or want, but Joe just looked at her as if he didn't understand the question.

Jamie started to rise at the sound of a knock on the front door, but sat back down and said, "I can't do it. I can't talk to anyone else." Joe put his arm around her as she started to break up again.

Moments later, a figure darkened the patio door and a face peered in. Sheets leaped up, pulled out the semi-automatic and stepped between the door and the table, shielding the others from view. He clearly saw a face as he moved toward the door, and felt his breath catch. It was Bubbles. A second later, the pulse of hope died. It was Bubbles' mother, he realized, and exhaled sharply. Joe had told him how uncanny the resemblance was.

 He stepped to the door and let her in. Her face looked haggard, red swollen eyes, hair covered with a black scarf, no make-up. Joe stood and put his arm around her shoulder and she turned into his arms, sobbing.

Sheets looked at the expressions on everyone's faces, realized he was still holding the black SIG and quickly tucked it back under his shirt. The group glanced between him and Bubbles' mother with wide-eyed stares, shocked into silence either by her resemblance to Bubbles or seeing him draw the weapon, or both.

Joe broke the awkward spell by saying, "This is Bubbles' mom,

Marie." He pointed to the people one by one. "You know Jamie. That's Egg, Buzz and… uh… your welcoming committee, Sheets."

Marie stared at him for a few moments. "She told me a lot about you," she said quietly, and Sheets felt oddly grateful to her or maybe to Bubbles, or maybe both. Before he could say anything, Joe steered her to an empty chair, then turned back to Sheets, who remained frozen in place between the table and the door.

"I guess you…we… have some explaining to do." Joe took a seat by Marie and the crew continued to stare at Sheets.

He quickly thought through his actions and could think of no way to explain them that didn't include the truth. But he returned their bewildered looks, unable to start.

"You brought a gun into my restaurant?" Jamie's sounded as if she were about to go on a tirade and Joe put his hand on her arm to calm her.

"There's a reason." Joe exchanged a glance with Sheets, then continued. "Her death wasn't an accident." His voice was barely audible.

Five sets of eyes turned to him and everyone seemed to speak at once.

"What do you—?"

"How do you know?"

"Not an accident?"

The anger in Joe's voice rose. "We know who did this."

"You need to go to the po—" Jamie started to say.

"No cops." Joe chopped off her words, picked up his chopsticks and stabbed them into the remnants of food on the platter. "I want this guy."

Sheets saw the shocked expressions on all their faces. Shocked not only by what they were hearing, but also from the change in

Joe. Sheets had always thought that Joe's face was reflected in his name. Unmemorable. Just an everyday Joe except for the expressive blue eyes, but now, the hurt and anger seemed to have carved new lines along his jaw, hardening his appearance. There was silence at the table for several moments. Joe appeared drained from his outburst. He stared in the direction of the door with the glazed look from earlier.

"The Coast Guard and State Police have already written it off as a boating accident," Sheets said quietly. "The fire was similar to one that killed two people in the marina a few years ago." He stopped and waited to see if Joe wanted to continue. He felt as if he'd already spoken more today than in all of the last six years combined. But Joe was still staring blankly across the table, so he added. "The people who caused this aren't here, didn't do it directly. The cops won't be able to connect them to what happened." Plus it's two different jurisdictions, he thought, though he didn't want to confuse them anymore.

"Assholes're gone. Probably in Idaho already," Joe spoke with venom.

The old Joe was all center, rarely high or low, Sheets thought. This new Joe had only the flat vacant state and the barely controlled anger. Nothing in between. It was almost unbearably sad to watch.

"Idaho? The wacko from the mountain?" said Egg.

"What wacko?" said Marie.

"He's part of it," Joe said, answering Egg's question, before turning to Marie and giving her a terse version of what had happened on the mountain outside Bonners Ferry.

"I'm confused now too." Buzz looked at Joe, then at Sheets. "What did any of this have to do with Bubbles?"

"There's more to the story." Sheets paused. How to explain something that he didn't fully understand yet himself? He turned to Buzz. "It was Joe they were trying to kill. Bub—" He swallowed hard. "She was in the wrong place at the wrong time."

"And this Idaho guy just, what, comes all the way to Dewey Beach and burns Joe's boat?" Egg's eyes were flashing. "How would he even know to come here, of all places? And why?"

"It's difficult to…." Sheets struggled to find a way to open this conversation. "Joe ran into some people out there from my past— ex-army guys— they'd been looking—"

"Ex-army?" Jamie slammed her hands on the table "I've heard enough." She looked at Joe. "And you two are seriously planning to go to Idaho to confront this psychopath who tried to kill you? That's bullshit. This is a matter for the police." She stood and said, "I'm putting an end to this before anyone else gets hurt," then turned to walk to the front of the dining room.

Joe jumped up and intercepted her before she reached the telephone on the reception stand. Sheets watched as he took both of her hands in his and spoke in a voice loud enough to be heard at the table. "James, please. I need this. I'm going one way or the other."

"Call the police, Joe, or I will."

She moved to go around him, but he drew her into his arms.

"Jamie, it's for Bubbles."

"No." She pushed him away, walked back towards the table and pointed at Sheets, fixing him with a glare. "You. You come to my restaurant, sit at my bar, rarely say a word, nobody knows a thing about you, including your name. I always knew you were trouble. And now you…with your gun…you want to take Joe across the country and get him killed too. Who the hell do you think you are?" Her voice cracked. "You got her killed. I don't know you. I don't trust—"

"Trust? Are you blind?" Joe grabbed her arm and pulled her back to her chair. "He's been like my brother for the last five years. No," he paused and looked Jamie in the eye, "No. He's *been* my brother from the moment I met him. I trust him with my life."

"But—"

"But nothing. It comes down to who you would kill for. If someone came and burned down your house and your daughter died, what would you do if you knew who set the fire? If you knew that the person responsible was beyond the reach of the authorities? You'd hope like hell you knew someone you trusted explicitly, someone that had the ability to track the motherfuckers down and kill them."

This wasn't Joe, Sheets thought, and glanced at the others, who looked as taken aback as he felt. He read the expressions in their eyes as confusion, maybe even fear. Joe never cursed.

No one said a word.

From the kitchen, came the loud clatter of a fresh rack of ice falling into its bin. Marie jumped and Buzz jerked his head towards the sound. One of the parakeets in the cage by the bar window chirped as if in response.

Joe let go of Jamie's arm and looking around the table, started to speak. "Bub—" He stopped, jaw clenched, eyes glassy. "I can't say it," he mumbled. He looked down. "She was the most important person in the lives of at least three of the people at this table. Think of what she meant to you, James." His voice caught and he stopped again. "Ah shit. I feel like half of me is gone..." He stopped.

Jamie started to get up from her seat, but Joe shook his head. "Let me finish," he said, and she sat. Everybody waited and after a moment, Joe said, "I need to tell them, Sheets."

"Joe," Sheets said. "I don't think—"

"I want her...they...." He glanced around the table. "They should know why you've kept quiet all these years."

Sheets just nodded, feeling numb inside, barely able to listen as Joe began to pace around the table, relating the story of Sheets' Afghan experience. For someone who hadn't slept much for three days and was devastated with grief, Sheets thought, Joe recounted the story nearly word for word. He tried to feel something, but hearing his experience—his worst experience—retold in Joe's anguished voice, only rekindled the hatred he felt for his father.

When he finished, Joe put his hands on Jamie's shoulders, paused briefly, then softly said, "He was just looking for a family, a place to be, like all of us." He stopped again. "I'm going to that ranch. One way or the other. Call the cops if you want, but they'll get nothing from me."

Sheets watched as Joe moved through the dining room to the bar, grabbed a bottle and sat in the darkness. Silence reigned at the table, but when Sheets looked back to the others, all eyes were on him, except Jamie's, who stared fixedly at the tablecloth she had bunched in her hand.

"I'm sorry." Jamie's eyes flicked up to his, then quickly returned to the table. "I had no idea. I'm just such a mess over her." She looked up again and this time she held his gaze. "But, she's gone and he's.... I couldn't stand it if...." She shook her head. "Look, please don't let him go with you."

How to explain the danger? Sheets thought. "He can't stay here, Jamie. They think he's working with me. But I'll try to get him somewhere safe until I...finish this."

Egg continued to stare at him. "Navy SEAL. All the swimming, sailing...the way you handled that drunk at my bar last summer." She shook her head. "How did we not put that all together?"

"Why would you?" Sheets said quietly. And then. "I'm glad you didn't. I wish you'd never had to find out."

"She knew," said Marie, crying. "She told me she just looked at you and knew."

Sheets could only nod, remembering that night.

Buzz had been silent for a long while. Now, he spoke in a strained voice. "You never answered Egg's question. How did they know to come to Dewey?"

"They've been here watching for at least a couple weeks."

"*What?*"

"A couple of weeks?"

"But Joe hadn't even left for Idaho yet!" Egg said.

Exactly, Sheets thought, so why? What had prompted The Admiral now, after six years? Did his father think his skills would have diminished, that he would be an easy target? And maybe he was. Look what had happened. "My father, The Admiral, is behind all this. I guess he couldn't leave the insult of my leaving unanswered, couldn't leave it—me— alone." He shrugged. "I guess they've been here waiting for an opportunity to get rid of me."

"Are you sure about this?" Buzz asked.

"I wasn't, but I am now." Sheets pulled the note from his pocket and handed it to Egg, who read it and passed it to Buzz. "It's my father's handwriting," Sheets explained. "Delivered to the marina office this morning by a military looking guy in a black SUV that the dockmaster said he's seen around town for a couple weeks. They obviously think they killed Joe. That's all I know so far."

"They've been watching the dock? Watching you and Joe?" Egg paused. "Jesus—all of us?"

"I don't know." Sheets shook his head. "Maybe."

Buzz stood and shook the paper at Sheets. "Burning boats. Killing innocent people." He was shaking. "Leaving this to brag about it. I want him, them, all of them, anyone who would do such a thing." He tossed the note as he spoke. "I'm going with you."

"No. This is for me to—"

"Me too. I'm in. She was the sister I never had. They need to be stopped." Egg stood and picked up the little man's hand. "We're going with you."

Christ, Sheets thought, this was out of control. "You have no idea," he said. "These guys are Special Forces veterans, they're trained killers with no conscience. People who wind up on a fortified ranch in Idaho are men who glory in killing." But as he looked at their faces, he could see them hardening into the idea.

"Could it even be done?" said Marie.

ψ ψ ψ

A bottle of Mezcal sat on the bar next to Joe's shot glass. Sheets poured it full and downed it, feeling smoky fingers spread from his throat to his stomach. The B-Dock crew was talking about the funeral plans in the dining room with Joe now. Sheets couldn't bear to even think about it. He refilled the glass, sat down and rotated it on its base, a photo of the Gypsy staring back at him from behind the bar.

Only one thing was certain, he thought, as he looked through the dim dining room at the five people at the table: he could not put them at risk. He decided that he would grab Joe the day after the service, jump in the pickup and go, just the two of them. Head to Idaho. Let Joe's need for revenge cool on the road, and then Sheets would go find The Admiral and settle things once and for all. Just get through tonight and tomorrow, he told himself, let their anger ease, let them come to their senses about getting into this.

ψ ψ ψ

"Is Three coming?" Joe was asking Marie, when Sheets sat down.

"He flew in from Europe today. I told him to meet me here."

Sheets had met Three, or Peter the Third, Bubbles' brother. He'd come to the marina with her once. Flamboyantly gay and hilarious, he'd been a huge hit with the B-Dock crew.

"And Peter?" said Joe.

"He's decided that you're to blame. He's probably meeting with his lawyers right now to figure out how to take away your money."

Joe shook his head and muttered, "So he won't be coming?"

"No," said Marie. She shook her head. "But it doesn't matter, I'm done with the man one way or the other. I've felt more love for my daughter in this room in a half hour than I've felt in thirty years with him."

For a moment, they were silent. Jamie gave Marie's hand a squeeze, her eyes welling with tears again and for the second time in his life, the first being this morning, Sheets wished he could cry.

The table was buzzing with plans for the service when Jamie spoke directly to Sheets. "If they came for Joe and didn't get him or you?" Her voice trembled. "Is he... Are we all in danger?"

Sheets hesitated, thinking again of the black SUV. "I think they're gone for now. They think they killed Joe. And this is only about Joe and me."

"Are you sure?" said Jamie.

"Not one hundred percent, but I checked and there wasn't anyone around the marina, her apartment or the restaurant. Still, if you can stay away from here until Joe and I...and...." He paused. "Once we leave town, you should be fine." Even as he said it though, dark feelings continued to roll through his head.

Chapter 40

It would have been a perfect day to end the summer, Sheets thought, already warm, with just a light chop on the water, but the whirring of the waterproof drill Joe was using on the hull of the Gypsy ruined that illusion. He was leaning out over the side of Sheets' inflatable Zodiac with his hands submerged. Sheets had towed the stricken boat out through the inlet into the ocean, beyond the sight of land. The rest of the crew stood on the deck of Sheets' sloop watching solemnly as Joe worked.

They had left in darkness, Joe wanting to scatter her ashes at dawn. Now the rising sun slipped through a slot in the clouds, blood orange, and seemed to ride each small wave toward the black-clad crew. They had passed the box with Bubbles' ashes down the line, each in turn saying a few words, Buzz, Egg, Sheets, Marie, Jamie, Three and finally Joe, who took the box and went to sit alone on the stern of the boat. After a few moments, he nodded at Sheets and they climbed into the Zodiac.

Sheets held Joe's belt with one hand, partly to keep him from falling out of the inflatable boat and partly because he felt Joe would be just as happy to follow Bubbles and the Gypsy down into the depths. And truth be told, he thought, if it wasn't for Joe, he might prefer to accompany her as well, unable to even begin to guess what a huge piece of himself had died with her. Now, as the trawler began to take on water, it listed to the port side Joe was drilling and Sheets maneuvered them around to the starboard hull. Three more holes and the Gypsy became level with the waterline.

The music from the speakers on the sailboat could be heard clearly across the water. *Late for the Sky,* Jackson Browne's most dirge-like album. The songs Sheets used to hear lines from in Joe's strong voice on Thursday nights when Bubbles was out dancing and he sat waiting for her in the hot tub. Joe had looped it on his IPod and now the sad tunes played over and over.

Joe reached over and opened the box over the deck of his stricken boat. Sheets could see his hands shaking as he mouthed the words to *Before the Deluge,* his voice trembling as he sang the lines;

'When the light that's lost within us
        Reaches the sky'

And then he released the box, heavy enough to sink in the rising water. Sheets detached the line from the cleat on the bow and within seconds, the Gypsy slipped from view, leaving only the sun's now bright reflection. Sheets felt as if his heart was descending with her,

When they re-boarded the sailboat, Joe again went and sat alone on the stern, staring out across the ocean. After a few moments, Marie joined him and took both of his hands in hers.

They seemed to speak for a while and then she led him back to the group sitting under the canopy in the cockpit. Sheets watched as the sun finished its transition from red to yellow and lit the faces surrounding him. He glanced at Buzz. The compact little man was wearing a three day beard which made him appear several years older. None of the men in the group had apparently thought or cared to shave since Bubbles' death.

Sheets handed Three a pair of binoculars and, as prearranged, he moved to the bow to watch for any approaching vessels. The crew still was discussing the plan to go to Idaho, a plan that Sheets had already discarded in his mind. He was just going along, because it seemed that the idea of revenge gave them an outlet for their grief and anger. Mostly he wanted to relax and enjoy the last couple hours of being in the sun and on the water, free from surveillance, safely away from any of The Admiral's eyes or ears. He knew it might be a long time before he had a chance to be on the water, a long time—if ever—before he had anything at all of the life he'd led for the last six years. He looked behind to the spot on the ocean where the Gypsy had sunk, the box of ashes with it.

Ashes, he thought.

Dust. He remembered his vow to never again travel to a dusty landscape and wondered idly if the hills of Idaho would be dusty. It was so far from the coast. He glanced at Joe's face, lined with pain, and thought of his father smirking while he wrote the note, feeling safe, sheltered from reprisal. Fuck you, he thought, there's no safe for you now.

Three was calling from the bow: "Company coming."

Chapter 41

"Let's all get below. Quickly." Sheets moved from the cover of the cockpit as the crew began moving down the stairs, looks of fear playing across their eyes. "Sorry," he said. "I'd just like to be careful." But already as he watched the boat approach, he sensed that this was more than a precaution. They were five miles offshore on a weekday in late September and they'd only seen a couple of boats the whole way out. This one was flying straight at them. Flying. His old battle alarms were being set off.

"Who do you think it is?" Egg elbowed him in the ribs as she waited her turn to climb down.

"Probably no one. Some guys out fishing." I hope, he thought, as the boat closed. It was an old Viking sport fisher with a tall flying bridge. He squinted: 1984 or 85. Forty-eight footer. Classic swept-back profile. Clean. The morning sun glinted against the white fiberglass and black tinted windows and a broad vee of churned white wake trailed far behind. One guy sat at the upper helm and two more stood on the back deck. Something wasn't right, Sheets thought. Had he been wrong about the Deltas pulling back? Had they followed the funeral procession out this morning? Put together a plan that quickly?

"No poles," said Joe. He had remained in his seat at the wheel and flipped his sunglasses down while staring at the approaching boat. "They're not out here to fish." His voice held none of the fear it should have, Sheets thought. It was as flat and dead as it had been for two days.

"Stay low and don't let them see your face. I'll be right back." Sheets took the stairs in two steps, unlocked the rear stateroom, his armory, and picked a sniper rifle from its rack.

Marie's eyes widened, staring at the guns, knife racks, drawers holding boxes of ammunition and shelves of gear. "Holy—"

Joe yelled, "They're not slowing down."

Sheets re-racked the gun, exhaling slowly. He was far too tense, the dark cloud hanging at the edge of his consciousness, causing him to overreact. Would The Admiral indiscriminately kill innocent civilians to get Sheets? But it was a stupid question. He knew the answer: An Afghani family was dead and they were certainly not the only ones. The man wouldn't hesitate for a moment.

Joe leaned down from the top of the stairway. "They're turning around."

Start the engine. Zigzag towards shore."

Sheets' mind flashed to *The Book of Five Rings.* The classic Musashi strategy of attacking with the sun at your back. Christ, he thought, how wrong could I have been? He felt sick. He had no plan and a boatload of untrained civilians to protect. A memory of The Admiral slapping him when he was eight years old stopped him. "Don't think. React," his father had screamed.

The crew stared at him as he began to gear up. He turned to the weapons locker and strapped a black knife to his right calf. He was about to order everyone into the armored stateroom when a thought came to him. "Can anybody shoot?"

Egg raised her hand. "Clay pigeons." Her voice tightened, "But it was…it was a country club." Her normally tanned face seemed to grow a few shades lighter.

Sheets pulled the sniper rifle down, flicked off the safety and gently handed it to her. "I just need you to keep them occupied. Off balance." He thought he detected a certain steeliness settle into her dark eyes. "It's ready, he added, "Just point and shoot." She nodded as he felt the rumble of the engine kicking in. "Distance?" he called up to Joe.

"Less than a mile."

"Stay low," he shouted, then turned back to Egg. "Crawl up and take cover behind the cabin roof," he told her. "Aim for the flybridge. Rise up. Shoot. Count to a different number each time, then shoot again. Keep the man at the helm on guard. Go." "Wordlessly, Egg slipped her arm through the strap of the rifle and moved up the stairs, pausing just once at the top, before disappearing from view.

Sheets looked at Buzz, pulled an AK-47 and an extra magazine from the locker and flicked the safety off. "Simplest gun in the world. Quick trigger pull for a single shot, hold for multiple rounds. Stay beside Egg. Alternate. After she shoots, you aim for the bow. Short bursts. Start low, the recoil will pull you up." He looked Buzz in the eye, saw only determination, and before he could say anything else, the little man stuffed the magazine in his waistband, grabbed the AK, and shot up the stairs with no hesitation. A picture of a desert fighter flashed through Sheets' mind.

Jamie had started to wail. Sheets nodded to Marie and Three, who seemed oddly calm, and told them to take her to the forward cabin. The hull was reinforced. "You'll be fine," he said, touching Jamie's arm. But she didn't respond, her panicked wail continuing.

He reached into the locker again and grabbed a machine pistol, then called up to Joe again. "Distance."

"Less than half mile. Closing fast."

If this was an attack, they were well within range of their guns, thought Sheets, and a thud against the hull confirmed it. He heard the distinctive report of the sniper rifle and a burst from the AK shortly after. Like a band starting up the soundtrack of his childhood.

So much for planning, he thought.

Chapter 42

Sheets crouched low as he came above board and moved beside Joe. He pushed him lower into the cockpit as a round from the Viking pinged off the mast. He started to tell him to keep the crew safe, but realized there was no safe and instead just looked into his best friends eyes. Cold and focused. Good. He tapped Joe on the shoulder and crept to the stern, hesitating, hating to leave the crew alone, but he knew he had to. Go with your instinct, react, he told himself. He untied the painter from its cleat and leaped into the Zodiac.

With two crab steps he was at the helm and the forty horsepower Yamaha engine roared to life. The inflatable quickly came on plane and he headed due south. The ocean remained calm, gentle swells, no whitecaps. Two targets for them to worry about now, he thought. Divert attention from the sailboat and they might survive. Might. Any doubts about returning to the old life disappeared. He felt a surge of elation as the onrushing air cooled him. Sea battles. His heritage.

As he flew south, Sheets was unable to see what was happening, but he could hear the exchange of gunfire and could tell that his two rifles were still in the fight. He arced a turn to the east, wanting to approach the big fishing boat from the rear port side. As he completed his turn, the two boats came into view and he assessed the situation.

Egg and Buzz were still popping up like armed and dangerous whack-a-moles. Two of her shots were nearly dead on, smacking into the base of the flybridge. The bursts from the automatic were keeping their riflemen below the gunwales. Way more than he could have expected. He felt a burst of pride, followed by a feeling of hope. Advantage B-Dock, Sheets thought.

Sheets could not even see Joe in the cockpit as the Morgan continued to weave towards the distant coastline. The guy at the helm of the fishing boat had slowed, probably thinking this was not turning out to be the walk in the park he had expected. A quick scan showed no other vessels approaching, just flat green water in every direction and empty blue skies above.

Just then, two more men appeared on the rear deck with what looked from a distance to be M-16s. These guys had access to U.S. military weapons, confirming his opinion that they were Delta. They immediately opened fire in his direction and he changed course to make his approach more directly from the rear. Keep the bright morning sun in their eyes, a taste of their own medicine.

The breeze was freshening, kicking up a little chop. He crouched lower behind the armored helm of the Zodiac. He steered with his left hand while he raised the machine pistol with his right, his mind racing: Viking sport fisher. Mid-eighties models usually had two side-mounted diesel fuel tanks. 300 gallons each. Diesel. Non-explosive, meaning less chance for fire, which was why it was used in military vessels. Less chance, he thought. But still. He hoped that they had thought to top the tanks off before their excursion.

Only a couple of hundred yards out now, he had taken only one or two hits from the men on the stern. One had crazed the Plexiglas window on the helm and the other had popped one of the multiple air chambers, which whistled as the air escaped. The two men were learning the difficulties of firing at a moving boat from a platform which was bobbing in the rhythmic swells.

At fifty yards, Sheets turned due west, parallel with the Viking, and popped a burst towards the rear deck. The two guys threw themselves down as the glass in the cabin doors behind them shattered. Sheets trained his pistol at the waterline below the silver fuel filler cap on the port side and raked the area for several seconds. Fuel began to pour through the holes made by the bullets. He flipped open a waterproof compartment below the helm, pulled out a flare gun and rammed home a cartridge.

A flare burning at 3000 degrees Fahrenheit. That should solve the problem of igniting the diesel fuel. Sheets steadied his arm on the starboard air tube, aimed the flare just below the waterline and pulled the trigger, ducking as he did. There was a ten second delay and then he was rewarded with a muffled thump as the diesel tank exploded below the water's surface.

He tucked himself tighter against the bottom of the Zodiac and waited as flying debris passed over his head, sizzling like sparklers. A couple of hot embers landed on his pants and he brushed them off. The chemical smell reminded him of the burned-out Gypsy. He pushed the thought away and poked his head above the side of the inflatable. Not the explosion he had hoped would destroy the Viking. There was a small hole above the waterline, but most of the damage had been directed toward the center. The rear deck had heaved upward and the two men were nowhere in sight. The fuel lines must have ruptured because the Viking had slowed and was now veering directly into the path of the Zodiac. At least it could no longer pursue the sailboat, he thought, realizing at the same time that he would be alone on the water.

With no time to get to the helm and turn his boat before impact, Sheets rolled over the side and pulled for deeper water. He heard the high pitched whine of the Yamaha engine as it passed over him and felt more than heard the ensuing thud as the two boats collided.

Collecting himself, he reached down and pulled off his boots, tapped his leg to see if his knife was still there, and clicked his watch into backlit dive mode. Sheets then pulled slowly to the surface, breaking the plane only until his eyes and nose were above the water. The fuel which had poured onto the surface of the water was burning and the smell of melted fiberglass hung in the air. The Viking blocked his view to the east. No way to tell if the Morgan had escaped, but there was no gunfire. No way to check if they were safe. Put it away, he told himself. React. Five men left.

The two men from the rear of the boat were paddling towards a dinghy which had been lowered from the foredeck of the Viking. Sheets couldn't see any of the others. He stroked toward the two in the water and slipped under when he was about ten feet away.

Late September and the surface water was still quite warm. As he swam under the first guy, he grabbed the man's boot and tugged him down, wrapping the guy's foot in a leg lock, as he pulled hard for the bottom.

Six to eight minutes. Even exerting himself, he could be under for that long. He figured the man he was pulling down was good for maybe one or two minutes at the most, flailing as he was.

There is nothing more frightening, even for seasoned fighters, than to be tugged underwater. There was no natural response. Well, except for himself. Maybe he should thank that old bastard, for holding him under the surface of the Ashley River when he was five. For waterboarding him when he was eleven.

Thirty seconds. The pressure in his ears changed as he passed through a colder thermal layer. He checked his watch— Thirty feet—and released the boot, pulling the man's foot above his head to disorient him. He then stroked for the surface.

The second man was now clinging to the side of the dinghy, either injured or too tired to pull himself over the side. Sheets surfaced silently behind the opposite canvas tube of the little boat and gathered his breath for another dive. He slipped beneath the man and yanked him as hard as possible to break his grip, locking the man's foot as he had done with the first, but as he pulled the man down there was no thrashing this time. He swallowed hard. Trouble. And before he could make a move, he felt a hand groping along the edge of his right calf. Felt his dive knife sliding from its sheath and though he twisted and grabbed for the knife it was too late. He felt a sharp pain as the knife penetrated the flesh above his knee. Felt it sink deeper yet.

Chapter 43

He raised his arms to propel himself downward to escape the knife and felt the pain magnify as the blade withdrew. After two strokes, he allowed himself a moment to settle into the pain. It focused his mind. He then shrank the pain and pushed it away. He moved his wounded left leg. Full range of motion, he thought, probably no great muscle damage. He glanced above and saw a shadow moving through the murky water. He guessed the man was thrusting blindly with the knife, hoping he had seriously wounded Sheets, hoping to finish the job.

What had he missed? He rewound his thoughts to the two men on the rear deck. He had assumed they were Delta, the man on the left stocky, muscled— typical Delta profile. He guessed that was the first one he'd dragged down. Little or no water training. He flashed to the second man. About the same height as the other, but leaner. He pictured him diving away from Sheets' fusillade and saw agility and economy of movement. And no panic in the water. A SEAL?

He didn't want it to be true. The one belief he'd held onto for six years was that SEALS were better, wouldn't participate in The Admiral's venal schemes. He thought they might still be his type of people. But, he knew he was about to test himself against a man with the same training and experience as himself. SEAL on SEAL. So be it.

The next move would determine whether he lived or died and likely settle the fate of his friends as well. He knew he was invisible to the man above, his only advantage. They were being inexorably drawn up at the same rate by the oxygen in their bodies. He risked a glance at his watch. Eleven feet to the surface. He couldn't let his opponent get there, get fresh air.

Underwater fighting was not a battle of punches and counterblows, the density of the water slowed momentum, preventing real damage. The survivor would be the one who could gain and maintain control, ultimately a test of strength, lung power and will. He pictured the moves he needed to make to pin the man's arms and prevent any further damage from the knife.

He stroked and pulled up under the shadow until he could make out a pair of boots in the gloom. He aligned himself below and to the rear of the boots. One shot, he thought and hoped the guy was right handed. He reached and tugged on the left boot and simultaneously propelled himself up behind the man. He saw the blade arcing down towards the boot he had pulled. Sheets crisscrossed his arms across the man's body and captured his wrists pinioning the knife to his abdomen and pulling with all the strength he had left.

The man's hands were now behind his back as if he were in a straitjacket, but he had incredible strength and was able to pull Sheets' hands forward, lunging back at the same time, trying to catch Sheets with a head butt. Sheets leaned back and got a knee in the guy's back for leverage and hauled back again. The effort left him in desperate need of a breath. And still the man thrashed, nearly pulling Sheets' hands free from his wrists. He had control, but the man's superior strength was turning the tide.

The knife glanced against his left leg several times with no effect. The man was only able to twist his hand slightly with Sheets gripping his wrist. Sheets felt the muscles in the guy's back bunching for another thrust forward in an attempt to break Sheets' hold. Sheets relaxed his grip slightly and when the guy started his thrust, yanked back with everything he had left. The right arm went limp in his grasp. Dislocated shoulder, Sheets thought, but did not loosen his hold. A stream of bubbles poured from the man's mouth.

And finally, as the two broke the surface, the arms went slack. Sheets, exhausted, sucked in air and pulled the man under again, taking no chances. They bobbed up behind the dinghy and Sheets checked the man's hand, but the knife had been released during the struggle. He pushed the body beneath the inflatable, aware that he had no weapon, was bleeding and in need of rest, but with no time. He had to try to finish this quickly. He took two deep breaths and then submerged. His chest ached and his throat felt as if it were on fire. Beyond the shadow of the dinghy, he could make out the dark outline of the fishing boat and pulled hard towards it.

The Viking had taken on enough water that, as Sheets broke the surface beneath the bow, he could reach the deck despite the upswept curvature of the hull. Silence except for the waves lapping against the hull. No shots. No sizzle of burning fiberglass. He had expected more damage, another explosion. The second diesel tank must have survived.

As he reached for the bow, a boat horn sounded. He turned to see the Morgan slowly approaching and he was flooded with relief, then fear. What the fuck were they thinking? Buzz was prone on the front deck and pointing to the left with two fingers held out. Sheets made a gun with one hand and looked back at Buzz, who again stuck out two fingers. Two gunmen left on the starboard side. Sheets then pointed at the flying bridge and Buzz gave him the universal "don't know" shoulder shrug. Sheets held up a hand to let them know they should keep their distance.

With that, Sheets swam to the damaged port side of the boat. The heavy tinting of the cabin windows would make him invisible to the men on the other side. He was counting on this and the fact that they would have no way to shoot with long rifles or handguns from the narrow companionway. Hurry, he told himself as he put both hands on the side rails. He pulled himself from the water in one smooth motion and without stopping, spidered up the side to the flybridge.

The helmsman was lying in a pool of blood, holding his upper arm. Egg or Buzz had hit the mark. The man glanced at him and reached for a pistol lying by his side. Too late, thought Sheets as he dived across the space and drove a forearm into the guy's temple. Three down. The pain in his leg amped up with the motion. He gathered the pistol and fired it twice, then said in a low groan, "got him."

A voice came from the starboard deck. "Sarge?"

"I'm hit," said Sheets in the same low voice as he crept silently and hid next to the top of the ladder to the flybridge. Blood pulsed from the wound when he bent the leg to crouch. He could hear the sloshing sound of someone moving closer on the now submerged deck.

And then a face appeared at the top of the ladder and Sheets slammed the pistol into the forehead and heard a splash as the man landed in the water where the rear deck had been. Four down. He pulled the unconscious Sarge towards him. Heavy, maybe 220 pounds. He took a deep breath, levered the body up and let it fall towards the starboard companionway. A shot rang out from the deck below, and a voice said, "Oh shit."

Sheets risked a look over the side, saw that the last man was still looking at the fallen comrade. He shot the gun from his hand. "Throw your shorts up to me." When the guy hesitated, Sheets fired another round close to him, spraying shards of fiberglass when the shot hit the wall by the man's head. He pulled off his pants and tossed them up to Sheets, who checked the pockets and threw the cell phone and knife he found into the water, then dropped the shorts back to the guy. "Your buddy Sarge still alive?" As if in answer, the prone man groaned.

Sheets glanced at the guy clinging to the dinghy, still coughing up seawater. He shouted at him to get into the inflatable and paddle up to the rear of the Viking. The dinghy was able to pull right over the transom of the foundering boat. Quickly, Sheets assessed the situation. One man dead. One badly hurt. Shot twice. One with a serious concussion. The other two should be okay. He wondered briefly why he even cared. He thought to check the rest of their pockets but hesitated, and instead just told the last man standing to get himself and the other two into the inflatable.

The situation now completely under his control, a strange feeling came over him. Like the old adrenaline rush he got after an engagement with the enemy, yet different. He felt something possess him and remembered the night Joe and he had been drinking and somehow wound up doing Tarzan victory bellows into the night air. So, he threw his head back and unleashed a roar. And was rewarded with an echoing response from his sailboat, but it wasn't the same now. The roars sounded haunting as if signaling death, the end of days.

He turned and raised his hand to the B-Dock crew and waved to motion them to keep their distance. No reason for them to see what would come next. He saw a spare magazine for the machine pistol on the helm, popped the old one out and rammed the new one in. Fifteen rounds. Enough to finish the job.

Chapter 44

The four guys, all together now in the dinghy, looked at him as if he were crazy, maybe wondering if these might be their last few moments alive. Sheets frowned at them and shook his head. "Your partner is below the dinghy." He paused. "Was he a SEAL?"

"*Beret Vert*," one of them replied.

French Navy Commando, Sheets thought. Tough bastard. He'd never done an op with one. He glanced down at the slice in his pant leg, blood beginning to crust on the edges of the tear, thinking, the guy was good.

He raised the gun. "Who burned the boat?" he asked. No one spoke. They exchanged nervous glances. Sheets saw the Gypsy sinking below the surface with the box that had slipped from Joe's hands just an hour before and his grip tightened on the pistol.

"Who burned the boat?" he yelled, this time, his voice hoarse. Again, none of the men spoke, but one glanced down. The only answer he would get from them, he supposed. The *Beret Vert*. The best of them. He flexed his arms, still feeling the strain in his muscles from holding the Commando while he fought to get free. He was already dead. Revenge enough?

No.

They were all part of this, all responsible.

She was irreplaceable. The woman he loved. The first. The only. Like him, she'd just begun to break out of the shell her father had placed her in. A gallery of moments with her filled his thoughts. That uncertain smile from the first time he'd spoken to her on the dock. The silvery hair glistening as she emerged from the ocean. The uninhibited touch of her skin against his as they rode together in Joe's pickup to rake leaves.

The gun had lowered from the fatigue in his arm, and he raised it and trained it on the men anew. They had to die. For her.

As he leveled the weapon, he heard The Admiral's voice: You're a weapon. You cannot think. Just kill them. If you don't, you'll only have to face these men again. Sheets pulled back on the trigger.

And Bubbles came to him again. Movie nights, when the slightest hint of violence caused her to bury her face in Joe's shirt. Her anger when she saw a man mistreating a dog. Five years, he could feel her saying, with disappointment written on her face. Five years to break away from the casual violence of your old life. He could see her point to the men in the dinghy and ask him; Is that you? Did those five years with Joe and three with me mean that little to you?

His arm was now trembling with what? Fatigue? Loss of blood? Sheets knew in his heart it was from relief. He eased back on the trigger and held the weapon to his side. His breath was coming in spasms.

The seriously wounded man was lying on the bottom of the inflatable. Sheets risked a trip into the watery cabin and found a first aid kit. As he tossed it to them, he said. "This is how it will go down. No engine until we're out of sight. We will watch until then. If you start the engine, I'll..." He paused and shook his head, looked at them quizzically. "The Admiral behind this?"

They exchanged glances, but didn't answer.

Sheets pushed the inflatable away with his foot. "Give him a message if you make it back. Tell him I'm coming."

Chapter 45

The Viking was nearly submerged as Joe pulled the sailboat alongside it. Sheets gingerly stepped from the flybridge to the bow of his sloop, favoring his wounded leg and still holding the machine pistol. He watched the dinghy drift away, carried south on the small waves, shimmering in the bright morning sun. As instructed, the four men had not started the small outboard engine.

Everyone watched him as he set the gun down and peeled off his soggy shirt. They were all on deck now and their eyes were wide and glowing with adrenaline from the encounter. Sheets started to say something, but a wave of lightheadedness washed over him and he slipped to the roof of the cabin. The motion pulled open the tear in his pants and he saw blood quickly cover his kneecap. He lay back, too tired to deal with it.

Voices swirled above him, but the struggle with the *Beret Vert* kept replaying in his head and he realized how close he'd come to losing his life and his friends in that moment.

"His arms are shaking," said Egg from behind him.

Sheets felt fingers dig into his deltoid muscles. His arms began to relax and he sank into the feeling. He opened his eyes and saw Egg's upside-down face leaning over him, an inch-long pink groove below her left eye. He shrugged out of her grasp and turned to her. "Are you all right?"

"I caught a splinter." She pointed to one of the many bullet pocked spots on the cabin. "It's nothing."

The sight of the serious damage brought him to full alert. There were at least a dozen gouges in the wood. He glanced at the others gathered around him—except Joe, who remained at the helm. "Anyone else hurt?"

"Untouched." Marie was holding a bandage, applying pressure to the cut on his leg. "We should sew this up."

"Wait." Sheets exhaled sharply and looked again at each of them in turn. "Seriously? No other injuries? Jesus." He shook his head. "You took fire from five men, four almost certainly Delta Force and one French commando." He started to say how lucky they'd been, but caught himself. The enormity of the danger they faced would set in as their adrenaline wore off. Let this high last a little longer. "Egg, Buzz, great shooting. One of you took out the driver." They turned to each other and bumped fists. Sheets wondered again if it had been sheer luck. He knew he had been good. Maybe as good as anyone six years ago. Maybe the best. But the response from B-Dock was totally unexpected.

He glanced at his watch. It seemed like hours since they'd spotted the fishing boat, but only fifty minutes had passed and he was reminded anew of how time slowed dramatically during battle. The ocean around them was empty, but for once it didn't calm him. Instead it was a reminder of how alone they were, with The Admiral's unseen forces waiting out there somewhere.

Marie was asking again about sewing the wound. He thought of all the work ahead of him. He didn't want to take a chance of ripping out stitches or having to sew the wound more than once. "Is it clean?"

"We ran water and hydrogen peroxide through it and there's Neosporin under the bandage. Marie relaxed the pressure on his leg. "The bleeding seems to have stopped."

Sheets thought for a moment. "Let's just duct tape it for now." He looked east, where he could now make out the distant shore. Carefully, he stood, leaning on Marie's shoulder, and then limped to Joe's side at the wheel. "I'd like to stay out of sight of land. Let's head northeast." He stared Joe in the eye trying to read the emotion there, but saw nothing except a flat blue stare. Sheets waved back in the direction they'd come. "Are you going to be able to set that aside for a while? I'm really going to need you now."

"Are you?" Joe's gaze never wavered, "You know she loved you and I know how you felt about her."

"Two hydrogens and an oxygen she called the three of us. Bound and unbound. I'll never get over her." Sheets broke his eyes away and looked back again in the direction in which they'd left her and felt her presence as strongly as if she were still here.

"Sheets, I gotta ask. I saw that gun you took from them. TEC-9's a drug dealer's weapon. Did her death have something to do with drugs?"

And Sheets felt pieces falling into place. The sudden attack. The TEC-9. The ranch. The Admiral telling him how much bigger his operation was than his sleazy films. Drugs and all the money they could mean. Money enough to kill for. Money enough to build and equip an army of men. He felt immensely tired and completely unequipped to deal with this. He glanced at Joe. "I hadn't thought of it, but…." He sighed. "It can't be anything else."

"Drugs," Joe repeated flatly. "That seems so…. She was so much…."

There were a million words and none could really capture what they both needed to say. Sheets stared at the line of white wake trailing behind them.

"So what do we do now? Run? Hide?" Joe's eyes flashed.

Joe's anger stoked his own and the fatigue vanished. What the hell. They'd taken the Deltas first shot today and won. And, he'd felt flashes of his old ability. Plus, he thought more soberly, we have no choice now.

"Yes. Scatter. Get Jamie and her family hidden somewhere. Send Marie with Three to Europe. Give Buzz and Egg the chance to opt out and take to cover. Sheets punched Joe in the shoulder. "Just you and me. We'll start in Idaho."

This brought a flicker of a smile to Joe's grief-ravaged face. "Let's do this thing."

ψ ψ ψ

"What about the restaurant? I can't just close it. People need money." Jamie looked back and forth between Sheets and Joe. "And I want to help. I promise I won't lose it again."

The crew had regrouped in the cockpit of the sailboat which was now headed north along the coast towards Dewey Beach, the hot sun high above them. Joe took Jamie's hands in his and said, "You're out. We can't take any chances with you being pregnant."

She started to protest, but Sheets thought she looked relieved. Joe spoke again, "I'll transfer enough money into the Emerald account so you can pay everyone for a couple months. This will all be over by then, one way or the other. Tell everyone to stay away from the restaurant until they hear from you."

As Joe continued to outline the plan they'd concocted to get her family to safety, Sheets did a quick scan of the ocean around them. No boats, except a fully laden container ship well to the east. The sun was raising the temperature so rapidly, that it already felt like a midsummer day. He turned back to the group.

"Lake of the Woods," he heard Jamie say. "There's thousands of islands. Rick's friend knows every one. They'll never find us there. Why don't we all go? Just wait for this to blow over." She looked at Sheets for her answer.

"There's no blowing over for me. The attack this morning means my father wants me dead and doesn't care about any collateral damage. Joe and I are going to Idaho. There's no choice. Buzz, do you have somewhere you can go? Family?"

A cloud passed above at that moment and it felt as if the temperature fell ten degrees instantly. Everyone's faces grew serious, as if the cloud were a reminder of their situation.

"Family?" Buzz swept his arm in front of him. "This is my family, and it was just attacked. Again. Don't try to cut me out."

Sheets felt a smile come to his face involuntarily. Something about the little man's demeanor in the fight told him that he could be an asset in the struggle ahead. He turned to Egg, the cut on her face making her look tougher than she was. "Egg?"

"Ditto to everything Buzz said."

"Three?" Sheets looked to the man whose calmness had never wavered throughout the day.

"I watched you all this morning and I was impressed by your reactions." Three looked around at the others. "I wish I thought I could help, but unless you're desperate for a french horn player, I think I'd be more of a liability." The group laughed.

Four, Sheets thought, all B-Dock, all people he knew and trusted. He was relieved that Three had opted out. "Where in Europe are you supposed to fly back to?"

"Paris. I have a flight out of Philly tomorrow."

"Philly's not a great option after this morning. We have to assume that they have names and pictures." He thought for a moment. If Three rode with Jamie, they could drop him at a different airport along the way. Sheets tried to picture the cities on the route from Delaware to Minnesota and had no idea. The Middle East he would know. Middle of his own country, no. Easier just to ask Joe. "Any international airports on the road to Minnesota, Joe?"

"Cleveland. No—Pittsburgh. You'd be driving right by it."

"To quote W.C. Fields. I'd rather be in Philadelphia." Three smiled. "But Pittsburgh is fine."

He looked at his watch. Time seemed to be crawling by. It had to be over 85 degrees. A day they would all be enjoying under any other circumstances.

"Three, come below for a minute. I'll tell you how to handle things at the airport." Sheets stepped below. Weak, he thought, but he had to try.

Three appeared moments later. "That was a little too obvious. She'll never go for it."

"What?" said Sheets.

"You want me to talk my mother into going with me."

"No—"

Three interrupted. "Look, my mother loves me…I've never doubted that, but Bubbles was her life. My mom stayed with that awful man to try to protect her. She was never happier than when Joe pried Bubbles away from him. Don't—"

"I assume you're discussing me—my future— without me."

Sheets turned. Marie was standing at the bottom of the ladder, hands on her hips, eyes blazing. The eyes. The anger. The flash. Bubbles. It took his breath away. He couldn't speak. He reached to a beam in the cabin roof to steady himself. In the two years he'd known Bubbles, he'd only seen her rise in anger twice, once over a guy beating a dog and once when she saw Moose hit Jason.

"She was my daughter," Marie was saying. "I'll be lost without her. Don't take away the chance for me to help stop the people who would do something like this."

"I just want you safe." Sheets put his hand on her arm.

She shrugged it off. "I don't want safe. I want revenge." Her voice broke, turned pleading. "I can help. I've got all the money we could possibly need."

Vehicles. Fake IDs. Sheets was too tired to compile a list of all the things they might need, but Joe had money enough for all that. But, he thought, she's possibly the only one that the Deltas don't know which means she could go places the rest of the crew could not.

"Please," she said softly.

He hesitated. Four had felt like a magic number. B-Dock. Friends. Tight. Five seemed well…odd. But he pictured Marie with Joe after they'd dropped the ashes, the calming effect she'd had on him. It wasn't really his decision anyway, she had as much of a stake in this as anyone.

Marie threw a couple fake punches at him and tried to smile. "Plus I'm a tough old broad. Zumba, Taibo, Crossfit, You name the exercise fad and I've tried it."

Throwing up his hands in surrender, Sheets said, "Stop. You had me at Taibo. Anyone who can throw a useless punch belongs on this team."

"Useless? Useless?" She launched another shot which landed solidly on his chest. "What about that, Mr. S.E.A.L.?" She grinned.

Crap, Sheets thought. He let the momentum from her punch collapse him onto the sofa. That face. That smile. Just like Bubbles. He wondered if would ever be able to get used to that.

Chapter 46

Two burly men grabbed Joe and began to hustle him down B-Dock towards the parking lot. Shit, Sheets thought as he lowered his binoculars and backed away from the lighthouse window overlooking the marina. In the darkness, he had not been able to see if the men were the same ones from the fishing boat this morning, but he supposed it didn't really matter. Joe hadn't gotten to Egg's boat, snatched by the Deltas, the plan already in shambles. Hurry, he thought, ten minutes to finish what he had to do, then get back and find Joe. Desperately not wanting to let Joe out of his sight, he reluctantly started to turn to go, when a motion from a third-floor condo caught his eye. He flicked up the binoculars and saw a third man motioning to the guys holding Joe.

ψ ψ ψ

As soon as night had fallen, they had sailed to within a couple hundred feet of the beach just south of Dewey. They'd been silent, morose even, and no doubt scared, since the enormity of the danger they faced had sunk in that morning. Sheets swam in and scouted the dunes for anyone watching. He found no one in the area for a hundred yards in either direction and returned to the water's edge and threw a stone out towards his boat, the signal to swim in. He wanted to rest while they swam, but his mind was racing, going over and over the plan.

The decision to approach from the ocean seemed to be the right one. The Deltas, as B-Dock was calling them now, had to be expecting them to sail up the bay if they came at all. Sheets had no idea how many men they had at their disposal. He'd stared up at the moonless sky. Still warm, over eighty degrees, the air heavy with humidity. The big houses of Indian Beach behind the dunes were all dark, metal storm shutters rolled down over most of the windows, creating the eerie effect of closed eyes watching him. He scanned the decks of the houses again for any signs of life. The wound on his leg throbbed when he moved it, but he knew he had to ignore the pain until the night's action was over.

Jamie, Three and Joe made their way in through the surf as Sheets watched from the dune line for any visitors. Buzz, Egg and Marie were taking the sloop down to Indian River Inlet where they'd wait for Joe and Sheets to arrive in Egg's motor yacht after they got Jamie's family and Three started on their trips out of town.

Sheets felt the need to hurry, had made sure they all had said what could possibly be their last goodbyes on the boat. He motioned Jamie and Three to stay low and begin moving north along the dune line to Dagsworthy Street, where Jamie's husband should be waiting in the van. Out of his control now, he thought, just focus on what he needed to do. After a two minute interval, he and Joe began to move north as well.

Sheets had made his way up the line of dunes to the big dark house on the beach at Dickinson Street. More than dark, he thought as he pressed against the black shingles, foreboding. He knew through Joe that the house belonged to the guy that owned the Rudder, The Cork and other businesses in town. Joe revered him for being the man who held the line against the 'make Dewey a family town' crowd and kept Dewey its traditional hedonistic self.

Six properties separated the beach and Route 1. Sheets made his way past the first five quickly. Each had the ubiquitous, wind stunted evergreens in front to conceal him. The sixth, the Dewey Villas, a nondescript white condo, had nothing in front, so he slipped into the parking lot behind it, stuck to the shadows under the rear balconies and made his way to the fence behind the adjacent Hawaiian restaurant. He scaled the wall and climbed to the roof fronting Coastal Highway He felt the thump of live music in his chest as he lowered himself to the warm shingles and raised his binoculars just above the roofline. The familiar smell of fried food rose from the exhaust fan churning away below him.

He slowly scanned from north to south and saw just one lone car making its way down Route 1. The parking lot for the Lighthouse Bar had maybe thirty cars, about right for an offseason Monday Night Football crowd, Sheets thought, as he looked across the divided main street. He needed to make his way undetected to the fake lighthouse which rose above the bar and had an unobstructed view of the marina. There were a couple of guys standing on the elevated walkway outside BookSandCoffee, but they were mostly concealed by the shadows of the building. Their posture alone screamed Delta—that way of always looking ready even when trying to look relaxed. Takes one to know one, he supposed. Shit, how many more out there watching and waiting? No way to cross the highway her without being seen. Move north, he thought.

As he climbed back over the fence, someone yelled, "Sheets." He pulled his SIG-Sauer from his waistband and rolled for cover onto a blackened patio. Fuck. Could he not have one thing go right today? He looked at the suppressor threaded on the barrel. Maybe just shooting a couple people would ease the frustration.

The voice again, but lower. "Sheets? Are you okay?"

He recognized the voice this time. Kim, a server at the Rudder, one of the fresh-out-of-college girls he'd taken sailing a couple times. He stuck his gun into his waistband behind his back and stepped out into the parking lot. Kim and a girl named Sara, another server who worked with Kim were leaning over the railing of the balcony. They looked ready to go out. Both with khaki shorts and tank tops. Dressed for the warm evening.

"Sheets. What are you doing down there?" said Kim. She sounded slightly inebriated.

A plan formed in his mind. "Sorry. I'm in some trouble. I could use a little help."

Kim leaned back from the railing. "Give us a minute. We're headed to the Lighthouse anyway. Be right down."

Sheets retrieved the dry bag he'd dropped in the parking lot and checked his watch. Only five minutes left before Joe would run across Collins Street towards the marina. He took a Hawaiian shirt with green toucans from the bag and buttoned it over his black T-shirt, tucking the gun in his waistband. His long black pants might look a bit out of place, but it was the only way to conceal the knife strapped to his calf.

A light appeared at the downstairs door and Kim and Sara stepped out.

"Wow. Something must be really wrong for you to wear that hideous shirt." Kim giggled and held up a palm for Sara to slap.

Sheets smiled. The two girls upholding a Dewey tradition. Have a few cheap drinks at home before going out, to save on the bar tab. They'd be relaxed which would work to his benefit. "I just need to avoid two guys on the deck by the bookstore."

"Why?" said Sara.

He said nothing and Kim smiled at him. "International man of mystery never gives anything up. I knocked on that door for two whole days of sailing. What can we do?"

"Just walk me to the deck of the Rudder. I'll be okay from there. Let me walk between you. Act like you're holding me up." Sheets handed them a fifty dollar bill.

They giggled. "Fifty bucks?" Kim said. "Come on then, Handsome."

And it worked. He had let his head fall onto Kim's shoulder as they passed the two men, while the two girls chattered away about nothing. They walked up the stairs onto the Rudder deck. All the outside bars were closed because the summer staff was gone. Everyone was inside watching the football pre-game show. At the door to the bar, he crouched down and crab walked behind the row of stools lining the bar facing across the little beach to the Lighthouse. He worked his way out to the little tiki porch area where the Island Boys entertained the tourists on summer evenings. If it wasn't Monday night, there'd be plenty of people out here enjoying the beautiful night. He could see stars out through the open sides of the hut.

He allowed himself a moment as he shed the gaudy shirt. Thursday, three days away, and she would have been here, just a few yards from this spot, and he let himself see her, arms raised, eyes closed, the world pushed aside. He realized he was holding his breath and exhaled slowly and thought of another night when the Island Boys were doing their reggae sets. The Jamaican lead singer had pointed at him when he was doing Peter Tosh's *Steppin Razor*. Joe had smiled and said, "Steppin Razor, Jamaican for bad ass," and sang the line, "*I'm like a Steppin Razor, you better watch my size. I'm dangerous, dangerous.*" Someone's about to find out, Sheets thought.

He raised his head just above the wooden railing of the hut. A man stood at the end of the long dock that ran a couple hundred feet into the bay from the Rudder deck. Sheets figured there was someone watching every dock along the north end of the bay, which was why they had decided to approach from the ocean. The man had his back to the beach. As Sheets watched, a green light appeared next to the guy's head. Night vision scope. He glanced back in the other direction and saw that the two men on the deck across the way were still watching the parking lot.

He pulled the SIG from his waistband, and slipped over the edge onto the sand. Staying crouched, he raced across the beach, ducking under the volleyball net and up onto the raised deck surrounding the restaurant. There was a murmur of voices through the open windows, but the game must not have kicked off yet or the roars from the fans would have started. Access to the lighthouse which towered over the Ruddertowne shops and restaurants, had been closed for years, ever since the Lighthouse kitchen had been reconfigured. But Sheets had some local knowledge courtesy of Joe.

Delaware bars had last call at 1AM. All drinks had to be finished by 2AM. So, the bartenders, still needing a drink themselves, would occasionally move the party up into the abandoned lighthouse directly overhead. If anyone wondered why there was a ladder lying in the sand beneath the deck, their question would be answered after 2 a.m., when it would be resting against the roof of the bar, allowing access to the door at the peak of the shingles, a door that was never locked.

Before hoisting himself up the four by four post to the roof, Sheets flashed back on the carefree times spent drinking with the bartenders and the few servers, always females, who knew the secret. And the even better times when he, Joe and Bubbles would sneak up in anticipation of the 360 degree view of a coming storm.

Chapter 47

Go Go Go, he thought. Save the family reunion. Sheets slapped his hand on his thigh in frustration as he watched Jamie hugging her daughter as they stood next to the van. He'd worked his way north from the lighthouse to the liquor store across from The Sand Palace Motel and had seen no other watchers. He could see Rick's profile in the driver's window. "Go," he said softly, and was rewarded as he saw Three usher them into the van. The door slid closed and Sheets breathed a sigh of relief. The taillights moved north out of sight and he waited one more minute and saw no one following. On their way.

He knew the real source of his frustration was that he had no idea how to get to Joe. The condo building had been constructed during his time in the marina, he'd watched it rise from what had been a gravel parking lot. With many of the design features you'd like in a prison. A rectangular, three-story concrete block box with two impenetrable doors. He pictured a Delta at each entry and one on the balcony. The whole building, easily defended by three men. Sheets had already seen six. How many more might there be?

And, as he jogged south, the warm air enveloping him like a second skin, another thought overtook him.

He wondered if his father was up there.

Waiting.

Chapter 48

"Keep moving. Don't slow down." Sheets tucked behind the freestanding ATM enclosure on the corner of the Rudder parking lot. He had been jogging back to the lighthouse to try and free Joe and was shocked to see him running toward him with two men in fatigues in pursuit. They had handguns pressed to their sides, which prevented them from pumping their arms, slowing them somewhat. Joe glanced towards the sound of Sheets' voice, but ran on, into the Sea Esta Motel parking lot. Sheets reached through the slit in the leg of his pants and slid out his knife.

The two men were panting as they passed the ATM. Almost identical from the rear; 5' 10" broad shoulders, both with dark windbreakers to conceal the holsters for their guns. Sheets silently moved in behind the guy to his left and when his foot lifted up, reached down with the knife and severed the man's right Achilles tendon. At the sound of his partner's roar of pain, the second man began to swing his gun around, but Sheets was behind him and his partner stumbled into him as soon as his damaged ankle touched down. To his credit, the guy tried to roll and shoot as he too started to fall, but his buddy was in his line of sight. Sheets was already airborne and brought both boots down on the second man's gun hand and wrist. He immediately shot his left foot out sideways and caught the first man in the neck, but his gun hand was free and rising. Sheets slashed with the knife, nearly severing the man's thumb, and the gun clattered to the pavement.

As he reached to scoop up the weapons, Sheets heard the thud of footsteps behind him and wheeled around to see Joe heading back towards him. Sheets couldn't help but grin, but Joe's expression was dead. Chilling almost. He took one of the guns from Sheets and drove it savagely into the side of one Delta's head, saying, "Payback's a bitch," then held the pistol to the head of the other.

"Don't shoot." Sheets touched Joe's arm lightly. "We don't want cops." The Dewey Beach police station was just down Rodney Avenue from the motel, no more than 100 feet away.

Joe's cheekbone was red and swollen and he fingered the swelling as he lowered the gun. "Bastard nailed me good." He kicked the man in the head. From the Ruddertowne parking lot came the sound of motorcycles roaring to life.

Sheets sheathed his knife and pushed Joe into the darkness under the support columns of the motel. "How many Deltas?" He wanted to ask Joe how he got away, but he needed information first.

"At least six in the condo and they were talking to others on radios." As if on cue, a radio crackled, then two motorcycles appeared just a few yards away. Shit, Sheets thought, they were now cut off from going back to the marina to retrieve Egg's boat. A third bike appeared at that moment on Route 1, cutting off any escape to the east.

"Pierpoint," Sheets said and they exited the parking lot onto Rodney and sprinted past the police station towards the marina at the end of the street. He saw Joe's shirt light up, caught in a headlight beam. When they reached the bait shack that stood on the grass at the edge of the water, Sheets pushed Joe to the right, past the ice and Pepsi machines buzzing away in front of the hut. The motorcycle was just hitting the loose gravel of the parking lot, stones spraying up and pinging off the exhaust pipes. Pierpoint marina was much smaller than theirs, and shallow. Only pontoon boats and small draft sailboats could dock here and frequently rested on the bottom at low tide. No way to swim for it. Their options were shrinking.

Joe glanced back at Sheets. "What's your plan? Wade to safety."

Sheets caught a glimpse of the old Joe smile, and though he wanted to believe it was the old Joe, he knew it was just an adrenaline rush. He'd seen it a hundred times before on ops and wondered again what it felt like. He had always been the opposite, dropping into a zone where everything slowed to half speed and his senses sharpened. The rotted fish odor from the bait shack was overwhelming, and he heard the far away sound of an approaching boat engine.

The grass ran out at a tall wooden fence which prevented the property owners next door from viewing the detritus that had accumulated at the end of the boatyard over the years: a stack of pallets, what appeared to be a tiny paddleboat with a dirty faded cover, a pontoon barge with a metal frame for a hoist rising from it and various rusting parts tossed around randomly. The metal frame looked like a guillotine in the low light.

The last dock was perfectly straight, running at least one hundred feet into the bay. A row nearly completely filled with pontoon boats, the empty slips looking like missing teeth. He tapped Joe's shoulder and pointed. "Go slowly out the dock." He then jumped over the low seawall into the shallow water on the right, ducking out of sight, the pain in his knee flaring. He reached up and uncoiled a hose from a piling.

The bike turned toward the dock, its idle loud, spotlighting Joe's retreating back as the rider bumped up onto the edge of the wood as he spoke into a microphone attached to his collar. "They're heading out the dock,"

Sheets stood, looped the hose around the guy's neck and pulled, dragging the man from the motorcycle into the foot deep water. As the man sputtered and thrashed, Sheets took another turn and held on as he called to Joe to come back. The sound of more motorcycles behind him caused him to turn and look up the bay. At least three more Harleys were idling at the end of the next street, their headlights illuminating the wavelets moving to shore. He heard a boat engine not far away. Surely heading toward them to cut off a water escape. Deltas to the North, East and West. An escape south through the marina was not an option.

Joe jumped on the bike that had fallen against one of the white plastic electric service boxes and pushed it back onto the grass. Sheets released his grip on the hose as the biker's struggling ceased. He found the cigarette pack sized radio on the guy's belt, pulled the receiver from his ear and stuck it in his own.

"We can't tell what's going on," a staticky voice said. "The bike's headed back in."

Another voice: "We've got the marina entrance blocked. Head back this way."

The headlights of the other bikes he'd seen began to turn away from the bay. Seconds away, thought Sheets.

"Get on." Joe was revving the engine.

I should be driving, Sheets thought, but there was no time to argue the point and Joe looked completely focused.

"They've got the entrance blocked." Sheets slid onto the seat behind Joe and drew the SIG from his pocket.

"Not unless they have a semi." Joe popped the clutch and they shot forward across the grass.

The ride was a blur and Sheets found himself just holding on for dear life as Joe navigated the streets he knew by heart at unbelievable speeds, the stink of burning rubber rising from the footpegs along with a shower of sparks, as he laid the big bike into the turns. And when he'd finally lost the pursuers, Joe turned onto a street that ended as a boat ramp into the bay, and never slowing, drove the Harley straight into the warm water.

As they stroked away from the submerged bike, Sheets pondered. Local knowledge. Hidden skills. Mixed with a little luck, it was keeping them all alive.

So far.

He wondered at the things he'd seen his friends do today. Had they kept as much from him as he had from them?

Chapter 49

It was as if had someone had just erased all the bar patrons and left the bar open. The shadows cast by the surfboards suspended from the ceiling formed perfect ellipses on the concrete floor, the light coming from a pole along the rail fence separating the bar from the bay. The rest of the barroom was dark.

Crouched behind a bar, knife out, Sheets listened for anyone approaching. He had checked to make sure the safety was off on the SIG-Sauer he'd given to Joe, and motioned for him to conceal himself back down the darkened hallway to the restrooms.

Northbeach. The last bar on the north end of the bay. Closed for the season, but the place looked like nothing had been done since the tourists left town. The TV's and speakers were still attached to the top rails of the canopies covering the outside bars. Condiment trays graced a few of the tables on the narrow strip of sand beside the bay. As he regulated his breathing and slowed his heart rate, Sheets wondered idly if they might even find beer left in the coolers.

ψψψ

"**W**here'd you learn to ride like that?" Sheets twisted his black shirt and water splashed onto the floor of the dimly lit kitchen. A fecund bay smell rose from the puddle.

"Nick and I rode Motocross for a couple years before he died." Joe hoisted himself backwards onto a narrow prep table after pushing aside a coffee carafe and several partially filled glasses. He pulled his soggy shirt off as well.

"Yeah but how does riding a little dirt bike twenty years ago translate to pushing a Harley through the streets of Dewey at sixty miles an hour?" Sheets could now see the damage the Deltas had done to Joe's face, a badly split lip and bruises that were beginning to discolor both cheekbones. If they could make it back to Sheets' sloop, he had a supply of the Percocet he knew Joe would need.

Joe shrugged. "I've been moving without thinking since they grabbed me on the dock. I saw that bike and just rolled with it."

"Adrenaline. The wonder drug. You saved our asses." Sheets glanced at his watch for the third time in as many minutes and restlessly moved to the back door and checked the lock. They were operating under his self-imposed thirty minute wait before moving from Northbeach. Let the Deltas get tired of searching. He moved back and sat on the stainless steel table by the dishwasher across from Joe, looked at him, and marveled at his escape.

Joe had already related the story of how the Deltas had turned their attention from trying to beat information out of him to listening to new orders coming in on their radios. He'd realized the sliding glass door was open and had made a run for it. Pure adrenaline rush, Sheets thought again. Twenty-five feet up. Approximately twelve feet out to the water. "To get to the water from the balcony, you had to go about twenty-three feet in the air."

"I didn't quite make it. Banged my toes on the dock and I belly flopped the entry. Hurt my face almost as bad as them punching me. Lucky there was no boat in that slip I landed in."

There was a single florescent bulb burning above the dish area, light enough for Sheets to see that the swelling under Joe's eye had nearly pushed it closed. Sheets went to one of the several refrigeration units still humming away and looked for some ice for Joe's cheek, but found nothing.

"Just cut me, Mick." Joe touched the inflammation.

"Can't do it Rocky." That sense of humor, thought Sheets. Even the new Joe couldn't shut it down. A wave of relief swept over him. He pulled two clean glasses from the rack inside the dishwasher and filled them with water, but he heard the outside kitchen doorknob rattle, slid out his knife and moved to the side of the door. He turned and saw Joe moving to the other side. There were no windows in the kitchen, no way for them to be seen unless someone forced the door.

Flashlight beams, looking like miniature spotlights began to move across the section of the dining area where the tables had been removed to create dance space. Sheets watched as the beams crept up the back wall to the raised DJ booth, then quickly disappeared. It would take a long time to thoroughly search even a tiny town like Dewey. Sheets guessed the search would rapidly become cursory and the men would withdraw to the condo above the marina and come up with a new plan. The Deltas only had so long before the bored cops noticed them poking around. He wished the stolen radio had survived the plunge into the bay. He checked his watch. Twenty more minutes. He was itching to move.

"How come you're not killing these guys?" Joe had moved back to the table, brushed off a couple desiccated lettuce leaves and laid down facing the ceiling.

Sheets ran a finger along the edge of the knife, his heart rate steadying with the departure of the searchers. Good question, he thought. He'd had a chance to permanently remove eight Deltas so far today and only the French commando had died. He tried to think of every man he'd killed as a SEAL. But the whole idea behind the ops he ran was to snatch and run. Only a couple had really gone badly, where their intel was bad. A couple firefights. The people he'd killed, he'd killed mostly at a distance. Impersonal.

"I honestly don't know."

"C'mon man." Joe raised his head and looked at Sheets. "I'm curious. Not judgmental."

There must be reason, Sheets thought. He seemed to have slid right back into his old abilities as a fighter this morning. Took the fight to them, rounded them up, and had them in his gun sights. And couldn't seal the deal, no pun intended. Why? Especially when he knew he'd probably see them all again. He tried to return to that moment with the four Deltas staring at him from the dinghy. He glanced at Joe, prone on the stainless steel table with the swollen face facing straight to the ceiling and the image reminded him of an autopsy scene in a movie, shaking him.

"I think it's your fault," he said as the image fled.

"My fault?" Joe rolled his head to see Sheets, his eye and a half peering at him across the room.

"Yeah yours. I was molded to fight and kill without thinking. Fight. React. Fight. React. Kill if necessary. I was Tarzan, in a way." He paused. "You made me think, showed me other possibilities. You...well...you and her, civilized me."

Joe turned back to the ceiling and Sheets could no longer see his face. "I ruined you," Joe said, and then Sheets saw the broken smile. "Contaminated The Admiral's petri dish."

Sheets had to laugh at this and relief washed over him once more. He'd been in love with Bubbles. But he loved Joe. He stepped over to him and turned his head to the light and checked the swelling. There was no way to tell if the suborbital bone was cracked or broken, but one way or the other, his head was going to hurt and they were at least an hour away from getting ice and painkillers.

"Leave me alone Doc. I'll be fine." Joe pushed Sheets' hand away. "We'll be dead soon anyway, from being in the bay so long. Man, we reek." Joe put his head back down on the table. "What are our chances?"

"Slim. We're outnumbered, and outgunned. We have no intel, no training."

"So we got em right where we want em."

Sheets thought back to Egg and Buzz in the firefight. "We found two shooters this morning and a motorcycle rider tonight. Marie's a wildcard. Can you talk her into going home?"

"She won't go and she could be an asset. I don't think the Deltas have seen her face." He paused. "And she looks just like her, doesn't she?" He didn't wait for Sheets to answer. "What happens if you run into your father again? If he's behind all this?" Joe lifted his head and looked into Sheets' eyes.

The ballast of the florescent light buzzed as Sheets wondered how to respond. A picture of the SIG in his hand that day in his father's study came to him. Lowering it from The Admirals' chest. "I wish I knew," was all he could say. He checked his watch. "Ten minutes."

Joe stared at the ceiling for a few moments. "I learned more about you in three days than in the last five years. Name. Background. Father issues."

Sheets stepped forward and touched Joe's leg with the point of the knife. "Bullshit. You learned some statistics. Bare facts. Are you saying you didn't know me? That she didn't know me either, because—"

"Whoa. No need to get angry. I'm just saying. Keeping your best friend in the dark." Joe tried to smile, but winced with pain from his cut lip. "By the way, I still don't know how old you are."

"Consider this a military op now." He tapped the flat of the blade on Joe's knee. "We'll be operating under the 'don't ask, don't tell rule."

Joe stared up at the grease stained ceiling tiles again. The smell of stale fryer oil permeated the air. "Did you ever tell her any of this stuff?"

"No." Sheets checked his watch again. Five minutes. "But with that weird intuition thing she had, she probably figured most of it out." He pulled the soggy T-shirt over his head."

Joe sat up and did the same. "Time?"

"Couple minutes."

Joe slipped off the prep table and touched Sheets' arm.

"We ever gonna be able to say her name again?"

Chapter 50

Best not to think about the bay water on his leg wound. He'd rinsed it in the dish sink and had Joe encircle it several times with duct tape they'd found in the kitchen. They had taken two of the surfboards from the ceiling at Northbeach and were paddling slowly south towards the marina, trying to stay in the shadows of docks and breakwaters. Sheets had come up with a makeshift plan which would depend largely on what the Deltas had done and where they were deployed.

The ache in his arms from the morning fight with the Beret Vert was returning. Six and a half blocks to the marina, he thought. Two hundred feet per block. Thirteen hundred feet. Four and a third football fields. Just under a quarter mile. One eighth of his regular morning swim. Hopefully, they were almost done for the night.

At least the weather was cooperating. It still felt like it was over eighty degrees. And no moon, giving them large patches of darkness between the lights from the few houses that hadn't been shuttered for the off season. They saw no one on the Rudder deck as they paddled silently by. From his position flat on the water, Sheets couldn't see if the Delta he'd spotted earlier was still at his post at the end of the Rudder's long pier, so he slid off the board into the knee-deep water and cautiously pulled himself up. Clear. He looked up to the Delta's third floor condo, less than one hundred yards away across the lagoon. The glow of the patio light made it impossible to tell if lights were on inside or if someone might be watching. He eased back down into the water.

Joe tapped Sheets' shoulder and pointed towards the outside of the bayside marina wall. An inflatable with two silhouettes visible against the dim lights from the docks was bobbing gently against the wall. The orange glow of a cigarette ember attached to one of the men moved as if punctuating some speech. Sheets nodded and then turned his face to the southwest. Same light wind from that direction that they'd had all day, he thought. He'd listened to the marine weather early in the morning. Southwest winds until late tonight, then a cold front pushing through with gusty west winds and thunderstorms. Temperatures dropping thirty degrees behind the storms. He craved a hot shower, but a cold one was looking much more likely.

A roar came from the open windows of the Lighthouse and a much more muted one from the Rudder. Monday Night Football. Giants versus Eagles, Sheets remembered. Even though they both cared almost nothing for the sport, Bubbles and Joe would have made one of their outlandish bets on the game. Bubbles had grown up around Philly and Joe had been a Giants fan as a kid in Connecticut. Once, Joe had won and Bubbles had been tasked with cleaning the beer cooler at the restaurant. Joe had told Sheets that she had showed up in a short skirt and as Joe supervised with a beer from a bar stool, the skirt kept riding up, and Joe got so worked up, he told her to stop. That's cheating, Joe had said, but she smiled innocently and said she was just doing the job.

"Eagles score." Joe said it in a sad voice that let Sheets know he was thinking of the same episode.

Sheets took the surfboards and pushed them towards the beach to the left of the dock where they wouldn't be seen, then turned back to Joe. A plan had come to him as soon as Joe had pointed out the men in the inflatable. "Here's what we'll do." He quickly outlined his idea to attach a line to the rear of the Deltas' boat with about twenty feet of slack while Joe untied Egg's motor yacht and readied it to move out on Sheets' signal.

Joe's face, which now looked like a red balloon in the strips of light coming through the spaces in the dock above, cracked open in a crooked grin that made Sheets cringe. "Evil. Better go with two ropes. I want to see that boat rip apart."

"Good idea. We've got to hurry. You're swollen up like the Elephant Man. Can you make it underwater to the old Gibson houseboat?"

Joe nodded and disappeared from view into the bay.

The water was only a couple of feet deep between the Rudder dock and the northwest corner of the marina and Sheets mostly just pushed himself along with his hands across the sandy bottom of the cove. He surfaced for air when he reached the breakwater. He poked his head around the wall and checked the inflatable. The two men were talking, but in low voices and he couldn't make out their words.

The Gibson was moored close to the entrance of the marina and Joe was already easing a line off on the north side of the boat. Perfect, Sheets thought, the southwest wind would keep it from banging on the dock and he began untying another rope. When they finished, he coiled the lines, pushed them onto his shoulders. They faced each other as they hung by a hand from the finger dock, neither wanting to sink their bare feet into the muck below them and he nodded to Joe. "I'm going to borrow a waverunner. When you hear it start, fire up Egg's boat and go. It'll take me less than ten minutes. The noise from the Lighthouse should cover you." He tapped Joe's shoulder. "Hang in. Almost over."

The inflatable was rocking against the wall about ten feet from the entrance, with the engine facing him. Sheets picked up the smell of a cigarette again. He wondered about their complacency. It seemed misplaced given the outcome of the events so far today and he grinned. One more hard lesson coming. He ducked under and felt his way along the wall until he could touch the big outboard motor.

He surfaced behind the transom. A Novurania with a seventy horsepower Yamaha. Must be at least fifteen feet long to handle an engine that size, he thought. He'd never seen a Novurania before, knew they were expensive. He could now hear the men's voices clearly. "Waiting at the bridge," one voice said. Another voice. "We'll pull out in ten minutes. Join them there." Good luck with that, Sheets thought, and set about his task.

It took him less than five minutes to secure the two lines to the inflatable, tie them off on a piling below the seawall and swim to the jet ski dock. Joe had the big Egg Harbor motor yacht half way out of its slip as he raced by. He heard the Yamaha engine roar to life as well and wished he'd had time to circle back and see the damage he'd done, felt some childlike glee when he heard what must have been the transom rip away when the inflatable moved to follow him as he flew by on the waverunner. Sheets did raise a fist in triumph as he did one quick turnabout to make sure that Joe had gotten Egg's boat safely through the marina entrance. Joe knew the bay almost as well as he did, thought Sheets, and would be able to navigate without running lights down the six mile long waterway even on a moonless night.

Six miles. Sheets eased down onto the seat and gave the machine full throttle, racing south at over fifty-five miles per hour. The lights of Longneck and Pot-Nets lit up the western shore while to his left the Seashore State Parkland was shrouded in complete darkness.

He was under no illusions, the waverunner was loud. If the Deltas were waiting at the bridge they would hear him coming. He wasn't sure he could handle any more action tonight. And he had a sudden inspiration in his tired brain. Why not let the Delaware State Police do the job for them? All he had to do was radio the Coast Guard and inform them that there were men with guns on the Indian River Inlet Bridge. The Coast Guard would call the State Police who had a troop in Lewes. It would take less than a half hour for them to respond, which they would be obligated to do and if the Deltas were anywhere near the bridge, they would see the flashing lights from miles away across the flat coast land. Quickly, Sheets turned the waverunner north to intercept Joe.

They idled in the center of Indian River Bay a mile west of the bridge and waited. Ten minutes later, blue and red flashers approached from both directions and crawled up the bridge, meeting in the middle. Just another bogus call, the cops probably said to each other. As soon as the flashers disappeared and the headlights made their way down toward each end of the span. Sheets breathed a sigh of relief and sank onto a vinyl settee. "Take us through, Captain."

Chapter 51

With his foot steering the sailboat south towards Wallops Island and his cache of military hardware that he knew they'd need, Sheets finished cleaning the sniper rifle and put the lid back on the little metal can of gun oil. Fatigue began to settle in on him and he wondered if only the tang of the oil had been keeping him alert. He glanced to his left where Buzz was sitting silently in the complete blackness of the moonless night. Probably asleep.

The light wind and heavy air caused the sails to luff and slow their progress, frustrating him. They needed to move. He glanced to the west, across the couple of miles to the coast, hoping for a freshening breeze. They were still not past Ocean City with the nearly forty mile long Assateague Island left to traverse, but he knew their slim chances would diminish to zero without some basic operational gear, night vision equipment, body armor, radios and more. Real military stuff he'd been given to test over the years and stashed away, never knowing why. Hidden in plain sight outside the fence of the Surface Combat Systems Center a super high-tech Navy facility. It made him smile now to think that The Admiral himself had posted Sheets there for a month, and he'd found the blind spot in the perimeter security where lay hidden the weapons he'd turn on the old man.

The unexpected day of fighting had worn him down, his leg throbbed with pain and his shoulder muscles still burned. He wondered if the day might have turned out differently if not for his last minute decision to arm Egg and Buzz. Definitely yes, he thought, The Deltas would have been able to concentrate on him, then turn their attention to the others. Maybe his only good decision so far. His planning needed to improve. He flashed back to Joe savagely slamming the man in the parking lot with the gun. It made him wonder if he was irretrievably lost, but he also had seen a spark of the old Joe while they hid out at Northbeach.

He rotated his aching shoulders. SEAL training included being worked to the point of exhaustion and then being forced to do more. 48 hours or more was routine. What ailed him? Was stamina the first thing to go as you aged? He smiled. Thirty-seven years old. It was probably just the adrenaline clearing his system. And maybe he was carrying the added weight of worry of splitting the crew into three. Jamie, her husband, daughter and Three, hopefully safely on the road to Lake of the Woods, but he had no way to know. Joe, Egg and Marie sailing north. He sighed; their safety was beyond his control now.

He looked up at the constellations and knew it was somewhere between three and four a.m. He pulled the AK-47 into his lap in and began to disassemble the automatic rifle.

Through the veil of fatigue, he heard a murmur from the seat next to him. He wondered if Buzz was talking in his sleep, then listened more closely and recognized distinct words. *Spring. Bolt carrier. Gas tube.* Buzz was listing the parts as Sheets removed them from the weapon.

The tiredness fell away. On alert, Sheets thought back to the firefight that morning and the way the little man had popped the magazine in and out without looking. He remembered seeing Buzz raise the rifle to his shoulder and fire in a way only a person with training would. He was sure now that Buzz had fired the shot that took the Delta leader down off the helm.

If the Tech-9 from yesterday morning had given him the drug connection needed to make sense of the attack, the AK-47 knowledge was even more troubling. Mr. Kalashnikov's rifles were the weapons of choice of every bad guy in the world. Ubiquitous in the Middle East. All terrorists everywhere trained with them and Yemen was a terrorist hotbed. Shit, he thought.

He moved his hand to the SIG Sauer at his side. "Mentally dismantling an AK in complete darkness without touching it, just by listening?" Sheets saw the reflection of the lights from the high-rise condos in Buzz's eyes turn his way. The Yemeni was otherwise invisible in the black night.

"Muscle memory." The eyes closed and Buzz disappeared.

"From where? When?" Silence fell and Sheets wondered if Buzz had heard, but the only other noise was the sound of the bow slicing through the water.

Finally, one word. "Camp"

"Camp? Weapons camp? Philadelphia has gun camps?" Sheets looked over, despite knowing he couldn't see Buzz in the gloom.

Another pause, then, "Not Philly. Yemen. Al Qaeda."

Warning signals blared in his head and he moved the pistol to his lap, finger on the trigger. Al Qaeda. Despite losing his faith in his father, the military and his country on his long trek out of Afghanistan six years ago, he retained his full measure of hatred for the Taliban and Al Qaeda. The faces of religious insanity. Unthinking ciphers dedicated only to hatred and violence.

"Al Qaeda?" Sheets could hear vehemence in his own voice.

Several moments passed before Buzz spoke again. Softly. "We all trusted you when we knew nothing about you. We had faith in you before and after we heard your story. Faith this morning when you left in the Zodiac that you weren't abandoning us."

The brown fingers, long for someone of his stature, appeared in Sheet's mind. Fingers next to his own, placing the parts of the engine of the ultralight on a blue tarp as he and Buzz took it apart for repair. He tried to picture those fingers piloting a plane into a tower or strapping a bomb to his body and couldn't. Somehow this reassured him. "Fair point." He eased back on the trigger, but remained ready. "Tell me."

The eyes appeared again and moved upward to the swath of stars, bright in the blackness. "I was twelve. My father was wealthy by Yemeni standards where nearly everyone is poor. He was in import and export. I was sent to private schools. We led a privileged life." Buzz began tapping a foot lightly against the cabin roof. "Then everything changed"

Sheets waited for Buzz to continue, wishing he could see the little man's face. He was trained in interrogation techniques, which relied in large part on reading facial gestures and body movement. The foot tapping was probably a sign of nerves, but hell, he thought, he had been nervous himself when he finally told his story. It had only been two nights ago. Two nights ago, sitting in Jamie's restaurant. He wondered again if she and her family were safe.

"I don't know what happened," Buzz was saying. "Why my father sent me. I only saw him one time after the terrorist camp and that was to receive a beating from him."

"Tell me about the camp."

"It was 1990. Al Qaeda was new in the country. Not many people even knew of it. The camp was near the border with Oman. There were maybe a hundred kids. We lived in tents. Exercise and weapons training from dawn until after sunset. We had breaks only for prayers and religious indoctrination." Buzz paused and the tapping stopped.

Sheets glanced to the shore. He could still see the lights from the pyramid shaped condo in Ocean City, which meant they were still less than halfway through the long beach town and the wind had yet to freshen. He looked around for lights from any other boats, but they were alone on the water.

When Buzz spoke again, his voice seemed to tremble with emotion. "Yemen is so poor. Half the people are malnourished.

The kids in the camp were the poorest of the poor. The two meals a day they got were probably two more than they ever ate regularly in their villages. They had never seen the inside of a school. But they were rock hard from scrambling to stay alive. They would have believed anything the trainers told them. Did believe. I must have looked like a soft fatted calf to them."

The emotion in the man's voice led him to believe the story. "How did you survive?"

"I learned to take apart the weapons faster than anyone else and I could spout the religious words and anti-American slogans better than the others. I think the leaders thought I would break, and I nearly did." The light tapping resumed.

"I think they experimented on us with drugs. To see if they could get even more out of us. It must have been in the food, for we would all get this burst of energy after meals. Looking back, I would guess crystal meth. Manic energy. We could run all night.

"One day, after the evening meal, they cancelled the training session and told us to go and read our Korans in the tents. The leaders had a meeting with their leaders. I sometimes wonder if it was Bin Laden himself, if he was there the night that I nearly died. Should have died." Buzz fell silent.

"Get it out," said Sheets. He set the SIG down, thinking of the similarities in his own early life to Buzz's.

"None of the kids could read, so I sometimes read verses to them. Love or hate the religion, it is still a beautiful book. But that evening, I felt crazy, like they had accidently overdosed us and we weren't even able to run it off. I started reading from the Koran and then began to change the words, mocking Allah, trying to get the others to laugh. I even began to imitate the voices of the trainers while I performed."

His voice falling to a whisper, Buzz continued, "A couple of the kids laughed. Thankfully, only a couple. They were shot. I might as well have pulled the trigger myself. I killed them."

Sheets heard the catch in the little man's voice and thought of the boy dying in Afghanistan. All he could think to say was, "No." And wished he had the words to comfort him. He knew if Bubbles was here, alive, she would have the right words, and he felt a spike of grief and a sinking feeling knowing she was gone. All that he said to Buzz was, "I still see the Afghani boy at night."

"It took ten years before I stopped seeing those boys every night in my dreams."

"How did the leaders know who laughed?" A gust of wind pulled the mainsail tight and the Morgan surged forward, but quickly slowed again as the wind died.

"Hidden cameras. As it turned out, we were watched at all times. They dragged me into the commander's tent and replayed my performance again and again as they beat me. Before I passed out, I heard two shots and they thanked me for identifying the other infidels."

"Why didn't they kill you too?" But he knew the answer. Buzz's father had been the Yemeni version of The Admiral.

"I can only guess that my father must have been funding Al Qaeda. The camps. I'll never know if he became a true believer or was just in it for the money. I'm sure at that point his importing included weapons. Maybe they wanted to let him deal with me. I was more dead than alive when he finished, but he couldn't bring himself to kill me and shipped me off to live with his brother in Philly."

Fathers, thought Sheets, as a flash of distant lightening brightened the sky while the squall line before the storm filled the sails, and the sloop shot forward into the dark night.

Chapter 52

The sign said, Mountain Time Zone. Sheets glanced at Buzz at the wheel of the Ford Excursion, his eyes locked in on the highway. He'd insisted on doing all the driving since they'd left Long Island. Rocky Mountain Time. That's what Sheets remembered it being called and wondered when it had changed. Joe would know, but he was a mile ahead with Egg in the old Hummer, the one that was an actual military vehicle. Buzz with his questionable connections in the Yemeni immigrant community had been able to find one along with the big SUV.

Time zone change or not, there were still no mountains. Just mile after mile of flat hypnotic fields with lights from the scattered farms providing the only breaks in the darkness besides the endless array of stars. Each house was protected by a row of trees on the west side—an attempt to block the constant wind, Sheets guessed. He thought of the movie *Raiders of the Lost Arc,* one of Joe's favorites, with the plane superimposed over maps to represent travel. That's what the trip had felt like so far. He had tried to picture a map of the middle of the country, but kept getting it wrong. He'd be expecting Iowa or a Dakota and get Missouri or Kansas instead. He could draw by memory an accurate map of Afghanistan, had been in all the Stans, Uzbekistan, Turkmenistan and every other country in the Middle East, but the middle of his own country was largely a mystery to him.

He glanced behind him. Marie was asleep in the cargo area atop the hidden compartment where the weapons were cached. He smiled. She'd been full of surprises. Said she hitchhiked across the country several times before settling down. The arguments between her and Joe reminded him of the mock bickering between Joe and Bubbles. She was able to pull Joe back from his anger and despair and keep him focused. The digital clock on the radio read 3:37AM. Let her sleep. Kansas couldn't possibly go on much longer, he thought. Wyoming was next, he guessed.

Five miles per hour over or under the speed limit. At least a one mile cushion between the two vehicles. Use rest areas, preferably during the day when there was more in and out activity. Park at opposite ends of the lot. The most anonymous route possible. A route which would carry them south and west of the target in Idaho. And a big empty place somewhere to rest and train for a couple weeks. Those had been Sheets' travel criteria.

Nevada, Joe had said, and reeled off some statistics. Seventh largest state, a little over 110,000 square miles. Population just over 2.5 million. Two thirds of them lived around Las Vegas, the rest mostly in Reno and the other towns along Interstate 80. That left a huge empty swath in the center of the state. He said he had driven the entire length of the old US Route 50, supposedly the longest road in the country, which started about twenty miles south of Dewey in Ocean City and ended in Sacramento.

There was a sign somewhere west of the Utah border, stating that Route 50 in Nevada had been designated the loneliest road in America and he couldn't disagree, Joe had told them. Marie hadn't argued, she just shook her head and told the crew that hitchhikers in her day were told to stay on I-80 or bypass the desolate state altogether. Sheets watched as a green sign appeared in the lights of the Excursion. Exit 438 Burlington, Colorado 5 miles. Wrong again, he thought.

A car had entered the highway behind them at the Kanorado exchange and Sheets checked the side mirror. It was maintaining a constant distance of about 100 yards. He glanced at Buzz. "You watching that car," he said softly, hoping not to wake Marie, but wishing she was at the wheel.

"Yeah, I can't tell if it's a cop."

"Slow down just a little. Let's see what he does." Sheets eased the Sig-Sauer from under the seat and double clicked the CB radio handset to alert the Hummer of potential trouble. They'd seen plenty of police vehicles along the way and hadn't received so much as a second glance. The Texas license plates on the SUV were supposedly traceable to a legitimate company in Dallas, but he still worried that The Admiral, with access to every computer of every agency in every state, in addition to every super-computer of all the intelligence agencies, could find a way to track them. And this isolated patch of dark highway would be a good place for an ambush.

"He seems to be matching our speed," Buzz said, as his gaze flicked between the road and the side mirror. "Wait. Someone behind him now. Shit. It is a cop."

And with that, the high beams of the police car came on, followed by a strip of blue and red flashers as the vehicle rapidly closed the gap between them. Trapped, Sheets thought, as he moved his hand to the door lever in preparation for rolling out. Calm, he told himself as he felt his heart rate amp up. The Excursion vibrated as Buzz crossed the rumble strip onto the shoulder. And with that, the police car moved to the passing lane and flew past, the trooper never even glancing in their direction. Buzz angled the SUV back into the travel lane, took the CB handset from Sheets and clicked an all clear signal.

He glanced at Marie who had slept through the incident and when he turned back, he noticed that Buzz was staring at him.

"Could you have…." Buzz glanced to the road then back to Sheets. "Taken care of the cop?"

The answer was clear to him, but he couldn't respond. Anyone sent after them would be filled with misinformation supplied by The Admiral, and Sheets would be put in the position of harming, possibly killing an innocent person. It roiled his stomach and he turned away from Buzz. He could only pray that he could find his father and end this before that happened.

"I understand," Buzz whispered.

ψ ψ ψ

He was fixing a map of the country in his head now. He'd loved Montauk, where they'd hidden the two boats. Hidden in plain sight in the case of Egg's motor yacht. Right back in the slip that she'd borrowed it from months earlier. Sheets saw the first evidence of sex as a weapon as well, as Egg charmed the young guy who watched the deserted marina in the off season. She talked the guy into hiding Sheets' sloop in the drydock facility and got him to let Buzz and Marie borrow his car to track down the vehicles that they needed. The ten thousand dollars they'd paid him hadn't hurt either, with the promise of that much more on their return.

Light filled the SUV, and Sheets twisted and glanced through the tinted rear glass. Jesus, he thought, not again, but it was only a semi with a tandem trailer that swung into the left lane and passed them, going at least 85, making up time on the nearly empty road. The edginess from the police incident had yet to settle in him. Another sign loomed out of the darkness as he turned back to face front. Denver 168   Salt Lake City 599. He knew the plan was to leave the Interstate before Salt Lake.

He saw the turn signal of the Hummer blink in the distance as it took the exit for Burlington, which offered the Kit Carson museum as an attraction. Buzz stayed on I-70. They had all agreed to have the vehicles drive on parallel roads when possible so they wouldn't always appear to be traveling as a convoy. He stretched his legs and felt a twinge from the wound above his knee.

Buzz had sewed up the leg while they were anchored off of Wallops Island, after Sheets had retrieved the weapons and communications gear he kept hidden there. Exhaustion had proved to be a much bigger problem on the three day sail to Montauk. The storm which had hit on their way south to Wallops had lasted for most of the trip up the coast including the eastward leg along Long Island. Sheets had remained at the helm to control the sloop in the high winds and seas. When they finally sailed into the sheltered harbor on the north end of Long Island, he had passed out from fatigue.

He'd slept for the better part of forty-eight hours in one of the staterooms on Egg's boat. The tossing of the ocean had also kept Buzz from sleeping and he crashed for two days as well. Before he slept, Sheets cautioned the others to rest while they could, the first lesson any soldier learned while on duty. The leg had felt better after the rest and Sheets had taped it up and risked a couple ocean swims in the frigid Atlantic water, even after Egg had regaled them all with stories of the great white sharks which migrated off the tip of Montauk. Great whites made him think of Jaws which of course made him think of a much more ominous danger: The Admiral.

He'd insisted on the Hummer. He wanted a real four wheel drive, one he was intimately familiar with, not something that was more like a family sedan with four wheel drive thrown in to make the man of the house feel better about his marriage and children. Sheets wanted to be able to knock something down if it got in the way. They all laughed at him, called him a caveman. In the monotone, they were beginning to get accustomed to, Joe had said it was what Tarzan would have driven, but Buzz went out and went him one better. He found a real one. Military model. Desert colors with the flip open armored roof panels. Big steel brush guard. Sheets spent a day going over everything and found it mechanically perfect. Sitting in the driver's seat made him feel confident for the first time, that their mission wasn't impossible.

But they had left the cross country driving of the Hummer to Egg and Marie. The crew thought it would be too obvious for anyone watching to see Sheets or Joe at the wheel. Buzz and Sheets were relegated to seats behind the heavily tinted windows of the SUV. They had all worked on changing their appearances. Egg's jet black long hair was now short and blond. He and Joe had exchanged glances when they first saw it, but neither one said how much it looked like Bubbles'.

Joe and Buzz sported the beards that they had been growing since Bubbles' death, which just made Buzz look more like a terrorist than ever. Sheets' own attempt at a beard had been less than successful and he'd wound up just shaving off the patches and he had resisted cutting his long hair. The thought of returning to a military style haircut made his stomach turn. He felt the need to maintain the connection to his new world and the memory of her threading his ponytail into the bandana.

Landlocked. As the mile markers flew by, Sheets kept returning to the word. No ocean. No bays. No coves. No lagoons. Estuaries, Inlets, Sounds. None. The rivers they passed after crossing the Mississippi in St. Louis were laughable, barely streams by east coast standards. Landlocked. He'd felt it constantly in the Middle East. All the Stans were essentially landlocked except Pakistan. He tried to think of a word for the feeling of discomfort he felt when he was away from the coast. Malaise maybe. He thought of calling

Queen. Queen of words. She'd have one. He tried to remember her book tour itinerary and wondered where she was tonight.

They'd rolled out of Montauk at midnight two days earlier, hoping to avoid the worst of the traffic around New York. The sun had come up somewhere along the endless up and down of I-80 in Pennsylvania where coal was evidently still king based on the number of semis crawling up the steep hills with hoppers filled with the black anthracite. One of Marie and Joe's arguments had been over which interstate was more anonymous. Marie said I-80, Joe I-70. In the end, they wound up using both and to Sheets' eye, there wasn't much difference.

Ohio had been flatter than Pennsylvania with lots of farms. They'd even seen some Amish fields with black clad farmers riding behind four horse teams. Indiana and Illinois blended together and he mostly dozed through them. Missouri struck him as weird. There were lots of religious billboards, but shortly after each one, there seemed to be a sign advertising an adult store or a strip club. When they stopped in the center of the state to switch drivers, Buzz had said that they should change the state motto to 'Missouri Loves Company'. In their road weary condition, it took them a while to get it, but they all wound up laughing.

Sheets glanced over at the little man; "Wake me up when we hit the mountains, Osama."

"Your mother shall know the flesh of Mohammad's mighty steed." Buzz tried to snarl, but laughed instead.

A sleepy voice came from behind them. "Nice talk gentlemen." And they rolled on through the darkness.

Chapter 53

One hour until sunset. Three hours until he dropped over the fence into the ranch. Sheets craved some action and despite the feelings he had for the four of them, he felt a powerful urge to be alone. Ten days in Montauk, three weeks in the desert and almost two weeks in Idaho with no breaks had bumped up against his tolerance for companionship. It had made him realize how much of the last six years he'd spent alone and how important that time was to him.

His frustration was also peaking because they had yet to spot The Admiral. The growing confidence he felt in their plan to assault the ranch and shut down at least one of the old man's operations was tempered by the knowledge that if they didn't find him, they were back to square one in their effort to return to their old lives.

The posse, as Buzz had jokingly named them in the desert, was sprawled around the perimeter of the abandoned fire tower's top enclosure. The tower that Marie and Buzz had found. A completely unexpected coup—it offered a direct line of sight to the front of the ranch house but was mostly obscured from view by the surrounding evergreens. It was in bad shape, but Sheets had climbed one of the legs to the top enclosure and it seemed to be sturdy enough.

He looked at the group now, everyone but Buzz in the corners they had staked out around the spongy rotted center of the floor where water had dripped through a hole in the roof for hours on the two bleak days it rained. Everyone had lost weight— haphazard meals mostly eaten cold from cans because they didn't want to risk cook fires. Matted dirty hair and grime laden hands were the rule, for they had found no stream nearby. They needed to hit the ranch tomorrow, he thought—no later—or he risked them losing the focus they'd need.

"How about Roach?" Buzz said now over his shoulder, then returned his eye to the spotter scope trained on the ranch as the late afternoon sun cast him in silhouette.

"I second that," said Marie. "All opposed?"

"Roaches are fastidiously clean. When I worked in the kitchen, we'd hang the rubber floor mats outside at night and by morning the roaches had eaten everything off them." Joe stood and moved towards Buzz on the outside deck. "Plus they can live up to a week without a head."

Egg made her way to Joe's side and gave him a two handed shove. "Get out. A whole week?"

Sheets readied himself to jump up, before he realized she was being playful. There had been tension building between the two since an incident in Nevada.

Joe broke out in a half smile. Something that had become increasingly rare. "I swear. I read it somewhere."

Buzz turned and stared at Joe. "Not independently tested and confirmed in your laboratory? I hate to take Roach off the board based on a rumor."

"Sheets, you're the boss. We need a ruling." Marie looked at him and the others followed suit.

He eased back against the wall. "This is a teambuilding exercise. If Joe loves and admires headless roaches, they're out. Joe please, another nomination."

Joe moved to the scope and looked briefly. "Chigger. The man has all the cuddly characteristics of a biting parasite."

Egg snorted, then began to laugh and one by one the others joined in and even Sheets found the morose state he fallen into begin to lighten.

The last of the Vermin had been named. The four regulars at the ranch were now called Slug, Tick, Maggot and Chigger. Buck remained Buck and Renee was called Mama. She had only been seen outside the ranch house once, setting out two lighted carved pumpkins on Halloween evening. Marie was the spotter at the time and said that Renee appeared to be limping. When full darkness fell, the B-Dock crew gathered at the railing on the tower

to check out the jack-o'-lanterns and Sheets thought that they all
seemed cheered by the glowing reminders of normal life.

The laughter seemed to have eased the tension that had built
since they'd arrived in Idaho. Close quarters in the shelter of the
tower made sleeping problematic and made everyone edgy. Joe
and Egg's dust-up in Nevada seemed to be resurfacing. He'd
accused her of enjoying herself and she'd reacted with her
trademark temper before Marie calmed them down.

Egg had pulled Sheets aside that night and said she needed to
talk. It had been pitch black, but the stars were bright enough to
illuminate the shining blond ends of the hair that looked so similar
to Bubbles' that it made his chest ache. Egg hadn't seemed to know
how to start, then finally blurted out—

"I'm so sorry. He's right. I know we're all in danger, but I love
everything about this, the guns, the fighting, everything. I've never
felt so alive...."

And she went on, stringing all her words together in her
excitement and he was struck with the thought that they were two
people passing in different directions on the same road—that his
only desire was to get this over quickly, so he could get back to the
life he hadn't known was possible until six years ago. She'd reacted
just as every guy in the Navy did when he got tapped for SEAL
training. Gung-ho, glowing and wanting more. It made him a little
nostalgic for the time before...but before what, he wondered, as a
line from the Don Henley song The End Of The Innocence
flickered just out of his reach.

As she'd continued, Sheets reflected on the time they'd spent
in the desert and what he'd learned about each person and Egg in

particular. Within a week, she could outshoot him with the sniper rifle. He knew from experience that great snipers were few and far between. It took someone with an innate ability to slow their heart rates and exude the patience to wait for the perfect shot. Which surprised him with Egg and her short fuse. Sheets was a good shooter, never great. He could control his heart rate, but he knew he was much better in a firefight, when speed and reaction time were of the essence. He felt she could be a champion if she had the time to learn ballistics and train with an instructor better than himself.

He didn't notice that Egg had stopped speaking until she put her hand on his arm. "Are you listening?"

"Yeah. I was thinking about how good you are. How fast you've picked everything up." But, he thought, it worried him at the same time, seeing Egg moving so quickly down the road he'd abandoned.

"Really." She squeezed his arm, but her voice became somber. "I just wish Joe didn't hate me for it. I feel terrible for him." Her head turned at the plaintive howl of a coyote and they fell silent waiting for an answering call which came seconds later, echoing against the boulders where they'd set up camp. "I love that sound," she said as she turned back and the stars set her hair alight again.

"It could be your hair," Sheets said. "From behind, it makes you look like her. I think it startles him sometimes. It does me."

"I can change it, cut it off."

"Don't. I—we—need you concentrating on what we have to do, not worrying. As my loving father beat into me: Don't think. React. Let me worry about Joe."

"Okay." Her voice lowered. "Sheets, if we make it through this, I don't think I could go back to the way I was living. It feels like I should be doing the stuff we're doing here. You've watched me for a month. Could I be a SEAL?"

He knew the answer was yes. She was as ferocious and committed as any man he'd ever served with, but he knew he'd do anything to try to stop her, for the real answer lay in that elusive Don Henley line that finally made its way to his lips.

'We've been poisoned by these fairy tales.'

Chapter 54

One last sundown quiz, he thought, as the sun fell through the trees behind the ranch, for he'd decided that they'd go tomorrow no matter what he found tonight.

No sense wasting time on the layout of the ranch, which was burned into everyone's mind at this point. The front of the big house faced the tower as did the matching building to the north which the posse assumed was a gym and living quarters, because Buck and the other four men frequently sat on its front porch in shorts with towels around their necks. The only other structure to be seen was an open-sided barn which housed vehicles, a black Suburban, two ATVs, a blue four by four Silverado pickup with a roll bar and four dirt bikes covered in dried mud.

Sheets turned to Marie to begin the quiz, but hesitated as he always did, wondering what would have happened if he'd gotten his way and she'd gone to Europe with Three. He really didn't need to wonder: having her here filled him with relief. Because she was the glue. He didn't understand how years of being the wife of a complete asshole, as Peter was universally described, could have prepared her for any of this, but she'd suppressed the anger he knew she felt and become the person the others turned to for everything that fell outside his limited expertise of weapons and tactics. She could calm the explosive Egg, handle Joe's volatile new personality and she had so totally charmed Buzz, that he rarely left her side.

And if he felt a tinge of embarrassment that Marie had become their leader, it was okay, he was more than willing to recognize his limitations and concentrate on bringing his own skills back to the level the posse would need to survive. The other huge bonus had been that if Egg was a sharpshooter, Marie was better. Quite a bit better. A natural. Her eyesight seemed perfect, even at long distances and she could put multiple shots into targets without resetting herself. B-Dock was awed by her ability and they'd decided she'd be the one they left in the tower to cover their approach to the ranch. Their backup and communications controller.

Sheet had used the military slang, Tango, to identify the four permanent guys at the ranch and the posse had just given them each a number. Until Marie noticed that one of them seemed to linger on the porch for long hours, eating, smoking, frequently doing nothing, and she'd called him a slug and the first of the Vermin was born. She also wondered aloud about how relaxed the people at the ranch seemed to be and it made him wonder as well.

They had to know that the tower was there, had to have scouted all the land within shooting distance of the property, but no one had approached the tower in their time there.

He and Buzz had patrolled the surrounding area while the others did the spotting and took notes on the personnel and their comings and goings. He finally chalked up the lax behavior to that feeling of invincibility and superiority Special Forces developed. Hell, he thought, he'd had that arrogance himself, but something about it felt wrong, like he was missing something important.

After Slug was tagged with his nickname, Sheets had watched as the posse haggled over the names for the other Vermin and it drew the B-Dock crew even tighter together.

"Marie," Sheets said. "Give me the rundown on your boy, Slug."

She looked up from her conversation with Buzz and without hesitation, reeled off the particulars, "6'3" 185. Lefty—"

"How do you know that?" Sheets tried his best Drill Instructor bark.

"Holster on the left. Looks like he carries Glock. Always unstrapped."

The vermin had never been seen leaving the ranch without visible side arms, like old fashioned gunslingers. Idaho reminded Sheets of the Middle East sometimes. Six years in Delaware and, until that day on the water, he'd never seen anyone with a gun besides the police and duck hunters putting in their jon-boats at the marina ramp. "What else?"

"He's always drives. Arm out the window, rain or shine." Marie grinned. "Easy head shot from here. Just a couple hundred yards to the gate."

Sheets stifled a laugh. It would be a piece of cake for her. "Head shot, soldier? Head shot? Troops, how do we shoot? he shouted.

"Center mass," Egg, Joe and Buzz chanted. "Take em down."

"Still," Marie said, and pointed a finger in the direction of the ranch. "Bam." And they all laughed, but Sheets felt tension behind the laughter, their thoughts of actually having to kill someone lurking there.

One by one they discussed the ranch crew. After a week, the Vermin had become easily recognizable. Sheets had taught everyone how to estimate size and distance through the scope. Maggot was the shortest, about 5' 9", but he weighed at least 220 and had thick muscles across his upper body. Tick and the newly christened Chigger could have been brothers, each about six feet even and a little over 200 pounds. Both had sandy blond hair. The Vermin all wore their hair buzzed short which suggested to Sheets that they were sparring in the gym. Many of the Deltas and SEALS he'd known wore long hair, liking the wild man look it gave them. But, short hair couldn't be used against you in a fight.

"Buzz, give us a run-down on the ranch routine," Sheets said and tuned out his answer because they all knew the rituals as well as they knew the layout. He watched Buzz as he spoke, but he found himself thinking more about Joe. The boys were only fair with long guns, but Buzz could handle the assault rifle like a pro and Joe was pretty good with a handgun. Sheets had had them practice shooting from the Hummer while approaching targets and they both proved adept at shooting while moving. And both were great drivers. Sheets could picture them crashing the fence and making their way up to the back of the house, the second line of attack they had decided to use with Sheets and Egg assaulting from the front. He thought that Joe would be fully engaged, with the opportunity to confront Buck finally here and it scared him to think that the outcome of that encounter might prevent him from ever seeing the old Joe again. Sheets pushed away the thought away. One problem at a time. Buzz had finished speaking.

"We go tomorrow." Sheets looked at each of them in turn. No one spoke, but he felt the need to elaborate. "We're as ready as we can be. Every additional day adds to the chance they'll see us. And…." Sheets tried to put on his most serious face. "I need a shower and I'm sick of cold food from a can." This brought smiles to their faces, but he could read the nervousness behind each one except Joe, who looked excited.

"Logistics?" Marie asked.

"You and Egg take the minivan to a motel in Libby tonight. Get as much sleep as you can. Egg, you need to look hot tomorrow. Be back here by zero six-thirty. Buzz, hold down the fort here. Joe can drive me to the fence in the Hummer. Any questions?"

As usual, Marie took the lead. "Do you really need to go in there tonight? It seems like an unnecessary risk and we can't do this without you."

He knew she was right. The constant parade of bikers to the back of the ranch house had spelled it out quite clearly. The Admiral was running a drug operation. But some need existed in him to see and feel something tangible, a bag of pot, a gram of coke, anything. The man was his father. He was trying to hold onto an admittedly childish fantasy that there was still a chance it was all a mistake, one last chance that his father hadn't completely sold out.

"Something I need to do," he mumbled. "I'll be okay."

Chapter 55

The ground grew warmer, as if he'd crossed a boundary line. Sheets backed away from the heat and felt his ghillie suit begin to cool. The night was cold, but he didn't feel it except for his exposed hands and blacked out face. He reached his hand out and there it was again, ground at least ten degrees warmer than the cool earth he was laying on. He kept his hand out and began to follow the line of warmth, already fairly certain of what he'd found.

ψ ψ ψ

As he and Joe had driven along the road to the fence, lights extinguished, the moon providing a ghostly grey line between the trees, he'd toyed with the idea of just taking everyone at the ranch out tonight, on his own, not put any of the others in danger. He was confident, given the strangely complacent attitude of the

Deltas, that he could do it, but if he was captured or killed, B-Dock would still be in danger.

Joe had suggested that they just wedge a ladder into the open hatch of the Hummer for Sheets to drop over the fence from. The Deltas had had the trees along the perimeter cut away so there were no overhanging branches and Sheets was reluctant to directly contact the fence and set off any possible sensors. As they were maneuvering the ladder into place, Joe stopped and looked at him, the moonlight casting shadows across his tanned face.

"Don't do it," Joe said.

"Don't do what?"

"Go after them alone. Don't cut the rest of us out."

Sheets remained silent, thinking that traveling with the four of them was like living with psychics.

"C'mon, Sheets. After six years, I recognize the game face. You've had it on all day. Everyone noticed."

He couldn't help but smile. "No hiding from you mind readers." He paused. "Yeah, I thought about it, but I realized that you all would be so angry, I'd have to take out B-Dock too."

Joe's expression softened. "You could probably handle Buzz and me, but you'd definitely have your hands full with Marie and Egg." He shook his head. "One housewife and one slacker. You couldn't have guessed they could do this."

"I would have said impossible. Now I think we have a good chance tomorrow." Sheets touched Joe's arm. "It looked like you were joking around with Egg earlier. You two okay?"

"Yeah. I was so far out of line in the desert. I apologized. It really had nothing to do with her. I've only felt two things since she died; this acute pain and rage. I'm glad it's tomorrow. Face Buck—see if that helps the anger—I don't think the pain is ever going away."

"Tomorrow," was all Sheets could think to say and they bumped fists.

ψ ψ ψ

Sheets had taken his desert ghillie suit and modified it by adding local foliage. He knew he was nearly invisible to foot patrols, but the Vermin also had All Terrain Vehicles with automatic rifles mounted so that the rider could shoot from a standing position and he knew he was vulnerable in any ATV encounter.

It was early November and Sheets could see his breath in the mountain air. There was enough ambient light from the half moon that he had taken off the night vision goggles. He heard the whine of a two-stroke engine. One of the ATVs was approaching and he wondered if he had set off an alarm sensor. He looked around and saw that the only cover was the twenty foot tall remains of a tree which appeared to have been struck by lightning. He crawled behind it, turned to see the oncoming headlights and held his breath.

The SIG felt warm in his hand from being holstered under the suit. The lights were coming directly towards him and he flipped the safety off. If he was spotted, he'd have to go with his plan of a solo attack and wished he'd brought one of the assault rifles, but when the ATV was about fifty feet away, it veered sharply to the right and sped away. He let out a long breath, watched it dissipate in the black night air, then slowly inhaled... He pictured Marie telling him to bail out now, but he knew he couldn't.

He reached out to the stump to raise himself, but yanked his hand back. It was hot. Quite hot, and he noticed again that the ground below him was warm. He rapped lightly against the stump and it sounded tinny and hollow. He pulled at the bark and a chunk came away revealing dull galvanized metal underneath. Sheets crawled several feet back from the stump and looked at the top of the thing. A distinctive heat signature could be seen against the light of the moon. The stump was a chimney.

He'd made his way around the perimeter of the warmer ground. A buried rectangle approximately twenty by forty feet. Something warm, hot even, that required a stack to carry away the heat. Now he lay on his back staring up at the stars which looked so close in the thin air. Meth lab, he knew, though he was still trying to convince himself otherwise. Some part of him that he didn't understand not wanting to believe—even now—that his father had sunk this low.

He continued to gaze up at the sky, knowing now he was just being—what was that word Queen had called him when he'd refused to concede a point about something in a book they'd been discussing? Obtuse. He was being obtuse. He'd known what the damn thing was the minute he felt the ground warming.

A section of the ground at the northwest corner of the rectangle began to rise up and fold back, startling him and he raised the SIG. A head appeared in the opening and as a body rose up, Sheets looked at the profile in the moonlight. Ponytail. The outline of a beard. He couldn't be sure in the darkness, but he guessed it was one of the two bikers who came every week, stayed for two days, then took off. He watched as a second man appeared, lowered the access hatch and smoothed the dirt and weeds that camouflaged the cover.

The two men shrugged on leather jackets and the moonlight reflected off the leather and the patches on the back. *Brother Speed* over a winged death's head with *Boise* below. Meth cooks, Sheets knew, and as if in confirmation, a strong chemical smell hit him, lingering even as the two men headed off toward the ranch house. Sheets remained still until they were out of sight, then eased the hatch back open. He asked himself again: what the hell am I doing? He tried to picture The Admiral, a man who'd dealt only with military people in the time Sheets had spent with him, interacting with outlaw bikers and felt an odd sadness. Crystal Meth. And his father.

He knew he had to look and stepped onto the ladder inside the hatch, feeling for a light switch along the wall. Something metal smacked into his forehead— a ball attached to a chain and a quick pull lit a row of fluorescent lights. His eyes begin to burn from the overwhelming chemical smell. Ammonia predominated, but there were many others. He climbed up the ladder, pushed up the cover and gathered several breaths as if preparing for a dive.

The heat in the enclosure was unbearable and he unbuttoned the Ghillie suit and let it hang from his waist as he surveyed the enclosure. Corrugated red walls and ceiling. A buried shipping container, although that didn't explain the size of the thermal outline he'd felt on the ground. Cargo carriers were not standardized, but they had to be less than nine feet wide to fit on semi trailers for highway travel. He surveyed the enclosure from the ladder. It was spotless— like any research lab he'd seen pictures of. Beakers, Bunsen Burners, flasks, tongs. A silver exhaust hood covered a portion of the center of the room. Right below the fake tree stack, he calculated. It was elaborate. Electricity and plumbing as well, he realized, noticing the three bowl sink centered on the wall below him and he wondered what kind of money an operation like this would generate.

The long wall opposite the one containing the entry ladder had a crude cut in it and hanging across it were strips of heavy plastic like he'd seen in supermarkets to keep cold air in dairy cases or meat cutting rooms. He pushed them aside and entered the darkened space, reaching out and swinging his arm at about eye level until he banged into another hanging light pull that revealed a second corrugated container identical to the first, dimly lit by two uncovered bulbs, one at each end of the forty foot space.

This side was filled with drums and other containers. He checked the labels. Red Phosphorus. Hydroiodic Acid. Hydrogen Chloride. A label on a box caught his eye, and he heard his own intake of breath. *Danas Pharma Islamabad Pakistan*. He opened the box, which was filled with packets of powder, each one stamped with the same information plus the word: Ephedrine. Ephedrine, the essential ingredient in Crank, Crystal Meth, whatever pop name it had these days. From Pakistan, the Middle East, The Admiral's stomping ground. Sheets could almost see the old man's fingerprints on the packets. He inadvertently took a breath and sat down on one of the two cots, pushing aside two military style gas masks that he pictured the cooks wearing as they worked.

He was dizzy from the chemicals now, but even more, he realized, as he looked down at the Ephedrine, sick at heart that the childish hope he'd been holding onto was gone. The man was dirty, and even worse, common, just another small-time crook. He started to lay back onto the cot, surprised by his feeling of bitterness, but caught himself. You've known all this and moved on, he thought. You've seen what you needed to see. Get out now. He thought of using one of the masks, but the thought of it touching his face made him queasy. He risked one deep breath and pushed through the divider. He made his way up the ladder and threw himself out into the night air.

He now felt truly sick, sweat dripping from his chin, the chemical smell seeming to be coming from his own pores. Quickly, Sheets eased the hatch down and rucked up the weeds to cover it. He began to crawl to the stack, but stopped when his stomach heaved and continued to spasm until it there was nothing left to come up. He pushed dirt over the mess, crawled away, then flipped over and looked at the sky, gasping for air. High as a kite, he thought, but the stars, the same constellations he looked at from the deck of his sloop, seemed to center him.

After several moments, Sheets realized that he was cold, the ghillie suit still around his waist and the temperature dropping rapidly. He buttoned up the suit, rolled over, began the slow crawl back to the fence, but stopped. Joe would be worried, but Sheets didn't think he could make it to the evac spot yet, still felt weak and dazed. He flipped onto his back again and after a few moments, the lines from the song Joe had been humming since they'd arrived in Idaho came to him:

'When I close my eyes I see you, no matter where I am.

I can smell your perfume through these whispering pines.'

And he realized he just wanted to be done with it all: Drugs, Delta, Idaho, The Admiral, all of this. He needed a sailboat, salt air, open water and the solitude of an empty patch of ocean.

Chapter 56

One click from Marie's radio in his ear broke the stillness of the mountain morning and alerted him that the Deltas were on their way. Sheets was concealed in the tall growth at the side of the road, peering up at the sun, surprisingly warm for early November. A solitary hawk rode thermals high above the road. Everything was in place, he thought. Joe and Buzz were in the Hummer waiting at the south fence. He pictured the big brush guard on the front, Buzz behind the wheel, Joe's eyes filled with cold fury, ready to take the action to Buck and his friends. Marie, in the tower spotting. The sniper rifle, she'd proved so adept with, mounted on its tripod.

Nearly a month of training, information gathering and practicing each step until it became rote, and in the end, their plan mostly depended on two hardened men being suckered in by a pair of legs. But what a pair of legs, he thought.

The black Suburban pulled to a stop behind the minivan where Egg was grappling with a jack, her short skirt flapping in the mountain breeze. Two men dressed in camo stepped from the SUV, the driver tall, the passenger much shorter, thick muscles stretching the arms of his T-shirt. They approached her, leaving their doors ajar. Perfect, thought Sheets as he crawled from his cover in the culvert, the ghillie suit matching the beige of the dormant grass. He silently moved behind the passenger door of the SUV and trained his Uzi on the driver's back.

"Freeze! Down! Down!" Sheets shouted. Both men spun toward his voice.

Egg let the jack fall and jammed the end of a tire iron hard into the mid-section of the shorter man, the one they had named Tick. As the taller man, they'd named Slug turned, reaching for a pistol on his hip, Sheets fired a suppressed round into the guy's left elbow and the pistol fell to the gravel of the shoulder, the man howling in pain. As Tick started to rise up, he also reached for the holster on his hip. Egg swung the tire iron and connected with the side of the blond high and tight hair at his temple, sending him to the ground with a thud. In one fluid motion, she tossed the tire iron into the back of the minivan and pulled a SIG-Sauer from the spare tire compartment.

"Hands on head," Sheets said and Slug raised one hand to his neck, unable to move the other. Egg trained her pistol on the man as Sheets stepped from behind the door, moved to the van and stripped off the camouflage suit. He had camo underneath, identical to the two men's. He grabbed a roll of duct tape, returned to the unconscious Tick and unsheathed his dive knife. He pulled off the man's boots and cut off the guy's clothing. Like clockwork so far. The twinge of nerves he'd felt while waiting was gone, the feeling of dead calm he remembered from his previous ops settling over him.

Egg looked exhilarated and pointed at the man on the ground. She turned to Slug, and said, "I hope the rest of you are better than that."

"You'll find out soon enough, bitch. We got twenty guys up there that'll be happy to see a slut like you."

Egg stepped toward the driver. "You do n—"

"Sshh." Sheets grabbed her arm. "Cool wins." He quickly checked for weapons and comms gear in Tick's clothing, tossed the man's boots into the culvert and the rest into the van, then pulled Tick's arms behind his back and took several turns of tape around his wrists. He lifted the man into the van and taped his ankles, slapping a piece across his mouth as well. He pulled a pair of black pants from the van and handed them to Egg. She pulled them on, tore away the skirt and pulled combat boots on in place of the flats she'd been wearing.

"Sit down." Sheets motioned Slug to the ground. The man eased himself down with the good arm, grimacing with the effort, sweat beading on his forehead. Sheets approached with the knife and glanced at Egg. "Keep the gun on him." He cut the laces from Slug's boots, pulled them off and tossed them into the ditch, then told him to stand up. The man struggled to his feet, gasping when he put pressure on the wounded arm, and Sheets removed everything from his pockets, dropping a cell phone to the gravel and stomping it to pieces before kicking it into the grass.

Movement across the road caught his eye and he raised his Uzi, but it was a white-tailed deer, more startled than he was, and it jumped back into the trees with a single bound.

"Walk to the driver's side." Sheets checked his watch. Seven and a half minutes. Perfect so far and no vehicles coming from either direction. Egg followed Slug to the SUV, her pistol held in a two-fisted grip as she covered him while he slid into the seat. Sheets set his Uzi on the hood of the vehicle and extended two arms into the air. In response, he received two clicks from Marie in his earpiece. He moved to the passenger seat of the Suburban and pressed the machine gun to the driver's ribs. Sheets waited until Egg had slammed the hatch on the minivan and returned to the driver's seat. She gave him a wave as a stream of white began to trickle from the van's exhaust pipe. His spike of anger at her earlier flare-up had passed and he hoped that it had only been first-op jitters.

"Eyes straight ahead. Hand on the wheel at eleven o'clock. If it moves from that position, I shoot. Proceed to the ranch gate. Look to the camera. Once, or I shoot. Do not exceed thirty miles per hour, or I shoot. Are we clear?" When Slug didn't respond, Sheets nudged the man's damaged arm with the Uzi. "Clear?"

"Shit," Slug said, wincing, but he nodded and pulled the SUV out around the minivan, sweat forming again on his brow.

One mile to the ranch gate. Two minutes. Sheets checked the side mirror. Egg was pulling out, thirty seconds behind. They passed a speed limit sign that had been shot so many times only a five was still visible and then the ranch house and gym came into view. No one in sight and no dust rising from the driveway. He keyed his mic and said, "Buck?"

"Buck plus two in the gym. Cooks in the kitchen." Marie's voice was calm in his ear. "No sign of mama."

Slug slowed as he made the turn into the ranch, stopping as the camera pivoted to the driver's window. As they pulled past the camera, Sheets leaned to the left and elbowed Slug in the temple, pushed him away, grabbed the wheel and stomped his foot onto the accelerator. The SUV shot forward, Sheets struggling to keep it on the rutted surface with only his left hand. Rocks pinged against the undercarriage as he gained speed. One half mile to the ranch house. Less than a minute. He heard three clicks from the earpiece. The signal for Joe and Buzz to ram the fence and make their way up the back road to the house. He envisioned Joe popping through the roof hatch with the AK-47 and he was hit with a fleeting fear that all their efforts were for nothing if the old Joe never came back. Sheets glanced up to check the rearview mirror, but the cloud of dust from the SUV obscured everything to the rear.

Slug's feet were blocking the brake pedal, so Sheets let the heavy vehicle coast to a stop on the uphill grade as he turned towards the gym building, ramming the lever into park. He grabbed a pair of flexcuffs from his pocket and locked the unconscious driver's hands to the wheel just as Buzz and Joe appeared on the road from the back of the compound. Egg pulled past the SUV, jumped from the van and ran to the front door of the ranch house. Like clockwork, Sheets thought again. Too easy. And no Admiral, meaning this skirmish was only the start.

He watched as the Hummer slid to a halt twenty feet from the gym door and Buzz jumped from the driver's seat and poked the fat black barrel of his suppressed Uzi through the window. He eased around to the west wall of the gym and peeked over the edge of the first bank of windows. A soft sound was coming from above him, but his earpiece came to life, taking his attention away.

"Mama secure. Jesus, she's covered with bruises." Egg's voice sounded shocked.

Joe's voice crackled over the radio, "Asshole."

Marie cut him off. "Stay on task." Perfect, Sheets thought, she'd keep everyone focused.

"Clearing the house." Egg had responsibility for Renee and making sure the house held no surprises.

The last three men were heading for the door of the gym dressed in shorts and sleeveless tees, towels wrapped around their necks, apparently thinking the noise was the SUV returning from town, not an assault. Chigger, Maggot and Buck, fresh from a workout. Sheets made his way back to the corner of the building and waited for them to appear. When all three were clear of the doorway, he screamed, "Freeze! Down! On the ground! Down!" The three men started forward, then apparently saw Joe and Buzz. Chigger and Maggot fell to their knees. Buck snarled and made a move towards Sheets.

"Down! One more chance before you die!" Sheets put a round between Buck's feet and the big man sank slowly to his knees. He was even bigger than Joe had described him, Sheets thought. "Crawl slowly to the back of the SUV. Both hands on the ground at all times. Buzz, bring some duct tape." Something was really tugging at him now. Something he'd missed. Too easy, he thought. He couldn't remember an op ever happening exactly as it had been laid out. It was that sound he'd been unable to place. Somewhere above him by the gym.

As Joe held the AK on the men, Buzz had taped all three of the men's' hands behind their backs and had them climb one at a time into the cargo area of the Suburban, then taped their ankles as well. Egg's voice came over the receiver again, "The house is clear. Coming out."

And it hit him, what he'd heard. Sheets looked up at the roof of the gym to where, mounted under the eaves, two tiny black cameras were in motion, tracking everything with a barely audible whirring sound as they rotated and no doubt transmitted their every move to someone, somewhere. He could see The Admiral's arrogant smile, triumphant at suckering his son in.

He frantically keyed his microphone as his heart fell. "Everyone hold their positions. Buzz, Joe, take the Hummer. Head for the fence." How could I have not thought of this, he wondered? And in disgust with himself, he pivoted and shot down the cameras. But as he waited for that familiar odor of combat to leak from the barrel of the Uzi, his vision narrowed and he was overwhelmed by another smell. Dust.

When he looked up, the Hummer was gone and Joe was glaring at him from the rear of the Suburban with a look that spoke of all the despair, pain and rage that had grown in him since Bubbles' death.

"I'm not leaving without finishing this." Joe pointed at Buck with the AK.

Before he could even decide on the words he needed to say—I understand or I'm sorry—a sound rose from the south.

A sound from his past.

Unmistakable.

Rotors churning in the mountain air.

Chapter 57

Not a Blackhawk. Not a Huey. Sheets ran through the sounds
of the various helicopters he'd memorized over the years. This was
new. Ominous. The crew had not seen a single chopper in the ten
days of surveillance. He keyed his mic. "Cover," he whispered, but
he knew in his heart that it was far too late.

And it appeared then over the southern tree line, backlit by the
bright sun. Bristling with mounted weapons, rocket tubes,
machine gun barrels. A Viper. They hadn't yet been deployed
when he was in. Still in trials, but The Admiral had gotten him a
ride in one, and its speed and maneuverability had been
incredible. It was over them in what seemed like a heartbeat,

pushing down waves of cold air followed by a rising cloud of gritty dust. Above the hammering roar, a voice came from a loudspeaker mounted below the cockpit, "Throw away your weapons."

Sheets hesitated, glanced down at his Uzi. It would be about as useful as a paintball gun against the heavily armored Viper.

With a whoosh and a roar, the B-Dock minivan, parked in front of the ranch house, turned to a ball of flames. Sheets stepped into the lee of the SUV as a wall of heat passed over. He glanced at Joe, who had taken cover in the driver's seat of the Suburban, his expression of anger replaced with fear. The speaker barked again, "No more warnings. Toss the weapons out of your reach." Sheets complied and watched as Joe opened the door and tossed out his AK.

The Viper touched down and four men poured out. Full kits, helmets with visors, M16s, body armor no doubt, Sheets thought. They rushed from under the rotor wash and trained their guns on Sheets and Joe through the dust and dirt being raised by the helicopter. Sheets glanced at the Vermin in the Suburban who were all smiling. "Oops," Buck said in a rasp.

The rotors began to slow as the engine of the Viper spooled down and a man backed out of the rear cockpit. Even after six years, Sheets recognized him immediately and guilt stabbed him for what he'd led his friends into. The Admiral. Crisp, as always, in desert camo, pants bloused out over unsullied combat boots, a matching camo fatigue hat. As the noise of the helicopter abated, he smiled at Sheets. "Son, good to see you again. In case you thought to make a dramatic escape, I brought along a friend to dissuade you." He made a rolling motion with the pistol he was holding and glanced at the helicopter. "Don't be shy. Join us." And the Queen slid from the Viper.

Confusion hit him momentarily, his mind unable to process the shock of seeing her here. She has nothing to do with this, Sheets thought. The despair that crushed him was quickly overwhelmed by a rising hatred for his father and that imperious smile. He would have thought it impossible to think less of the man than he had last night in the meth lab, but that was nothing compared to what he felt now.

Wrinkled jeans, the shoulder length dirty-blond hair she took so much care with, flattened and sticking to the side of her face, but somehow smiling at him. She was wearing a military sweater in olive green, many sizes too big for her, sleeves pushed up in big rolls. Waiflike. Sheets tried to think of the cities she was scheduled to visit on her book tour, but remembered mostly cold weather places, Minneapolis, Chicago. Only one that he could recall, San Diego, had weather in which she might have been taken while not wearing warm clothing.

He thought it had been near the end of her tour, but it still meant they'd had her for over a week. He started to speak, wanting to tell his father she had nothing to do with this, but he knew it was a waste of breath. Their last encounter, the note he'd received at the marina, and what he'd seen on the ranch had told him everything he needed to know about the man. The Admiral would have no regrets about killing an innocent bystander.

The dust continued to settle around them and the acrid scent from the burning minivan seared his nostrils, reminding him of the aftermath of the fire on the Gypsy, and he wondered if Bubbles would have understood his need to have made this apparently futile crusade. Sheets tried to quickly picture where the rest of his crew was. Buzz couldn't have made it to the fence. Egg was still in the ranch house and Marie should be in the tower. The best he could hope was that the three of them could make their way out. His only goal now was to get close enough to The Admiral to kill him.

"Lambada, Lambada, you're going to die now." Buck was rasping out a little tune from behind Joe in the SUV.

"Don't react," Sheets said, but it was too late. Joe had turned from the driver's seat, fist raised, and one of the armed men now surrounding the vehicle yanked open the door, hauled Joe out and slammed him against the SUV. Breathe, Sheets told himself, as his heart raced. Nothing you can do. Two men approached Sheets and trained their guns on him from a safe distance. The Admiral walked to within five feet of Sheets, his left arm tightly around Queen, the pistol pressed to her ribs.

"Cut these men loose," said The Admiral, gesturing to the Vermin in the rear of the Suburban, and the Viper pilot who had followed the armed men, moved to comply. The Admiral looked back at Sheets. "William, William, William. Did you really think you'd get away with this?"

He saw Joe glance at him from the other side of the SUV, obviously as startled by the use of Sheets' real name as he was. Sheets first thought was not to reply, but he thought of the three crew members who had an outside chance of escaping if he could buy them some time. Buck and the Vermin were stretching their unbound arms and Slug wound up and launched a punch towards

Sheets with his uninjured arm. Sheets turned away and the blow grazed his chin and Slug's hand slammed into the window of the SUV. A broken hand to go with his elbow, thought Sheets, as the man bellowed in pain.

"Stay away from him. I told you he's mine to deal with." The Admiral pulled the gun away from Queen's side and leveled it at Slug.

"Frank was in the minivan." Slug shook his damaged hand and everyone turned and looked at the smoldering hulk. "And that bitch is still in the house. She's got a SIG."

The Admiral motioned at two of the men. "Clear the house. Do with her as you please, but no survivors. We'll track down the Yemeni when we're done here." He looked at Sheets. "Did you know he was Al Qaeda? A terrorist for God's sake. How low have you sunk?" When Sheets didn't respond, The Admiral continued. "The question stands. Did you expect to get away with this with a band of civilians?"

"Why did you wait so long to come for me?" Sheets ignored his father's question. He wanted to keep him talking, knowing that if The Admiral got a little closer and began gesticulating with the gun, Sheets might have a chance to get to him.

"Believe it or not, we couldn't find you. We were looking all over the world. I thought you'd hole up on some far-away island. Brilliant scheme, hiding in plain sight. Right under our eyes." The Admiral shook his head. "Delaware."

Over his father's shoulder, a movement in the barn caught Sheets' eye and he realized that he was looking at the rear end of the Hummer which was mostly covered with a tarp. Buzz. No one else seemed to have noticed. He took a half step in The Admiral's direction, trying to keep attention focused on himself. "Are you proud of your operation here? A United States Admiral running a skeevy little drug ring."

"Step back." The Admiral pushed his pistol hard into Queen's side and she gasped. "This little operation, as you put it, grosses close to two million a week. You have no idea how badly America needs its meth. I consider it a huge public service. I was hoping to talk you into joining us. Big money. You could have lived like a king."

A gob of spit landed on The Admiral's immaculate pants. "Fuck you," said Joe. He looked across the hood of the SUV at Sheets. "This can't be your father." The man closest to Joe grabbed him and slammed his head into the side of the Suburban and he slid off out of Sheets' view. The man raised his M-16 and pointed it where Joe had disappeared.

"Wait." Sheets heart fell. He looked at his father and was certain from The Admiral's expression that Joe's life was over. "I'll help you, just let the others go."

The old man smiled and hugged Queen closer to him. Her face seemed to reflect Sheets' own desperate feeling that there was no escape from this nightmare. The Admiral continued. "I trained the finest fighter in the world and forgot to teach him how to lie. Don't worry son, Buck has other plans for your filthy friend." He motioned toward the gym with the pistol. "Take him to the ring and watch him." Maggot and Chigger moved around the SUV and dragged Joe by the feet to the gym, his head bouncing from side to side, creating a furrow in the dirt.

Sheets turned his attention back to his father. The gun had not been returned to Queen's side. Keep the man talking, Sheets thought, and get just a little closer. "Where do you find all these war heroes willing to turn their backs on their country?"

"Delta alumni mostly. A few active. The country they swore to protect leaves them high and dry when they muster out. The finest and best trained men in the world, used to living on the edge, trained to kill. What can they do in civilian life? How can they get that high?" The Admiral again broke into his superior smile. "They're particularly good at eliminating the competition."

The two men who'd gone to the ranch house were walking back and Sheets' heart ticked up a beat. Egg wasn't with them. Maybe she at least had escaped.

"She's gone," one of the men said, the visor flipped up on his helmet now, and Sheets thought the eyes looked familiar.

"Are you sure," said The Admiral, the smile gone, and as he turned towards the men, he let the pistol fall to his side.

Without hesitation, Sheets launched himself at his father, closed his hand on his throat, and then felt the world go black.

Chapter 58

A look of doubt lit Joe's eyes momentarily. As well it should, Sheets thought. The man across the octagonal fighting ring probably outweighed him by sixty pounds. Mass increases force, he thought, remembering physics class at the Academy. The reason a cat doesn't tangle with a dog or a wolf with a bear.

Size matters.

Sheets watched as Joe's eyes returned to the flat dead state they'd been in since Bubbles' death. A good sign.

He glanced up at his own hands cuffed on the outside of the chain link surrounding the octagon, high enough up that he had to stretch to keep from losing feeling in them. He glanced behind him at two of the men from the Viper who had dragged him in and locked him to the fence. They had flipped up their visors and had Heckler & Koch HK416 rifles trained on his back. How fast had this all gone south? He looked out the big bank of south facing windows at the helicopter, motionless now, reminding him of a giant dragonfly and making him wish for one last look at an ocean.

Chigger and Maggot were stationed by the door, still wearing their workout clothes, but armed now with what looked like M-16 assault rifles. The sun coming through the windows was bright enough that no interior lights were on in the huge building. The rectangular space was precisely one hundred feet long and half as wide with twelve foot high windows filling most of each wall. The smell of stale sweat rose from the canvas floor of the octagon, an odor that had been pervasive in Sheets' old life and took him back to his childhood and the ring in the Charleston house where he'd tasted his first blood at The Admiral's hand.

The raised platform of the fighting ring centered in the space was eighteen feet in diameter and the fence surrounding it rose ten feet above the floor of the ring with the last few feet angled in toward the center, leaving only a small opening at the top. No easy way out. The rest of the space was filled with equipment, free weights, heavy bags and a climbing wall at the north end.

Blood began to trickle again from the wound above Sheet's right ear where one of the men with The Admiral had hit him with the butt of his rifle. He looked out at the sun trying to gauge the time of day wondering how long he had been unconscious. He shook his head. Pain lanced from the wound throughout his head, actually making him more alert. He began taking stock of the situation.

Hopefully, Egg, Marie and Buzz were on their way out of the state. Sheets knew now that The Admiral was unaware of Marie's existence. Buzz could probably hide out in the Yemeni community until the Deltas forgot about him. But what about Egg? He sighed. Feisty Egg. Sharpshooting Egg. She'd taken to his old lifestyle like a duck to water. He could only pray that she could find a safe place to hide if she had escaped from the ranch house and he felt a trace of sadness that this life that had so attracted her might end so quickly.

As for the Vermin, Tick was dead, incinerated in the minivan. Slug was out of commission with the wounded arm. Chigger and Maggot were at the door and Buck was in the ring with Joe. Two of the helo men were behind him, the whereabouts of the other two unknown at the moment. He glanced to his right where a narrow wooden grandstand rose ten rows high next to the octagon. Slug was sitting in the second row from the top, his wounded arm in a sling. In the top row, the Viper pilot sat next to The Admiral, who had an automatic pistol in one hand and an arm around Queen.

Queen, the brilliant Queen. At least the others had volunteered to be here. She managed a wan smile and it broke his heart.

Chapter 59

The Admiral looked for all the world like a Roman emperor above a gladiator pit, a big smile on his face, the shaken looking Queen, held tight against his side. Sheets realized the black pistol in his right hand was probably the SIG-Sauer Sheets had threatened him with six years ago. The Admiral spoke into a microphone attached to his crisp fatigue shirt collar as he looked down at his son. "You look a little peaked. I hope you'll be up for your match."

Sheets returned his father's gaze with no response. The man looked good for his age, just the spreading patch of grey in the high and tight hair giving him away. Sheets promised himself that no matter what else happened today, if they released him from the handcuffs, he would find a way to hurt or kill the man. Any lingering hesitation was gone.

The sound system came alive again. The Admiral spoke, "Our first bout of the day is a rematch." He paused to consult a note card. "Joseph Rath of Dewey Beach, Delaware versus Buck McGuin of Bonners Ferry, Idaho. Their first match went to Mr. Rath, but Mr. Mcguin disputes the outcome, due to Mr. Rath's use of illegal substances. Last man standing or alive wins. Gentlemen, please consult your seconds."

Joe walked over to the fence and looked up at Sheets. "What the fuck ails this man? This is like the ending of a movie where you keep asking yourself why the bad guy doesn't just end it. What's the show for?" He looked down and whispered. "She's dead and it's a game to him."

Exactly, Sheets thought, a ridiculous self-serving game. "I humiliated the man, nearly killed him, and it's been eating at him for six years. Plus, he's always seen himself as larger than life." Sheets paused. "If he wants a game, all we can do is try to make this end like those movies."

Joe reached up, weaving his fingers through the chain link into Sheets' hand.

The man to Sheets right moved in a step and stuck the muzzle of his HK through the fence and prodded Joe's arm. "No touching, faggot."

Joe didn't even look at the man. "Spoil The Admiral's big show if you shoot me, so why don't you just shut the fuck up." He left his hand on the fence.

As the man pulled the gun back through the fence, the front sight caught briefly on the metal. Sheets tightened his grip and leaped up, striking out with his right boot, and caught the guy with a vicious blow high along his jaw, just below his helmet, which flew off. The cracking of the bone breaking was loud enough to be heard throughout the gym, and the man collapsed without a sound. One more down, Sheets thought, as something smashed into his knee and he lost consciousness again.

Water dripped into Sheets' eyes as he regained awareness. Buck was standing in the center of the ring holding a water bucket. Pain was arcing up from his knee through his thigh. When he tried to lift the leg, a wave of nausea stopped him, but it was pain he recognized. Almost certainly dislocated. Something was touching his hand and he realized Joe was still there, his shirt drenched, a look of fear in his eyes.

"Jesus, Sheets." Joe's voice wavered.

He managed a half smile through the veil of pain. "Right where we want em."

Maggot had left the doorway and had his M16 trained on Sheets, while the other man knelt next to his fallen friend. "He's dead. Fucker broke his neck." The man stood and advanced towards Sheets, holding the carbine by the barrel like a baseball bat and Sheets knew what had happened to his knee and he tensed, ready to react. As the guy pulled back the gun in preparation to swing, a shot rang out from the grandstand.

"Put the gun down." The Admiral's voice thundered. "We'll do this my way. I warned you all to keep your distance from him. You'll get your chance."

What's he saving me for, Sheets wondered?

The man lowered the HK, ripped off his helmet, threw it to the concrete floor, glared at the old man, but said nothing.

The Admiral smiled and tightened his arm around Queen. "Do you see what a magnificent weapon I created? He said to her. "I think it's only fitting that we're here together to witness his last fight." When she continued to stare vacantly without responding, The Admiral paused, stared at his son, then circled the barrel of the gun in the air. "On with the show."

Sheets curled his fingers down onto Joe's and squeezed. "Watch my knee. Tell me when it's centered in one of the fence holes. I can't feel it."

Time slowed as he rotated the leg, fire radiating out from the wound until Joe, after what seemed like an eternity, said, "Stop. What are you doing? Oh Christ. Your knee's not facing forward."

He ignored Joe and focused on remembering what the medic had said when he'd dislocated his knee in a ship boarding training exercise. *Relax the quadriceps to straighten the tendon.* He pulled himself up and tried to let the leg hang loose. *Slowly ease the patella back into place.* He pushed the kneecap as firmly as possible into the fence and began to turn the leg. And was met with an impenetrable wall of agony. He found himself panting, heard his father's voice, but couldn't make out the words and realized Joe was shouting for them to get him down.

He closed his mind to everything else. Slowly wouldn't work. He had one chance. One slim shot. Sheets pictured the move. Jam the knee tight into the diamond shaped hole and wrench the leg to the left. Hurry, his arms were tiring. He made the thrust and pivoted and everything turned black.

When another splash of cold water brought him around, Sheets glanced up and saw Queen was squirming under The Admiral's grasp.

"Stop this, you asshole. He's hurt," she said.

The old man placed the pistol to her temple, and with a dead-eyed stare said, "It ends today. He will fight. Buck, Rath, center of the ring."

An anger as diamond hard as he'd ever felt took hold of him, and Sheets knew that whoever was put into the cage with him would probably die.

Joe turned away from Sheets' and peeled off his camouflage overshirt to reveal a tattered orange Miami Hurricanes T-shirt."

Sheets looked at the T-shirt, one that Bubbles had worn almost every night when she stayed on the Gypsy. Joe must have found it at her apartment and worn it like a talisman. Sheets thought back to all the nights he'd spent with Joe or with Joe and Bubbles on the dock, frequently just sitting silently, listening to the waves slapping against the hulls or the breeze rustling the ropes into the masts. He always came away feeling as they'd had a deep conversation, even when nothing was said.

The pain was still radiating out from his knee and it flared when he hung as far down as the cuffs would let him and planted his foot on the canvas, but he could move the joint again. He called Joe back. "Hold Buck off as long as you can. I think I can go. We have a chance."

Glancing down, Joe said, "Not with that—how the hell…? It's back in front."

"Lambada. Time to get it on." They both turned to Buck, snapping high kicks at the center of the ring.

As he looked at the man, Sheets wondered anew how Joe had survived their first encounter. At least 6'4" and 240 pounds, muscles rippling across his chest and shoulders, Buck was imposing to say the least. He wore an olive drab wife-beater and loose camo pants. His feet were bare and he bounced up and down, pounding his fists together.

"Stick and move," Sheets said, "If he tries the Brazilian shit, hurt him."

Joe tapped his fists together, glanced skyward, mumbled, "I want to hurt him," then turned to the center of the octagon.

"Thought about how you'll do without pepper spray?" The big man smiled malevolently, his voice a low rasp.

"Does your steroid swollen head still hurt?" Joe replied.

Sheets watched as the rash on the guy's shoulder and neck began to redden. Joe stood with his hands still down at his side, making no apparent move to protect himself. Joe was not a small guy, Sheets thought, but he looked half as big as Buck and he looked away sickened by the thought of what might happen. Sheets flexed his damaged leg to try and keep it from locking up. He didn't think this mismatch could last long and wanted to be ready.

Buck moved slowly towards Joe, still hammering his fists together. When he was about five feet away he launched himself, his right leg leading, the flat of his foot heading straight towards Joe's head. Stupid, thought Sheets, he'd never been a fan of leaving his feet in a fight—you sacrificed leverage and power. When Joe told him that Buck was practicing Capoiera, he'd shown him a few simple countermoves in the desert.

A smile came to Sheet's face as he watched Joe duck in towards the big man and move slightly to his left, Buck's foot passing harmlessly over his shoulder. At the same time, Joe brought both fists up from his side and slammed them into Buck's crotch. Buck moaned as Joe winced and backed away, shaking both hands. His opponent had obviously been wearing protection. Some damage had apparently been done though for when Buck landed, he fell to the mat with an audible gasp.

Joe circled in and managed to get a kick in to the back of Buck's leg. Sheets guessed he was trying to keep him down, but the big man was able to move to a crouched position and then to his feet. He did a slow shuffle towards Joe, still hurt, with his hands raised in a boxer's stance. Joe raised his hands as well and circled counterclockwise. Buck threw a left jab. Joe flicked his head to the left and the blow just grazed his temple. It was apparent that Joe had a speed advantage and that maybe he could keep Buck at bay for a while. Sheets put as much pressure on his knee as the handcuffs would allow and felt that the pain had diminished.

The left jab had left the bigger man off balance and Joe was able to step in and get off a solid roundhouse right to Buck's nose, bringing a trickle of blood. Backing away, he dropped his hand and shook it and Sheet's realized that the shot to the groin Joe had delivered had seriously damaged his hands. The good news was that Buck was probably not going to be doing any more kicking given the way he was barely moving his feet. He's got a chance with the big man hobbling, Sheets thought.

But now, Joe had become tentative, apparently afraid or unable to punch with his damaged hands. Buck was slow enough that Joe was able to slip most of his punches, but it was only a matter of time before he caught Joe with a big blow. Sheets continued to flex the leg, preparing himself for whatever was coming.

The end came quickly. Buck hit Joe with a vicious left hook which Sheets could not tell if Joe had partially slipped or not, but Joe fell to the canvas and didn't move. Buck moved in for the coup de gras and kicked him in the back of the head, but the damage from Joe's first blow seemed to weaken the impact and Buck gasped with pain again. The latch on the door to the ring was opened and two men entered, each grabbing one of Joe's legs and pulling him out to the edge of the canvas. Two men that Sheets would never forget—and another rationale for this ridiculous show became clearer.

As one of the men unceremoniously kicked Joe off the raised platform, Sheets couldn't be sure from his angle, but he thought he saw one of Joe's eyes open briefly, almost like a wink, before the orange shirt disappeared over the side.

Chapter 60

His knee flared again as he moved across the ring and sat with his back to the grandstand, not wanting anything to distract him. He pushed on the kneecap. The pain was intense, but it felt as if it was back in place. Closer now to the canvas surface he could see dark brown stains. Blood had been spilled here. Frequently. Sheets pushed himself back to his feet and shook out his hands. They tingled as the feeling returned.

Maggot had left his position at the door and uncuffed Sheets from the fence as the guard had held his gun on him. With one arm pinned high on his back, Sheets was pushed through the door into the ring. He put up no resistance—all of his concentration was on measuring the space and plotting the moves he'd need to make. It could be done and he let his mind go blank in anticipation. They'd had to skirt Joe's unmoving body and he'd quickly glanced away, knowing to worry about him or Queen or anyone else would pull his mind away from the one thing that mattered now. Their last slim chance. One jump.

A man entered the enclosure and The Admiral began to speak. Sheets tuned out the sound. No introduction needed. He would never forget the name or the face. Stan, the leader of the three guys from the mission in Afghanistan. The man who had told his guy to shoot the little boy. A chill run up Sheets' spine as the events of that night replayed in his head.

Stan was dressed like Buck had been, same bare feet. Sheets glanced down at his own outfit. Black T-shirt, black pants and his old stained combat boots. He had never understood the barefoot fighting thing. Steel shank boots could do some serious damage to flesh and bones. The guy wasn't as big as Buck, but he easily had thirty pounds on Sheets.

No smile on the man's face.

No posturing.

Sheets heard Stan mutter. "For Donnie."

And it took him a moment to remember. Donnie, the Delta he'd shot all those years ago. For innocent children, thought Sheets.

The bell rang.

The man raised his fists and moved in slowly. Sheets moved away from the fence and planted his feet, raising a sharp but manageable flare in the knee. Stan launched a kick towards the damaged side of Sheets' head. Sheets turned his head away from the blow, but it caught him on the wound above his ear. A shot of pain that traveled all the way through him, but he had largely slipped the kick. He had done this in every fight he'd ever had: Let the other guy have the first shot. See what he had, how he moved. Give the guy some confidence.

He shook his head as he circled to the center of the ring, acting hurt. He heard the sound of the door to the octagon squeaking open and risked a look behind him. The other surviving member of the mission, the guy with the camera, who the other two had called Boogie or Booger. Sheets turned back to the first guy just in time to catch a shot from the man's big right hand. It put him down onto the filthy canvas with a thud, but once again, he had ducked his head quickly enough to take most of the blow on the top of his forehead.

From his back. Sheets heard another sound behind him, the unmistakable click of a folding Ka-Bar knife blade locking into place. Doubt flashed through his mind. Had his skills deserted him? Two guys. One with a knife and one who had already gotten two decent shots in on him. He glanced up at The Admiral, still with the supercilious smile that told Sheets he believed there was only one way this could end. A feeling swept over him. The feeling of complete control he'd always felt in fights before. That smile would soon be wiped off the old man's face.

Sheets kipped to his feet, focusing on the pain in his knee, which seemed to be diminishing and backpedaled away from both men, while unbuckling his belt. He pulled a piece of molded plastic from the end of the buckle revealing a razor sharp edge. He took three wraps of leather around his left hand and looked to the man with the knife. Take out the weapon first. The Ka-Bar guy was much smaller than the other, maybe 5' 10" and 200 pounds. He gestured with the knife, telling Sheets to come fight.

Sheets moved to put the smaller man between him and the big guy. He didn't want anyone behind him. Sweat had broken out on Boogie's brow and Sheets realized that he hadn't even noticed that the hot overhead lights had been turned on. He closed the distance between himself and Boogie and swung the belt backhanded towards the man's knife arm, knowing that Boogie would be expecting him to slash from the outside in. Sheets grinned as the heavy buckle caught Boogie on the inside of the elbow. Bingo, Sheets thought. He knew the shot would cause a temporary spasm of the ulnar nerve, and he watched as Boogie's hand flexed and the knife fell to the canvas. Sheets flicked a straight right hand toward the man's head, stepping in simultaneously to kick the knife back to the edge of the ring.

Boogie stepped back and rubbed the joint. "Lucky shot," he spat.

"Funny bone's a funny thing," said Sheets.

Boogie bull rushed him then, trying to take him down, but Sheets easily sidestepped out of the way and grabbed Boogie's shirt collar as he went by, using the man's momentum to slam his head into one of the metal fence supports. As he slumped to the canvas, Sheets stomped on his foot and felt the crunch of small bones fracturing.

"Shit," he heard Buck say from the seat he'd taken in the grandstand before silence settled over the room.

Stan eyed the Ka-Bar laying at Sheets' foot. Sheets followed his stare and bent to pick it up, then tossed it to the man and smiled. "You're going to need that." He looked up at The Admiral again. The smirk had been erased and he'd let go of Queen, who'd moved a few inches away. "You should have ended this charade while you had the chance," Sheets said.

Sheets rushed to the center of the ring, feinting a kick to bring Stan's knife hand down, then swung savagely with the belt, the razor edge slicing open the flesh on the man's forehead, sending a torrent of blood into his eyes. He let out a roar of agony and the knife fell away as his hands moved to the pulsing wound. A chorus of groans rose from around the octagon as Sheets let the belt fall from his hand and knelt to pick up the knife.

The big man was down on one knee in the center of the ring pawing at his eyes to clear the blood. Sheets started to move towards him, then stopped, looking up at the opening at the top of the octagon. One shot, he thought, and bent to retrieve the belt. He tied it off in a figure eight around the damaged knee, then stepped back until he was against the fence. A movement caught his eye. Maggot was moving toward the door to the ring and raising his gun. Hurry, Sheets thought. He risked one last glance at the stands. Queen had edged a little further away from the old man and had her head in her hands. Perfect.

Stan hadn't moved, but the pool of blood around him was so big that Sheets feared he might bleed out and topple over. He gathered himself and took three long strides toward Stan, leaped to the man's knee, pushed himself to his shoulder, then launched himself towards the small opening in the fence top. He had just enough lift to grab the top pole and pull his body through the gap with one hand. As his free arm came above the level of the fence, he pulled it back and hurled the knife towards The Admiral.

Chapter 61

He supposed he would always wonder if he had missed on purpose. Three inches to the center and the man would be dead. The knife had entered The Admiral's head on his left temple, but had only succeeded in opening a flap of skin and hair which hung over his father's ear, bleeding profusely. Sheets had fallen back through the small opening at the top of the octagon, but had managed to hold onto the fence rail. As he hoisted himself back through the space, he saw The Admiral raising the automatic pistol.

The distance was no more than ten feet. A smile broke out on The Admiral's face as the blood coursed down his jawline and dripped off his chin. The gun continued to rise. "I guess it's fitting. I created you as a weapon. I should be the one to decommission you."

Sheets glanced at Queen, still seated just a foot away from his father. She had been spattered by the blood, but she looked more angry than frightened, and after a momentary glance at Sheets, she reached out and pushed The Admiral's gun arm with both hands while leaning into him with her shoulder, pushing him into the helicopter pilot sitting next to him. Sheets heard the gun discharge, but he was already in motion. He jumped from the rail onto the fencing and got enough bounce to clear the distance to the grandstand. He planted one boot in the face of the pilot, knocking him backward off the stands.

The Admiral was trying to raise the pistol again. Sheets had only managed a glancing blow to his father's shoulder. Sheets fell backward, his impact broken by Slug who was sitting in the row below Queen and The Admiral. He lashed backward with his head, but Slug had already begun to stand and he only connected with the top of his spine. Then he saw Queen rise and land a solid right hand to the wound on the old man's head while she unleashed a string of epithets. It sounded as if she were punching a sponge. She shrieked, hit him one more time and pushed him off the grandstand.

And then all hell broke loose.

The huge room filled with the sound of the helicopter roaring to life. It had landed only a few dozen yards from the gym, so the noise reverberated throughout the space along with a cloud of dust. Everyone's attention was drawn to the Viper sitting outside the south facing windows. Sheets pushed off the seat above him, driving Slug forward and toppling him onto the seats below. Weapon, he thought. He was now laying on his back on the flooring of the second row from the top. The top rows were now clear except for Queen and Sheets motioned for her to take cover in the footwell.

There were several climbing ropes suspended from the rafters just a few feet behind the seating. Sheets cautiously rolled up onto the seat above, crouched, sprang to the top level and leaped to one of the ropes. He pulled himself up a couple feet until he had a clear view. All heads were still pointed towards the south window. Sheets scanned the room quickly. The Admiral and the pilot lay still on the floor below. Chigger was still by the south door, now facing out towards the Viper. Maggot and one guard stood by the ring. Only Buck was unaccounted for.

Sheets saw the guard spot him and bring up his HK. Sheets released his grip and fell. A burst from the gun passed through the space he had just vacated, one bullet close enough to sever some strands of the rope. Sheets grabbed the line again to try to break his fall, but it slipped through his grasp, burning flesh from his palm. His good leg landed on the pilot's midsection, but the damaged leg hit the concrete floor causing an involuntary groan. He tried to stand, but the pain forced him down and he knew the fight was probably over for him.

The Admiral was finished as well. A bloody pool was already accumulating around his head. Sheets picked up the SIG that had landed on his father's chest. The chaos continued, blocked from his view by the grandstands. A sound he could not identify jarred him and the whole building seemed to shudder as the helicopter engine's roar ceased with a shrill whine. A brief silence was quickly filled with staccato automatic rifle bursts followed by another silence. Completely frustrated by his inability to see, Sheets pushed himself to one of the steel supports of the stands and pulled himself up on his good leg. He immediately fell down again as a loud thud and a tremor shook the floor. It felt like the aftershock of a bunker buster bomb. What the hell was happening? he wondered.

The unmistakable roar of a Striker shotgun reverberated through the gym and any hopes Sheets' had for the crew fled. Called a Streetsweeper in the U.S., a couple rounds from the gun's twelve round magazine could kill everyone in the room, and his people didn't have one. Shit, he thought, and glanced up, maybe he could still save Queen and escape somehow. If he could only move. As he began pulling himself to his feet again, he heard a shout above the mingle of voices on the other side of the grandstand.

"Down, motherfuckers!" And the Striker blasted again, followed by the sound of debris falling from the ceiling.

Not possible, Sheets thought, as he hopped towards the front of the stands. It had sounded like Egg.

"Clear." The sound of Marie's strong command voice came from the direction of the entrance.

"I think it's over," said Queen from above him. He looked up and saw her head poking out from the footwell. "Jesus, where did you find these people?" she asked.

All Sheets could do was smile at her through the pain and the draining feeling of relief that overwhelmed him. As he made his way to the edge of the stands, he could see Joe and Egg herding Maggot into the ring, where the other Deltas sat, dazed looks on their faces. Glancing past the octagon, he saw Marie on her knees near the door.

Buzz was down.

ψ ψ ψ

They sat side by side on the bottom row of the stands looking like partners in some kind of one-legged race. Sheets and Buzz each had a pant leg cut off at mid-thigh as Marie ministered to Sheets knee and the gunshot wound that had made a clean groove on the outside of Buzz's leg. Sheets had passed out for a few moments again when Marie pushed the kneecap back into place once more, but he felt the tape she'd wrapped tightly around it would hold it in place.

The story that Buzz, Egg and Marie were telling was almost unbelievable. The loud shuddering he'd heard was Buzz bouncing the helicopter into the gym entrance and severing a support column in the process. The Viper sat blocking most of the entryway, looking as ominous as it had when it first appeared on the horizon. Egg had found the ranch armory, buried like the meth lab. She'd liberated the Striker and then tossed a grenade into the access hatch, resulting in the ground-shaking thud that had knocked Sheets down. She still held the nasty looking weapon, cocked on one hip, as she glared at the Deltas sitting in the ring. Marie had directed the final three pronged assault on the remaining Vermin from a hiding spot outside the gym. And Joe had probably saved Buzz's life when he rammed into Maggot as he was drawing a bead on the onrushing little man.

The details of the battle ran together in his head as the crew talked over each other, high on their success and lingering adrenaline. Sheets' feelings of relief and pride in what his people had done had masked the lingering pain in his head and knee. Queen, who had witnessed everything from her perch in the stands and was now seated at his side, had not uttered a word until the others had fallen silent.

"You all were fucking." Queen shook her head. "Amazing."

Marie finished bandaging Buzz's leg and stepped away, and Sheets was startled to see Chigger staring up at him from the floor outside the octagon. He reached quickly for the SIG before realizing that it was only Chigger's head. He glanced at Buzz.

"Helicopter rotor," Buzz said.

They all stared at the severed head for a moment until Joe walked over and stood next to it. He turned to the others and smiled. "Maybe we should have kept the name Roach. He might have lived for another week."

And Sheets watched as one by one, they dissolved in laughter. His people.

Chapter 62

The old man looked diminished to the point that Sheets was left to wonder how he could ever have been in awe of him. Queen had wrapped duct tape around The Admiral's head as Sheets held the flap of scalp in place. She hadn't questioned, never said a word, which, after what the man had done to her, spoke to the levels of understanding she had that he knew he'd been blind to. Time, he thought, he needed time to sort it all out and hoped that the nightmare she'd endured wouldn't turn her away.

He tried to lift his father, felt his knee giving way, and Queen slipped her hands under the old man and helped until Sheets' legs were under him. They exchanged a glance and he turned to the door of the gym. A half hour ago, his only wish had been to see the man die, and now he was cradling him in his arms, hoping he'd survive. Senseless, he thought, and wondered if his friends thought he'd lost his mind. But Egg and Marie looked up from their seats where they were finishing bandaging Buzz's leg, and the expressions on all three faces seemed sympathetic.

The sun lit The Admiral's face as they passed through the door and Sheets could now see the creases that spoke of the man's true age. Joe was cuffing the last of the survivors to the helicopter skid and Sheets looked from his father's face to Joe's. If there was a reason left to hate the man, it was the lifeless glaze of Joe's flat stare, but all Sheets felt was emptiness. Joe stood and pulled open the door to the Viper and watched as Sheets set the old man on the seat, Joe's expression never changing.

The Admiral's eyes fluttered open and he stared at Sheets and said, "I would have killed you."

"That's the difference between us."

Chapter 63

"Cut him loose." Joe motioned with the barrel of the SIG towards Buck.

Everyone left alive—the ranch Deltas and the men that arrived with The Admiral—were cuffed to the skids of the helicopter. The dead were left where they'd fallen. Sheets did another count of the men in his head. It matched the number of men he saw. Everyone was accounted for. Renee, the ranch owner, was secured in the main house. They hadn't had the time or the inclination to figure out her role in whatever was happening at the ranch.

Sheets checked his watch. 3:35. They should go. March all the men to the meth lab, secure them inside and go. Every moment spent on the ranch was a chance for someone else to show up. Someone else to deal with.

The sun was well along in the southern sky and would soon disappear behind the trees. The thin mountain air would not hold the warmth of the day for long. Sheets wanted to be gone. "It's over Joe. We need to go."

"I need to finish this."

Sheets put his hand on Joe's arm. "There could be more people coming and Buzz is—"

"There's no need for the rest of you to stay." Joe shrugged off Sheets' arm and motioned again with the gun. "Just cut him loose"

I can't leave him, Sheets thought. He stepped forward and cut Buck's flexcuffs. Buck had a vacant look as he rubbed his wrists. Sheets was sure he'd been tweaking before his fight with Joe.

"Back to the ring," said Joe.

Buck said nothing as he stepped into the gym. Sheets glanced up to the support timber which had been severed by the rotor blade. The roof was sagging, but would probably hold in the light wind. Dark threads of resin had seeped from the cut wood, filling the air with an evergreen scent. Joe followed Buck through the door. As he passed, Sheets looked into Joe's eyes. Blue ice. Hard.

Marie, Buzz and Egg looked to Sheets. "He's right. It's not over," said Marie. Their faces were etched with fatigue. Capture. Recapture. Adrenaline highs and lows. A long day. Sheets needed to get them out soon. He looked at Queen sitting with her back against the wall of the building, sweater torn, hair tangled, face traced with dirt and sweat.

"We can't—won't leave him here." Egg walked into the gym.

Buzz and Marie each raised a hand and clasped them together. "B-Dock," said Buzz.

"Like a rock," said Marie.

It had become their mantra as they trained and traveled. Sheets looked at them and couldn't help but smile. Rode hard and put away wet, as Joe would say. Tired, dirty, yet unwilling to let each other down. He felt some measure of pride. He had never served with better. They turned to enter the gym.

"Buzz, can you watch from the door, keep a gun on these guys?" Sheets said.

"I'll watch them. He should be with the rest of you." Queen stood and held her hand out to Sheets.

"Do you know how to shoot?" Sheets glanced down at The Admiral's SIG. He'd already checked that a round was chambered. "The safety's off."

She took the gun from his hand and pointed it at Boogie, who still looked dazed from his encounter with Sheets in the ring. "Like this?" she said and fired twice, kicking up dirt between the man's legs. "How's that feel, asshole. Pervert. Ten days of you watching me. It made my skin crawl."

"Did he—?" Sheets stepped toward Boogie, who was fully alert now.

"No. Your father stopped him. At least I can give him that." And then Queen took two steps forward and kicked the man in the crotch. Even Sheets had to turn his head and wince, thinking that Boogie would have to be carried to the meth lab. She turned back to Sheets and smiled. "I won't need much of an excuse to shoot. Go on."

Buck was at the top of the three stairs to the octagon. Joe set his pistol down on the ring apron and mounted the stairs, flexing his hands. Buck moved to the far side of the ring as Joe closed the chain link door.

"One last dance, Lambada." Buck bounced on his toes and shook out his massive arms. He smiled at his own joke, but his eyes no longer held that steroid confidence from earlier. False bravado, Sheets thought. Joe didn't respond, just raised his fists and moved to the center of the ring.

There was still the huge size differential. Joe could not afford to let the big man catch him flush with a power shot. And it became clear quite quickly to Sheets what Joe was doing. Each time the big man threw a punch, Joe used his quickness to avoid the blow and then land counterpunches, all aimed at Buck's upper arms. Sheets smiled and shook his head in wonder.

The Rumble in the Jungle in 1974. Ali versus Foreman, Joe's all-time favorite fight. George Foreman was huge and seemingly indomitable. He landed punch after punch as Ali cowered against the ropes while the crowd in Zaire chanted Ali's name, fearing for his life.

It looked to Sheets as if Buck's arms were tiring from punching and absorbing Joe's relentless shots to his biceps and shoulders and they began slowly dropping, as a flag being ratcheted down a pole. When Buck's arms fell to his sides, Joe began to work on Buck's face, much as Ali had with Foreman, waiting for him to tire in the hot jungle air, then going to work chopping the big man down.

Blood was now everywhere. Joe's fists were turning Buck's face to hamburger. Buck was out on his feet, no longer capable of defending himself, his right eye swollen into a cowl covering the whole socket. When Joe shook out his arms between punches, blood from his own mangled fists mixed with Buck's, and showered out from his hands.

And, much like Foreman collapsing to the canvas in the eighth round from a combination of punches and sheer fatigue, Buck finally went to his knees, no longer having the energy to support himself. He brought his hands over his face to stop any further punishment. Done, Sheets thought.

Joe stopped punching, put his head back, looked up through the opening in the ring and said, "For you." Although he'd spoken in a normal voice, the words seemed to echo in the now silent room. Sheets watched as Joe stepped to the door of the ring, picked up the pistol with a swollen red hand and placed the gun to the back of Buck's head. A sharp intake of breath broke the deadly silence and Sheets glanced to his left where Egg and Marie were huddled in each other's arms, eyes averted from the ring. Buzz stood behind the two women, his eyes filled with sadness. Sheets felt all emotion drain from him except a hollow feeling of doubt. Was this why they came? Was this what she would have wanted?

Sheets started to move towards the stairs, needing to stop Joe. The reason he hadn't finished The Admiral and all the others crystallized in his mind. He didn't want the weight. He didn't want to carry these peoples' lives with him forever. Did Joe understand this? Sheets knew he didn't. He also knew that the old Joe would never consider doing what the new Joe was about to. He felt a hand on his arm, holding him back. Marie

"It's his decision," was all she said.

Silence in the big room. "She was better than you," said Joe, as the sound of metal sliding on metal rose as he racked the slide, checking to make sure a round was in the chamber, exactly as Sheets had taught him.

Joe pushed the barrel of the pistol into Buck's neck. A bubble of blood formed on Buck's lips as he attempted a word. Joe pushed harder, forcing Buck's head down.

"Better than you," Joe whispered.

Sheets lowered his head expecting the bark of the pistol.

He heard the sound of the wind outside and saw the glistening drops of blood on the canvas. He smelled the gunshot odor still permeating the air. And waited for the shot that would break the silence and his hopes for the return of the old Joe.

It did not come.

Sheets looked up and saw tears running down Joe's cheeks. Marie and Egg were stepping into the ring as Joe lowered the gun. Egg took the gun and set it outside the door. Marie took Joe in her arms and Egg joined her, tears streaking the dust on both their faces.

Sheets realized he hadn't been breathing. When he did, relief seemed to course through him with the oxygen intake. He felt the little man's arm around him. Buzz was shaking.

Sheets looked through the tall windows. The orange ball of the sun was disappearing through the trees. It looked distorted. He realized that he had something in his eyes and raised his fingers to them. Moisture. He glanced down to his chest then, and saw the single drops on his shirt.

Tears.

Chapter 64

"You're just going to let him go" Egg turned a fierce glare towards Sheets.

Buzz and Marie stared at him balefully as well. They were standing next to the Excursion, watching Joe's back as he pulled open the door to the terminal at Glacier Park International Airport, whose name seemed to promise more than the one small building could deliver. The place had a deserted feeling with just one other vehicle in the unloading area, a taxi, with its trunk open and its two passengers, standing at the curb waiting for their bags.

No baggage. No coat. No ticket. Joe had stood in the grey November morning, pulled a toothbrush from his pocket, given the crew a wan smile, said, "Just like Reacher," and turned to go. They had all given him a hug and begged him to stay with them. When the others were done, Sheets stepped in, put his arm around Joe's shoulder and turned him away from the others.

"I'll find you," he whispered.

"I don't want to be found."

"I'll find you anyway."

"It won't be easy. I don't even know where I'm going."

"You forget who you're talking to. Lord Greystoke—Tarzan—master tracker."

Joe shrugged out of Sheets' grasp and faced him. "I let her down. Didn't do what I came for." He turned to the terminal.

Sheets called softly after him. "It ended the way she would have wanted."

Joe gave a half wave and kept on going.

ψ ψ ψ

They hadn't made it far from the ranch after putting everyone who remained in the meth lab and parking the Suburban on the access hatch. Everyone except for The Admiral and Renee. Sheets had just left his father in the helicopter. The battered Renee had asked for a ride to her sister's house in downtown Bonners Ferry which was on their way to Route 2, the fastest way out of Idaho. She had collapsed in Joe's arms and he wound up laying her in the cargo area of the crew's SUV.

There was nothing left of the minivan but a blackened hulk and they'd stashed everything else back in the other two vehicles, leaving only blood on the floor of the octagon as evidence that they had ever been there. Sheets guessed that by the time all the different alphabet groups arrived—DEA, FBI, DIA—that the crew planned to call when they were safely out of Idaho, even The Admiral would be unable to explain away the lab and the damaged helicopter. It would probably never even make the news, swept under the carpet in the name of national security.

They had decided to caravan to Lake of The Woods and pick up Jamie and her family. Sheets drove the Hummer for the first time since Long Island and watched as the camera at the ranch gate tracked their departure. He idly wondered if someone was still watching. It seemed unlikely that The Admiral or his people would have wanted a permanent record kept of the ranch's activities. He glanced to the passenger seat at Queen, already curled up and asleep. She'd said she would write the narrative, take everyone's stories on the way home. The story that the various parts of the government would not want published, the stories that hidden away, would keep them safe.

Their combined smell and fatigue had stopped their retreat from Idaho on the outskirts of Kalispell, Montana, only about 150 miles. They had picked a motel based solely on which one looked the least likely to run out of hot water. Buzz had said just pick a national chain, preferably the biggest one. He said there would be big motels to catch the overflow from the national park, but would be mostly empty in November, so there would be no competition for hot water.

Possibly the best shower of his life, Sheets thought. Queen hadn't even woken up, he'd just carried her in and put her in one of the big beds. She'd said that for the ten days she was held by The Admiral and his crew, she'd only slept for a few hours. Egg had ordered pizza and they gathered in her room and ate their first hot meal in two weeks and decided to sleep as late as possible in the morning. Which turned out to be until almost 10 a.m., when they convened, still looking like zombies, and made their way to a restaurant where they proceeded to eat nearly everything on the menu. Joe was leading the way out of town in the Excursion, but only made it a couple of miles before turning into the airport.

ψ ψ ψ

As Joe passed through the door to the terminal, the others, continued to stare at him from beside the Excursion.

"You can't let him go. He's a mess." Buzz grabbed the sleeve of Sheet's jacket as the others looked at him with concern.

"Alright. Buzz, get some duct tape. We'll throw him in the SUV. I'll go get him." Sheets turned towards the terminal.

"Wait. Sheets is right. We can't do that," said Marie. "What are we going to do? He might try to hurt himself."

"I told him I'd find him." Sheets said.

"He could go anywhere in the world," said Buzz.

Sheets pulled a passport from the pocket of his cargo shorts. "Not without this."

"It's still a big country. Lots of hiding places." Egg shook her head.

"You forget who we're talking about; Joe Rath." Sheets smiled. "What do we know? He's hurting, he'll go for something he knows."

"The ocean," said Buzz.

"Warm water," said Egg.

"That eliminates the west coast. He always complained that the Californians mislead everyone, that the Pacific never gets warm enough to swim in. And it's November, so nothing north of say—Georgia." Sheets looked at everyone in turn. "One more thing."

"Bars," they said as one.

Chapter 65

T he bartender tapped the bar.

"Bottle of Krug," the man said without raising his head from the wood.

"Krug." The bartender laughed. "Look at this place." He swept his hand around, inviting the guy to gaze at the rickety tables and chairs, the only lighting coming from archaic neon beer signs. *Mabel Black Label* said one. Another extolled the virtue of Stroh's: *Fire Brewed in Detroit.*

"This is the second worst dive in Key West. Even I won't go in the worst." Which was saying something, since the bartender looked to be about 250 pounds and not fat.

The man put his hand in his pocket and slapped bills down on the bar. "One thousand dollars for a bottle of Krug."

Sheets sat in darkness at the back of the barroom, baseball cap pulled low over his eyes and watched the scene unfolding. He swirled a beer bottle on the greasy table top moving a ring of condensation outward. The only other occupied table was close to the bar where two men sat, each wearing yellowed wife beaters and cut off jean shorts. They rose and moved to the bar, taking stools on either side of the man. The bartender nodded at them and moved to the other end of the bar.

Maybe brothers, Sheets thought as he watched the wiry guy on the left ease the bills out of the drunk's hand. "Come on, we'll get you home," one of them said, as they lifted the man, wrapping his arms over their shoulders and carrying him towards the door.

As Sheets stood when the men passed him, the bartender said, "Stay out of it."

"I'll be back for you." Sheets smiled and turned to the door.

The drunk was already face down on the pavement in the alley next to the bar when Sheets walked by. The two thin men were rifling his pockets while holding him down.

"You're gonna want to let him go and put his money back." Sheets stood at the entrance to the narrow walkway, hands hanging loose at his side. Dim light was provided by a single bulb enclosed in a wire cage above the delivery entrance to the bar. Cases of empty beer bottles were stacked against the wall.

One of the men rose from the drunk, grabbed a bottle and smashed it on the wall, leaving a stub with three sharp points which he held out towards Sheets. The other glanced up, but continued searching the pockets.

"And you're gonna want to get the fuck out of here before you end up down here with him," the guy with the bottle said.

Sheets felt a little offended. A bottle? The guy would have to get real lucky to do much damage with a broken bottle. "Honestly. Last chance. You need to go."

But the guy surprised him. He didn't slash as most people might. He made a straight thrust which could have actually hurt or killed someone if he connected with the carotid artery he had aimed for. Sheets pushed the hand with the bottle aside and used the man's momentum to slam his head into the alley wall. His partner was scrambling to his feet. Sheets pulled a matte black knife from his pocket and snicked the blade open.

The second man took a couple steps away from Sheets further into the alley. He held up his hands. "I don't want no trouble."

"Set the money on his back." Sheets motioned towards the drunk with the knife. "Empty your pockets as well. Then do the same for your partner's." When the man had finished, Sheets pointed at him with the knife. "Pick up your friend and carry him into the bar. Tell the bartender that your hustle is over. I highly recommend that you leave town. I'll be back to check, but you won't see me this time and you won't walk away."

When the two men were out of sight, Sheets leaned over the drunk and stuffed the money into his pockets. "Joe," he whispered, "How much longer?" But he knew it didn't matter.

A week.

A year.

A lifetime.

This man had saved his life—given him a life. Sheets would protect Joe forever if that's what it took. My brother, he thought, as he hoisted Joe over his shoulder, the pungent garbage aroma of the puddle Joe had been lying in spreading to his own shirt.

Joe burped and muttered. "Krug."

"Home," Sheets replied, and headed down the street.

Epilogue

Paradise in April

3oz Admiral Nelson's Coconut Rum
3oz Pineapple Juice   3oz Hawaiian Punch
Serve over ice in Hurricane Glass

"Joe? Joe? Is that you?"

The phone in the center of the table was nearly vibrating from the sound of Egg's voice, the speaker loud and clear. The dappled shade of a palm tree swayed across the platter of fruit and coffee mug in front of him. We may need to add another rule, Joe thought; bars are just better with palm trees. Of course, the warm April sun reflecting off the ocean in Key West didn't hurt either.

"Yeah, it's me. Where are you?" The sound of her voice had warmed Joe even more than the island air.

"Joe?" Egg's voice crackled with intensity. "If this is someone fooling around…"

"No No. It's really me. Where are you? Sounds like wind."

She sniffled. "On the boat. Dewey. Oh, Joe. You're alive."

"What boat?" Joe winked at the man seated across from him. "Did you steal your father's boat again?" He pictured her dark eyes beginning to flash.

Egg didn't take the bait. "Borrowed. Re-borrowed."

Joe could hear her crying softly.

"Are you okay? Where have you been? Nobody's seen Sheets. Crap. I miss you guys so much."

Alcohol still seemed to ooze from his every pore. This was only the third day he'd awakened with a clear head and listening to Egg cry made Joe aware of what he'd been putting everyone through. "In order. Okay is relative, but I'm gonna live. I've been in Key West. And he's right here."

This time the phone did move as she screamed. "Sheets is there? Sheets?"

Sheets set down his coffee mug. "I'm here. How's my sniper?"

"You bastards. Laying in the sun while we all worried. Take me off speakerphone. I've got questions."

Joe watched as Sheets pressed the phone to his ear. Joe reached for a slice of fresh pineapple and when he looked up, Sheets was smiling at him.

"Fat." Sheets paused. "No, more like he swallowed a soccer ball."

But I was able to jog a whole mile on the sand this morning, Joe thought.

"Greyer. Right down the center like a skunk." Sheets reached for his mug.

"No. Yellow, but tanned. What color is yellow crossed with brown?"

Sheets laughed, then said, "Joe, take off your sunglasses. To Egg, he said, "Bloodshot. Some blue here and there." Sheets' voice became serious and he averted his gaze. "Maybe." He paused. "I'm not sure. Time will tell." He held out the phone. "She wants to talk to you."

"Asshole." Egg had arrived in full fiery vent mode. "You—"

Joe cut her off. "Hey Hey Hey. I just wanted to come to a warm place and drink myself to death. But no, some hulking good samaritan kept getting in the way. What kind of country do we live in, that a drunk can't lie peacefully in the gutter without interference from some lunatic ex-SEAL?"

Egg snickered. "Christ, listen to you. Sounds a little like the old Joe before—" She stopped. "Sorry."

Maybe a couple Mimosas wouldn't hurt, Joe thought. He looked out across the startlingly sharp pastel colors of the Atlantic. Light green turning darker then finally a deep blue reaching the horizon. No. He'd learn to say her name again without craving a drink. He'd learn to pack the memories away somewhere safe, so he could bring them out and examine them without pain. He put the sunglasses on and stared at Sheets. Lord Greystoke. He was gazing out at the ocean. Joe was suddenly hungry for news of the others.

"Joe?"

He had forgotten about the phone. "Give me an update. Jamie have that kid yet?"

"She's big as a house. Marie's fussing over her, helping run the Emerald. She's living at Ang...sorry."

"It's okay. You can say her name."

"Everyone's gone back to saying Angel. It just seems... easier. Anyway, Marie's living in her apartment. Even the cat came back. Marie financed a new ultralight for Buzz. Tell Tarzan to get his ass back here. I'm afraid of what will happen if Buzz tries to put it together by himself."

Joe felt a pang of remorse. He hadn't thought nearly enough about these people he cared for. "How is the little man?"

"I made him shave the beard. He really looked like a terrorist. Jamie said he couldn't wait tables with it."

"At the Emerald?"

"Yeah. Me too. I took your job. We all, all three of us, seem to need to be together. Talk about what we did out there. We send Jamie home and hang around the bar until late. It's weird, Joe. We all went from zero to sixty on one morning in September and back to zero two months later.

The talk of the restaurant and the bar, his bar, and all his people, made Joe want to be back in Dewey and Rehoboth. He looked around. Key West. Paradise. Palm trees and tropical breezes. Umbrella drinks and bikinis. And he realized right then that he would trade it all for April, chilly wet April, in slower lower Delaware.

Backup Dedication

I met Maribeth Fischer through a bartending friend in 2005. As we became friends and she learned that I had a background in finance, she suggested that I be the treasurer for the Rehoboth Beach Writers Guild. "Absolutely not," I replied.

When I finished filing the tax forms for the RBWG, she told me that as treasurer, I needed to start attending the monthly Guild readings. "Absolutely not," I replied.

After attending my third reading, Maribeth insisted that I needed to participate as a reader. "Absolutely not," I replied.

And so it went. When she needed one more person to fill one of her novel classes, I was volunteered, despite telling her that I had no story, no characters and no plot. For better or worse, three years later, *Down on B-Dock* is a reality.

Maribeth Fischer is a brilliant writer, terrific friend and the best editor you could possibly find. She was, however, completely unsympathetic to any of my sorrowful excuses for lack of writing production during this process.

So Teach, thanks for all you've done, and if that spot in the next novel class needs filling, I have only one thing to say—

"Absolutely not."

ACKNOWLEDGEMENTS

It couldn't have happened without the following people who were my classmates in The Rehoboth Beach Writers Guild novel classes over the last three years, and I apologize if I am leaving anyone out: Chris, Chanta, Heather, Another Heather, Marian, Dick, Steve, Carl, Lisa, Betty, Lynne, Alan, John, Lauren, Ceil, Eileen and Barbara.

A special thank you to another classmate, Kent Schoch, a talented local singer/songwriter, for taking the time to read *Down on B-Dock* and provide me with extremely helpful feedback and encouragement.

And lastly to the final four: Terri Clifton, Crystal Heidel, Kathy Winfield and Jenifer Adams-Mitchell, the advanced novel class attendees who excoriated, cajoled, threatened and occasionally praised me every Monday for the last year. Each is a terrific writer, with books of their own coming soon. Their savage weekly beatings pushed me to the finish line. Thank you all.

The cover and title page designs were also done by Crystal Heidel, wonderful writer, great graphic designer, thoughtful reader, and sparkling wine connoisseur. Our weekend bubbles for Bubbles editing sessions were very productive. I think. I appreciate every moment of your time and effort.

Made in the USA
San Bernardino, CA
06 June 2013